for Sondra
Best Wishes

Dorsey

THE
BACCHUS
CLAIM

P9-APQ-916

THE
BACCHUS
CLAIM

Dorsey Price Salerno

iUniverse, Inc.
New York   Bloomington

THE BACCHUS CLAIM

Copyright © 2009 by Dorsey Price Salerno

All rights reserved. No part of this book may be used or reproduced by any means, graphic, electronic, or mechanical, including photocopying, recording, taping or by any information storage retrieval system without the written permission of the publisher except in the case of brief quotations embodied in critical articles and reviews.

iUniverse books may be ordered through booksellers or by contacting:

iUniverse
1663 Liberty Drive
Bloomington, IN 47403
www.iuniverse.com
1-800-Authors (1-800-288-4677)

Because of the dynamic nature of the Internet, any Web addresses or links contained in this book may have changed since publication and may no longer be valid. This is a work of fiction. All of the characters, names, incidents, organizations, and dialogue in this novel are either the products of the author's imagination or are used fictitiously.

ISBN: 978-1-4401-6421-7 (pbk)
ISBN: 978-1-4401-6422-4 (ebk)

Printed in the United States of America

iUniverse rev. date: 3/19/2010
Second edition

To Robert

ACKNOWLEDGMENTS

I am grateful to the following friends who were kind enough to read the manuscript of *The Bacchus Claim* and offer comments and suggestions: Elizabeth Barrett, Tracy Barron, Jane Beers, Deb Dahlem, Bigna Francis von Wyttenbach, Emily Hanlon, Florence Kaplan, Mark Kramer, Kathleen Lea, Judy Levine, Tullia Maffei Lynch, Mary Ann Marshall, Shirley Reisch, Marly Rusoff, Leonardo Salvaggio and Margot Travers.

During the writing of the book, e-mails flew back and forth to and from Padua. I thank Professor Gilberto Muraro of the University of Padua and his wife Heide Muraro for researching many of the historical details of the story. My thanks also go to the Chief Rabbi of Turin and to the librarians at the Jewish Theological Library in New York.

Lee Laster of the Westchester Holocaust Commission helped me enormously when she spent an afternoon explaining how the *Anschluss* affected her and her family.

And *In Memoriam:* Hilda Goldsmith of Gelnhausen, Germany and Armonk, N.Y. shared many cups of coffee with me in her immaculate kitchen while she explained what life was like in Germany for a little Jewish girl just before September 1, 1939. Dr. Raffaele Lattes, Professor of Surgery and Surgical

Pathology at the Columbia University College of Physicians and Surgeons, answered dozens of questions about how and why he fled to this country from Turin in 1940. Professor Lattes urged me to go to Italy and talk to his "baby brother" (age 83). Signor Giuseppe Lattes and his wife, signora Yolanda Lattes welcomed my husband, my daughter and me at their home in Turin. There we learned how it was to be a hidden Jew, married to a Catholic girl, in Italy in World War II.

And most of all, I thank my husband Robert for his constant and loving encouragement and support throughout the long process of researching and writing the book. I dedicate this book to Robert, of course.

CHAPTER 1
NEW YORK—2009

Tullia Cantarini was determined not to seem nervous, but the two people she was speaking to were looking at her as if she was a liar or a con artist. "You mustn't do this!" she insisted. "It's stolen property!"

She dropped into the chair Henry Prentiss and Adelaide Bunning had offered her at the long conference table of the Winthrop Auction House, and swung her briefcase firmly against her leg. Hoping to look professional, she lifted her chin and straightened the jacket of her dark blue suit. She wished she looked older than her twenty-eight years, and was certain that she shouldn't have worn her shoulder-length blond hair in a ponytail.

Henry Prentiss, Managing Director of the Winthrop Auction House, tucked his folded handkerchief deeper into the pocket of his dark gray suit and pressed his lips together. He closed the door to the mahogany-paneled conference room and gestured for Adelaide Bunning, Head of European Paintings, to sit across from Tullia. Ms. Bunning lowered her ample hips into her leather chair and pushed a stray wisp of gray hair away from her severe face, before glancing impatiently at her watch.

Mr. Prentiss took a chair next to Ms. Bunning, looked straight at Tullia, and said, "Ms. Cantarini, don't think you're the first person who has tried to claim art work from the Second World War."

Ms. Bunning nodded. "And mostly the people who come in with these stories are living out a family myth or creating some fantasy of their own."

Tullia drew a deep breath to steady herself. How could she convince these two people that the drawing they were about to auction belonged to her family and not to some other person claiming it as his own? In the silence that fell while Mr. Prentiss and Ms. Bunning awaited her response, she was aware of the indistinct rush of traffic five floors below. She knew she'd be out on that street in two minutes if she couldn't convince these people that her grandfather was the true owner of the four-hundred-year-old Bacchus sketch.

"My grandfather," she began, "Beniamino Cantarini, found a preliminary sketch of Caravaggio's *Bacchus* painting in 1939 in Venice. Since Beniamino's father, Claudio, was a well-known art dealer in Padua, it was not difficult for him to gather his associates to consider the possibility that this was an original work of Caravaggio. To a man they agreed that the sketch was indeed authentic. They were amazed and overjoyed that the only known preliminary drawing Caravaggio had ever sketched was now found after four hundred years!"

Ms. Bunning tapped her pencil against the palm of her hand. "If this were true, why would your family wait fifty years to come forward with this claim? And why would someone as young as you be challenging the Winthrop Auction Gallery at this late date?"

Tullia explained that the invaluable sketch had never resurfaced in her lifetime. Her grandfather, now eighty-seven, wanted more than anything to reclaim the drawing that had been stolen from him during the Second World War, but didn't want his name to appear in the newspapers. Tullia's father, Raffaele Cantarini, could have come, but was at the moment teaching a course in Renaissance Art in Padua, Italy. Tullia further explained that her doctorate in Fine Arts from Yale University and her work for six years at the Cantarini Art Gallery gave her grandfather confidence in her ability to speak for the family.

"You have proof of your claim?" Ms. Bunning asked, her tone indicating that she seriously doubted that.

Tullia nodded, touching her briefcase. "I have all the relevant documents right here."

"Really?" Ms. Bunning said, her skepticism unassuaged.

Mr. Prentiss gave a deprecating smile and wiped his glasses with his handkerchief. "The present owner of the Bacchus drawing has asked that his name not be revealed until after the auction." Under the table, Tullia rubbed her sweating palms against her skirt as she explained that her family definitely did not need to be told the name of the person. They were quite certain who it had to be.

Then she finally made her bold request. "Mr. Prentiss, Ms. Bunning, I would like to ask you for one hour of your time, so you will know why I am certain this rare and invaluable Bacchus drawing belongs to the Cantarini family and not to the person claiming it."

Ms. Bunning looked at her watch again. "I think not. We really have no time for this."

Tullia's heart sank. She looked at Mr. Prentiss. He was frowning, obviously thinking, and she took that as a good sign.

"One hour?" He glanced at Ms. Bunning. "I feel that we have an obligation to give Ms. Cantarini an hour of our time. After all, Beniamino Cantarini is a respected colleague in the art world."

Tullia's heart leaped at the opportunity. She was aware of the portrait of J. L.Winthrop, founder of the Auction House, staring down at her, his regard as cold as that of Ms. Bunning. She focused on Mr. Prentiss and began.

"My grandfather, Beniamino Cantarini, discovered Caravaggio's only extant sketch in 1939. Most people don't know that it is the preliminary drawing of the *Bacchus* painting in the Uffizi Gallery in Florence. Grandfather found it in a mask shop in Venice and purchased it. When I was little, he often told me stories of Caravaggio, and how he found the drawing and how the Gestapo stole it from him. His life's dream was to survive the war and find the Bacchus sketch again. My grandfather always said it was like losing a child and forever hoping to find it."

Tullia felt more at ease now, explaining how her grandfather often talked about his life spiraling out of control when the Nazis took over Italy in September 1943, how it was a chilling time, with German soldiers on the prowl, ready to carry anyone off for any infraction of their rules.

"My family was Jewish, and even in Italy the Jews were especially targeted by the Nazis. My great-grandfather Claudio and my grandfather Beniamino, who was twenty-one at the time, were taking a train to Rome to fetch the Bacchus drawing. It was their last valuable possession and they desperately needed to sell it. They had taken the sketch to Rome several months before, thinking the chances of a buyer would be greater in a larger city.

But as luck would have it, a good offer came instead from nearby Venice. Claudio was afraid to leave his wife and daughter alone in occupied Padua, but he was more afraid to take them along with him to Rome. The story, as my grandfather tells it, goes like this."

CHAPTER 2
PADUA—1943

The early morning sun filtered through the glass skylights of Padua's railway station. The air was redolent of oil and the steam of departing trains, as families and friends said good-bye on the train platform, casting nervous glances at the German soldiers patrolling outside the passenger cars. Grim-faced and arrogant in their green uniforms, the young soldiers marched up and down in pairs, occasionally stopping to listen in on conversations.

Near the sign announcing *Partenza per Roma,* Claudio Cantarini and his wife, son, and daughter stood in a tight circle. Claudio bent his gray head over his family and said the blessing he had given his children every Shabbat of their lives: "May the God of our fathers keep you safe." Ben, tall, blond, and strong from hiking in the hills north of Padua, wished his father wouldn't say those words so near the German soldiers. One of them might understand Italian.

Claudio's wife, Constanz, touched her husband's pale face and gray sideburns tenderly, then pressed down the lapels of his black coat. She drew their eight-year-old daughter close to her, smoothing her long, dark braids, and made her son promise to take care of his father when they reached Rome.

"Of course," Ben said. "I'm twenty-one and I know how to stay out of the Germans' way. Don't worry, Mamma."

Claudio took hold of his wife's hands. "Constanz, *cara mia,* promise me that you and Monica will stay in the apartment while Ben and I are gone." He lowered his voice. "You don't want to be stopped in the street by German soldiers before Rabbi Coen brings your Christian documents to you. He told me he'd found someone to forge them. Don't venture out without those Aryan papers and remember that your names will be different."

She nodded, then looked up at her son and pushed the blond hair back from his forehead. She asked him if he had his father's pills in his briefcase, reminded him to give the cheese to signora Bovenzi in Rome, and made him promise to telephone her in case the train couldn't make it through to Rome. Earlier that morning the family had listened to the forbidden Radio London and had heard about Allied bombings south of Venice and Padua.

Ben gave his mother a final embrace. It was unsettling to feel her shoulder bones through her brown tweed coat. Everyone had lost weight since the war began three years before, but why hadn't he noticed it in his own mother? She was still lovely, with her chestnut hair, high cheekbones, and fair skin, but now she seemed so vulnerable. It would be better for him to go to Rome alone and leave Papà to take care of his mother and sister. Wrapping one arm around Monica, he kissed her forehead, and said, "And you, *briccona,* you little scamp, behave yourself and do whatever Mamma says."

Just as Ben turned to follow his father up the train steps, two SS officers in their black uniforms, lightning bolts on their collars, strode across the platform toward him. Careful not to make eye contact with them, Ben sprinted up the steps after his father.

In the train, Claudio walked quickly down the long corridor, looking for an empty compartment. As he and Ben settled on the blue plush seats, the small overhead lights flickered, indicating that the train was about to move.

"You have the food and my heart pills?" Claudio asked his son.

"Mamma already told you she's put them in there, Papà." Ben pointed to the briefcase he'd placed in the overhead net. He saw through the large window that the SS officers on the platform had moved down to the next passenger car.

"No need to be short with me, son."

"Yes, Papà." Ben searched the platform for his mother and sister. He spotted his mother bending over to tie Monica's shoelace. She should hurry up and move along. The SS officers had stopped to watch her. At last she took his sister's hand and started to walk away.

Claudio opened his newspaper, then looked up to ask Ben if he wanted to tell him about his meeting at his friend Giorgio's the evening before.

Ben glanced through the glass door to the corridor. For the moment it was empty. Nevertheless, he lowered his voice. "I learned from one of the Resistance people how they make the four-pointed nails. This is tremendous." He sat forward. "All you have to do is take two metal rods about two inches long and pointed at each end. You bend them in half and solder them together. No matter how you throw them, they end with one sharp point sticking up. You pick a place where a German convoy is going downhill around a curve, and when the trucks pile up you throw grenades and run."

9

Noticing his father's worried look, Ben asked himself why he had bothered telling Papà about the four-pointers. He looked away, trying to think of cellars where he and his friends could set up a clandestine shop. Once back from Rome, he'd join Giorgio in the Resistance. There'd be time enough to tell Papà then.

The train was under way and already moving along at a fast clip, passing through the outskirts of Padua and rushing by the outlying farms of the valley. The morning mist lifted, revealing roads and highways empty of traffic, except for occasional German trucks filled with troops. Ben cursed inwardly at the invaders taking every last gallon of Italian gasoline.

His father spoke, as if something had just occurred to him. "I don't blame you for being disappointed that we have to sell the Bacchus drawing. You just have to remember that, no matter who owns it after this, you are the one who found it."

Ben shrugged, hiding his deep disappointment. No one could ever know the thrill he had felt discovering that sketch, tucked in between two papier-mâché masks in the window of a *Masquerìa* in a Venice side street. Lost for four hundred years, rumored to be hidden in one private villa after another, and then he, Beniamino Cantarini, had recognized it. Ben's heart leaped as he pictured the drawing. It was as small as a man's hand, drawn in brown and white wash, but it had the same energy, the same dash as the *Bacchus* oil painting in the Uffizi Gallery. It foretold the masterful painting that Ben had gazed at so many times. When his father's friends saw the drawing, they too couldn't look away from it. On the spot they declared it a miracle that Ben had found Caravaggio's lost preliminary sketch. Priceless, thought Ben, but he hadn't wanted it because it was invaluable. He was swept away with it because the hand of the master had drawn it.

His father folded his arms across his chest. "I never thought it would come to this, Jews not permitted to own a business, my own son not allowed in the university." He shook his head. "We lived in a golden age until 1938, our family respected, no one caring that we were Jewish." He sighed. "And then the government passed the racial laws and we were called enemies of the state." He shook his head. "But someday things will go back to normal."

Ah, Papà. First he fussed and worried over details, and then he saw the future in a golden haze.

His father smiled wanly, as he reminded Ben that they were fortunate to have a Catholic partner to take over the gallery until the war was over.

Ben cut in. "Fortunate! Some partner! Aldo Lupino doesn't care that the percentage he's giving us isn't enough to live on. And why don't you ever question the stories we hear about him?"

"Son, you know that in the art world rumors are rife. After all, Lupino may not have known that he was selling a fake painting to the Griffino family. Besides, I heard those stories after I took him on as a partner. Maybe others were jealous, or … "

As Papà talked on about Lupino, Ben studied him. Even though he was still neat and professional in his dark blue suit, the war and his worries about the gallery and the family were turning him into an old man. His hair was completely gray now, his frown no longer occasional, but constant.

Claudio continued, "If the drawing is sold again, we'll follow it. It won't be lost."

"And if the next owner sells it?"

His father smiled. "Someone will always know. We will follow it like a father would follow a wayward child."

The door to the corridor slammed back, crashing against its

frame. A stern-faced, sharp-featured Nazi soldier shot out his hand. "*Papiere!*"

Ben's heart slammed in his chest as he reached into his breast pocket for his forged Aryan passport.

Claudio stood up, holding on to the iron rack above his head to steady himself in the swaying train. Damn, Papà shouldn't stand for him. But that was his father, ever the gentleman. Claudio reached into his pocket and with a courteous nod handed over his papers.

The soldier gave the two men a scornful look. "Campano, Arturo, art dealer. What is your business in Rome?"

Claudio answered. "We're meeting with a colleague."

"In the middle of a war?" the soldier snapped. "You have time to meet about art?"

An affront! Ben jumped up and took a step forward.

The soldier kept his eyes on Claudio. "Your son is a factory worker. What factory?"

Ben answered sharply, "I can speak for myself. A factory in Padua. I have a leave of absence."

The soldier glared. "You've got a mouth on you! Why aren't you in the army?"

Claudio gave his son a warning look, but Ben thrust out his chin. "Doing work for the war effort—like you."

"*Saukerl!* Dirty Italian swine!" He poked a finger against Ben's chest, announcing that he was keeping their papers. They'd get them back if they were cleared by the authorities. He opened the door, turning back to say, "Do you know that the SS has requisitioned all taxis and automobiles in Rome? I hope you like to walk." With a smirk, he slammed the door shut.

"You annoyed him," Claudio said. "That temper of yours has cost us our Aryan papers!"

"*Porci* Nazi, they make me ashamed to be half-German."

"When are you going to learn to control yourself?"

"Did you see how rude he was? No respect."

Claudio sighed. Ben remembered how many times he'd been told that you catch flies with honey, not vinegar. But he couldn't bear to grovel in front of a Nazi soldier. And how were they going to walk everywhere? He thought of the heart pills in the briefcase and Papà's shortness of breath.

When he mentioned that problem, though, his father simply put up his hand, saying that God would protect them.

Ben leaned back and folded his arms. Really, how did his father think God would look out for him especially, when people were dying all over Europe? Arguing with him was utterly useless.

His father spoke again, changing the subject entirely, talking about Caravaggio and how it was for him when he lived in Rome. Not so different from now, he told Ben. "They had one kind of plague in those years and we have another." Claudio warmed to his subject, alive in the world of art and history. "At the end of the century, oh, in the 1580s, there was a terrible famine and the Romans were forced to eat bread made of barley."

"Yes, yes, I know, Papà. You've told me lots of times before."

"Caravaggio was so poor and unknown that he was forced to live with a distant relative in Rome who fed him only greens. Our painter called him Monsieur Salade and Caravaggio left him after a few weeks, hungry as he was." He smiled.

Nothing to do but let Papà talk, but had it ever occurred to him that the Allies might bomb the tracks so badly that they'd never get to Rome at all? Or that if they made it to Rome, that some *carogne* Nazi might not return their papers? And this so Ben could go after a drawing that he was being forced to sell, when all he wanted was to keep it forever.

*   *   *

On Constanz's way back from the train station with Monica, a young German soldier stepped onto the sidewalk in front of her. Putting his face an inch from hers, he said, "*Guten Tag, gnädige* Frau!"

"*Nein*, Klaus," his partner said, a big, meaty fellow. He pulled the smiling, fresh-faced soldier away from Constanz. Her heart in her throat, she held Monica's hand more tightly and kept walking. She wasn't ashamed to be Jewish, but sometimes she wished she hadn't been born in Germany.

Constanz asked herself if she should go to someone else's apartment rather than their own. After all, signora Mondini would let them in. Or would she? Neighbors had become less friendly since the racial laws were passed five years before. As she neared her building, she heard the soldiers' heavy footsteps gaining on her. "Monica, don't look back," she whispered.

Approaching the entrance to her building, she stopped short. Two more German soldiers, both muscled and hefty, were blocking the entry and staring at someone kneeling on the pavement. Constanz put her finger to her lips, cautioning Monica to be quiet, and edged her way past the soldiers.

Good Lord, the man on the pavement was her neighbor, Professor Roth! He was sweeping the sidewalk with a toothbrush while the soldiers stood above him, taunting him. How degrading! What if that were Claudio? His heart could never take it. She forced herself to continue on to the door, her legs shaking.

"*Entschuldigen Sie, gnädige* Frau!" One of the soldiers, another of Hitler's adolescent recruits, turned and smiled at her. "You see what a Jew is good for?"

Constanz wanted to scream at them to leave him alone and tell them that he was an honorable man. But the words died in her mouth. She pulled her daughter up the steps to their apartment. As she was turning the key in the lock, she heard a voice at the bottom of the steps.

"*Halt!*"

She opened the door, pretending she didn't understand German. Footsteps came fast up the stairs, and then a firm hand grasped her shoulder. It was the same two soldiers who had followed them in the street.

She spoke sharply to keep her voice from shaking. "What is it?"

"*Wo sind Ihre Papiere?*"

She stared at the soldiers, paralyzed. Why hadn't she listened when Claudio warned her not to go to the station?

"*Carta d'identità!*" the younger one repeated, staring at her and thrusting out his hand.

Constanz opened her purse and rummaged for her papers. She should have stayed at home and waited for the rabbi to give her Aryan papers. She held out her documents with a trembling hand.

The soldier read aloud: *Prefettura di Padova*— Prefecture of Padua. Cantarini, Constanz Lehman, 18 Piazza delle Erbe, apartment 3, being of the Jewish race, is herein designated as an enemy of the state.

Constanz tried to keep her voice steady. "Excuse me, why are you stopping me? We haven't done anything wrong."

Smiling, he said, "So you're a Jewess. You don't look like a Jewess. You could pass for a very attractive German woman."

15

The older soldier frowned while the young one put his hand on Monica's dark hair and stroked it. Constanz shuddered but stood still, afraid to move.

"Where's your husband?" the younger soldier asked in broken Italian. "Away in the war? No, Jews aren't allowed in the army, are they? We're always patrolling this street and if you ever feel lonesome, just come and find us."

Her heart slamming in her chest, Constanz kept her eyes down and pretended she hadn't understood.

"*Ach, nein.* Leave her alone," the older soldier said.

The young soldier gave her a broad grin. "Next time you come downstairs, don't be in such a rush." He bowed sharply. "*Arrivederci,* Signora."

Constanz jammed the papers into her purse, clutched Monica's hand, and hurried into her apartment. She double-bolted the lock behind her and in the living room dropped into Claudio's brown leather armchair. She turned on the Tiffany floor lamp next to her, comforted by being in her own home, even though she was still shaking. Looking around at the flowered chintz chairs, the maroon velvet sofa, the cream curtains at the window, and her beautiful black Bösendorfer baby grand piano, she felt the wild beating of her heart start to slow. Pulling Monica onto her lap, she soothed her, saying, "Don't worry, darling, they're just nasty soldiers with no manners."

Monica gave her a confused look. "What does an enemy of the state mean?"

"It's a mistake. But it won't always be like that." Maybe not, but now she was trapped in her own apartment and called an enemy of the state.

She took Monica's hand and walked to the closet where the radio was hidden. Tuning in to Radio London and keeping the sound low, she leaned in close, hoping she wouldn't hear that the Allies had bombed the tracks between Padua and Rome. *Grazie a Dio*, no mention of the rails, only a list of the cities bombed, Turin the hardest hit. Would the Allies start bombing Padua?

She moved to the window and peered down at the street. Two soldiers armed with rifles were patrolling the block. They looked up at her window and walked past.

The afternoon hours dragged on, and by evening Constanz was exhausted from listening for footsteps coming up the stairs and from telling Monica that they were safe. All her reassurances didn't help. At suppertime the little girl picked at her food and looked at her mother with wide frightened eyes. She kept Monica up late to have her company, but after she put the child to bed, the silence in the apartment pressed in on her.

The next morning and afternoon, she waited and waited for the telephone to ring, jumping at the sound of German jackboots marching in the streets, and peering out the window to see if Claudio and Ben might be coming up the sidewalk. Dear God, where were her two men? Another day had gone by and finally, when it was evening, still dressed, she stretched out on her bed and fell asleep.

A few minutes later, the shrilling doorbell shattered the quiet. A fist hit the door hard, three times. Constanz leaped to her feet. Her heart banging in her chest, she approached the door.

CHAPTER 3

More bombings on the tracks ahead. Each time the train started moving again, it wasn't long before another raucous announcement came over the loudspeaker in the corner of the compartment. There would be a further delay. The normal seven-hour trip to Rome was taking a day and a half. Finally, Ben and Claudio saw through the window of their compartment the bustling outskirts of Rome. And still no return of their documents. At last, at nine in the evening, the train shuddered to a stop in the Stazione Termini in Rome.

"Thank God we're here," Claudio murmured to Ben, as they made their way along the crowded train corridor. "I prayed all day not to be under the bombs."

Father and son descended from the train and pushed through the crowds on the platform. At the street entrance of the station, a printed sign announced a Return of Document Desk. The two men rushed to be the first in line. A sour-faced soldier behind the desk thrust their papers at them, saying, "*Ja, hier, aber—*" He continued in Italian. "We'll be watching you. No one is supposed to be moving around Rome. After nine-thirty … " He drew a line across his throat.

Unshaven, his mouth tasting of the grit from the long ride, Ben asked his father if they could make it to the Bovenzis' apartment by nine-thirty.

Claudio stepped onto the sidewalk, moving ahead quickly, calling over his shoulder, "It will take us about three-quarters of an hour. I hope the telephone lines are working. Mamma will be frantic by now."

On the darkened street, they realized that the blackout was going to make it difficult to find their way. They set out in the direction of the Bovenzis' apartment, guided by the occasional white curbstones. When they arrived at the first cross street, Claudio slowed down and sucked in his breath. Two German soldiers were positioned behind a machine gun. Claudio cautioned Ben to walk past them quietly and keep his eyes down. Ben obeyed, but felt his rancor rising. He wasn't going to be humiliated by foreign vultures picking at his country's flesh.

They walked for a half hour, passing soldiers at each cross street. When they reached a long empty stretch of wide boulevard, Claudio grasped Ben's arm and stopped him. "We'll end up in prison if you walk with such an angry gait. I resent them as much as you do, but you have to make yourself invisible."

"Resent! Is that all you do, resent?" Ben said in a fierce whisper. "I could grab each one of them by the throat and kill them. We have to get rid of them, the way we should have rid ourselves of Mussolini years ago."

A few minutes later, Claudio nodded toward a nearby park protected by a high wall. Two soldiers stood guard by the gate. "Villa Torlonia, Mussolini's residence," he murmured.

"Too bad he fled. We could have gone in and thanked him

for the troubles we've had for the past five years," Ben whispered in return.

"Hush," his father said. "Here's Via delle Alpi."

They stopped in front of a three-story stucco building. Claudio pushed the buzzer on the gate, saying softly that he hoped the concierge wouldn't remember him from other visits. He supposed that Campano sounded a lot like Cantarini.

When the door to the building opened, a short, plump balding man in broken-down carpet slippers shuffled over the paving stones toward them. He stood on the other side of the gate without showing any intention of opening it.

"We're here to see signor Bovenzi," Claudio said.

"He didn't tell me he was expecting you." Reluctantly, the man opened the gate. "I have to have your identity papers." He turned his back, letting them follow him into the apartment building and down a dimly lit hallway. "How long are you going to be here?" he called back.

"We're not sure," Claudio answered respectfully.

The concierge's office smelled like cabbage, and the dust lay thick on his banged-up black desk. Through a doorway Ben saw a heavyset woman in a dark blue apron bent over a stove.

The concierge studied their documents, moving a fat forefinger under each section: name, place of birth, occupation. Ben realized that the man didn't read well, if at all. He was a little man with new big power. This gave Ben the courage to speak up. "In Padua we aren't asked for our papers when we visit."

The concierge snapped back, "Well, you're not in the provinces. You're in the Eternal City." He reached in his desk and handed Claudio a piece of paper. "Read this. It was sent a week ago by the German police."

Claudio read the paper and handed it to Ben, who saw: "It is forbidden to ride a bicycle, to stock up on food, to telegraph or telephone outside Rome, to walk on the sidewalks herein listed, to cross the streets herein listed, forbidden to enter or leave the city."

"Worse than I thought," Claudio murmured. He picked up his documents and opened his wallet, putting a large lira bill on the man's desk.

The concierge slid the money inside his desk drawer and motioned for them to leave the office.

Claudio and Ben closed the door behind them and crossed the hallway to a door marked Edoardo Bovenzi, *Negoziante di Incisioni* (Dealer in Engravings).

Ben complained to his father that they shouldn't have to pay off the concierge.

Claudio pressed the buzzer. "Youth wants it the way it should be. A Jew understands that you work with the way things are."

"Papà, as soon as we say hello to signor Bovenzi, see if he'll give us the drawing. I'd like to have it next to us tonight."

The door inched open, an eye peering though the crack. A pause and then a surprised voice called out, "Claudio! Ben!" The door opened wide. An older gentleman, wrapping his bathrobe around his generous waist and pushing down his white flyaway hair, grinned broadly. "You look like two dusty cadavers, my God! Well, come in." Edoardo Bovenzi took Claudio's elbow and pulled him and Ben into the foyer of the apartment, quickly closing the door behind them.

Ben saw a stranger in the mirror over the credenza in the dark, narrow hallway and realized he was looking at himself. His blond hair was darkened by the soot of the train ride. With his rumpled clothes and unshaven chin, he looked like a vagrant.

Bovenzi clapped Ben on the shoulder. "It's a good thing I

know you or I would have been frightened." He peered at him closely. "But you're still a handsome young man."

"You're good to let us come," Claudio said. He handed his friend the package of cheese Constanz had sent.

Bovenzi turned, calling out for his wife Yolanda. Ben asked eagerly if he could see the drawing right away. To his disappointment, Bovenzi said no. It was perfectly safe in the vault in the other room. It would be ready for Ben in the morning.

Signora Bovenzi appeared in the foyer, her face pinched and drawn, one hand holding her dressing gown together, the other pressing back her shoulder-length gray hair. When her husband handed her the cheese, she took it and nodded, barely looking at it.

Bovenzi gave a hurried glance at the hallway door. "It's better if we move into the living room to talk. The walls have ears nowadays."

In the past Ben was always struck by the refinement of the apartment, with its antique engravings and softly cushioned beige sofas. Now he didn't care to study the Old Master paintings and bronze busts. He only hoped this would be a safe haven.

"Please excuse the lateness of our arrival," Claudio said, "but there were so many delays. We had to wait for bombed trestles and tracks to be repaired." He held his hands up in a helpless gesture.

Yolanda Bovenzi pursed her lips and bluntly said that they mustn't stay.

Bovenzi cleared his throat, explaining that every concierge in Rome had to keep a list of who came and who went. The German soldiers came by regularly, banging on doors.

Signora Bovenzi interrupted to say they were looking for anti-fascists and runaway soldiers.

Ben protested, saying that they didn't talk politics and they weren't runaway soldiers.

Signora Bovenzi agitated the sash on her dressing gown. Her voice growing louder, she said that no one was allowed to spend the night at friends' houses and the rumor was that all Jews were suspect.

Ben looked at her, wondering how these people who were dear friends before the war could now be so changed. She went on to say that there were punishments for harboring undocumented people and it was selfish of Claudio and Ben to stay under these conditions.

An expression of relief spread over Claudio's face. He reached into his breast pocket and held out his papers. "See, Aryan papers."

Signora Bovenzi shook her head, telling him that the concierge probably remembered them from the last visit. They hadn't always had those Christian papers, after all.

Her husband winced, and said, "Last week the SS came into our cousin's apartment at three in the morning and took away two friends who were staying with them. The SS insisted that the friends were anti-fascist. You've heard of Via Tasso—Gestapo Headquarters?"

"Wait a minute," Ben said. "I'm not naïve. I know what the Gestapo does—worse than the fascists' castor oil treatment—but don't we have a neo-fascist government here?"

"An Italian neo-fascist government in league with the Nazis." Bovenzi pushed his hand nervously through his hair. "At least, so far they've only put people in prison."

Signora Bovenzi clamped her hand around her husband's wrist. "Our cousins are allowed to take food to their friends only every other day. They can bring back their clothes to wash, but there is no word of their friends being released." She took a deep breath, unable to stem her outrage. "There were bedbugs and lice in all the dirty clothes." She looked hard at Claudio. "We still don't know who denounced them. People are doing all kinds of things for money." A pained look crossed her face. "Please," she said, her voice rising to a wail, "please go away."

Her husband tapped his finger on his lips. "Darling, do you want the whole building to hear?"

Three sharp raps sounded on the hallway door. Signora Bovenzi's hand flew to her mouth. "Oh, dear Lord. The SS!"

"Maybe not," whispered her husband. "They kick with their boots." He raised his hand for silence and walked to the door.

When Bovenzi opened the door, the concierge entered, breathing heavily. "What is all this noise about? They'd better hurry the hell out of the building."

Bovenzi straightened up and excused himself. In a moment he returned with his wallet, murmured something to the concierge, and beckoned for the man to step into the hallway.

After a whispered conversation around the corner, the concierge shuffled away. When the door was closed, a long moment of heavy silence hung in the air. Yolanda Bovenzi broke it, telling Claudio and Ben that they really must go.

Her husband shook his head, reminding her that the taxis were all requisitioned and that the hotels were taken over by the Germans. He couldn't stand the thought of his friends walking past the SS and being arrested.

God damn it, Ben thought, that was enough! "Signora Bovenzi, you can't toss a man like my father out into the street. He has a heart problem!"

"Yes, I know, but I thought he was better, now that … " Her words trailed off.

Ben continued, "We just need a few hours sleep, then we'll take the drawing and catch the early morning train."

Signora Bovenzi gritted her teeth in resignation. "All right, I'll put out the towels. Edoardo, you explain what they would have to do, if—" She turned abruptly and left the room.

Keeping his voice under control, Bovenzi apologized for his wife, explaining that her nerves were even worse than his. He motioned for them to follow him across the living room to a small bedroom.

Ben could see that since his last visit all the elegant furnishings had been removed. Now there was only a dark green sofa piled with a sheet and blankets, a ladder-back chair, and a small writing table. A blackout shade covered the window's elegant carved frame. Their host explained that the rest of the furniture was in their country home because they never knew when they'd have to run and hide.

Bovenzi walked to the sofa. "Claudio, you can sleep here. I'm afraid Ben will have to sleep on the floor." He removed an etching from the wall. Ben saw a wooden ring the same color as the paneled walls. "If anyone comes to the door tonight, you must go in here." He pulled the ring and a panel slid to the side, revealing a dark closet jammed with leather satchels and odd pieces of furniture. "Take everything in here with you—suitcase, briefcase, bed linens, everything." He took a flashlight from the closet. "Keep this next to you, so you can find your way."

Bovenzi motioned for Ben to step into the closet by straddling two empty suitcases. Ben found himself in a three by five foot opening, empty except for a bottle of water and a chamber pot. Bovenzi cautioned him to take two more suitcases from behind him and pile them up in the opening. Ben could see that he and his father would be completely hidden, even if the panel were

26

opened. When he climbed back into the room, Bovenzi looked at him apologetically. "We hope you won't have to go in there."

"We're very grateful," Claudio said.

Bovenzi put a hand on his friend's shoulder. "I would have called you about how bad things are here in Rome, but for the past three days all calls are forbidden. I wanted to write, but Field Marshal Kesselring has suspended all private correspondence."

"I only wish we could call Constanz," Claudio replied. "She'll be frantic by now. She expected us to arrive in Rome yesterday."

"Sorry, old friend." Bovenzi turned to go, but remembered something. "You can shave and clean up in the morning. The rule in the building is that we don't run water after nine o'clock at night." Leaving the panel open, he added, "If you have to hide, put the etching back first. Then once you're inside, pull the string so the ring won't show. Good night." He left, closing the door behind him.

Claudio dropped into the ladder-back chair with a sigh. "You see," he said, "they let us stay. God is good."

Ben wanted to say, if God is so good, why are we in this mess? But that would be blasphemous and only upset Papà. So he pulled back the covers on the sofa and asked, "Can you sleep here all right?"

His father's wan smile was barely visible in the shadows. "Better than you on the floor. If it's too much for you, we'll trade places in the middle of the night."

"Papà, come on! Besides, you know I can sleep anywhere."

Claudio lay down on the sofa and reached for the blanket, but Ben was already pulling it up for him. He snugged it around his father's shoulders. "We'll be all right, Papà. All we need is the Caravaggio drawing and we'll be home before you know it." He patted his father's shoulder.

Ben put a blanket on the floor. Before lying down, he turned off the dim bulb and pulled back the blackout shade to look at the street. The wind was blowing the rain in gusts and fits. He could just make out a soldier, flashlight in hand, making his way to the gate in front of the apartment building. He held his breath as he watched the fellow grab the gate lock, shake it, and walk away. Those Nazis never let up, he thought, and lay down on his blanket, folding his jacket into a pillow. He resisted falling asleep, thinking he should be ready to help his father into the closet. Gradually, though, his body relaxed, and he drifted off to the soft sound of his father's nighttime prayers, a sound he'd thought was a lullaby when he was a child. *Sch'ma Israel, Adonai Eloheinu …*

*   *   *

Clutching her sweater closed, Constanz peered through the peephole of the hall door. It was Rabbi Coen who had knocked, thank God! She started to breathe again. But what was he doing there at that time of night? She opened the door, shocked to see his face so serious, his hand nervously brushing back his red hair. She stood aside to let him in, anxious to lock the door again. "Did you see soldiers outside my apartment building?"

He shook his head. "No, I saw no one. I came to bring Aryan papers for you and Monica." He handed her the documents. "You are now Celeste Campano and Monica is Maria Campano. You should learn some Catholic prayers, in case the German soldiers provoke you and test you." His fedora pressed to his chest, the rabbi walked past her and into the living room. "May I sit?"

"Yes, of course, Rabbi."

He sat on the maroon velvet sofa, saying he wanted to get right to the point. He had come because Claudio, before going to Rome, had discussed with him the idea of the family moving.

His voice urgent, the rabbi told her to think of her family and remember how badly things were going for the Jews in Germany. Constanz winced when he spoke of her cousins in Berlin who had disappeared two years ago.

She put up her hand to stop him from talking. "Where was I in this discussion?" She saw it now, the two men sitting in the rabbi's study deciding what was good for her family without including her. "I'm offended that you and Claudio spoke of our family moving and never said a word to me." From the street came the sound of soldiers marching in lockstep. "Sometimes Claudio coddles me like a little girl, perhaps because I'm so much younger than he is, but he shouldn't."

The rabbi assured her that it had been merely the beginning of a discussion and that he had been waiting for more information, which he now had.

"Oh." She shouldn't have mentioned that Claudio sometimes treated her like a child. It was an irritation that should stay inside the family.

The rabbi continued, describing a Catholic family in Turin—Italian, of course—who were willing to hide her family. It was rumored that the Germans might start taking foreign Jews to Germany.

"Turin?" she repeated. "But Radio London says they're getting some of the worst bombing raids. Besides, I'm not a foreign Jew. I'm Italian! I have been since Claudio and I were married."

The rabbi's face wore an expression of patience wearing out. "The Baldisseras live well outside Turin, in a small village. Now, as far as your nationality goes, it's rumored that Hitler won't make a distinction between foreign and naturalized Jews."

"But the Italians would never permit that."

"Dear child, you've been taken care of your whole life. It's time you—"

"Mamma?" Monica appeared in the doorway in her nightgown. She rubbed her eyes and looked at the rabbi. "*Buona sera, Rabbino.*" The little girl padded across the room, climbed up on Constanz's lap, and hid her face in the folds of her mother's sweater.

The rabbi stood, patted Monica on the head, and picked up his black fedora, urging Constanz to think about what he had said.

Through the window she watched the rabbi cross the street below, her shoulders relaxing only when he slipped away into the darkness. She tucked Monica under her covers and sat at the foot of her bed until the child fell asleep.

A village outside Turin? Good Lord, that was all the way on the other side of Italy, in the mountains. She had never even been there. Her eyes stinging with held-back tears, she curled up next to Monica. *Claudio, Ben, please hurry home.*

CHAPTER 4

Where was he? Ben couldn't move. He was exhausted, his mind at the bottom of darkness, unable to think. From far away it came again, *brring-brring*. Ben's body felt as wooden as his mind. Something was wrong, but what was it? *Brring-brring*. They were in Rome—in the Bovenzis' apartment. It was still dark. A doorbell was ringing furiously. The SS?

He came fully awake, his heart pounding. He had to find the flashlight. He swept his arm in a wide arc, groping. Come on! Where was it? He heard voices in the next room. A man's voice, signor Bovenzi. A woman's voice, his wife. They were arguing, whispering harshly—angry words about what to say when they opened the door.

"Papà, get up!" Ben whispered.

"Yes, I'm awake." The rustling sound meant he was gathering what lay around him.

Rapid footsteps approached and the bedroom door was flung open. Edoardo Bovenzi's voice rasped out, "Quick, hide yourselves. Take everything with you."

"We are ... we are," Ben called back, still scrambling for the flashlight.

The door closed. Their host's slippered footsteps scurried away.

Ben's fingers touched metal. He wrapped his hand around the cold cylinder of the flashlight, feeling for the switch. The beam found his father's weary face. He looked like a wraith, struggling up from the sofa, arms filled with blankets and sheets.

Over the insistent jabs of the doorbell, Ben heard Bovenzi call out, "*Sto arrivando*, I'm coming!"

Ben flashed the light on the wall, spotted the etching, and pulled on the wooden ring. He heard the apartment door open just as his flashlight beamed into the closet. "Quick, Papà, get in here," he whispered, pushing the blankets through the opening. He pulled at his father's arm. "Come on, Papà, move faster." Ben helped him straddle the suitcases. "Good, sit down on the blankets."

Ben replaced the etching, climbed in next to his father, and slid the panel shut before turning off the flashlight. He shoved the suitcases against the panel and crouched on the floor. In the darkness fear clutched at his stomach. For a moment his eyes retained the circle of light from the flashlight, and then he saw only complete blackness. Was this what it was like to be buried alive? All he could feel was the hard floor beneath his bones and the rough edges of the suitcases at his fingertips. The dry, musty air parched the back of his throat. Only the sound of his father's labored breathing spoke of life. Papà's heart—not now, please God.

"My pills," his father struggled to say.

Ben felt for the clasp of the briefcase and opened it carefully. Even the slight sound of metal clicking against metal made him cringe. He extricated the pills, shone the flashlight on the bottle of water at his feet, and gave them both to his father. Papà's breathing filled the cramped space—wheezing in, wheezing out. Slowly, slowly, the breathing grew more even. Finally Claudio's icy hand reached for Ben's wrist. "I'm better."

The closed panel and barricade of suitcases blocked any noise from outside. How long would they be trapped in there? Long enough to run out of air? Would they die quietly, Ben wondered, or would they push the panel aside and burst out of there, only to be dragged away to Via Tasso? They had gone back to their own private ghetto. He remembered someone saying that even though modern-day Italians never thought about a person's religion, Jews were still only eighty years out of the ghetto—and that they could always be sent back.

Ben remembered that you should breathe slowly if you're using up your oxygen. If they ran to the street the soldiers at the corner would turn their machine gun on them and rattle them down, no questions asked. And his father couldn't even run twenty feet. He strained his ears for voices or footsteps but heard only the drumming of his heart. Impossible to tell how much time was passing—minutes or hours? Suddenly, with a rush of sound, the panel was yanked open. Edoardo Bovenzi's disembodied voice called in through the blackness, "Come out."

Rising stiffly to his feet, Ben grasped his father under the armpits. Clinging to each other the two men stepped from their hideaway. Were the SS standing behind Bovenzi?

First light was creeping in at the edge of the blackout shade. Ben figured it was about six in the morning. Bovenzi must have dressed hastily, because his necktie was loosely knotted and his suit jacket hung open. Brushing back his white hair with both hands, he said, "It was Ugo Foà at the door. He's gone now."

Claudio stared at him in surprise. "Really?"

"Who is he?" Ben asked.

"Ugo Foà is the president of your Jewish Community here in Rome—and a close friend." Frowning, Bovenzi tugged the knot of his tie into place. "Let's have coffee and a piece of your cheese. I'm sorry. Yolanda couldn't find bread yesterday. We'll talk in the dining room."

Ben and his father exchanged looks. Claudio assured Ben that Foà's arrival at that early hour meant trouble.

A few minutes later, faces washed and shaved in haste, clothes brushed by hand, Ben and Claudio went to the dining room to join signor Bovenzi. He was standing at the window staring down into the street, his shoulders rigid. He motioned them to sit at the long mahogany table. Ben was glad there was no sign of his wife.

Their host sat, gulped a mouthful of coffee, and then spoke. "Foà told me that last night at six o'clock Major Kappler called him and Almansi to his office."

"Who are Kappler and Almansi?" Ben asked.

Bovenzi's expression said that he had no time for questions, but he explained that Kappler was chief of the SS in Rome and Dante Almansi was president of the Union of Italian Jewish Communities. "Kappler told Almansi he wants 110 pounds of gold from the Jews—in the next thirty-six hours."

"*Oy vay iz mir!*" Claudio exclaimed, raising his arms in supplication. "God in Heaven!"

"What right do they have?" Ben asked angrily.

Bovenzi threw his hands in the air with exasperation. "At first it was bad for the Jews, now it's bad for the rest of us too. We're in a nightmare, afraid to cross the street, terrorized in our own homes."

Ben saw what was happening. Jews not allowed in the army or navy, not permitted in the university, having to give away their businesses—and now 110 pounds of gold in thirty-six hours.

"It's been done forever," Claudio said, shaking his head. "It goes along well for us, just long enough that we feel comfortable, and then the trouble starts all over again."

Bovenzi groaned, saying that the Jewish Community in Rome could never raise that kind of money. He pushed away his coffee cup, explaining that even though the Jews in Rome were poor people, Foà wanted everyone to turn in their jewelry—watches, necklaces, rings, any gold at all. He added that Foà and Almansi had spent all night trying to convince the Italian police to help and they couldn't, or they wouldn't. He stood, throwing down his napkin. "The deadline is now noon tomorrow." He looked at his watch. "That gives the Jewish Community twenty-nine hours."

"Wait a minute," Claudio said, raising a finger. "Will Kappler take money instead of gold?"

With a snort of deprecation, Bovenzi told him that Kappler had told the Jews not to bother him with lire, that he could print as much money as he needed.

Claudio shook his head. "In Belgium, France, and Germany—and now here too."

Bovenzi narrowed his eyes. "Kappler says he wants gold, not the lives of the Jews or their children. Do you understand what he's saying? 'Not your children.'"

Ben shuddered, thinking what monsters the Nazis were.

Bovenzi went on. "If the gold isn't delivered exactly on time, he's going to take two hundred of the Jewish Community and deport them to Germany."

"Barbaric," Claudio breathed. "After giving away their gold, no Jew will have money to run from the Nazis."

Ben looked at his wrist. "My watch is gold. Where shall I take it?" He felt foolish. It was so little to give.

His father pulled out his pocket watch. Grandfather's watch—how many times he'd seen his father rub his thumb over it lovingly, speaking of Nonno. Claudio lifted his wrists, saying that his cufflinks were gold too.

The telephone in the hallway jangled. Bovenzi moved quickly to answer it and in a moment returned, saying that Foà was opening the synagogue offices to start collecting.

Claudio stood and put down his napkin. "We can be there in three-quarters of an hour."

Ben objected. His father could never walk there and then back to the train station.

Claudio insisted. "Ben, I want you to see this. These are your people. These are the things you must someday tell your children."

Their host gave his lips a last wipe with his napkin. "I respect your wishes, Claudio. Your Caravaggio study is on the front hall table." He took Claudio's hands in his. "Be aware that the Germans are starting to block off streets and then it's—*hup*—they sweep up the men and boys into trucks and take them God knows where."

Bovenzi took hold of Ben's shoulders. "I hadn't seen your drawing before your father gave it to me for safekeeping. It was a privilege to see it. It's … it's captivating. I was moved by its energy and verve and I'm so very sorry you have to sell it." He looked into Ben's eyes. "But it's what an art dealer has to do. He must resist becoming emotionally attached to the work. I'm sure your father has told you that."

Ben nodded, his bitter disappointment rising once again.

In the hallway, Bovenzi took leave of Claudio and Ben. "Good luck, old friend. Let's hope for better days."

"Thank you for taking us in," Claudio said, squeezing the man's hands.

Ben approached the box with the drawing reverently. Unrolling the small sketch, he marveled again that it had survived almost four hundred years. The sight of it brought the same rush of feeling as the day he'd first found it in Venice four years before. Caravaggio had sketched in brown pen and wash the young, muscular Bacchus raising his glass of red wine. Ben was overcome again by the play of dark and light, the realities of life in the ripe grape next to the withered leaf, the careless robes, the sensuous, full lips of the young god, the serene, commanding eternal Bacchus, God of Wine.

His father's voice startled him. "Remember, we own nothing, neither possessions nor people. All of life is on loan for a generation."

Ben returned the drawing to its box and put it in the briefcase, wondering how his father could speak with such tranquility. He knew that if he lost Caravaggio's drawing, he'd do anything to find it again. Although he had to sell the drawing now, he was determined to buy it back when the war was over. He'd fight to make certain that the Bacchus sketch always belonged to Beniamino Cantarini.

CHAPTER 5

The third day after Claudio and Ben left for Rome, Padua's autumnal rains began in earnest. Sheets of water pounded the streets and overflowed the curbs. Hoping that the bad weather had driven the soldiers off the street, Constanz pulled back the blackout curtain and looked at the sidewalk below. *Grazie a Dio*, no one there. What had become of poor Professor Roth on his hands and knees? She hadn't seen him since the soldiers had forced him to clean the front steps with a toothbrush. Should she go to his apartment and see if he—

Suddenly, two soldiers in rain slickers stepped out from a doorway below and began their usual patrol. She quickly drew back from the window.

Hearing Monica washing her face in the bathroom, Constanz mechanically prepared a simple breakfast—bread and milk for her daughter and chicory for herself. When Monica came into the kitchen, Constanz kept her voice soft, trying not to betray her shakiness. "Good morning, *amore mio*." She gave her daughter a reassuring hug.

While they ate their breakfast, Constanz tried to appear calm, but her thoughts were racing wildly. Where were Claudio and Ben? Why hadn't they called her? Claudio always told her to be brave, but she counted on him to give her strength.

"Mamma, do we have any cheese?"

Constanz took the remaining cheese from the cool box and sliced it. She attempted to talk cheerfully to Monica, all the time telling herself not to dissolve into tears. "When Papà and Beniamino get home, we'll go out to the country again and buy more cheese and maybe a chicken from the farmers."

"Did Papà and Ben call last night, Mamma?"

"They would have, my darling, but the telephone lines must be down. I'm sure they're on their way home." Monica was frowning. Constanz could tell she was not reassured, so she tried to sound more convincing. "We'll be together soon, you'll see."

The morning and afternoon crept by. Still no word. By ten in the evening, Monica had eaten her supper and lay asleep on the sofa.

A knock at the door! Constanz jumped up and tiptoed to the door. Looking through the peephole, she saw the older of the two soldiers who had followed her up the steps the day Claudio and Ben had left for Rome. She spun around and ran back to Monica. Shaking the little girl by the shoulders, she pulled her up.

Monica rubbed her eyes. "What, Mamma?"

"Don't talk, just come with me down the back steps."

Please, Constanz prayed, don't let there be German soldiers at the back door.

Holding her doll, Monica scrambled behind her mother, asking, "Why did you wake me up? Are Papà and Ben home?"

"No, not yet. Hurry now."

Constanz's hand was shaking so badly, she had trouble knocking on her neighbor's door one floor below. Scuffling footsteps approached and a woman called through the door. "*Chi è?*"

"Signora Mondini, it's Constanz and Monica Cantarini. Please open the door."

Cautiously, the door was drawn back. The sight of signora Mondini in her comfortable chenille bathrobe and the homey smell of warm bread made Constanz want to throw herself into the younger woman's arms. Instead, she hurried inside with Monica.

Signora Mondini, pushing back her dark hair, whispered in alarm, "What in the world is it, at this time of night?"

"Could you please close the door behind us and lock it?" Constanz said.

Signora Mondini pushed the door shut. "Keep your voice down. My baby is asleep."

Constanz poured out her words. "Claudio and Ben went to Rome three days ago, so we're alone and there's a Nazi soldier at my door."

Signora Mondini's face paled. Monica clutched at her mother and began sobbing, but Constanz's neighbor shook her head vehemently, explaining that her husband was away on business and she wouldn't do anything that would endanger her baby. She wanted Constanz and Monica to leave.

Constanz begged to stay, just for a few minutes.

The younger woman was adamant. "No, Signora Cantarini."

"Please, I can't go back to my apartment. I'm terrified."

When Monica began crying harder, signora Mondini put her hand on the doorknob. Opening the door, she said, "I'm sorry about the racial laws, but it isn't fair to bring innocent people into your problems."

Constanz suppressed the anger bursting inside her chest. She put her arm tightly around her daughter and led her into the hallway. Signora Mondini called after them, "Perhaps the soldier has word of your husband and son. You had better speak with him." With that, she slammed the door shut.

Constanz felt faint. Breathing hard, she turned and climbed up the steps, pulling Monica behind her.

* * *

As he and his father entered the first street inside the Jewish ghetto, Ben tightened his grip on the briefcase containing the Bacchus drawing. "How safe are we here?" he asked his father.

"These days a Jew is safe nowhere," his father answered.

Ben glanced around, but there was nothing except a wash of noise, neighbors calling to one another, people dashing in and out of the winding alleyways and crisscrossing the small piazzas. Even at seven-thirty in the morning, the air was electric with energy and intent. He was amazed by the confusion of sights and sounds.

"Five years since we've been here, but it'll be the same in a hundred more," Claudio murmured. "This is how old Rome was for your Caravaggio, hectic like this, only even more dangerous."

"More dangerous? Have you forgotten last night?" Once again Ben was amazed by his father's naïveté.

"In those days, each man had a knife in his hand. At least I see no knives."

Was his father trying to protect him again, or was he trying to fool himself?

"Look around you," Claudio went on. "These are your roots, which you never see in Padua. Sometimes I regret that we've become so assimilated. A man who doesn't appreciate his tradition is not a full man.

The scene was a mosaic of color and frenetic activity, men on street corners behind stands of old clothing calling out in voices made nasal to rise above the cacophony of the crowded district—*qui, qui, guardate!* It's here, the best, the best. As they passed a fruit stand, his father shook his head and smiled, saying you'd think the man was selling the finest food in Rome. The wares the vendor was calling "better than you can imagine" were wrinkled potatoes and questionably fresh apples he had scrabbled together in spite of the food shortages.

Even though he was nervous, Ben drank in the sights and the ghetto dialect, Roman mixed with Hebrew. Children called out and scrambled over the ancient marble columns lying neglected and cradled by weeds. Here and there he spotted Hebrew inscriptions carved into the façades of shops.

His father pointed to the end of the Via del Portico d'Ottavia. They were approaching the synagogue. Ben looked up with awe at the old building, venerable with its century-old Babylonian-style architecture. Seeing the towering domes, he expected his father to comment on the land of the East that had been their ancient homeland. Instead his father stopped abruptly at the wrought iron gate enclosing the empty courtyard.

"Where is everyone?" he exclaimed. "I expected a line to be formed already. News travels fast in the ghetto."

Ben followed his father through a side door and climbed the cold, poorly lit stairway to the Jewish Community offices. The large gray room had a musty odor, as if the windows hadn't been opened in a long time. Rows of filing cabinets lined the walls, and on a semicircle of plain wooden tables stood empty boxes. Five bleary-eyed middle-aged men walked up and down behind the tables, gesturing, all talking at once. The fear in the air was palpable.

"See that fellow across the room?" Claudio asked. "He is signor Foà."

Tall, young, energetic, his dark eyes capped by bushy black eyebrows, Foà looked like a natural leader. Coming over to them, he called out, "Ah, Signor Cantarini, what a privilege!"

Claudio greeted Foà and introduced Ben. "Outside this room, we are using the name Campano. We have Aryan papers."

"Yes, of course." Foà shook his head, explaining that barely anyone had come. The Community had been telephoning all night, but people were afraid. He nodded toward an owl-faced older man bent over a table, adjusting a scale. "We managed to reach our jeweler, signor Anticoli." The old man nodded.

Claudio and Ben put their watches on the table. The jeweler took them, pried open their backs, and unscrewed their stems and inner workings. Handing back the detritus to the two men, he said, "They'll still tell time."

Ben slipped the weightless remains of his eighteenth birthday gift into his pocket. He felt a welling up of pride at being the first to help. Then he silently cursed the SS, wishing they could all burn in hell. He thought of the ancient prayers of the Seder: "In every generation, in every age, some rise up to plot our annihilation."

Much more gold was needed, something bigger than a few people bringing bits of jewelry. Ben approached Foà, who seemed annoyed at the interruption, and asked, "Don't you need a better idea than waiting for people to come in?"

Foà gave him a hard look, explaining that he had boys running through the streets trying to exchange lire for gold. Then he told Ben to go sit with his father. Feeling like a schoolboy who'd been admonished, Ben returned to his father, frowning and grumbling. Claudio put up a hand. "We came to help. Just follow instructions."

Ben couldn't simply sit, so he strode over to Foà again. "Look, do you have a telephone and a list of the Community?"

"We've tried that. Nobody is answering the phone." Foà pointed to a room off the office. "It's all in there."

In the smaller room, filled with dusty files and stacked up chairs, Ben sat at a card table in front of a telephone and a list of names. The names A-K had been checked off, so he started by dialing Lasky. After five rings, he gave up. Lautenberg—no answer. Licheri—no answer. He slammed down the telephone, saying aloud to the room, "Have you run away, or are you hiding in your houses?" Next he called Luseni. After three rings a man answered in a nervous voice, "*Pronto.*"

"Ah, Signor Luseni," Ben said, "I am calling from the Jewish Community offices and—"

The man interrupted. "I know about the extortion, but I'm busy packing and I have no time to come."

"But these are our people. They need help!"

"Don't tell me my business," signor Luseni snapped back. "My family comes first and we're going away." Click—he had hung up.

"You bastard!" Ben cursed into the telephone. He dialed a signor Luzzati. After three rings, a timid older woman's voice answered. "*Sì, pronto.*"

"Signora Luzzati, I'm calling from the Jewish Community offices. Have you heard about the deadline?"

"Yes, but I'm afraid to leave my house."

"We'll send someone over."

"All right. I'm four blocks away." She gave her address.

Fifteen calls later, Ben had five addresses to run to. He showed his list to Foà, who shook his head. "You'll be back in an hour with three ounces of gold. What good is that?"

Ben started for the door, but Foà pulled him back by the sleeve, taking him to the window, telling him to look at the sidewalk below. In the nearly empty street, two men stood under a chestnut tree, looking around, not talking. "They're checking our progress. Keep clear of them."

"Nazis?"

"Of course. Gestapo. The SS wants to know how we're doing." The serious-faced men were more chilling to Ben because they had no uniforms. They both wore trench coats and dark fedoras.

Ben gave the briefcase to his father and said, "Please don't let this out of your sight." Downstairs he waited until the two Gestapo agents had turned away for a moment. Then he walked quickly in the direction of the first address he'd been given.

An hour later, his trouser pockets filled with coins, necklaces, and rings, he again passed the two men still standing outside the synagogue. He walked in a nonchalant manner, waiting until the last moment to duck in under the archway of the entrance. At the top of the steps, he looked for his father and found him sitting where he had left him, still clutching the briefcase. Pulling the gold from his pockets, Ben gave it to the jeweler. Signor Anticoli shook his head, pointing to the one box holding gold, now three-quarters full.

Foà, perspiring profusely, called out to the knot of men milling around the room, "We have lire. I want everyone to take the lire I give you, go in the streets, and find people who will give you their gold."

Ben realized that it was hopeless and looked at his father

again. Claudio, his face ashen, beckoned to Ben. "Find me a glass of water. I need my medicine."

Ben gave his father his pills. "Papà, we've done all we can and maybe we need to get on the train."

"No, we can't leave yet. So many times our people have been backed against the wall. And yet we survive. But I'm too tired to think."

"Papà, isn't the Vatican near here?"

"Less than half a mile," his father answered, shrugging.

"Don't they owe the Roman Jews something for having kept them cooped up in this ghetto for hundreds of years?"

Claudio shook his head. "You think all debts are paid?"

"But they could talk to the Nazis. Aren't a lot of Germans Catholic?"

Foà shouted to two young men who had appeared at the top of the steps. "Ah, Adriano Ascarelli and Renzo Levi!"

Claudio stood from his chair. "Renzo Levi, *buon giorno.*"

A slim fellow with an angular face put out his hand to Claudio. "Oh, Signor Cantarini, forgive me. It's been a few years—the dinner at your apartment—" He introduced Adriano Ascarelli.

Ascarelli turned his penetrating black eyes toward Claudio. His permanent frown lines deepening, he gripped the older man's hand, and then he looked impatiently around the room, asking where the people were.

Ben spoke up. "I'm signor Cantarini's son. I have an idea—what about going to the Vatican? Maybe they can influence the Nazis."

Ascarelli exploded. "If the Germans knew we were going to the Vatican, they could arrest all of us!"

Ben insisted that he was willing to take the risk.

Claudio agreed that it was dangerous, but wanted Ben to go with Ascarelli and ask for help.

Foà thought for a moment and gave his permission. Ascarelli sprinted for the stairs. Ben again handed the briefcase with the Caravaggio sketch to his father and raced after the young man.

"Ten o'clock," Ascarelli called over his shoulder. "Twenty-six hours left. Move faster, will you, Cantarini?"

CHAPTER 6

Ascarelli raced through the ghetto, the tails of his long black coat flying behind him. Ben kept pace with him through the crowded, winding streets. He knew that Ascarelli wished he hadn't come along, but dammit he was here now. The clock in the tower of the last street in the ghetto marked ten minutes past ten. With precious time speeding by, the push to the Vatican made Ben's face hot and wet with perspiration. Finally the streets widened and led to a bridge over the Tiber.

"Who are we going to see?" Ben asked.

"Monsignor O'Flaherty," Ascarelli answered curtly. "He's close to the pope."

"Has the pope ever helped Jews before?"

Ascarelli smirked and gave him a sidelong glance, and then told him that in the Middle Ages the Jews had to pay three hundred scudi a year to the Vatican and kiss the foot of each new pope. Did Ben call that a help?

Ben persisted. "I mean in our lifetime."

Ascarelli stepped up the pace. "Once in a while, but you can't count on it."

In a few minutes they had reached the threshold of a vast piazza. Ben remembered, five years before, seeing St. Peter's Square thronged with people, but now only an occasional priest or nun ventured across the open area, head down, acknowledging no one. Embraced by a huge double row of marble columns, the square was dominated by an enormous marble structure, the Basilica. Though built to glorify God, Ben decided it had been designed to make a person feel insignificant compared to God. The image of his synagogue in Padua came to mind, impressive enough, but with more comfortable proportions. Here, seemingly endless mosaic designs spread across the square, leading the way to the overwhelming edifice.

"German soldiers," Ascarelli hissed, slowing down. In front of the Basilica a group of German soldiers eyed the square. "Don't act rushed. Go at a normal pace."

Ben lifted his chin and kept walking. The soldiers glanced at them as they passed, but said nothing.

A Swiss guard, in his medieval costume of red and yellow ballooning pants and striped vest, looked oddly colorful in these grief-filled wartime days. He thrust out his halberd to stop them. How would they ever get past all this? Ben was surprised to hear Ascarelli speak with quiet authority. "We're from the Jewish Community. Monsignor O'Flaherty sent for us."

The guard moved his halberd to the left and let them pass. Ben's heart was racing. Could they be entering some kind of trap? Their footsteps echoed as they walked up a wide marble staircase. At the top, a young priest in a long black cassock stared at them through his round eyeglasses. "What is your business, please?"

Ascarelli removed his black fedora, holding it to his chest. "We're looking for Monsignor O'Flaherty."

The priest shook his head, gesturing for them to return to the street. "He's not in the Vatican today."

"We're from the Jewish Community and we need help, immediately," Ben said.

The priest's voice took on an edge. "Everyone else is in a meeting, not to be disturbed." He added, "Come back tomorrow."

"Tomorrow!" Ascarelli exclaimed. "Two hundred Jews could be taken off by the Gestapo tomorrow!"

The priest insisted that he had no authority to disturb the meeting.

Ben shot back that the priest would find authority in a hurry if two hundred Catholics were about to be taken hostage.

"Don't be insolent, young man," the priest snapped back. "I said I can't help you."

Ben bit his lip, realizing he'd made a mistake. Still, he persisted. "Don't you see, we're desperate. The Gestapo wants 110 pounds of gold and the Jewish Community doesn't have it. The deadline is tomorrow at noon! How long will the meeting take?"

"Perhaps until early afternoon. Look, the war has made problems for everyone."

Ben pressed on. "When I was little, a Catholic boy used to call me a Christ killer. I didn't kill Christ, but the Germans are killing Jews. We are desperate *innocenti*. We need your help!"

The priest's face turned red. He hesitated, then gestured for them to follow him. Walking with Ascarelli and Ben down a long hallway, he left them in a high-ceilinged waiting room. He indicated a long white sofa and walked out, his footsteps sounding on the marble floor.

Ascarelli muttered, "You Jews from the north can be insistent, can't you?"

"Well, dammit, it had to be said." Ben paced the room, looking at the tables topped with enormous golden vessels. He saw so much wealth, so much gold everywhere; even the windows were swagged with golden velvet draperies. The heavy rococo tables were lavishly gilded, and the stiff brocaded sofas were run through with golden threads. Those people could help in two minutes, if they chose to. Anger was boiling inside him, anger at the Nazis for their sadistic ways, anger at this priest for his insensitivity.

The room was silent as the tomb, with only occasional tapping of footsteps somewhere in the distance and now and then the faraway ringing of bells. Ben kept pacing, studying the looming paintings of saints with their otherworldly gazes. Even the ornate frames were thick with gold paint.

Ascarelli, who had thrown himself onto an overstuffed gilt sofa, began muttering imprecations at the "stupid Vatican hierarchy." He glared at Ben. "Will you stop walking around like that? Where do you think that will get you?"

"Well, I could do without looking at you twirling those tassels on your sofa!"

"Oh, shut up!" Ascarelli stood and walked to one of the windows. "Now look at that. The SS are all around this place. I heard that they were going to do this."

Ben went to the window. Three SS men were painting a broad white line parallel with the front of the Vatican. "What's that all about?"

"That white line says everyone inside is safe. Once you go past that line, you're in the Third Reich's territory and your life—"

"*Caspita!*" Ben cut in, muttering that it was bad luck that they hadn't gotten in and out of there sooner.

Ascarelli pointed at him. "Your father is so proud of his up and coming art dealer son? You have no patience. You're walking like a rat on a treadmill! Sit down!"

Another half hour passed. Church bells sounded in the distance, then silence again. Finally Ben heard footsteps approaching. He and Ascarelli shot to their feet.

A priest walked into the room, his black robe swinging, a red sash around his waist. "Good afternoon, I am Monsignor Izzo. His Holiness has given your situation his most earnest consideration."

"And—?" Ascarelli said.

"The Vatican is willing to lend the Jewish Community that part of the gold which they are not able to raise."

Ben breathed a sigh of relief, but Ascarelli didn't look reassured. Would it come in time, he asked the priest, before hostages were taken?

The priest nodded, saying that the loan would not have to be returned until after the war.

Ben spoke up, asking why the pope didn't speak to the Gestapo about stopping this blackmail altogether? Weren't some of the Gestapo Catholic?

"I have told you what we have to offer." The priest's tone was final.

Ascarelli shook his head and reached for his fedora. "Thank you, Monsignore. Good-bye."

The two young men raced down to the great piazza. The Swiss Guards looked at them with cold faces. At the white line Ben averted his eyes from the SS men. Passing them, he waited for a hand on his shoulder. Once he and Ascarelli were a safe distance from the soldiers, he said, "God in Heaven, why doesn't the pope protest to the Gestapo—make them stop this inhumane extortion?"

Ascarelli glanced at him. "Are there always answers?"

Ben grimaced. Ascarelli sounded like Papà. "Do you think they'll keep their promise?"

"Who am I—the pope? Maybe yes, maybe no." Holding his hat against his chest again, Ascarelli took off at a rapid pace. Ben followed, thinking, would the Vatican really give them the gold to fill the shortfall, or was that just a pretense to get rid of them?

*　　*　　*

Standing with Monica in the foyer of her apartment, staring in fright at the front door, Constanz half-expected the door to be kicked in. Wasn't that what the SS did when you refused to open the door right away? She put her eye to the peephole—thank God, they'd gone away.

She stepped back and heard the telephone ring. Maybe one of those soldiers had gone back to headquarters and was calling her. Should she answer? Her thoughts swirling, she tried to make sense of everything that was happening. Maybe it was Claudio. She turned on the table lamp and gingerly lifted the receiver. "*Pronto.*"

A man's voice said, "Constanz?"

The voice was familiar, but who was it? "*Sì?*"

"This is Rabbi Coen."

His voice was strained and hoarse. Could it be someone trying to deceive her?

"Hello? Are you there, Constanz?"

Now it sounded like the rabbi. He cleared his throat. "I am sorry to call so late, but I wanted to tell you that something is going on in Rome."

She stiffened. "What do you mean?"

The rabbi continued hurriedly, telling her that a member of

the congregation had just returned from Rome and had reported that there was a very difficult situation with the Jews and the Gestapo. The rabbi didn't know all the details—

Constanz cut in, "Are Claudio and Ben all right? They only went to Rome to get the Caravaggio drawing. You know they have Aryan papers, so they are traveling as Catholics."

The rabbi's voice was suddenly stern. He said there seemed to be no immediate danger, but should they telephone her, she should tell them to get away from Rome as soon as possible. And she should be careful herself. It was getting very dangerous for Jews.

As she put the receiver in the cradle, Constanz's gaze fell upon a piece of paper that must have been slipped under the front door.

She picked it up. In German script, it said:

"*Liebe* Signora, I have stopped at your apartment to apologize for the poor comportment of my fellow soldier. I will stop again to present my apologies. Sgt. Kurt Wildmann."

Feeling dizzy, Constanz sat in the chair and re-read the message. What did he want from her? She imagined him returning with other soldiers and … No, she mustn't think like that.

"What does it say, Mamma?"

"Nothing important, darling. I think the person who left it had the wrong address. It was all a mistake." Monica didn't answer, and Constanz wasn't sure the little girl believed her. "We'll go to bed and I'll sleep next to you, my sweet one."

CHAPTER 7

A block away from the synagogue, Ascarelli stopped short. "Good Lord, look at that!"

A throng of people filled the courtyard, overflowing through the iron gates to the street and the wide parapet overlooking the Tiber. It looked as if half the city was there. The two young men pushed through the crowds and entered the side door of the synagogue.

Upstairs Claudio approached them, pale but smiling. Ben put his arm around his father's shoulders. "Are you all right, Papà?"

His father put his hand on his chest, assuring him that he was fine and that they mustn't stop now. When they returned home, Mamma would understand why they had taken so long. Pulling Ben's head down, he whispered in his ear, "Your grandfather would be proud of you. All your telephone calls got the people to start coming, and to tell their neighbors to come."

The onrush of people continued until evening, the staircase and landing jammed with people wanting to donate. Young boys pushed by with wads of lire, running out to the street to buy gold on the black market. Calls continually rose above the crowd:

"How close are we? What's happening? How many pounds do we have?" Ben, with an eye on his weary father, helped to direct people. He ran back and forth to the courtyard and tried to calm people and keep them moving faster up the stairs to the collecting room.

When nightfall came, Foà called out in a hoarse voice for the ten-man committee to come into the next room. He shut the door and stood on a makeshift wood dais to announce that the Community had collected enough gold.

Murmurings and sighs of relief ran through the assembled men. Ben heard his father mumble a soft prayer, ending with a whispered, "God is good."

"But wait." Foà put up a warning hand. "We need more gold."

"Why?" Ben asked, amazed. Ascarelli put his finger to his lips and shook his head.

Foà continued, "We'll go to Via Tasso with extra gold. Everyone should come back in the morning, ready to start collecting again."

"Why extra gold?" Ben asked once more.

Ascarelli leaned into him. "A Jew from the north wouldn't understand a Roman Jew's problems. Promises that are *false*, that's what we're used to. And so we have to be *furbi*— you know *furbi*?"

"Sure," Ben said. "Crafty."

When the committee returned to the collecting room, Claudio told Foà that he and Ben would like to spend the night there.

Foà nodded, saying he could take them to his apartment, but it would safer there at the synagogue.

When the room had cleared, Ben pulled blankets from the

closet and pushed two overstuffed chairs together for his father to sleep on. Lying on the floor, he put his hands behind his head, angry that the goddamn world had been turned upside down. Sitting up again, he looked inside the briefcase. The drawing always made him feel secure and worthy—even now it filled him with excitement. Bacchus's indolent look and suggestive smile, the young god's muscular arms, the tempting fruit, all gave the promise of the painting in the Uffizi. In spite of the corrupt world Caravaggio lived in, he had survived to produce a masterpiece. It sickened Ben to think of selling the drawing, of not seeing it again—for how long? It had once been lost for four hundred years. Could it disappear again, perhaps forever? The thought sent a shot of pain to his stomach.

"You did a good thing today, Beniamino." His father's voice was soft and indistinct.

"Yes, but let's see what happens tomorrow. Good night, Papà."

*   *   *

Constanz checked that the front door was double-locked; she wished that the kitchen door had an extra lock too. It was midnight by the time she had tucked Monica back into her bed and had readied herself for sleep. She decided not to change into her nightgown. The thought of it made her feel too vulnerable. Instead she lay down in her clothes and pulled the down-filled *piumino* around her. Would Claudio really insist they leave this cozy bedroom with its antique cherry armoire and its porcelain Hümmel statuettes of children and kittens? Leave all this to go to some stranger's house? She heard the bells of the Catholic church marking each hour until four in the morning.

At seven, out of habit, she awakened, grateful that no one

else had knocked on the door during the night. She was groggy but ready for news of Claudio and Ben. Tiptoeing out of the room, she went to the kitchen to prepare breakfast for herself and Monica.

By nine she still had no word from her two men. How long must she wait? She tried not to imagine what could have happened to them, but her mind wouldn't obey. She saw them being questioned—and then what? She imagined the train being bombed and Claudio and Ben running from it—but running where? Stop, she had to stop this! If only she knew *something*.

Finally, Monica appeared, sleepy and dragging her doll behind her. "*Tesoro mio!*" Constanz exclaimed, hugging the little girl, never wanting to let go. The bright sunlight slicing through the living room windows comforted her, and she felt confident that only a few more hours would pass before some good word would come. Claudio was so wise and had such a dignified way about him; everyone would feel his presence. When at last in the middle of the morning the doorbell rang, Constanz's spirits rose with joy. She knew they must have misplaced their key. Tears filled her eyes, something that always happened to her at moments like this.

"Here they are!" she called to Monica, who was struggling with her schoolwork at the kitchen table. Mother and daughter dashed to the front door.

Constanz opened the door wide, saying, "Ben! Claud—" She stopped. It was the older, beefy German soldier who had spoken to her before. Seeing him was like having a hand encircle her throat. She saw his serious expression, his tightly-fitting uniform on his stocky body, the wide black leather belt around his hefty waist, and the pistol strapped to the belt under his left arm. She stepped back, clutching the doorframe. "What is it?" she asked.

The soldier stood stiffly in front of her. "Frau Cantarini? *Sprechen Sie Deutsch?*" Putting his heels together and giving a quick bow, he continued in German. "I saw on your document that you were born in Berlin, so I'm sure you speak German."

She knew she couldn't deny it. *"Ja, das ist richtig."*

"Entschuldigen Sie, dear lady, but may I come in?"

"Why? Do you have news of my husband?" Her heart was banging in her chest.

"Nein, Frau Cantarini."

"Then what is it you want?" She looked at his leathery face. He must have spent his fifty-some years out of doors. His thick fingers said that he did manual work. He took off his cap and leaned down to Monica, saying in a heavy German accent, *"Buon giorno, come ti chiami?"*

Monica looked at her mother. Constanz said, "She's shy. She doesn't like to give her name." And Constanz wasn't going to give it either.

He pointed to the inside of the apartment. *"Bitte,* may I come in?"

She wanted to say no, but didn't dare. She put her arm around Monica and stepped farther back into the foyer. The soldier followed, until the three of them were standing in front of the telephone. Constanz thought of seating the man in the living room and coming out to telephone for help. But who would help? Nobody. She had learned that the night before.

"Frau Cantarini, I am Sergeant Wildmann. I have come to apologize for the way in which my partner addressed you."

What kind of trick was this? What *did* this man want? He had the kind of politeness the Germans had—until you knocked against them.

"I come from a small town in Austria," he added.

Angry that he was standing in front of her like this, in her own home, and talking about things she didn't care about or want to hear, she said, "Why are you here?"

She realized he was holding one hand behind his back. She swallowed hard. He pulled his hand forward, offering her a paper bag.

"What is this?" she asked.

"We get good coffee now." He pressed the bag into her hand. "From the colonies, you know."

"I really can't accept this."

"Why, *gnädige* Frau? For me it was disagreeable to hear my fellow soldier speak to you the way he did. Please accept my apologies in his stead."

She wanted to scream, Take your coffee and go back to Austria! "I really have nothing to say," she said, "except that one cannot apologize for other people."

His face turned red. A bead of perspiration trickled down from his temple. "I hoped that you would make a cup of coffee for me."

"I know how to boil the water," Monica said. She ran off to the kitchen.

"No," Constanz said. "We have no milk or sugar."

"I don't use them in my coffee," the soldier replied. His smile pushed back his fat jowls. "I would like to sit at a kitchen table again and wait for a cup of coffee."

Was it better to close the front door, or leave it open? If she closed it, then she and Monica would be alone with him, but if she left it open, other soldiers might come in. She closed the door and led the way to the kitchen.

CHAPTER 8

Shortly before noon the next day, Ben helped carry fifteen cartons of gold earrings, cufflinks, rings, bracelets, and necklaces down to the street. The total weight was one hundred and ten pounds of gold, plus three extra pounds. Claudio lifted his hand in a blessing as Ben hefted his box into a waiting van and jumped in to sit beside Foà and an Italian police escort. At the last minute a chunky fellow wearing a black fedora slid into the van. Foà introduced him as His Excellency Almansi, president of the Union of Italian Jewish Communities.

The driver of the van roared off, skirting the banks of the Tiber and wheeling through the wet streets. Ben held the railing over his head to steady himself. He glanced at Foà, but the man's expression gave no clue to his thoughts—his unruly black eyebrows were furrowed as usual, but otherwise his face was a blank mask. The group rode in silence, until Almansi pointed at the Arch of Titus, muttering, "There's a celebration of Jewish slavery—a triumphal arch."

Ben looked at the carvings of chained figures being dragged

through the streets of Rome and heard Almansi mutter how two thousand years later, we're here again.

A few more blocks and the van pulled up in front of a dull fascist-style building pressed next to an old villa. A tight-lipped SS officer opened the rear door of the van. Ben, Almansi, and Foà, followed by the Italian police, jumped out. Each one of the Jewish contingent lifted a box onto his shoulder and proceeded into the villa. Ben, his box grinding into his shoulder, pulled at Almansi's sleeve to tell him that someone should stay with the gold in the van.

Almansi nodded and spoke to one of the Italian police. The group trudged past some offices and through a garden behind the rear of the building. Raindrops trickled into Ben's collar and rolled down his back. Inside another building, Ben and the others were led into a large conference room. The only furniture in the room was an antique mahogany table. Blank rectangles on the blue stucco walls showed that pictures had once hung there. Probably taken to Berlin, Ben thought—more "safeguarding" of Italian paintings. Three SS men stood guard by the window, their hands on the guns at their waists.

Despite the tremendous weight of the box, Ben felt triumphant that they were making the deadline. An SS officer pointed to the table, saying, "*Stellt die Kisten auf den Tisch!*" The Italian police escort stood back while the Jews obeyed the command and set their boxes on the table. Ben rubbed his aching shoulder and followed Foà and Almansi back to the van. They repeated the trip until the van was emptied of its gold.

Back in the conference room for the final time, Ben saw that a balance scale had been placed on the table. He edged close to Almansi and whispered, "Should we have brought our own scale? Can we trust theirs?"

"Just watch their hands on the lip of the tray each time."

The SS men pushed the cartons toward the scales, grinding ugly scratches into the patina of the mahogany. The lack of respect for even the furniture gave Ben a sick feeling. A balding, sour-faced older man, his eyes down, entered the room, a jeweler's loupe hanging from his neck. He was followed by a German officer who said, "Signor Foà, I am Captain Schultz."

Ben took note of the officer's proud bearing, his searching watery-blue eyes. This was a man with no heart.

"Yes," Foà responded. "This is His Excellency Almansi, and—"

The Captain cut him off. "Yes, yes."

"Major Kappler is not here?" Foà asked.

"No, I shall represent him today. We will take careful note of the weighing."

To Ben his expression implied distrust of the Jews.

Foà replied evenly, "His Excellency Almansi will also take note of the weighing."

"If he wishes." The captain's tone of voice said that it made no difference, that it was *his* calculations that counted.

The jeweler drew a crisp, folded handkerchief from his pocket, pursed his lips, and thoughtfully rubbed his loupe. The captain's assistant, notebook in hand, moved next to him. With his little finger, he adjusted his nickel-rimmed round glasses.

Foà handed Ben a notebook and pen, murmuring, "Calculate carefully."

"The scale measures ten pounds at a time," Captain Schultz announced. "We must weigh eleven times to reach one hundred and ten pounds of gold."

Foà nodded. The SS assistant eyed the gold and then looked at the Jews with distaste. He dipped into the heap of cigarette cases, wedding rings, and necklaces, his expression saying that he was fingering filth. He lifted two handfuls of gold onto the scale. A wedding ring slipped out of his grasp and bounced back into the box. The assistant frowned, adjusted the weight, removed a bracelet, slid the weight again, added a wedding ring, and then a locket. The scale balanced at slightly over ten pounds.

"Captain, if I remove the ring, it is less than ten pounds." The assistant lifted the ring from the scale. "I leave it, and it is over ten."

"Leave the ring and move on."

Ben's face was hot. So that was the trick. He looked at Foà, whose face was impassive. He wrote in his notebook: #1 - ten pounds, and added a plus after the number.

The SS assistant reached in the box for the second weighing of gold. How did that feel, Ben thought, to have your hands rooting around in ransom? As he recorded the second weighing, he looked at Schultz. He was probably there because Kappler didn't want to dirty himself. Even Schultz didn't want to touch the loot.

On the third weighing, Ben was shocked, thinking he saw one of Papà's cufflinks. He closed his eyes until it had been slipped onto the scales. He studied Schultz with loathing, until Foà kicked his ankle.

The only sounds in the room were the *thrush-thrush* of the gold being shifted and set on the balance scale, until Schultz walked out of the room, his boots clicking across the parquet floor. He returned in the middle of the fourth weighing with a gun in a leather holster. Why a gun now? Ben had to force himself not to stare at the Luger, the German soldiers' proud symbol of power.

By the sixth weighing, Ben was cold with fear. Had the

Germans decided to shoot them on some pretext? He looked at Foà, who kept the same tense but impassive expression. Or would the Germans just arrest them and send them to Germany?

Shifting, Ben glanced at Almansi. His full lips were pressed together in deep concentration. The seventh and eighth weighings had finished. Almansi, perhaps sensing Ben's fear, took the pencil and paper from him and made the notations for the tenth and eleventh weighings.

Foà broke the silence. "Eleven times we have weighed—we are finished." His face was ashen, but his lips curved in a thin smile of satisfaction. Almansi nodded, a relieved look on his face. Foà continued, "Now we place three extra pounds of gold on the scale as a show of our good will." He pointed to the remaining gold in the last box.

Captain Schultz opened his eyes wide with surprise. "*Nein,* we have weighed only ten times. Put ten more pounds of gold on the scale."

Almansi pointed to the empty boxes. "But no ... " He held out Ben's notebook. "Look, we have weighed eleven times."

Captain Schultz slapped his hand against his thigh, like a man not accustomed to being contradicted. "How many?" he asked his assistant.

The assistant looked at him impassively. "Ten," he answered.

Ben flushed with anger. "I have eleven in my book." He took the notebook from Almansi and pointed to the numbers.

A vein stood out on Schultz's temple, a muscle moved in his tightening jaw. He exploded, "First you ask to have the deadline extended, and then you try to cheat us. Did you plan this deceit, sitting around that synagogue of yours?"

The sting of the man's words took Ben's breath away. Foà kept calm, but couldn't hide the fear in his eyes.

"Captain Schultz," Ben blurted out, "we want to re-weigh the gold."

Schultz glared at him. "You? Who the hell are you? *Zehn, zehn!* Put ten more pounds on the scale, or we take what's here and send you and two hundred like you to Germany."

"Look," Ben said, pointing to the empty boxes. "We have no more gold. Why would we make trouble for ourselves? It's only … " He searched for the right words. " … honorable to let us weigh again."

"Honorable? Did you say honorable? To me, you said that?" Schultz, his face scarlet, motioned to his assistant. "Take everyone into the next room while I call Berlin." He strode toward the telephone.

Ben, Foà, and Almansi walked into the anteroom, followed by the policemen, and stood looking at one another, shaking their heads.

Finally Almansi asked Foà, "Shall we tell him we'll go back and get more gold?"

Ben took Foà by the coat sleeve. "No, we have to insist on another weighing."

The Italian policemen eyed each other. In the long silence, Ben heard only the ticking of the ormolu clock on the wall behind him.

Foà spoke up. "Is this an excuse to take hostages?"

The three men stared in silence at the floor. Minutes went by. Occasionally an Italian policeman cleared his throat. Almansi wiped beads of perspiration from his temples. Ben could finally stand the wait no longer. He started for the door to the conference room. As he opened it, Captain Schultz entered. Ben was stunned by the man's pleasant smile.

"I have decided," the captain said in a cordial tone, "that we will weigh again."

The Italians looked at each other in surprise. Wondering if Schultz had really called Berlin, Ben followed the others back into the conference room. The weighing proceeded in silence. As the work progressed, the room grew warmer. Ben could smell the sweat of the Italian policeman next to him.

Finally, the eleventh box was weighed and found correct. The extra three pounds of gold remained aside. Captain Schultz motioned for them to be added to the tray, saying, "The required gold has been delivered." As the boxes were carried to the adjoining room, Ben studied Captain Schultz's face, trying to read his thoughts. Triumph? Greed? Arrogance?

Schultz dismissed the Jewish leaders with a wave of his hand. He turned his back and started for the adjoining room.

"Captain Schultz." Ben took two steps after him. "We need our receipt."

The captain wheeled around, frowning. "For what? For what you agreed to bring us?" His lips were in a tight line. "First you cause us to weigh twice, as if we had nothing else to do, and then you ask for a receipt. Get out! My wife and children are waiting for me to have tea. You've wasted my time too much already."

"But if someone should ask if we have delivered the gold?"

"Tell them to go to hell." The captain's face darkened. "Get out of here, you filthy swine."

In the street, Ben was relieved to see that the Italian police were still waiting for them. He climbed into the van with Almansi and Foà.

Foà lifted his hat and wiped his brow with his handkerchief. "He thought he could get ten more pounds of gold out of us and keep it for himself. He probably decided to be satisfied with three pounds. But what is three pounds of gold? So far our people are safe."

Listening to Foà, Ben envied the Roman Jews' sense of community. But was this the price they had to pay? Having to surrender everything, remembering to keep their eyes down?

When they arrived at the synagogue, Claudio greeted them, looking happy yet drained.

"We did it!" Ben exclaimed, throwing his arms around his father.

"I'm so proud of you." Claudio smiled wanly. "I wish we could call your mother. I would feel better."

"We've done everything we can do. Let's go for the train," Ben said. "Can you take the half-hour walk?"

Claudio handed Ben the briefcase with the Bacchus drawing. "To get home, I could walk for hours."

Outside the synagogue courtyard, Ben glanced around, thankful that the street was almost empty. No sign of the Gestapo. Father and son walked quickly through the darkening fog, ducking their heads to keep away from the overhanging branches of the chestnut trees.

Suddenly, sharp footsteps approached. Two SS officers appeared, flashlights aimed in their direction. Ben sidestepped them, pulling his father with him.

"*Halt!*" one of the officers shouted.

Ben's heart lodged in his throat. Run? Could they disappear into the fog? But he knew Papà couldn't run a quarter of a block. Both flashlights shined into his father's face. Claudio raised his arm to screen his eyes.

"*Come si chiama?*" the first officer asked in heavily accented Italian.

"Campano, Arturo."

The taller of the two soldiers clamped a hand on Claudio's shoulder. "Art dealer, *nicht wahr?*"

Art dealer? How did they know that? Ben asked himself.

"*Sì,*" his father answered in a shaky voice.

"Come with us."

"But why?" Ben demanded. "We haven't done anything. My father is ill."

"We have orders. You can explain yourself at Via Tasso."

From out of nowhere metal crunched against Ben's cheekbone. His legs gave way as a knee slammed into his groin. He gasped for air and fell to the pavement.

A car pulled up, its tires squealing. A rough voice said, "*Hinein! Schnell!*" and the car screeched off. Papà and the soldiers were gone. Ben was alone on the sidewalk, tears of anger stinging his cheeks.

Straining to get up, he thought of the words, "Art dealer, *nicht wahr?*" He pushed himself up on one knee, grasping his suitcase and briefcase. The Caravaggio drawing was still there. Why Papà? He was old and ill. Where should he go for help? Ignoring his pain, he hobbled as quickly as he could in the direction of the Bovenzis' apartment.

*   *   *

As Constanz walked toward the kitchen, her legs threatened to fold under her. It flashed through her mind—Nazi soldiers raping women, killing children. No, this mustn't happen to her. She stopped for a moment to lean against the back of a chair. The furniture in the dining room, the table and chairs, the Meissen china and brass chandelier, whirled around her.

"What is it, dear lady?" the soldier asked, holding her arm.

"Nothing, nothing," she snapped, yanking her arm away. Her

breathing became more regular and her head cleared. Anger rose within her that this intruder had pushed his way into her home.

"Mamma," Monica called from the kitchen. "I put the water on. It's almost boiling."

"Be careful. Don't burn yourself." Constanz walked to the kitchen cupboard and reached for a cup and saucer.

The soldier had not advanced beyond the kitchen doorway. He must be waiting to be invited in, she thought. "You may come in," she said firmly, "but only for coffee."

His cap pressed against his chest, he stepped into the kitchen. He looked around and pointed to a pine chair at the yellow linoleum table, his eyebrows raised as if asking permission.

"Yes, sit down," she said.

He dropped into the chair and nodded toward Monica, who was staring at him. "You will sit too?"

Monica looked at her mother who, unwillingly, nodded assent.

He set his cap on the rung under the chair. When Monica sat down, he said, "I have a little girl about your age. Can you understand my Italian?"

"Yes. What is her name?"

"Frederika. We call her Freddy for short."

Monica frowned in confusion. "Isn't Freddy a boy's name?"

"*Ja, ja, aber* it can also be a little name for a girl."

Monica ran to her room and came back with paper and a pencil. She sat down again and began drawing a picture of a family.

"So," the soldier said, "you can draw a nice picture. My little Freddy also likes to do that."

Monica looked up at him, glanced at her mother, and went on drawing.

Constanz took down the coffee mill. Her mouth watered at the aroma released from grinding the beans. How long since she'd smelled real coffee? Two years, maybe three? She yearned for a cup herself.

She poured the water over the grounds, pressed the grounds and poured the coffee into a cup. And now, instead of enjoying this, she was serving it to her enemy. Her throat tightened with rage as she set the cup down in front of the soldier.

Monica jumped up and rushed to the cool box, pointing to the milk.

"No!" Constanz almost screamed the word. "We're saving that for Papà and Beniamino."

"*Bitte!*" the soldier said, waving his hand. "I do not take milk." He bent over his cup, inhaling the fragrance, and then sat back. "Dear lady, I am ashamed to drink this alone. I brought this so that you could have some too."

Constanz shook her head and began washing the breakfast dishes. She stood at an angle, so she could see the soldier from the corner of her eye.

Monica seemed to understand that she should not make conversation with the soldier. She watched him stir his coffee, drink from the spoon, and then lift the cup and saucer to his lips.

Constanz heard a familiar whirring sound, and then—*cuckoo*. The bird jumped out from his brown wooden nest to announce eleven o'clock. The soldier grinned broadly.

"Oh, I have just such a clock in my house in Mondsee." He put the cup and saucer down and glanced at Constanz.

"We were not always German." He looked away from her and spoke to the air. "When the German army came into Austria, you know, the *Anschluss,* that's when it was decided that we were to be German." He paused a moment. "I have such a beautiful farm outside Mondsee, up in the mountains. But I was told I had to be in the army, so now my wife has to milk the cows and bring in the hay. Such a lot of work but I tell her that we have no choice." He finished his coffee and carried his cup and saucer to the sink. Constanz hastily stepped away from him.

Good, he's finished, she thought. *Let him get out of here.* She took a few steps toward the dining room, hoping he would follow her.

In German he said, "I never expected to find in Italy a lady who can speak German. I once took a trip to Salzburg. It's a long trip by horse and wagon. My brother milked the cows when my wife and I went on that trip. My brother can't help me now, because he's with the German army in Yugoslavia. Now I should be always in Mondsee. You know that cows are in pain if you do not milk them every day." He walked to the end of the kitchen to the cuckoo clock. "You have sometimes to clean such a clock or it won't work anymore. I hope my wife is cleaning our clock."

He stared at the clock, his arms hanging by his side, his thick fingers drumming against his thighs.

Suddenly he wheeled around. Constanz turned to face him, her shoulders tense, her arms crossed over her chest.

The soldier bent down to the rung of the chair for his cap. "Thank you, dear lady, for making me a cup of coffee. It was good to hear a little German. Now I must leave."

She followed him to the door, shutting it behind him and double-locking it. Sitting on the chair near the telephone table, she fought to push down any pity she felt for the poor creature, trapped against his will by the war. No, she would spare him no compassion. After all, who had spared her family any kindness, any sympathy?

"Mamma, why are you crying?"

"Because I'm glad he's gone." She stood and wiped her eyes with the backs of her hands. Walking back to the kitchen, she took the Austrian's bag of coffee and locked it away in the cupboard.

CHAPTER 9

Outside the Bovenzis' darkened apartment building, Ben punched the buzzer and banged on the gate. The concierge finally shuffled down the steps, telling him he'd wake the dead with all his noise.

"I don't give a damn," Ben shot back. "My father has been taken to Via Tasso. I need to see signor Bovenzi."

"They've gone to the country." He rubbed his wrist. "It's no picnic when the SS comes around asking who's been here."

"You denounced us, you bastard!" Ben put his hands through the bars, grabbing hold of the man's shirt.

The concierge shoved him back. "Get the hell out of here."

"You son of a bitch!"

The man beat it up the stairs and disappeared into the darkness. The door to the hallway slammed shut.

Ben set off at a run for Via Tasso, the rain splattering against his leather jacket and his face. He made his way through the streets with the help of headlights from patrolling police cars. In twenty minutes he reached Via Tasso, his shoes filled with water, squishing with each step.

The SS man on duty shot out his arm. "*Heil* Hitler!"

"I'm here to find my father," Ben said, trying to catch his breath.

"You will have to speak to Herr Feltzer." The SS man took Ben's papers, looked at them, and then with his flashlight pointed to the entrance door.

Inside, a guard knocked on the door behind him and opened it. At the far end of a large room, a round-faced, heavy-set man sat behind an ornately carved desk. Brown business suit, perhaps in his middle thirties, his blond hair already receding, he didn't look up from the papers in front of him. Looming behind him was a large portrait of a glaring Adolf Hitler, set off by two enormous red and black swastika flags. Steel file cabinets lined the wall behind the man. Ben told himself to stay calm. The man finally looked up and pointed to the chair facing him. Ben sat down, noting the nameplate on the desk.

"You are Herr Feltzer?" he asked. "I have come to find my father, Arturo Campano. He is an Italian citizen."

Herr Feltzer held out his hand. "Your identity papers." He glanced over the papers and tossed them onto his desk. "Why have you come to Rome?"

"My father is an art dealer. We are here on business."

"Your father is an art dealer and you work in a factory? That must give him pleasure!" The man smiled thinly.

"We both know about art," Ben answered.

"And your father likes impressionist art?"

Ben hesitated, aware that the Nazis tolerated only Teutonic art. "My father will look for whatever his clients want," he said, hoping that was vague enough.

Feltzer reached into his breast pocket and removed a pack of Nazionali. "I've grown to like some of your Italian cigarettes."

Lighting one, he sucked in deeply and blew the smoke through his nostrils.

Ben leaned forward. "Herr Feltzer, my father—"

Feltzer waved his hand to stop him. "Only German art expresses the vitality and grandeur of our *Volk*. Street women and debauchery will not lead our people where they want to go. The heroes of German mythology express our ideals."

His face growing hot, Ben thought of the *Bacchus* hanging in the Uffizi—a gorgeous, unashamed rendering of debauchery. And the small, exquisite drawing in his briefcase was the inspiration for it.

Feltzer opened the top drawer of his desk and slipped Ben's identity papers inside. "*Mein* Herr," Ben said, "excuse me, but I have come—"

Feltzer shook his head. "I've studied art in my time and I have an understanding of the basic problem." He fiddled with the ashtray. "You know Carl Jung, of course, and his 1936 article entitled 'Wotan'."

Ben nodded, at a loss for words. Feltzer drew a deep breathful of smoke and exhaled. Then his words poured out. When the world was in trouble, Feltzer said, it was because the artists had been leading the way, their creativity gone amok. Art should follow the lead of the state. He paused for a moment, searching for the right words, then plunged on, assuring Ben that when civilizations had too much money, they became interested in art. That was when the problems began, because the artists were all homosexuals—or at least debauched—and then homosexuals were forcing their sick morality onto the *Volk*. Feltzer flicked the ashes of his cigarette into the ashtray without stopping his lecture. "The Reich wants painters who work with the symbols and motifs of German mythology. Therein lies our strength."

Ben sat forward. "I am here to find my father."

"You already said that. Do you think I have the memory of an eighty-year-old?" Feltzer beckoned to the guard at the other end of the room. "Take him with you."

His throat dry, Ben picked up his belongings and followed the guard. They climbed a staircase whose carved white balustrade contrasted with the slashes of red and black swastika flags decorating the stucco walls. The old villa was a maze of passageways, alcoves, and doorways. Finally, the guard stopped in front of a closed door. Unlocking it, he took Ben's suitcase and briefcase. Before Ben could protest, the guard had pushed him inside and slammed the door. Ben heard the key turn in the lock.

In the dim light, he saw his father, looking smaller, almost shrunken, seated in a chair in the middle of the empty room. "Papà?" Ben called softly. His father looked up, meeting his eyes. "Are you all right?"

"Of course, Beniamino. I was just asking the Master of the Universe how long I would be here until you came to me."

Ben leaned over to embrace him. He saw that his father's cheek was swollen. "Papà, what happened?"

"It's a sport for Nazis, you know, beating up Jews."

"But your Aryan papers—"

"They find a way to learn everything. How naïve to believe that the concierge wouldn't recognize me." He shook his head. "When you don't have enough food to eat, I suppose you turn in a Jew to get your supper." His father pointed to the ceiling, put a finger to his mouth, and began speaking in Venetian dialect. "The Gestapo wants money. It costs to get out of prison and they believe that an art dealer has money."

"Then how are we going to get you out of here?"

"They're going to send you for money. Herr Feltzer says he wants two thousand lire by the end of the week."

"That's enough to live on for six months! Where does he think we can get that kind of money?"

"In the picture vault, in the living room at home, I have lire enough for half of what he's asking."

"But where are we going to get the rest?"

"Go to Lupino and ask to borrow the other half of the money."

Ben stared at his father. Lupino? That so-called partner of his father? Why did Papà think he would lend him a thousand lire? The man had barely hid his pleasure when Claudio had to turn over his gallery to him. Now Papà was instructing Ben to offer twenty percent interest.

"To be paid when? He'll want to know that."

"*Ahi!* That throbs." His father rubbed his cheek. "When times are better."

"When times are better? Now that the Germans are here?"

"If Lupino can't help, then take the Bacchus drawing to the buyer in Venice." He sighed, looking at his hands. "But see your mother first and tell her not to worry. She depends on me." His eyes pleaded with Ben. "Listen to me, my son. I haven't given your mother the kind of life she grew up with."

Ben turned his head away, afraid his father would start confiding things he didn't want to hear. His voice apologetic, Papà explained that Constanz's life in Berlin had been filled with concerts and operas. She had reminded him of Italian girls, the way she laughed so easily and loved to dance and sing. A look of adoration filled his eyes. "It was magic, the way she played the piano. She was on her way to a wonderful career."

"I know," Ben said. The sound of his mother's fingers flying over the piano keys was part of his childhood.

His father continued, lost in his thoughts, saying that the first time he had seen her, she was playing in a concert for friends. When he heard her performing Beethoven's *Appassionata*, he knew he had to see her face and talk with her. When she finished playing and looked up at him, he knew that he loved her.

He gave Ben an urgent look, as if he must understand every word. "She gave up her music just to marry me. I've always felt guilty about taking such a talented, beautiful young woman away to Italy. I had no connections to help her with a career."

"I'm sure Mamma did what she wanted to do."

"Her father told me when I asked to marry her that I was too old for her. Fifteen years older." He looked at Ben as if asking forgiveness.

"It doesn't matter, Papà."

His father gave a wry smile. "I told her I was taking her to the land where the sun always shines, but think how it rains in Padua—and it's very provincial for her."

"I love you just the way you are, Papà, and I'm sure Mamma does too."

Claudio cautioned Ben not to be hard on his mother if she should get upset, and to tell her that he really had been certain they'd be back in a day or two at the most. He stood and held Ben's face in his hands, telling him he had always been a good son and that his sweet Monica was better than a father deserved.

The finality in his father's voice frightened Ben. He promised to do everything he could to get his father out of there.

Claudio looked relieved, but then said that it was time for the family to leave Padua. So many Jews had already fled to Switzerland. They should have gone months ago.

Ben thought of his friends who had crossed the border at Lugano, but reminded his father that the Swiss weren't taking any more refugees.

His father waved away his hesitations, telling him there were other places and that he'd been speaking to the rabbi about this. He sighed. "He's trying to find us something. He thinks our best chance is to hide with a Catholic family. Beniamino, if Rabbi Coen says it's time to leave Padua, you are to do as he tells you."

"You'll be home by then, Papà." Claudio looked down, saying nothing. Unable to bear his father's silence, Ben asked his father where he would sleep.

"Where should I sleep but where they tell me?" His father shook his head. "Why do we make small matters urgent, when it's the large ones that have us by the neck?" He looked into Ben's eyes. "Yesterday you were an Italian who happened to be a Jew. Today you have become a Jew who happens to be Italian. You are a Jew, whether you observe the traditions or not." He waited, watching Ben's expression. "You must never forsake your heritage. Remember that your name is Cantarini, from our ancestor who was a *cantore* in the Scuola Levantina synagogue in Venice."

Ben nodded. "I know, Papà."

"Tell me that you will always be proud to be a Jew."

"I promise, Papà." He swallowed hard. "Papà, did you ever think we'd have the troubles our grandparents had?"

"For so many years, when I came home to my family in the evening, I thanked the Master of the Universe for all he had given me. My family most of all, but then my paintings. No matter how weary I was with all the problems at the gallery, I used to take a little glass of vermouth and sit with my paintings and drawings. Everything unpleasant fell away and I was at peace."

"Papà, why aren't you angry?"

"People make the troubles," his father answered, "not the Master of the Universe."

Ben knelt down, putting his arms around his father's knees. "I'm sorry, Papà, I'm so sorry."

His father leaned down to embrace him, and then urged him to stand. "Hush now." He kissed Ben's forehead. "I love you, my son. Take care of yourself and your good mother. Tell her I love her and remind her that she must be brave and that God will help her. And Ben, watch over your sister Monica." Claudio put his hands on his son's head.

His eyes wet, Ben fought down the helplessness encircling him. He kissed his father on each cheek and turned away to rap on the door. A moment later, he heard a key in the lock. The door opened, and the SS guard stood in the doorway. Ben told him he was ready to leave and that he needed his belongings, as well as his papers from Herr Feltzer.

As he left the room, Ben heard his father murmuring the old, familiar words, the ones he said when he entered the temple: "How lovely is Thy tabernacle, O Lord of Hosts. My soul longeth, yea, even fainteth for the courts of the Lord."

The guard shut the door behind them and walked ahead of Ben until they arrived at Herr Feltzer's office. It was empty. "He said to give you this." The guard handed Ben his suitcase and identity papers. "He wants your father out of here in one week."

"I understand," Ben said, trying to control his anger. "My briefcase, please."

The guard shrugged. "He didn't say anything about a briefcase. By the way, he said to tell you that we don't keep people here longer than a week." The guard smirked. "Like eggs, they go bad."

Ben jabbed his forefinger against the guard's chest. "That's my briefcase, and I want it—now!"

Without answering, the guard pulled his gun from its holster and shoved it against Ben's chest. "*Raus, Jude!*"

Ben stumbled out of the office.

In the hallway, he stood for a moment, shaken, catching his breath. He retraced his way to the entrance of the building, walking slowly at first, and then quickly. Hurrying into the street, he broke into a wild run toward the station.

Twenty-four hours later, the train from Rome arrived in Padua. Ben jumped down the steps before it came to a full stop and ran for his father's gallery. He took the stairs to his father's office by twos, hurried through the anteroom, and knocked on the office door. Eight o'clock in the evening—Lupino should still be there.

Aldo Lupino was sitting at Papà's desk, telephone pressed to his ear, a mass of papers spread before him. In his dark suit, his brown hair carefully combed, and his pencil moustache, he looked older than his thirty-five years. He was telling someone on the other end of the line to call him because other potential clients were interested. Waiting for the end of the conversation, Ben surveyed the office to see if Lupino had changed anything since he had taken over. A richly colored oriental carpet that his father had wanted to sell still covered the floor, since Lupino had insisted it should stay in the office. The same file cabinets stood along one wall, but Lupino's bronze statuette collection now cluttered the credenza. Lupino put the phone back in its cradle, still looking at it.

"Signor Lupino," Ben began.

"So … " With his narrow-set brown eyes, Lupino studied Ben's face. "You're looking a bit the worse for wear this evening. What happened to you?"

Ben had thought of a thousand ways to begin. Should he insist? Should he beg? And now, facing Lupino, he burst out, saying he needed help—his father and he needed help.

Lupino's face clouded over in consternation. "What is it?"

"My father is in Rome. The Gestapo has him." His voice broke, and he cleared his throat. "They beat him up, for nothing! They want money—two thousand lire. We have half of it, but that's all! We don't have the rest!"

Lupino leaned forward. "What happened in Rome? He told me he was going to pick up the Bacchus drawing. What else was he doing?"

Ben understood the implication of guilty behavior. "I don't have time to tell you the whole story but we need your help."

"What did he do?"

"He didn't do anything! It's a kidnapping. They want ransom, don't you understand?"

"*Caspita!* But wait, don't you have a buyer for the Bacchus drawing?"

"The Gestapo kept it!"

"What?"

"I need the money right away. I can't leave my father in that place."

Lupino shook his head. "It was so unwise—"

"You were on the telephone when I came in. Have you sold any paintings?"

Lupino put his fingers over his mouth and eyed Ben thoughtfully. He explained that very few paintings were selling in the midst of the war and when they did sell, buyers wanted them for nothing. He tapped his fingers on the desk, adding that he was having a hard time paying the mortgage on the gallery.

Ben leaned forward. "Get a second mortgage. My father will pay you twenty percent interest when things return to normal."

Lupino's eyebrows furrowed. "If I'm having trouble paying the first mortgage, how could I handle a second one?" He spun his chair around and looked out the window. "Your father is a real gentleman. And your mother is kindness itself, a lovely lady." He turned back, contemplating the palms of his hands for a moment before looking up and assuring Ben that he was really shocked and sorry, but the problem would simply have to be solved in some other way. He stood. "Perhaps a bank would give you a loan."

"But I have no assets to borrow against!"

"Look, Beniamino, doesn't your father have family you could go to?"

"None at all."

"Isn't there someone in his coterie of friends?"

Ben shook his head. "They're all Jews. They have their own problems."

"Yes, of course. Listen, Ben … " He looked away, biting his lip in thought, and then faced Ben again. "Frankly, I can't put my hands on that kind of money. I'm heavily invested, but in companies where there's no liquidity. I'm really sorry." He glanced at the papers on his desk. "I'll be away on business tomorrow, but I want you to let me know how you work this out."

Ben pounded his fist on the desk. "For God's sake, Signor Lupino, I'm desperate!"

"Come now, there's one good thing here. Your father is too old to be sent to a work camp." Lupino began sifting through his papers.

"You son of a bitch!" Ben strode out of the room, slamming the door so hard the glass panes rattled. Halfway down the staircase, his suitcase bumping against the wall, he realized he hadn't turned on the light. It didn't matter, because he never would have seen through the hot tears. Not bothering to wipe his cheeks, he felt his way down to the door.

By the time he reached his apartment building, he could not think of anyone who could raise that kind of money. With the image of his father sick and sad and alone in a dark room vivid in his mind, he climbed the steps.

When he put his key in the lock and entered the apartment, he could hear his mother talking to Monica in the dining room. He walked down the hall and stood in the doorway.

His mother jumped to her feet. "Ben, thank God you're home! Where's Papà?"

He shook his head, not knowing where to begin.

"What happened to your cheek?"

"It's nothing. Papà is still in Rome."

"What?"

Ben said to Monica, "You'd better go to your room."

Constanz took the little girl by the shoulders. "Go to your room, sweetheart, and shut the door."

Monica stood her ground. "I want to know too."

"I'll tell you later. Go on!"

"Grownups don't understand," she said, her face twisting, ready to cry. "No one tells me anything."

Ben watched the little girl stomp off to her bedroom. His mother turned to him, demanding to know why his father was still in Rome.

"Mamma, we had to help the Jewish Community. The Gestapo was demanding gold—with a deadline!"

The look of terror in her eyes frightened him. He told her that they had stayed to help, and then the SS had stopped them and taken Papà to Gestapo headquarters, and now the Gestapo wanted money before they would release him.

His mother's face was ashen. Ben guided her to a chair, suddenly flooded with doubt that he had done enough to help Papà.

"Did they hurt him?" she asked.

"He's all right, Mamma," he said, not wanting to tell her more. "But they want two thousand lire."

"Oh my God! We don't have that kind of money." Ben thought she was going to cry, but she pulled herself together, narrowing her eyes with resolve. "Let's take the Caravaggio to the buyer in Venice, get the money for it, and we'll go get Papà in Rome."

Ben lifted his hand. "No, Mamma. The Gestapo kept the briefcase with the drawing."

"What? Why did they do that?" Her voice rose. "Don't you realize … Why did they … " She stopped in mid-sentence. "Your father's pills were in the briefcase. You took them out, of course."

"Mamma, you don't know what it's like there."

She put her hands over her mouth and squeezed her eyes shut, then strode to the other end of the room and lifted a painting off the wall, revealing a small safe.

"Mamma, don't even look. Papà told me he has only one thousand lire in the safe. He told me to go to Lupino for help. I was just there and he won't help."

Anger flared in her eyes. "Your father has too much faith in that man." She grasped his arm with sudden urgency. "You and your father talk about that drawing all the time. Selling it, keeping it, amazed by it, getting it back someday. That Caravaggio drawing is the source of all our troubles. It's as if Caravaggio's criminal ways have chased us down through the centuries."

Ben put his arms around her to stop her trembling and told her she couldn't blame the drawing. But was she right? It was true that the sketch enthralled him and everyone else who had seen it. Why? Because it was four hundred years old and evoked both the life on the streets and the lust that Caravaggio had experienced? Ben knew it fascinated him and drew him in more each time he looked at it, but that didn't mean it was the cause of their troubles. The sight of his beautiful mother so undone was horrible. Finally, he said, "The last thing Papà said was to tell you to be strong and to trust in God. There has to be an answer."

His mother straightened up. "The rabbi!"

Brushing strands of hair off her wet cheeks, she reminded him that his father was always at the rabbi's office giving him financial advice and having coffee with him. The rabbi would know how to help.

Ben thought of all the times he had dragged his heels about going to synagogue. His mother must have understood what was going through his mind, because she told him he had to go to the rabbi's office. She reminded Ben that Rabbi Coen was there until all hours nowadays. Ben should go there now but watch out for the German soldiers.

Ben pedaled wildly through the blacked-out streets, rattling over the ancient cobblestones, hoping the patrolling Germans wouldn't catch him. At last he was under the medieval arcades near the synagogue office. He threw his bicycle against the brick wall of the building and pressed the bell two, three, four times. Why didn't the rabbi answer the doorbell? Finally, he heard footsteps behind the door.

Rabbi Coen opened the door enough to pull Ben in by the elbow. His usually stern eyes opened wide in mock surprise. "Ah, Beniamino! Is it Yom Kippur? Did I make a mistake?"

Ben felt his cheeks turn hot. "Rabbi, I know I don't come to synagogue often enough, but we need your help. Something awful has happened."

The teasing expression left the rabbi's face. He walked to his office, beckoning Ben to follow. In his musty office, crammed with books, the rabbi sat at his desk while Ben told him that his father was being held by the Gestapo in Rome, and that Ben and his mother needed money to get him out.

The rabbi sat forward, asking to know everything.

In a hoarse voice, Ben explained exactly what had happened. Rabbi Coen sat back, sighing.

Ben held out his hands in supplication. "We don't have the money! Please, Rabbi, can you help us?"

The rabbi opened a desk drawer and drew out a file folder. "Your father is not the only one being detained in Italy. Everything is changing—very fast." He held the folder up, waving it slowly in the air. He was going to put his father's name in that folder, Ben thought. He was burying him.

The rabbi took a pen and a clean sheet of paper and began writing. Ben could see: Cantarini, Claudio. New identification papers: Campano, Arturo. Art dealer. Padua. The rabbi's demeanor was all business. Ben wanted to yell, *This is my father!*

The rabbi proceeded steadily. "What is the name of the man holding him?"

"His name is Herr Feltzer. I don't know his first name."

The room was silent except for the scratching of the pen. Too slow. Why didn't he hurry? The clock on the wall said ten o'clock. Ben looked around the room, filled with bookshelves and boxes of Bibles, skullcaps, and prayer shawls. "Is that all you're going to do?" he asked. "Add his name to a list?"

"It took six days to make the world and you want your father out of German hands in five minutes?" Rabbi Coen set down his pen. "Are there paintings you could sell?"

Ben shook his head, explaining that when his father turned his gallery over to signor Lupino, the agreement was that Claudio would get twenty percent of any sales. Signor Lupino swore that nothing had sold recently. "My father and I went to Rome to get our last drawing and now the Gestapo has it." Ben shut his eyes for a moment, trying to hold back the panic.

"Ah yes, the Caravaggio drawing. What a regret for you!" The rabbi shook his head. "Your father never spoke much of family. Does he have brothers?"

"No, my father is an only child and my mother's only brother is dead. He was killed by Hitler's SA thugs."

"Yes, your father told me that. I'm sorry." The rabbi's eyebrows met in a frown. "While we're talking, I'm thinking. Any cousins, second cousins?"

Ben shook his head. Rabbi Coen sat back, pressing his fingertips against his forehead. If the rabbi told him to pray, Ben thought, he'd get up and walk right out of there.

"I am going to call some of the wealthy in our congregation. It won't be the first time they've helped a brother." He looked at Ben hard. "Remember from your bar mitzvah that we are our brothers' keepers? Nothing means anything until we live it."

Ben wanted to stay while he telephoned, but the rabbi told him to go and take care of his mother and sister. He walked to the door, ready to turn the knob. "You have to know when things are out of your hands. *Shalom*, Beniamino."

In the waiting room a well-dressed woman sat with her young

son. Ben glanced at them, thinking, why hadn't the rabbi sent them away and started telephoning?

Rabbi Coen seemed to read his thoughts. "First things first, Beniamino," he said softly. He nodded to the woman. "*Buona sera*, Signora Lattara." The rabbi held out his hand to the boy. As the mother and son followed the rabbi into his office, Ben heard him say, "I'm sorry, Signora Lattara. I'll explain what you must do to get your husband ... " The door shut.

Pedaling his bicycle through the center of town, Ben rode by the Caffè Pedrocchi. Laughter and German beer songs drifted out to the street through the beaded curtains. Who could be happy when the world had gone insane?

All was quiet when he entered the apartment. Only the night-light shone dimly on the telephone table. Eleven o'clock. How could Mamma go to bed and not wait up to hear what the rabbi had said? As he walked toward her room, the door to his father's study burst open and for one moment, Ben imagined his father appearing, saying, I am not so foolish. I found a way out. But it was Mamma in her pink dressing gown. She called to him, animated, waving a booklet.

"Ben, I found it! I knew your father had savings in Zurich. He told me two months ago that he was going there, and here's the account book." She pointed to the page. "See? Five times what we need! Why didn't Papà tell you about this? He must have been so upset that he forgot." She thrust the passbook into Ben's hand.

He leafed through the book. "Mamma, we can't use this."

"What do you mean?"

He showed her the last page: "Withdrawals in person and only with authorized signature."

"But if we explain, really, how could they refuse us?"

"Hasn't Papà ever talked to you about Swiss bankers? They don't change their rules for anybody." He shook his head. "Let me tell you what Rabbi Coen said."

She wrapped her dressing gown tighter around herself and sat in a chair, her hands knotted in her lap, while Ben talked. When he had finished, she asked, "How quickly can he do something?"

"He'll call us when he knows something."

His mother buried her face in her hands.

"Mamma, we have no choice but to wait. Let's try to get some rest." They embraced in silence and went to their rooms.

Ben lay in his bed, staring into the dark. Was there cash in the gallery? He could go down that night and search around. He would repay it later. But then that bastard Lupino would have the police after him and there would be more trouble. Ben replayed his conversation with Lupino over and over, growing angrier each time. He went through the sales Papà had almost completed before going to Rome. Yes, of course. Now Ben knew what he had to do.

CHAPTER 10

Early the next morning, before the secretary arrived at the art gallery, Ben sat at Lupino's desk. The same file cabinets, the same chair by the desk for a visitor, but no new paintings, he noted. The hum of traffic from the street below meant the world was getting to work and the secretary would arrive soon. He felt an edge of guilt as he opened the top drawer. Inside he saw only pencils lined up in a perfect row and notations on scraps of paper held together with a large paper clip. He riffled through the papers. What was this? "Lunch with G. M. Monday Caffè Fiorentino." That must be Giovanni Mauro, the art dealer. He found other names and initials he recognized. Some dinner dates too. He found a notation from the previous day—"Call E." Was that before or after he had talked to Lupino? The telephone number written under the initial wasn't a Padua or Venice exchange. He jotted down the number.

What else was Lupino up to? He opened the desk's file drawer. Nothing unusual there. He looked hastily through all the drawers but saw nothing useful. Slipping everything back in place, he gave a final glance around the room. Feeling dissatisfied, he walked quickly through the still-darkened outer office and down the stairs to the street.

In fifteen minutes he was back at the apartment. His mother was standing by the kitchen sink, her face blotched from crying. "Did the rabbi call?" he asked.

"No! I can't stand this waiting any longer." She wiped her raw eyes with her damp handkerchief and pushed it into her sleeve. "Signora Marcello stopped by to tell me how sorry she was to hear about Papà being detained by the Gestapo. I suppose Lupino has been telling people about your father." She bit her bottom lip. "Monica overheard her and she's so upset." She wiped her cheeks. "And here I am trying to cook. I don't even know what I'm doing."

"I'll help you, Mamma."

"Heavens no, I can't have my son helping me in the kitchen."

Ben pulled the paper from his breast pocket and showed it to her.

She studied the number. "That's a Berlin exchange."

"It's in Lupino's handwriting, dated yesterday. I'm calling it. I want to see who answers."

She held on to the piece of paper, telling him not to call because the government listened in nowadays and they might ask why he was calling Berlin.

He took the number from her and walked to the telephone. He placed the call with the operator. After two rings, he dropped the telephone back in the cradle as if it were hot. "Good God! Gestapo Headquarters!"

His mother put her hand to her mouth. "Do you think they could trace the call?"

"I hung up right away." Before he could think, the telephone jangled. He picked up the receiver. "*Pronto.*"

"Rabbi Coen here."

Ben gave a huge sigh of relief. "Yes, Rabbi Coen."

"All of you, come to my office right away."

Ben hung up and looked at his mother. "He wants us now."

At the synagogue office the rabbi opened the door, led Monica to the waiting room, and hurriedly took Constanz and Ben to his office. Once there he spoke slowly and distinctly. "I'm sorry, but we simply cannot raise the money you need. I have five hundred lire for you, but the congregants are being squeezed by the racial laws just as you are."

The rabbi explained the only thing to do was to send Ben back to Rome. He would have to take Claudio's one thousand lire and the five hundred that the rabbi had raised. He must convince Herr Feltzer that it was absolutely all the family had, and that Claudio was an ill man and that Herr Feltzer must release him, unless he wanted the poor man's demise on his hands.

Constanz felt the blood drain from her body, but she shook her head and said, "Ben, it isn't *you* who will go to Rome. *I* will go."

"No." The rabbi was firm. "It's a man's job. Ben will go."

Constanz stood. "I know you mean well, Rabbi, but it's my husband and I am going to bring him back."

Ben jumped to his feet. "You can't go. You have no idea what goes on there."

"Constanz," the rabbi cut in, standing as he spoke. "I feel responsible for you in the absence of your husband. You will not go to Rome."

"I'm sorry, but I *am* going and that's final." She picked up her pocketbook.

The rabbi frowned, insisting that she was being irrational.

Ben pleaded with her, trying to make her understand that she wouldn't know from one minute to the next what those people were going to do, that they were totally unpredictable and crazy.

She turned to her son. "The whole world is crazy, but it's my job, don't you understand? I am going. You've been to Rome and that's enough."

"And who will take care of Monica?" he asked.

"You will. You can tell Aldo Lupino that you can't work for him for a few days." In a quiet voice, even though her stomach was in a hard knot, Constanz said, "Rabbi, do you have the five hundred lire now? That way I won't have to come back in the morning before I go to the train."

"Rabbi," Ben said, "my mother and I will talk about this at home." He took her by the elbow. "Thank you for all your help."

"Yes, we appreciate it," Constanz said. "But there's nothing to discuss at home."

The rabbi walked to a safe on the other side of the room. Shaking his head, he withdrew an envelope and handed it to Constanz.

The next morning Constanz put on her best suit and the hat she wore on special occasions. She had made up her mind to seem perfectly calm, even though her stomach hurt so much she had to resist doubling over. Monica was clinging to her skirt, saying, "Mamma, I don't want you to go. I'm afraid."

"I don't want to leave you, sweetheart, but I have to help Papà get home. We'll be back soon and everything will be fine." She straightened the ribbon on Monica's braid and gave her a tight hug and a kiss.

Ben was leaning against the doorframe, quiet and frowning.

"You know that there's a curfew in Rome. Where do you think you'll stay?"

"We've done nothing but discuss this trip since yesterday, Ben." She checked that the lire were in the zip compartment of her purse and picked up her satchel. "I'll be all right. I'm going to bring your father home and we'll have the drawing to sell. I can tell this man Feltzer that I'll send the rest of the money from the proceeds of the sale. Now take Monica to the kitchen and get a card game going." She hugged her daughter again, and then gave Ben a last kiss and motioned with her head toward the kitchen. "Please, Ben."

Going down the steps she called back one soft good-bye, hoping her neighbors wouldn't know she was leaving. She set out in the direction of the train station, walking quickly. No telling what would happen if she caught the eye of the German patrol.

By the time Constanz reached Rome, it was early evening and her fears had been replaced with anger at what had befallen her family. But when she saw the plain, block like entrance of 155 Via Tasso ahead of her, she knew she must keep her emotions at bay—so thoroughly contained that the SS man at the door would see only a confident woman on an important mission. She quickened her pace.

"*Guten Abend,*" she said. "Herr Feltzer, *bitte.*"

The SS man stood taller and gave her a long look. "*Ihre Papiere.*"

She handed him her papers, grateful they were Aryan papers. The soldier gave back the documents and opened the door for her. "Herr Feltzer," he said to the guard inside the hallway. Trying to maintain her composure, Constanz followed the guard to a closed mahogany door. He knocked.

As they waited for an answer, she heard an inhuman scream come from farther up the hall. Again she heard it. The howling of an animal? She shuddered. "God in heaven, what was that?" she asked the soldier.

He only shrugged.

From behind the door, a man called out in German, "Come in."

She entered a large office, empty except for a chair, the swastika flags draped on the wall, and a man sitting behind a large desk. The man fit the description Ben had given her—mid-thirties, thinning blond hair, plump body, and thick lips.

"*Sie sind* Herr Feltzer?" She spoke in German, hoping it would help her cause.

"And who are you?" he asked, coming around from behind his desk to shake her hand.

"I am Frau Cantarini." She was certain he must know her name was not Campano. "Herr Feltzer, Herr Cantarini is my dear husband and I have come for him. Where is he, please?"

Feltzer indicated the chair next to his desk. "Please, sit down. Your husband is quite well and we have put him in a room in a nearby villa."

Constanz sat down, setting her purse and satchel next to her. "I am concerned that he may not have received his medicine. You know, he is not a well man."

"We could see that he was suffering, and as soon as he told us that his pills were in his briefcase, we gave them to him." He pulled his chair around to sit next to her. "My dear lady, this must have been very difficult for you." His thick lips parted in a smile. "Perhaps I shouldn't say this about my own countrymen, but some are not as kind as they ought to be."

Constanz was bewildered. Ben had said Herr Feltzer had been

arrogant toward him. Now he seemed quite courteous. "Herr Feltzer, my son told me that we must pay a fine for my husband's release … " She searched for the proper words and decided to leave the sentence unfinished. "How much is required?"

"Ah, well, you see … it's not my doing, really. My superior wants two thousand lire. He feels it's necessary for the war effort."

Constanz felt the pulse in her neck throb with anger, with the horrible injustice of it all. Trying to keep her voice under control, she insisted that her husband had done nothing except walk down the street. And did that deserve a fine?

Herr Feltzer's expression showed deep apology as he explained that, after all, her husband and son had been walking on the street after the curfew.

She stood up, clutching her purse. "You know that my husband's detention and his fine are a disgrace! What kind of German manners do you have?"

Feltzer stood as well and held her elbow firmly, telling her to sit down and be reasonable.

Constanz dropped into the chair again, chiding him for keeping her husband's briefcase with its personal items.

He walked to a safe box behind him, unlocked it, and removed the rolled-up Bacchus drawing, slowly opening it.

"Yes," she said, "I will want that as well as the briefcase."

"My dear lady, any kind of drawing or painting has to be sent to Germany to be safeguarded. Imagine if something should happen to all these Italian treasures. These are dangerous times to have things lying around loose."

Constanz sat back in her chair, the breath gone out of her. Finally able to speak, she said, "I have most of the money you require and we have a buyer for that drawing—in Venice. With the money from that sale, we'll be able to pay the rest of the fine. So we must have that sketch, don't you see?"

Feltzer ignored her, wondering aloud why this was the only sketch Caravaggio had made, and had Caravaggio himself been the model for Bacchus?

When he turned to Constanz, the look in his eyes was chilling. "You must know," he said, "that Caravaggio was a rogue, and he wanted to send his libidinous desires down through the ages." He smiled at her. "That's what I see in this, just as I see lust in the *Bacchus* painting in the Uffizi."

"So then you will return it to me. Please roll it up again, give me the briefcase, get my husband, and we'll be on our way." She stood, trying to look masterful.

Feltzer's expression grew impatient. "I cannot let you have the drawing."

She felt ill. Now how would she get the rest of the ransom money? "But that belongs to our family! You can't imagine how horrible this is for us." Her voice rose. "We have only this!" She removed the gray envelope from her purse. "I have fifteen hundred lire and we can get no more. Do you understand?"

"My dear, you are breaking my heart. Such a beautiful lady should not suffer like this."

"Herr Feltzer." Her voice was barely audible. "Please say that fifteen hundred lire is enough."

Feltzer set the drawing on his desk and picked up a telegram. "Let me read to you. 'Any citizen found walking the street after the curfew is liable to execution.' This telegram came from Berlin a week ago. Dear lady, do you see how fortunate your husband is to have only a fine hanging over his head and not to be facing a firing squad?"

Her heart stopped, but with effort she spoke, asking him if

he really thought that a stranger to the city deserved death for walking down a street.

In a stern voice, Feltzer said, "He had a briefcase with him. The Partisans are forever walking around with pipe bombs and grenades in briefcases and suitcases."

"Well, did he have anything like that in his briefcase?"

"It's already done. Berlin wants two thousand lire for his release."

Feltzer walked toward her and took her hands. Constanz pulled her hands away and took a handkerchief from her pocketbook to avoid his stare.

"You are very beautiful," he said, still standing too close. "Of course, you know that."

She dabbed at her eyes and said nothing.

"Look at me," he said softly. She did, hoping desperately that he had decided to accept the fifteen hundred lire. "I know that I can find a way to help you. I can see that you really do not have what Berlin wants." He reached for her hands again.

She tried to free herself, but he held on firmly. "Please ... " she said, leaning away from him.

"Can you be very good to me?"

She yanked her hands away from his, her mind swirling. "What are you saying?"

"It would not be difficult for you to enjoy an evening with me. I'm really very pleasant company." He smiled.

Constanz stared at him, stunned. "No. I just want to take my husband home. How on earth could I, as you say, 'enjoy an evening' with you when you're holding my poor husband prisoner?"

"Your husband is very comfortable. He isn't in prison at all. First thing in the morning, we'll go to him, he'll be released and all will be well." He smiled again. "Won't you give me a chance? If your husband is released now, you two will run into the curfew and the same thing will happen all over again. Spend the evening with me. We'll go to a lovely restaurant." His cheeks were high with color. "I love to dance, do you?"

"I just want to see my husband and take him home," she said, almost inaudibly.

"Of course. And you will. I'll find the other five hundred lire for you—I'll have to do that to help you, you know. And your part is just to enjoy yourself with me this one evening." He nodded persuasively. "I hope you won't find that too difficult. I can be a very entertaining fellow."

"No." She stepped back, shaking her head. "I cannot do this. I love my husband very much and I could never do such a thing."

"Well," he said, his tone growing serious. "And who will come to help you and your husband if you are caught in the streets after the curfew?"

Constanz looked around the room. She was trapped. Who could help her? And where did Feltzer expect her to spend the night after he was through with her? Not with him, dear God, please no. She put her head in her hands.

"Don't be so distressed, dear lady." Feltzer walked to his desk. He began shuffling through some papers and told her he would give her a moment to decide.

If she did this, how could she face Claudio? She wouldn't tell him, but he knew her so well. She took her handkerchief out again and blew her nose. She could just tell Claudio that Feltzer had accepted the fifteen hundred lire and been satisfied.

Feltzer looked up at her, his face still flooded with color. "Well?"

"If I do this, when will I see my husband?"

"Together we will go to find him at eight o'clock tomorrow morning. My driver will take you and your husband to the train station, I promise."

Reluctantly, she nodded. A feeling of nausea rose within her. "I will give you the fifteen hundred lire when I am ready to go with my husband to the train station."

"*Ja, das ist richtig,* just so!"

"And not until then, do you understand?"

"Of course. Now, I already have a reservation for dinner at a fine restaurant, the Foro Romano III. We can leave in a half hour." He held out his arm. "Would you like to freshen up a bit before my driver picks us up? I know that you've had a long day on the train."

"Yes." She walked past him, deliberately not taking his arm. "What you have done and what you are asking are totally immoral. But I can see that you leave me no choice."

Feltzer said nothing as he rolled up the Bacchus drawing and returned it to the vault.

CHAPTER 11

When Constanz opened her eyes, the room was still dark with early morning shadows. She pulled the covers up to her neck and drew away from where he had been beside her for an hour at midnight. A shower, she wanted a shower. She could still smell his cloying cologne on the sheets, on her skin, still feel his sweaty, rough hands stroking her arms, caressing her breasts ...

Oh, stop! Stop thinking about it, she told herself. It was over and Claudio would be safe. Or was there something worse to come? She clutched her head. An exploding headache banged behind her eyes. She had drunk four, or was it five, glasses of Champagne to dull the fright of what she might have to do when they left the restaurant. And he had urged her on, pouring more into her glass, calling her *Liebchen* and *Schatzi*.

As she stumbled across the room toward the bathroom, she shuddered, remembering how he had stroked her leg under the table, asking if she liked that and calling her *Bonbon*. She took off the bathrobe he had left for her and stood under the hot shower. There was only a bar of harsh wartime soap, but, sobbing, she washed every inch of herself. When she walked out of the shower and picked up the towel, she saw that it was a brand her father used to sell in his department store in Berlin years ago. Thank God Vati wasn't there to know what had happened to her and to their poor Germany, to know what monsters had taken it over.

She pressed the towel against her eyes, telling herself to stop crying. She mustn't let Claudio see her like this. She dried herself off and put on her underclothes and then her traveling suit.

"Uf!" she groaned. The smell of cigarettes from the restaurant still clung to her clothes, reminding her of how he had insisted she take his arm as they entered the restaurant. He had nodded, smiling, to the tables of SS officers. Several officers had looked her over and nodded in return. She wanted to weep afresh, at the humiliation of being paraded the length of the restaurant like a courtesan.

Once dressed, she struggled with shaking fingers to find brush and lipstick in her purse. When she turned to the mirror, her mouth fell agape. She looked ghastly. Gray circles ringed her eyes, and her skin was as pale as a person in shock. She was putting on lipstick, trying to conceal how grim she looked, when she heard a knock at the door.

Her heart leaped with fear. What now? "Yes? Who is it?" she called.

A man's deep voice replied. "Eric Feltzer."

"Are you ready to take me to my husband?"

"Of course," he said. "First we'll have breakfast. Come, open the door."

She called out that she was not hungry. He should come for her when he was ready to take her to her husband. He tried the door handle, and suddenly she feared he would leave her in this room and never come back for her. She could be his prisoner. She decided to open the door.

"I am not ready," she told him, her stomach churning at the sight of his face. "But I shall be in a few moments. Please wait outside."

"A gentleman waits for a lady," he said with a mock pout. Lowering his voice, he added, "But was I not a tender lover?"

His fingers were on the doorframe. Constanz fought with herself, resisting the desire to slam the door on them. "Step back and wait for me!" she ordered. She closed the door firmly. Sweeping up her purse and satchel, she looked around the room to make certain she hadn't left anything. The sight of the rumpled sheets brought another stab of nausea. She turned her back to the bed and tried to regain her composure. Once she was in Padua, it would be as if the horrible nightmare had never happened.

She stiffened herself and opened the door again. "I am ready to see my husband now."

"Are you certain that you don't want breakfast? You have a long trip ahead of you."

"No breakfast. I told you I want to see my husband."

"My dear," he said, "if we had more time to enjoy each other, you would not be so indifferent to me. I do admire you."

She pressed her lips together and looked away.

At the villa next to 155 Via Tasso, Feltzer held the door for her. As they entered, he said, "I made reservations for you and your husband on the Rapido in first class."

She opened her purse and gave him the envelope containing the fifteen hundred lire. In return, he handed her Claudio's briefcase. "We will need to be taken to the station," she said. "My husband, I am sure, is in no condition to walk there."

"Of course," he answered smoothly. "Didn't I promise you that?"

They stopped in front of a locked door. Feltzer motioned to

the guard to open the door and announced, "Herr Cantarini, *hier ist Ihre* Frau."

A gray-haired man, thin and bent, stumbled toward them. At first, Constanz wasn't sure, and then she cried out, "Claudio!" For a moment she was unable to move, but then she rushed to her husband and embraced him. She felt him shaking, no sound coming from him.

Weakly, he put his arms around her and let his head fall on her shoulder. "My darling, darling Constanz," he whispered. "What are you doing here? Here in this dreadful place."

"I've come to find you and take you home, my dearest Claudio."

"Home," he murmured, his head still on her shoulder. "We can go home."

"Yes, we're going to the train right now."

Supporting him, Constanz led him past Feltzer and into the hallway. Slowly they shuffled their way to the street where Feltzer's driver opened the car door for them. Feltzer handed the driver train tickets as Constanz helped Claudio into the car. She turned to Feltzer. She knew the man could snatch her back again, but her fury overcame her.

She said, between gritted teeth, "You have soiled the dignity of my family and stolen the Bacchus sketch from my son. You will rue the day you did this to us."

Feltzer lifted his arm to check his watch and turned from her, as if he had not heard her. Constanz stepped into the car. As the limousine sped away, she saw the back of Feltzer's heavy-set body as he walked toward Via Tasso.

Constanz and Claudio walked along the train platform until they found the first class car. He was so weak that she had to take his elbow and push against his shoulder to help him up the steps.

What had they done to him to make him ... She turned away from the word *frail.*

When they found their compartment, she put the briefcase and her satchel in the overhead netting. As they sat down, she avoided Claudio's eyes, hoping he wouldn't ask to look in the briefcase. How would she tell him that the Caravaggio would be taken to Germany? Her anger flared again, but at least Claudio was alive and safe, and she would see that he became strong once more. She reached over to pat his hand, just as the door opened and two Nazi officers stepped in and took seats across from them. One of them, middle-aged, serious, and frowning, didn't acknowledge Constanz and Claudio. He sat next to the window, opened his briefcase, pulled out a paper, and began making notes. The younger one had an open face and obviously wanted conversation.

"*Guten Tag!*" he said, looking past Claudio and smiling at Constanz. She nodded, quickly averting her eyes. Had Feltzer sent the officers to follow them? She told herself to be calm. There was no reason for more trouble.

The train's engine was steaming, ready to pull out of the station. On the platform, a young boy was calling up to their window, "*Pane, pane!*" The younger soldier lowered the window and beckoned to the boy. "*Comprate il pane!*" the boy screamed. "*Il treno parte subito!*"

The soldier looked at Constanz. "*Ja,* he's right. Who knows when we can buy food again? Permit me to buy a loaf for you."

She shook her head. Claudio, who had been looking out the window with a dull stare, turned to the soldier but said nothing.

Hastily the soldier added, "And for you too, *mein* Herr."

"No, thank you," Constanz said crisply. "We will buy our own."

Claudio whispered into her ear, "I have no money."

She took money from her pocketbook and realized that it was the first time Claudio hadn't reached for his wallet to buy whatever they needed. She leaned out the window, handing the boy his money and taking the round loaf of bread.

The soldier smiled. "We have Bratwurst with us, and beer. Perhaps you and your father would like some."

Her father! Did Claudio really look that old? She saw a wave of pain cross his brow. She shook her head and made up her mind to speak only to Claudio, who was slumped back in his seat, his eyes closed. She leaned her head against his shoulder and held his hand.

"What is it, dear?" Claudio asked. "You shivered. Are you cold?"

"It's nothing. I must have dozed off."

"Yes, of course."

From the soldiers' conversation, they seemed to be going to Austria on leave. Good, they would be getting off and changing trains in Verona. Her mind was eased.

Many hours later, the train slowed down for Verona. The officers stood, said *"Auf Wiedersehen"* to Constanz, and left. She was relieved to see them go, but now she felt defenseless against any question Claudio might ask. She cringed, thinking of Herr Feltzer.

"Constanz!" Claudio exclaimed. "What is it?"

She straightened quickly, saying she was just tired.

"You seem in pain."

"No, no, not at all. Look, the train has started up and we have no one in the compartment. Let me give you some bread." She tore off a piece of the round loaf. "Here, darling."

Claudio swallowed the bread and wiped his lips with the back of his hand. "Don't you want some bread?"

"In a little while." She had to forget what had happened to her. She must.

Claudio sat up straight and waved his hand in the direction of the empty seats across from them. "Now we can talk. How is it that you came to Rome instead of Ben?"

"Ben wanted to come, but I insisted that I would do it."

"I never would have let you do something so dangerous. I can't imagine that Ben permitted you to—"

"Darling, I am your wife. It was only natural for me to go."

Claudio brooded for a long moment, and then asked about Lupino. She explained that in the end he couldn't help. She knew Claudio was coming back to life and soon he would be peppering her with questions faster than she would be able to think of good answers.

He leaned toward her, asking her where she had gotten the money for Feltzer. When she told him that the rabbi had raised only five hundred lire, his forehead beaded with sweat. He wanted to know where she had found another five hundred lire. She lied and said that Feltzer had accepted fifteen hundred lire in all.

Looking down at her hands, she wondered how she could change the subject. "Tell me how they treated you at Via Tasso. Did they give you enough to eat?"

"They left a tray of food on the table twice a day."

"Only twice a day? That wasn't enough! Tell me more."

"I was warned not to speak about Via Tasso. Please, don't ask anything." Claudio looked straight at her. "How is it that we have first class reservations on this train?"

She avoided answering his question. "Don't you think it's more comfortable?"

"I'm asking you if you bought these tickets."

"No." Her throat closed up.

"Then where did they come from?"

"The driver gave them to me when we arrived at the station in Rome." She put her hand over his again. He drew his hand away.

"And who gave them to the driver?"

"Well, I don't know. I suppose perhaps Herr Feltzer did."

With relief she felt the train slowing down. Fifteen more minutes and they would be at the Padua train station. If only she could fend off his questions for a little while longer.

"You're holding something back from me," Claudio said. "Did Feltzer touch you?"

She tried to look surprised. "What do you mean?"

"The Gestapo don't give away first class tickets to men they've kept in prison for a week."

She put her hands in her coat pockets to hide their shaking. "Darling, stop this! Why are you saying things like that?"

"You went to that evil man when you were five hundred lire short of what he was demanding ... *Oy vay iz mir!*" He clutched his hair. "I've lived long enough to know what happened!"

"Not true, no, not true! You mustn't say that!" She thought of the Caravaggio sketch. She knew her husband would be devastated, but better they talk about that instead of what had happened to her at Via Tasso. "But Claudio, there is something I have to tell you."

He had sunk back against the seat. He looked at her, confused.

She stood and pulled down the briefcase. She held two fingers against her temple—oh, the pain! How was she going to mention his name? In a barely audible voice, she told Claudio that Herr Feltzer had said all art work was sent to Germany—to be safeguarded.

Claudio's face turned white. He made a little choking sound.

She took his arm. "Darling, our family is safe. Nothing else matters."

"Ben's Caravaggio?" His eyes filled up. "How will I tell Ben?"

"You'll tell him that his father came back from where people are insane and he's safe. He must be grateful to God for that."

Claudio put his hand on his chest.

"Claudio!" She reached into the briefcase, took a pill from the glass bottle, and gave it to him.

"At Via Tasso, they always told me they'd bring the pills when they had time." He swallowed the pill and reached for his collar.

She loosened his collar for him, thinking how Feltzer had lied to her, in addition to everything else. Claudio's lips were turning blue. Should she run for help? No, she mustn't leave him. She helped him lie down on the seat. "Be calm, darling. This will pass." Would it really pass?

With a cry of pain, Claudio grasped his left arm. His lips were moving in silent words. She put her ear against his mouth. "My fault … my beautiful wife … touched … " He took a shuddering breath. *"Sch'ma Israel."* He gasped for air, his face bloodless. "Forgive me … "

His head rolled to the side, limp, his mouth agape. Constanz, in disbelief, held him in her arms. He couldn't be! "Claudio! Speak! Speak to me!" She put her hand near his mouth. "Claudio! Claudio!" There was no breath. "No, no! Oh please, no!"

The train was pulling under the platform overhang in Padua.

She saw the conductor hurry by outside the compartment and called to him. "Please, help me! My husband ... "

The conductor rushed in, looked at Claudio, and said, "I'll call for an ambulance." He returned quickly. "Signora, they're coming to take him to the hospital." He leaned over Claudio and shook his head. "But I'm afraid it may be too late."

*　　*　　*

In a cubicle of the emergency room Constanz heard Rabbi Coen speaking to Ben, but she was too stunned to understand what he was saying. All she could do was stare at Claudio's motionless body covered to the neck with a shroud. His eyes had been pressed shut and his face was blue. Silent tears flooded her cheeks. She shook her head, unwilling to believe what had happened.

Rabbi Coen put his hand on her shoulder, urging her to leave Monica with the nurse and find a quiet place where he could talk to her and Ben.

In a small office nearby, Constanz nervously fingered some brochures on a table, wishing she could be left alone with her shock and sadness. The rabbi spoke with authority, telling her and Ben they must give themselves time to absorb their loss. Constanz could only turn her face away.

The rabbi continued, talking softly. "Perhaps you have heard that Jews may not put death notices in the newspapers. My announcement in the synagogue will have to do. I'll find ten men to form a minyan, so we can say Kaddish. And since Jews are no longer allowed to use the telephone, Ben, you will tell your friends that the family will sit shivah starting tomorrow after the funeral."

Constanz shook her head. "I can't."

"You can't what?"

"I can't face sitting shivah."

"But, my dear ... the solace of your friends will be—"

"They'll ask what happened in Rome and then they'll know that I am responsible for Claudio's death." She slumped in her chair, her hands over her face.

Gently, the rabbi asked, "How could it be your fault, Constanz? Tell me, what happened in Rome?"

She put out her hands, as if to stop the question, and whispered, "I should have taken Ben with me. Then it never would have happened. No matter how much I protested, the Gestapo wanted more money." She could not bring herself to say the name of the man who had degraded her.

"I see ... A woman trying to save her loved one." Rabbi Coen sighed. "You were forced to pay another price, weren't you? The SS are well known for this." He paused. "You were given an impossible choice."

She put her hands over her face again, hiding from Ben's anguished stare. "Stop, please."

"And if Ben had gone with you, you both would have been turned away—and Claudio never would have been released."

Her face burning, she whispered hoarsely, "I should have refused."

"And then what would have happened to your husband? You are not the first woman to have given herself to save her husband."

She dropped her hands and faced the rabbi. "How can I ever forgive myself? On the train coming home, Claudio knew. Don't you see, Rabbi? And that's what made his heart give way. It was my fault."

Rabbi Coen assured her she was wrong. Claudio had had a

weak heart and Constanz knew the Gestapo had not given him his medicine. The rabbi laid his hand on hers. "I tell you that you have a duty. Do you hear me? A duty to forgive yourself—as surely as the good Lord forgives you. And furthermore, if you don't, you are weakening yourself for the enormous task ahead."

Ben put a hand on her shoulder. She shuddered, whispering that she was not worthy to be touched.

"What task is that?" Ben asked, moving closer to her.

"Constanz, you are the head of the family now. You must gather your strength and do everything you can to keep Ben and Monica safe."

She shook her head, as if in a stupor, and said that perhaps in her mind she would be able to forgive herself, but never in her heart.

Rabbi Coen started to say more, but Ben spoke first. He had just been in Venice, speaking with a signor di Stefano, an art dealer and an old friend of Claudio's. He'd been offered an opportunity to work with signor di Stefano, but he would have to prove himself.

The rabbi looked dubious.

Ben continued. "Signor di Stefano is in a wheelchair. He had an accident a week ago and needs someone to help with his gallery. All his assistants have been called up to the army, so he really needs me. The first thing he wants me to do is to go to Bolzano to show a painting to a prospective buyer." Ben's eyes lit up for a brief moment. "And I think I could handle that."

"Bolzano?" Constanz stared at him in alarm. "Oh no, Ben. The Nazis are calling Bolzano part of Germany now. No, stay away from there."

Ben insisted that with his Aryan papers, it wouldn't be a problem. Besides, on the way home he had run into his friend

Giorgio, who had told him he was going up to Bolzano for the weekend before joining the Partisans. Giorgio wasn't afraid of Bolzano.

"All that may be," Rabbi Coen said, "but we need to talk about an entirely different matter. Let's get to the point. This is not the moment I would have chosen to tell you this, but Hitler is calling for all German Jews to be sent back to Germany."

Constanz shook her head, unable to believe what she was hearing. She was certain Mussolini would never allow that, and besides, she was an Italian citizen. The rabbi put up his hand, insisting that she was Jewish and born in Germany. That was all Hitler cared about.

"But the government wouldn't dare send me away," she said. "Not after what happened to Claudio."

"My dear Constanz, there is no Italian government anymore, just the neo-fascists controlled by the Nazis." His expression grew more serious. "The Jews of Padua are deluding themselves, just like Jews all over Italy. They're all playing ostrich."

"But what in the world can we do about it?"

"After the funeral, you'll sit shivah for two days, discussing none of this with your friends. When they've all left, we'll make a plan for your family."

He stood. "I'll go now and find the hospital papers you'll have to sign. I'll stay with you for that and then I'll drive you home."

Once again Constanz realized that she had no choice.

CHAPTER 12

The last of the mourners had paid their respects and left, hoping to reach home before the Nazi-enforced curfew. Only Rabbi Coen remained with the family in the living room. Constanz sat on a low chair, no makeup on her face, as was the custom with sitting shivah.

"Rabbi," she asked, "why are you telling me to take the covers off the mirrors? Shouldn't we leave them on for seven days?"

"No. You will not sit shivah after tomorrow noon." He reached into his breast pocket and pulled out a piece of paper. "I don't want to shock you, but I must. These are the words of Hans Frank spoken three years ago in October 1940, to a Nazi assembly. Have you heard of him?" Not waiting for an answer, he said, "He is the German Governor General of Poland—he's always been one of Hitler's favorites." The rabbi pressed open the page. "My dear Comrades ... I could not eliminate all lice and Jews in only one year. But in the course of time, and if you help me, this end will be attained."

Constanz clapped her hands over her mouth.

He folded the paper, asking her if she still doubted that

Hitler wanted all the Jews he could get his hands on and that he intended to work them to death.

Ben put his arm around his mother and Monica climbed on her lap, huddling against her chest.

The rabbi gave Constanz a hard look. "This could happen to you. Once in a while a Jew escapes one of these camps." Constanz winced. "Our hidden friends in Munich and Berlin have met these walking skeletons. I warn my congregants again and again—and what happens? The men don't want to give up their businesses and the women don't want to disturb the families. Do you want this family to survive, Constanz?"

Speechless, she nodded.

"Then listen to me. The war is not going well for the Germans. Never mind what the *Gazettino* says. The Allied bombings are wiping out all the industrial sites in northern Italy." The rabbi spoke more quickly. "Do you think the Nazis will put up with losing the war? There are fifteen thousand German troops in Italy right now—foxes in the chicken coop!" He raised his arms in exasperation, exclaiming that Hitler was a madman who considered Jews vermin, filth to be ground under his heel. He took a deep breath and lowered his voice, telling Constanz that they could come for Monica first, to make her follow.

"Oh, that's horrible!"

"Yes, Constanz, it *is* horrible. That's why you must sell this apartment and get out, as soon as possible. I'm in contact with a Jesuit priest in Turin—Monsignor Pietro—who's helping refugees. He's found a family for you."

She leaned forward, her arms crossed on her chest, as if to protect herself.

"Who is this family?" Ben asked.

"Signor Baldissera is an industrialist. He has a factory which makes automobile parts. The Baldisseras are Italian—Catholic and sympathetic to our problems. They are willing to take the risk of having you live in their home as servants, but you'll have to pose as Catholics. Monsignor Pietro in Turin will arrange for backdated baptismal certificates."

A sick feeling in her stomach, Constanz asked the rabbi to assure her that the family wouldn't have to be baptized. His answer came back without hesitation. "A Jew does whatever he must to save his life."

To save his life. Constanz was stunned. An involuntary shiver ran through her.

The rabbi went on to say that the Allies were bombing Turin every night, but that fortunately the Baldisseras had a home outside the city. They would say that Constanz was their housekeeper and Ben their gardener.

Ben pointed to himself in surprise. "Me, a gardener?"

The rabbi nodded, adding that they must pack just one small suitcase each, so they wouldn't look as if they were running away. The Baldisseras would be ready for them on Wednesday. The rabbi was working with a Catholic real estate person who could sell their apartment quickly. He wouldn't be able to get them much, but he would do as much as any of the agents making deals for Jews.

Constanz turned to Ben. "How about your work with signor di Stefano? You could stay in Venice and find a *pensione.*" She was talking faster and faster. "We'll be all right in Turin by ourselves."

"No, I won't work for him now. I'll explain that I have family obligations. How can I leave my mother and sister alone in Turin?"

The three adults argued back and forth until Constanz

decided that Ben would work for signor di Stefano for a month, and then come to Turin.

"But how do you know he won't turn Ben in?" Rabbi Coen asked.

Ben answered. "If you knew signor di Stefano … he is incensed about what the Gestapo did to Papà in Rome. He knows he can't tell anyone that my name is Cantarini."

"So, Constanz," the rabbi said, "I can see you're no longer the shy young woman I met some years ago. This signor di Stefano will understand that a family without a father needs the son. One month, then."

Constanz looked at Ben. "But tell him you can't go to Bolzano."

"Mamma, I told you, signor di Stefano is in a wheelchair and he needs me to go to Bolzano."

"Honestly," she said, "you're so like your father, so stubborn."

"Be careful, whatever you do." The rabbi stood and started for the front door, and then turned back to tell them something else. Because the Baldisseras were putting themselves at risk, they expected the Cantarinis to do things their way. Their charity didn't extend to letting Ben and Constanz make any decisions.

He looked at Ben. "Beniamino, before you go to Venice, I want you to stop by my office. We need to talk—and don't forget."

"Yes, Rabbi."

"May the God of our Fathers keep you safe. Good-bye."

Listening to the rabbi's hurried footsteps fading on the stairs to the street, Constanz had the sinking feeling that her life had just been snatched from her. "These people make all the decisions?" she exclaimed. "Before they've even met us, they're telling us what to do, what not to do?" She walked to the fireplace and smacked her fist on the mantelpiece. "Well, it's still *my* family."

Looking around the room, she saw so much that she loved—the credenza Claudio had given her for their tenth wedding anniversary, the silver she'd inherited from her grandmother, and her dearest possession, the ebony Bösendorfer piano her father had sent her from Germany. *"Porci* Nazi*!* They have nothing to do with the Germans I grew up with! And I have to leave all of this for some strangers?"

She marched to the crystal cabinet and opened the door. "Do you see this?" She picked up a fluted Champagne glass. "One of a dozen that your father and I were given for a wedding present." She lifted it above her head.

"Mamma, what are you doing?" Monica cried out.

"Don't, Mamma," Ben yelled. "There's no use."

"Oh yes, there most certainly is. If we can never enjoy these together, then neither will anyone else." She threw it with all her force across the room into the fireplace, where it shattered against the stone. "Now there are only eleven. No one will have a complete set." She stared at Monica, realizing what a shocking thing she had just done. "Please don't be upset, sweetheart. Mamma is angry, that's all. It has nothing to do with you." She turned to Ben. "Please get me the broom and a dustpan and let's start packing."

*   *   *

The next day, Ben went to see the rabbi as he had promised to do.

"Beniamino," said Rabbi Coen, "I asked you to come here

because you've said nothing to me about your father's death. All the time you were sitting shivah, you never spoke of it."

Ben looked around the rabbi's old-fashioned, dreary office and shook his head. How could this man surrounded by dusty books and prints of the land of Israel ever understand the problems in the real world? He shrugged, saying he hadn't wanted to upset his mother and sister any more than they already were.

"Then you're trying not to think about it?"

"No, I have my own feelings about it." He willed his voice not to shake.

"I know that you somehow feel responsible for your father's death. Tell me why."

Ben bit his lip, afraid he would cry if he spoke. The rabbi waited. Ben breathed deeply, and then the words poured out. He should have stopped his father … everyone had been saying how dangerous it was in Rome … he should have made his father listen. Hot tears stung his eyes.

The rabbi sat silently, letting the torrent flow.

"I should have gone alone," Ben said again. "It's my fault … about my mother, I mean, what happened."

The rabbi shook his head.

"And maybe I could have convinced Feltzer to give back the Bacchus drawing. Now we have nothing!" Ben asked the question that was burning into him. "Why did God let this happen? My father loved God."

"We don't understand these things, but we know that we're given free will."

"I'd rather be *told* what to do every day of my life than have this happen! Did God ever think that we might like that better, or does He only think of Himself?" The rabbi's face was swimming in front of him. "Rabbi, what's wrong with you that you don't understand?"

Rabbi Coen leaned forward. "Right now it is hard for you to understand anything. I can't tell you that you were fortunate to have grown up with such a wonderful father, because you won't hear me. But some day you will understand."

"And I suppose you're telling me I have to accept this?"

"I'm telling you to take care of your mother and your sister. Your father loved you more than his own eyes—he would trust you to take care of what he no longer can. This means you won't try chasing down that Caravaggio drawing in Rome, or anywhere else. Go wisely and carefully and be the man your father hoped you would be."

Ben thought how his father would have wanted him to say thank you, but he couldn't bring himself to do it. He stood, shook hands with the rabbi, and left.

CHAPTER 13

NEW YORK 2009 Later in the morning

Sitting at the long table of the Winthrop Auction House conference room, Tullia was relieved that she had not been stopped from giving so many details of her grandfather Beniamino's story. She knew it so well that sometimes she almost believed it was her own story, that she had lived through those years herself. It was her legacy as much as the Meissen porcelain and the Italian silverware her grandmother Silvia had left to her.

Every time she paused for a sip of water, she took a moment to study Henry Prentiss and Adelaide Bunning, who were sitting across from her. She hoped that by now they would be firm believers in her story and persuaded that they mustn't go ahead with the auction. The more Tullia spoke, the more the two heads of the auction house seemed willing to listen.

Henry Prentiss nodded, meaning she should continue. Tullia leaned forward and took up her story.

"My grandfather would have moved heaven and earth to track down the drawing, but he knew that his first responsibility was to his family. The next step was to help his mother and sister get ready to move to Turin."

CHAPTER 14

For Constanz, selling the apartment was shutting another door on Claudio. She felt that she was abandoning him forever. At least in the apartment she could have kept some part of him alive.

"Only one suitcase, imagine." She walked through the living room, checking the tabletops and bookcases to make certain she had put away everything important. She thought about the Rinaldis, the new owners of the apartment. They had come in so shamefaced, but still had allowed her only a corner of the cellar for storage. Constanz jammed what she could into the small space—Meissen plates, books, and a few mementoes she and Claudio had brought home from trips over the years.

She ran her hand over the polished black wood of her beautiful Bösendorfer piano. To think she had to leave this source of comfort behind. She would ask the Rinaldis to keep in mind that she'd like to buy it back from them after the war. After the war? Would she be dead or alive after the war? No, she mustn't let herself think like that. She opened the piano bench, swept up the pile of music, and put it in her suitcase. Maybe there was a piano where she was going.

When should she tell Monica where they were moving? She imagined her daughter saying something to the concierge. No, that wouldn't do. She would wait until they were on the train. Something her father used to say came back to her—"Jews have ears in their skin, they scatter before the storm." If she could remember all the words Mutti and Vati and Claudio had said, at least she wouldn't be completely alone.

On Wednesday morning, Constanz stood with Monica and Ben on the platform of the Padua station, waiting for the train to Turin. The light breeze of a surprisingly warm late October morning tugged at the dotted veil of her traveling hat. She pulled it down in front of her eyes, wishing it were darker. She knew she looked anxious and desperate, her face pale, her eyes red from exhaustion and weeping. Could the armed German soldiers chatting at the coffee bar twenty feet away tell that she and Monica were running away? She prayed they wouldn't ask why Ben wasn't in uniform.

Monica moved close to her mother, hugging her doll tightly. Constanz touched the edge of Monica's felt hat, straightening the grosgrain ribbons floating behind it. She looked at Ben. "Do you have everything you need?"

"Yes. I'm only going to be in Bolzano for the weekend, and signor di Stefano says my landlady in Venice will do my laundry."

She pulled Ben close. "When we were sitting shivah, I heard your friends talking about going to Bolzano for a final fling. What was that about? Nothing to do with you, I hope."

"I'm going there strictly on business. Don't worry."

She straightened. "Ben, please take good care of yourself. Don't let me worry that you'll do anything foolish."

"You know me better than that, Mamma." He gave his sister a warm hug. "Look, here comes the train, right on time."

For five hours the train chugged through the wheat fields and rice paddies of the Po river plain. Mother and daughter sat pressed against the other passengers in their third class compartment, Constanz scouring the skies above for Allied bombers. Claudio would say God was good, she thought, because not one plane flew overhead. In the few minutes they were alone in their compartment at a station stop in the town of Novara, just before Turin, Constanz explained everything to Monica. They would live with a nice older couple, they would answer to their new Christian names, and they would be Catholic. Monica seemed frightened, but at least she wasn't crying or protesting.

The memory of Claudio's death had settled like a gray cloud over Constanz's shoulders. Then when she least expected it, she shivered, remembering the German's eager fingers stroking her arms. And the Bacchus drawing! It would always be her fault that it had been stolen and that Ben would never be able to follow its trail and find it again.

On the station platform of Porta Nuova in Turin, Constanz looked into the faces of the people rushing to meet the passengers, wishing she had asked the rabbi if he knew what the Baldisseras looked like. Was one of them coming to meet them or would they both be there? If they didn't show up, she didn't even have their address. Would she look them up in the telephone book in Turin or in Montebello? Did a little village like Montebello even have a telephone book?

Before her worries could overwhelm her, she spotted a middle-aged couple hurrying toward her. The woman was out of breath, either from her portliness or from rushing. Her short gray hair was held back by a black velvet ribbon and her ample figure was stuffed into a handsome blue English tweed suit. She held out her hand to Constanz, saying, "Celeste Campano?" Then she leaned forward and breathed with lavender breath into Constanz's ear. "It's you, isn't it?"

So there was her new name and she would have to accept it. Constanz shook the woman's hand, explaining that her son was delayed and would join the family in a few weeks.

"I see. Well, I'm Francesca Baldissera." The older woman stood back. "And this is my husband, signor Baldissera."

He smiled broadly. "Celeste is going to call us by our first names, Francesca and Gianni."

Constanz felt again the shock of being called by her new name, but she was reassured by the man's ruddy face and charitable smile. He was as portly as his wife, but in a handsome, contained way. Dapper in a double-breasted suit and muted silk tie, he wore deep worry lines on his forehead. Constanz smiled, because there was something roguish about him, this man with the semicircle of gray hair.

"And this must be Maria," Francesca said, putting her hands on Monica's shoulders and looking into her eyes, as if trying to see what she was all about.

"You're very pretty," Gianni said to the little girl, "with your dark eyes and shiny braids." He bent over and patted her on the shoulder. "Maria, how old are you?"

"I'm eight," she answered shyly.

"Eight years old? Well, we'll want to find out all about you, Maria. You look like somebody who's fun to be with."

As they walked together, Francesca explained that it was unfortunate to start with a problem, but they'd all have to stay in the Turin house for one night. They had intended to go straight out to their country house in Montebello, but there was no methane gasoline for the car. She frowned and looked over at her husband. "Gianni couldn't find any."

"Now don't be so hard on me. I'll find gas." He smiled at Constanz. "That's why we were late. We had to take the streetcar."

Suddenly, Constanz felt completely weary, not caring what this couple had to say to each other, or where she had to lay her head. She just wanted to go someplace quiet and be alone with her daughter.

"We think Turin is beautiful," Francesca said, boarding the streetcar. "We hope you will like our old, aristocratic city."

Constanz pulled herself out of her weariness and tried to seem interested. True, the city was elegant, with miles of stately arcades and centuries-old buildings in the French style. The snow-tipped Alps far to the north embraced the city, but it was all so distant from her homey Padua. A few stops later, Gianni helped his group down from the streetcar and led them to a street lined with ancient plane trees. Behind an iron fence stood a large brick villa. Unlocking the heavy iron gate and pushing it open, Gianni announced that this would be their home for that night.

Her home for that night? For how many nights and how many days would she and her daughter be wandering and hiding?

Upstairs Constanz gazed around the room she and Monica would share. It was a pretty little room with yellow and pink chintz bedspreads and matching chintz curtains framing tall windows that overlooked a brick walkway. An enormous beech tree spread its branches over an adjacent courtyard.

Francesca sat next to Monica on the bed and searched the little girl's face. "Has Maria been told not to say that she is Jewish?"

"Yes," Constanz answered. "She understands."

"Well, I hope she really does." A look of resignation on her face, Francesca stood up and turned to Constanz. "My husband wants me to tell our friends that you and my daughter-in-law were old school chums, and that you're lonely with your husband in the army in southern Italy. That's why you're here with us."

"Claudio in southern Italy? You know that's not so, don't you?"

"Yes, of course I do. I'm very sorry about your husband, my dear, but this is the safest thing to say."

Francesca must have seen Constanz's distress, but she pressed on. "Frankly, I would never have taken you in, but my husband is insisting on doing this." Beads of perspiration dotted Francesca's upper lip. "The Gestapo has started arresting people who help Jews and it terrifies me."

Constanz nodded wearily, asking herself why Rabbi Coen had sent her family here. With this woman being as frightened as she was, she wouldn't be able to stand up to German soldiers for two minutes!

"I'm too old for all this," Francesca continued, "but as I said, this is what my husband wants." She reached into her pocket and produced two small white boxes. She handed Monica one of the boxes.

The little girl lifted the lid and folded back the tissue paper. "Oh, look, real jewelry! A gold cross! I've never had anything gold before! Just like what my Catholic friends have. Will this make me Catholic?"

"Put it on her, Celeste," Francesca said.

Constanz lifted the delicate gold chain with unwilling

fingers. As she reached around her daughter's neck, she
vivid memory of Vati, her dear father. He was standing ne
her in their living room in Berlin, saying how fortunate she was
to have a happy childhood and not be forced to hide behind a
cross. Wasn't it awful, her father was telling her, that during the
pogroms the Polish Jews had to pretend to be Catholic and wear
crosses and memorize Catholic prayers, in case they were tested
by the mobs of Jew-haters. And now the curse had snaked its way
down the years to find her.

"Ooh," Monica said softly, stroking the cross. "Thank you."
She hugged Francesca's ample waist.

After Francesca left, Constanz walked to the window and
stared outside, seeing and yet not seeing. The big house was
silent, magnifying her despair. Her thoughts fell on Ben, so far
away now. She turned and stroked her daughter's hair. "We have
to stay here, because we want to be safe. Now, remember, you're
Maria and I am Celeste. We have to pretend that we are Catholic
and that we have a different papà, whose name is Arturo and who
is in the army."

How was Monica going to keep all of this straight? And
would Ben let go of his obsession, or would he try to track down
the Caravaggio drawing? If he did, surely even more trouble
would follow. She asked herself again how long she could hang
on while the world was spinning wildly around her.

*   *   *

Signor di Stefano rolled his wheelchair to the front of his
showroom, crowded with paintings and easels, and smelling of
paint and turpentine. He looked out at the street and smacked
his fist on the window ledge. "I never thought to see Nazi soldiers

in Venice strutting up and down in front of my gallery. *Porci Nazis!*"

Ben nodded, agreeing with his new boss. When he had first met di Stefano, he'd been surprised to see such a hearty man in a wheelchair. Middle-aged, stocky, but not yet gray, di Stefano had a booming voice that belied the pain he still felt in his leg. Now he watched Ben pick up his rucksack and asked if he had everything he needed.

"Yes, Signore, the painting is in here." Ben patted the portfolio resting against his leg.

"You've caught on to the business so well. I can't believe you started here only three days ago. Now let's see how you do in selling this Monet." Momentary anger crossed di Stefano's face. "Be careful walking at night, or you'll get rammed by a Nazi sidecar like I did." He gave Ben a worried look. "Do you have a flashlight? They're blacked out in Bolzano."

"The train gets in at four o'clock. It won't be dark yet." Ben picked up his portfolio. "I'd better move along now."

Signor di Stefano gave his wheelchair another push and reached for the door. "Just one more thing, Ben. Signor Heinrich von Mühlenberg is a knowledgeable art collector. Dealing with him will be difficult, because he's shrewd and he's tough. He will challenge you and try to outsmart you, so be alert. If you reach an impasse, telephone me—they may let a call go through—and let me intercede. This deal mustn't fall through."

Ben straightened up and tried to look authoritative. "Signore, I never shrink from a challenge. I look forward to this."

"One more thing, Ben. If he starts asking you about the Caravaggio, play very dumb. I know you want news of it, but discussion of it could lead right back to you being Jewish. I've told von Mühlenberg that you aren't in the army because you have a bad leg."

Ben waved good-bye and headed off for the Stazione Santa Lucia. He wondered if he really was up to the job of selling this Monet painting to a well-known art collector. As he walked through the damp streets of Venice, crossing the bridges over the back canals, he told himself not to feel nervous but instead to think of something pleasant. Wouldn't it be great if his friends did go to Bolzano this weekend? They had seemed pretty certain of it when they had come to sit shivah. Then he could have a little fun and maybe even hear news of the Partisan activities.

The train was jam-packed. Ben stood in the corridor running alongside the crowded compartments, pressed against the other passengers, holding onto his portfolio with the Monet painting. It was a relief that for once German soldiers and SS officers were not in evidence. After three hours of gazing out the train's wide window, when the chalets had given way to mile after mile of vineyards, Ben's thoughts returned to the Caravaggio drawing. He could picture it so clearly, every line and shading, the curve of the God of Wine's bare arm and shoulder, his look of seductive invitation as he held out the glass of wine. Who had the drawing now? Herr Feltzer? Or had he already sent it on to Hermann Göring? That bastard of a *Reichsmarschall* would love to get his hands on it.

Soon the pinnacles of the Dolomites turned pink in the late afternoon sun, and the train slowed down. Ben saw with disgust a wooden sign draped with swastika flags announcing Bolzano as the next stop. Even here, in this quaint little tourist town, the Nazis had to show their muscle. When the train ground to a halt, Ben checked that his Aryan papers were in order, picked up his belongings, and jumped down to the platform. He was amazed to see that even in wartime, geranium-filled flowerpots hung from the wooden beams outside the station.

Great! He spotted his friends on the platform ahead of him and smiled. Freckle-faced Raffaele, rucksack over his shoulder, waved at him, and Cristoforo, a head taller, clapped him on the back. Giorgio, grinning his crooked smile, gave him a false punch in the chest.

"Did your family move?" Giorgio asked, walking along beside him.

"Yes." Ben hoped his clipped answer would stop any questions, though he was sure they wouldn't ask where the family had gone. "I have a painting to sell in Bolzano."

"So you got the job. Good!"

Ben spotted German soldiers at the other end of the platform and automatically put his hand on his breast pocket where he kept his Aryan papers. He lowered his voice and said to Cristoforo, who was dressed in hiking pants, "I thought you were in the army—good Catholic boy like you."

"I was, but when the Nazis took over, I got myself some new ID papers and deserted. I'll be damned if I'll fight for those swine. On my way back from Bolzano, I'm going to Trento to join the Partisans in the hills. They'll have rifles by Tuesday."

Giorgio spoke in a soft voice. "We're making more four-pointed nails. We've already got a good idea of the German truck movements."

"I wish I could join you," Ben said quietly, "but you know things are different for me now."

"I know. Cristoforo was supposed to fight somewhere near Russia—didn't even have lined boots. He was issued cloth to wrap around his feet inside his boots. They say the Germans send the Italian troops to the front first, the bastards. We all want to fight

140

against the Germans, not for them." He looked at the outsized flags hanging from the station eaves—black swastikas on fields of white and red, curling and flapping in the mountain air—and pulled Ben aside. "Yesterday Mariana broke off our engagement. She said the authorities warned her father to put an end to any thoughts of marriage between a Catholic and a Jew like me."

"Will she still go on seeing you at least?"

"No. She does pretty much what her parents tell her to do."

"Maybe after the war is over, I mean, it can't be too long. With the Allies bombing the hell out of the cities, some people think they'll be in Rome in a couple of weeks."

Giorgio grimaced. "Maybe. But now the Germans are ruining our lives. The more Nazis I get rid of, the better I'll like it. I'm already a good shot from the days you and I used to go hunting in the mountains."

As the group crossed the piazza in front of the station, Ben elbowed Giorgio and nodded toward the Park Laurin hotel, telling him that he had a reservation to stay there. He'd have to go past the SS soldiers who were drinking coffee on the hotel's veranda and already scrutinizing Ben's group.

A hand clamped the back of his shoulder. Ben spun around, reaching for his papers. Behind him was not a soldier but another familiar face—Bruno.

"*Ciao,* Ben. You made it here too? We're going to have a great weekend—if these German blockheads don't bother us."

Ben was relieved to see good old Bruno, a real southern fellow, hands flying as he spoke. Of course Bruno was there ahead of the pack and had already found a *pensione* on the mountain, a great little chalet. He was already having a good time—bonfires and an accordion at night, and he insisted that Ben join them. He wouldn't hear of Ben's excuses about having to show his boss a receipt for the night's stay at the Park Laurin. It would be simple just to say the hotel was full when he arrived.

The sight of the Nazi soldiers eyeing them convinced Ben. Looking neither left nor right, he strode up the steps and into the hotel. At the reservation desk he cancelled his room, and then quickly descended the veranda steps and caught up with his friends.

Walking through the center of Bolzano, Ben saw that Hitler's soldiers in their drab blue-gray uniforms had replaced most of the tourists. Since he'd last been there with Papà, the fascists also had removed the statue of the noble poet Walther, which used to stand atop the fountain in the central plaza.

His friends didn't seem bothered by the new look of Bolzano. Jostling and calling to one another, they climbed onto the funiculare. As the cable car inched up the steep ascent, climbing high above the deep valley, Ben turned to watch the town fade into the distance. The red roofs melted together into a solid pink mass, with only the lacy spires of the cathedral standing out against the evening sky. He remembered taking this same ride years before. How startling it was then, in the dusk, to see the lights of Bolzano far below twinkling in the growing mist. But now the inky darkness of the wartime blackout would envelop Bolzano, reminding him nothing was the same.

When the mountain train stopped, Ben and his friends walked a half block to a two-story chalet, a stand of spruce trees on one side, a meadow on the other. Inside the chalet, Bruno led the group down a long corridor lined with old black and white photographs of Alpine scenes, until they reached a dormitory room.

"Throw your rucksacks on a bed," he said, "and let's go outside. The accordion is going full blast."

Once the landlady had locked his portfolio away, Ben stepped outside, pulling a sweater over his head and breathing in the mountain air. For the first time since his father died, his spirits lifted a little bit.

"Come on," Giorgio urged. "Let's have a beer now, and later we'll have supper at the Caffè Montagna. More music, more singing, it's all arranged."

What was he doing? He'd been sent up to the mountains to make an important sale, and here he was going off to have a good time. He'd go, but he wouldn't stay long.

CHAPTER 15

After sitting in the Baldisseras' living room for a half hour after dinner, Constanz felt it was time to excuse herself. Taking Monica's hand, she headed for the stairs. Monica raced up ahead. Constanz hesitated long enough to hear Francesca say to Gianni, "How are we going to prepare Celeste for Hans Hauptmann's visit?"

A German in the house? Constanz shuddered.

"Hans won't be here very long," Gianni said. "Besides, Celeste seems to be a strong woman. She'll handle what she has to." He paused. "Tomorrow I'm going with you to see Monsignor Pietro. Celeste and Maria need baptismal papers now, not in six months, and the religion lessons will just have to wait."

"Good. Monsignore will pay more attention to you than he would to me."

Hearing Gianni's heavy footsteps coming toward the hallway, Constanz reached for the banister and retreated up the stairs.

In their bedroom, she read the story of Cinderella to Monica, her eyes on the words but her mind on their new life. Finally, she tucked Monica into bed, telling her to repeat their new names until she fell asleep. "Tomorrow we'll all be going out to the country to live." She tried to sound enthusiastic. "Another house, imagine."

"If the planes drop bombs on us, will we be killed?" Monica asked.

"No, we'll be safe, my little sweetheart."

In her bathroom, Constanz pressed her hands against the sink to keep them from shaking. Leaning toward the mirror, she looked at herself. "Just for the blood in my veins, I'm bad. How could that be?" She closed her eyes and whispered, "Claudio, I'm becoming one of those widows who talk to themselves. Help me! Watch over me!" For a moment she listened to the sound of her own breathing. "My name is Celeste Campano. My husband is Arturo. He is a colonel in the army, stationed in southern Italy." She opened her eyes, forcing herself to continue. "My son's name is Bernardo and my daughter is Maria." She reminded herself that Claudio used to say that you mustn't pray for God to change the world, but only to help you get through it.

She prayed softly, "God, if you are there, help my sweet girl to remember her new name. Grant us one favor—don't let anyone suspect what we are."

The next morning Gianni, Francesca, Constanz, and Monica went to the center of Turin to find Monsignor Pietro. Outside a dark stone church built in the last century, ornamented with gargoyles and heavy molding, Gianni pushed hard on the bell. A stooped, elderly priest edged open the door, bringing a rush of stale, cigar-laden air. On the frame of the door, where she was accustomed to seeing Rabbi Coen's mezuzah, was a small bowl of water. Francesca dipped in her fingertips and crossed herself.

The priest led them down a hallway lined with paintings, and

Constanz darted a look at the first one. It was Jesus on his face resigned to his suffering. Farther along was a of a woman being visited by an angel. Would she be expected to believe these things? Impossible. She would never understand the depictions in this gloomy hallway. But she must accept all this so that her children would be safe. Just before entering the waiting room, she glanced up at a sepia photograph of the pope, a visionary look on his drawn, ascetic face. Claudio used to say "Christians make the trouble and then we need the Christians to help us." He was right, she thought. Yes, he had known.

Francesca sat on a fringed settee and patted the seat next to her for Monica to sit. Constanz's love of elegance repudiated every dusty rococo item in the room, obviously donations from a dozen old houses. What was wrong with her, she asked herself, that she was noticing furniture at a moment like this?

A middle-aged, athletic-looking priest with a shock of white hair introduced himself as Monsignor Pietro. Leaving Francesca and Monica in the waiting room, he ushered Constanz and Gianni into his office.

"Now, Monsignor," Gianni said, easing himself into the chair next to Constanz, "let's get right to the point. I'm asking you to baptize Celeste and her daughter immediately."

The priest looked up at the ceiling, as if composing his thoughts, and then formed his words carefully. "But, Gianni, you know that six months of instruction is a requisite. The bishop insists on it."

Constanz's heart sank. As much as this man's religion was distasteful to her, she wanted it, oh Lord, she needed it. She looked from the priest to Gianni. They were talking as if she weren't even in the room. The priest picked up a pen, twirled it between his thumb and forefinger, and set it down again.

"Monsignore," Gianni said, "we can't take a chance that this lovely lady, a widow, and her little girl will be sent back to that madman's country. Doesn't it say in the Bible to watch over widows and orphans?"

The priest closed his eyes in thought. Finally, he said, "But they still must have six months of instruction after the baptism."

Gianni waved away any problems. "The priest in Montebello will help with the instruction. We're leaving this afternoon."

Monsignor Pietro nodded. Opening a drawer of his desk, he pulled out a sheet of paper and handed it to Constanz. "Read this, dear lady, and understand what you are signing."

Constanz took the paper. It read: "I am in full agreement that my child/children _____ be baptized in the Roman Catholic Church and that he/they be instructed in the Catholic faith. Furthermore, I have no objection to him/them being brought up as Roman Catholic. Signed _____ parent/legal guardian."

"Brought up?" She tried to swallow the hard lump in her throat. She had imagined … Well, what *had* she imagined? A month? Three months? At most a year? But *brought up?* That could mean her little girl's whole life. She shook her head and handed the paper back to the priest.

"Celeste," Gianni said, placing his hand on her wrist, "I don't want to force you, but you need this for the safety of your family. After all, it's not a den of thieves you'd be entering. And the Monsignore won't do this again tomorrow."

"No, I won't," the priest said, standing. "And I'm not going to sandbag you into this, either."

"Wait," Constanz said, reaching for the paper. "I'll do it. I need to … I really want to do it. I'll sign."

The priest led Constanz, Monica, and the Baldisseras to a

small room off the sanctuary, crammed with old books and dusty statues. He carefully placed on a small table vials of oil and water and a container of salt. Lifting one vial and then another, his lips barely moving, he murmured a monotonous blur of Latin consonants and vowels. He was like someone in a trance, his arms and hands moving in a deliberate pattern. As she watched him, Constanz's heart raced. Was she doing the right thing?

The priest's thumb touched her and Monica's forehead, with oil and water, and then their tongues with salt. Gradually the cool shadows of the room and the priest's soft, toneless murmurings worked their way into Constanz, bringing a welcome numbness to her body and mind. For a few minutes she was lifted away from reality, from the world of loss and confusion and terror. The noise of the outside world was far away; all she heard was the hypnotic droning of the priest's voice. Watching Gianni's and Francesca's faces, she saw tranquility and confidence. They must feel it, too, the safety of this place, isolated from the terrible world outside. Yes, now she and her daughter, and even Ben, had a chance to be safe.

The priest removed his white stole. Would he give them a final blessing in Italian, in words she could understand? Contrary to her hope, he said nothing as he packed the vials of oil and water and the container of salt into their mahogany box and closed it firmly. He gestured toward a side door to the street, dismissing the group.

"Good luck, everyone," he said. "Move away from the rectory quickly."

After hurrying everyone along the sidewalk for a few minutes, Gianni said, "It's almost ten o'clock and I'm going to the office. We'll leave for Montebello at four o'clock this afternoon. Be ready."

"Of course." Francesca gave Gianni a light kiss. "Come along, Celeste and Maria. We have to cover the furniture before we leave. The trip takes about an hour by car. Then tomorrow in Montebello we'll get ready for Herr Hauptmann."

Hearing the German's name again, Constanz remembered the terrifying dream she'd had the night before in which she was chased by faceless men. "Who is Herr Hauptmann?"

"A business acquaintance. He's arriving in a few days." Francesca lowered her voice. "I should have explained. The government ordered Gianni to retool his factory to make tank parts."

"Why would you risk having a German in the same house with us?"

Francesca stopped and gave her a sharp look. In a whisper, she said, "Gianni arranges for all the strikes and slow-downs he can. It's the best we can do. Now let's not discuss it further."

The peace she had felt in the rectory had vanished, evaporated into the chill autumn air.

CHAPTER 16

Bruno was right. The Caffè Montagna was welcoming and warm, with its knotty-pine walls, logs crackling in the huge stone fireplace, and ivy overflowing the copper pots on the darkened mantelpiece. Sitting with his friends at one of the long tables, eating pasta and tiramisu, Ben tried to let go of his concerns. Mamma and Monica were no doubt safe. The rabbi would only send them to people who really wanted them. Tomorrow he would face signor Heinrich von Mühlenberg, but tonight he would let go and have a few beers and a few laughs with Giorgio and his other friends.

His good mood ended when a group of German soldiers burst through the door. They took the table next to his group, calling out, *"Bier, bringen Sie Bier!"* and filling the room with their cigarette smoke. From the corner of his eye, Ben saw them ordering drinks for the local girls and urging them to sit on their laps. He watched the Nazis, wishing he could drag the bastards outside, push them against the wall, and press his thumbs into their throats.

"How long are you staying in the village?"

A local girl had edged in to sit next to Ben. She smiled engagingly and pulled at the ruffle of her Tyrolean blouse. It took Ben a moment to calm his rush of anger.

"Until Monday morning."

"Would you like to dance?" Not waiting for an answer, the girl stood and pulled Ben onto the dance floor, leading him into a country waltz. Her waist was small and neat under his hand. It felt good to have a girl in his arms again.

As they danced Ben saw an older woman, tall and angular, smartly dressed in a city suit, walk into the smoky, crowded room. With her was a young woman.

"What are you staring at?" the girl in Ben's arms asked.

"Nothing." But it wasn't true. The young woman who had just entered the room was eye-catching, in her blue skirt and high heels, her dark hair pulled neatly back.

"Oh yes, you are staring at someone else. Maybe I should go and talk to the German soldiers. They love to dance and they've got plenty of money for drinks. Not like you students." She looked in the direction of his glance and wrinkled her nose. "Is that your girlfriend?"

"Of course not."

The girl tweaked his chin. "Come on, let's sit and have a little beer. You're not even paying attention to the music." Ben realized he had slowed his step below the beat of the accordion.

He sat with the girl on a bench against the wall, making small talk. Still he darted glances at the dark-haired young woman across the room. Now a man kissed her on both cheeks and turned to embrace her older companion. The fellow took the attractive young woman by the hand and led her onto the dance floor. Then, when the music stopped, she walked with him and the older woman out of the crowded room. Ben felt strangely let down, as if she had teased him and then left him. Oh come on, he told himself, how could a girl he didn't even know play games with him.

But the incident had brought him back to reality. He thought of the job he had to do the next day and how much he and his family needed the commission from the sale of the painting. Ben stood, picked up his sweater, said good night to his friends, and headed back to the *pensione*.

The next morning, outside the Park Laurin hotel, the autumn sun glinted off the polished finish of the limousine drawing up to Ben. The driver stepped from the car and said, "Signor Campano? I am Konrad, signor von Mühlenberg's man." As the chauffeur opened the rear door of the car, Ben made a quick study of the man—not much older than Ben, unsmiling eyes and hard features. Not a person he'd like to make conversation with.

Ben glanced at the SS officers on the front veranda of the hotel and silently thanked Bruno for convincing him to cancel his reservation there. Once seated in the car, he laid his portfolio with the Monet close to his side and tugged the knees of his trousers to maintain the crease.

After a half hour, the driver called over his shoulder, "Better part of an hour until we reach the castle," and snapped the partition shut. With each passing mile, Ben felt himself growing more tense. What were the words signor di Stefano had used to describe von Mühlenberg? That he was wily? No, shrewd and tough. The road grew rougher, the hairpin turns coming more often.

At one point the driver slowed to a crawl. "What is it?" Ben asked.

"Sharpest turn in the road. A car flipped over here last week. Now there's no guard rail."

Ben peered over the edge of the precipice. Far below, the Adige River gushed from a hidden tunnel and plunged over rocks and broken trees.

How old was this von Mühlenberg, this lawyer from Venice who had the wealth to spend his weekends in the mountains shooting game, leading the gentleman's life? Ben looked up at the hills crowned by the distant Dolomites, the highest summits already touched with snow, and felt his own insignificance.

Ahead of the car, on the top of a steep, chalky hill, stood a stone fortress, no doubt built centuries ago as a protection against marauders. Ben lowered the window to have a better look, but quickly raised it. The air this far up was cold and cutting.

When the car reached the crest of the hill, it traveled through an allée of evergreen trees and pulled up at a massive wrought-iron gate. The driver's tap on the horn brought two wolfhounds lunging at the iron fencing. A groundsman ordered them into their dog run and pulled back the gate. Before stepping out under the porte cochere, Ben snugged his tie and brushed the cuff of his sleeve.

Inside the castle, the aroma of antique furniture and polished wood greeted him. Coats of armor lined either side of the long entrance hallway. A servant indicated an open door halfway down the hall, saying that signor von Mühlenberg would meet him in the library.

Ben gazed in awe at the beamed ceiling of the great room. Two walls were covered with leather-bound books, and in the massive stone fireplace, large enough to walk into, enormous logs burned and crackled. He stepped over to read the titles of the books—his father always said that books gave a clue to the interests of the owner. Nietzsche, *Der Antichrist,* Adolf Hitler, *Mein Kampf* ... Slowly Ben gathered his forces and his ideas.

"Good morning," a gruff voice called out. A man in a gray tweed shooting jacket strode into the room, his hand out, his footsteps heavy on the dark carpet. "I am signor von Mühlenberg."

"Bernardo Campano," Ben said. "I'm pleased to meet you." He quickly assessed the man he was dealing with—mid-fifties and heavy-set, gray hair parted in the middle and neatly combed back, nickel-framed glasses, a no-nonsense man of means.

"Come." Signor von Mühlenberg nodded. "Sit by the fire."

Ben judged that the man had grown up in the Dolomite area. His Italian had the typical soft sound of Austrian German. His host reached for the tapestried bell pull next to him and asked if Ben wanted a schnapps. Ben agreed and sat across from him.

Konrad, apparently now acting as butler, came into the room, poured two schnapps, handed one to von Mühlenberg and one to Ben, and then left.

"So," von Mühlenberg said, raising his glass toward his guest, "Konrad tells me you were not to be found at the Park Laurin hotel last evening."

The man's opening thrust succeeded in putting Ben off balance. Hoping his surprise was not apparent, he lifted his glass and took a sip. "You are quite right, Signore. I met some friends on the train and decided to join them for the evening. But, of course, I was ready for your driver this morning." He smiled. "And, by the way, I very much enjoyed the drive up the mountain."

Von Mühlenberg gave Ben a perfunctory smile. "I see that di Stefano sends me a rather young man."

"I'm not as young as I look," Ben said, and quickly changed

the subject. "Signor von Mühlenberg, how did you discover your interest in art?"

The older man studied his schnapps. "More to the point, signor Campano, how did *you* get your introduction to the art world?"

"It's always been a passion of mine since I was a youngster. My family taught me much that I know, and then of course there are the university courses. And you, Signore, how did you decide that you loved art? Were you fascinated by one particular school of painting, or perhaps a particular artist?"

"My father had a large collection, to which I have added and which I will show you."

When Konrad appeared to ask if they needed anything else, Ben had the feeling that he had been listening outside the door. Von Mühlenberg waved him away, and then explained to Ben that the man had been with him for years and was very solicitous.

"In fact," he added, "since I have no wife or children, I have taken him under my wing." He smiled with satisfaction. "He's a distant cousin of mine, from the Austrian town I grew up in, so it feels rather like home to have him with me." He lowered his voice. "He was born on the wrong side of the sheets, as they say, and fortunately has a different family name. Konrad Grünewald had a rather checkered past until I took him in. I straightened him out, you know." He chuckled. "Hard to get yourself in trouble up here in the mountains."

He continued. "Anyway, to answer your question, my father took me to galleries all over Europe and taught me to appreciate modern art, as well as ancient and Renaissance works."

"Did your father have a favorite period, Signore?" Ben felt himself gaining more confidence. There were always preliminaries to discuss before a client would ask what the dealer had brought with him, and he was on solid ground discussing art.

"The more modern, the better for my father." Von Mühlenberg paused, and then added, "Of course, you and I both know about the present dislike of 'degenerate art,' but … " He shrugged. "I may not agree with the Nazi rejection of modern art, but I do favor Germany taking back this area of Italy." Ben knew that the loyalties were often different in this Alpine region, but he'd never been faced with it. Von Mühlenberg continued, "After all, Signor Campano, we were Austrian until the Great War. Look at the cathedral in the center of Bolzano, so dear to us, all the writing carved in German. The customs, the food … we're more German than Italian, even our names." He lowered his voice. "Signor di Stefano assures me that our discussion may lead us where it will and that it stays in this room."

"Of course, Signore. I know about the concept of irredentism, that the Germans want to reclaim the territories lost in old wars."

"Yes, we understand that this war won't last forever. It's difficult to know which way it will go, but I have a good idea. However, I don't state my opinions publicly." He stood. "I want to show you my gallery. I had all the paintings hung yesterday for your visit."

Leading Ben down the hallway, past medieval pennants and suits of armor, von Mühlenberg explained, "Of course, I usually keep my paintings covered and propped against the walls, facing away from the sunlight."

So the man was a real collector, Ben thought.

Entering the large whitewashed room, devoid of furniture except for a polished bench placed in the middle, Ben had a difficult time masking his surprise. Works of well-known modern painters lined the walls, Modigliani, Braque, Manet, Picasso. My God, a priceless collection, hidden up there in a remote castle in the mountains!

Von Mühlenberg's expression had softened. "Modigliani is Jewish, you know, but for me it's quite all right, art knows no religion, no nationality." Together they studied the elongated, peaceful figure of Modigliani's mistress. Ben had always been drawn to the artist's cool, enigmatic paintings.

Suddenly, von Mühlenberg turned to him. "Did you know signor Claudio Cantarini of Padua?"

The shock of the question numbed Ben. He could only nod.

"I was prepared to ask him to help me with my collection, but before I could be introduced to him, he died. What a shame."

"Yes, a terrible loss," Ben said, his throat dry.

"We were all astounded to hear that his son had found Caravaggio's Bacchus drawing, in a mask shop of all places!"

Ben knew that he would stammer if he tried to respond. He nodded again.

"That young man must be about your age. Do you know him?"

Ben told himself not to look away. He gazed steadily at von Mühlenberg as he answered that he had heard of Ben Cantarini and that the drawing had certainly been a remarkable find.

"What I would give to see that drawing." Von Mühlenberg gave a sly smile. "Perhaps even to own it myself! You were at university with the Cantarini son?"

He was pressing him. Did he know? Was he playing games with him? Ben forced himself not to wipe his sweating palms on his jacket as he shook his head. "I suppose our paths must have crossed at some point."

"Have you heard anything about what's become Caravaggio since Cantarini's death?"

"No, I haven't." Ben leaned in toward the Modigliani painting. "This is a particularly beautiful painting. The sinuous line of the model's torso is extraordinary." He looked at the older man. "You have a most impressive collection here."

"For a collector, nothing is ever complete." Von Mühlenberg's voice ill concealed his eagerness. "As I told di Stefano, if I could find the right work by another French painter, I could possibly be interested."

"Ah, yes, Signore, allow me to get my portfolio."

Retrieving his portfolio from the library, Ben noticed that the window opposite the fireplace gave onto a meadow. The wall next to the window was empty. He smiled as an idea came to him.

When Ben returned to the gallery, the older man was extricating a large easel from a closet. Together they placed the stand in the middle of the room under the skylight. Ben opened his portfolio and removed the Monet, carefully clipping its edges to the easel. He stepped away from the painting, allowing it to have its full effect on his potential client.

The meadow in the painting shimmered under soft sunlight; three poplar trees stood one behind the other, leading to a path that beckoned the viewer on to a larger meadow.

"Ah!" A sigh escaped von Mühlenberg. "Claude Monet."

There followed a moment of silence. When the man turned to Ben, his eyes brimmed, his voice was unsteady. "*Ach!* If only we could hold on to such moments," he murmured to himself in German. "The peace, the quiet, the beauty … " Abruptly, von Mühlenberg's expression was businesslike again. "It's lovely, but I doubt one would be able to hang it for years to come. If the Germans win, how can I show anyone this 'degenerate' art?"

"But what a pleasure if one could enjoy it in the privacy of one's own home." Ben added, "The painter has died. There will be no more such masterpieces from his hand."

"Of course, I know that," came the irritable answer. "How much does signor di Stefano want?"

Ben waited for a moment. He could hear his father saying, "Don't rush a client. Pause before you speak."

"He would let it go for six thousand." It was a thousand more than his employer had told him to ask, but this man was going to be a hard bargainer. And a larger price would bring a larger commission for him.

"What?" Von Mühlenberg wheeled around to look at Ben. He shot out his hand toward the painting. "For this? Do you think I'm Croesus that I can invest that kind of money in a painting I can't even let anyone know I've acquired? I have some important people coming up here from Rome this evening for dinner. I'd have to hide it."

Ben's heart skipped a beat, but he kept his voice calm. "I can imagine hanging this painting next to the window in—"

"Which window?" Von Mühlenberg cut in.

"The window in the library giving onto the meadow. The view is very like this, except that you have no poplar trees. I have seen landscaping created so that it is a doubling of a painting. Cypress trees in your meadow would create much the same effect. The imitation gives more pleasure in the viewing of both."

The man drew in a long breath, saying he was willing to settle on a figure of five thousand lire.

Ben assured him that signor di Stefano would insist on no less than fifty-five hundred lire.

The older man turned and walked toward the door, announcing that he wanted to telephone the gallery owner.

Ben was firm, telling him that a phone call would not help. The answer would still be the same.

Von Mühlenberg looked at the painting again. Ben knew the man had been seduced by the beauty of it when he said, begrudgingly, "I would have to move the painting every time someone comes."

"Yes, of course, I understand."

"What do you see when you look at it?" he asked unexpectedly.

"I like the way that path calls a person to follow it."

"Hmm." Von Mühlenberg stared at the painting, his arms folded across his chest. There was another pause, the silence Papà said was usually followed by the decision to acquire the painting. Ben's host nodded. "Yes, it is beautiful. Come to the library. I'll make a check for fifty-five hundred."

Ben had never witnessed a decision made quite so fast. Von Mühlenberg gave the painting a lingering look, and then walked with Ben to the library. Dashing off the amount and his signature, he handed over the check. "There's something else I want. Find out for me where that Caravaggio drawing is. I'll make it worth your while."

Ben couldn't stop a sharp intake of breath. "Of course, if I'm able to."

"Good. I'd be the happiest man in the world if I had that drawing! Now, perhaps you could spend some time with me this afternoon and tell me what you know about my paintings. And I'd like you to stay and spend the evening here with my dinner guests."

Ben's heart quickened. "You are too kind, but I have other business in Bolzano. I must return by late afternoon."

"Too bad, because one of my guests is the head of the Gestapo in Rome. He's up and coming—it never hurts to be friendly with such personages. But, anyway, we'll have lunch now and talk about where to plant the trees. And I want to know more about you."

Good God! Feltzer here in Bolzano! Ben could barely force a smile.

As the two men took their lunch at the long, polished table in the regal dining room where banners and coats of arms decorated the walls, they spoke of von Mühlenberg's paintings. Ben was able to keep the discussion so lively that he steered it away from himself. His client only learned that he had grown up in the Veneto area, no more. At two thirty Konrad appeared with the limousine. The check in his portfolio, Ben eased himself into the backseat.

"Sold him a painting, did you?" Konrad asked as they drove under the allée of evergreen trees.

"Hmm," was Ben's only response. Konrad wasn't going to get him to talk out of turn. Still, he could barely contain his excitement at his first sale on his own, and how well he had done. But the thrill was dampened by the politics of his client. He had sold a beautiful painting to a Nazi sympathizer. Damn! And did that man think he was the only one who wanted to know where the Caravaggio drawing was? What Ben would give to search for it, but he knew where his duty lay. He had to stay alive and take care of his family.

CHAPTER 17

Late in the afternoon of Constanz's and Monica's baptism, Gianni drove them with Francesca to the outskirts of the village of Montebello. He turned onto a dirt road and stopped in front of an iron gate set into a high wall. After opening the gate, he drove into a broad, pebbled courtyard.

"This is our house," he said, pointing to an elegant half-timbered two-storied villa. On one side of the house a gravel path curved through a dormant rose garden; on the other side a large English garden was neatly clipped and staked for the winter.

A stoop-shouldered man, wearing patched overalls and a shapeless sheepskin jacket, came around from the rose garden. He touched an imaginary hat and walked on to close the gate. Returning to the group, he said, *"Buona sera,* I hope your ride out here was pleasant."

"Si, grazie," Gianni said. "Signora, this is Giacomo."

The gardener nodded. "Is your son here?"

Constanz tried not to look nervous. Would this man figure out that her family was in hiding? "He'll be here before too many days."

Giacomo blotted his eyes with the back of his hand, telling Constanz that his boy was off in the army. He had been sent to Russia and Giacomo hadn't heard from him in a year and a half. He paused, and then asked Constanz if her son had ever worked in a garden.

She shook her head, but promised that her son would learn fast.

When they walked into the library, Monica broke away from her mother and ran across the room to a baby grand piano. "Look, Mamma, isn't this like our piano at home?"

"Yes," Constanz murmured, surprised to see such a beautiful instrument in a country home. She set down her suitcase and walked across the room to run her hand over the glossy wood. "It's even the same kind, a Bösendorfer."

"Celeste," Francesca said, "why don't you play something for us? It will be nice to have music in the house again."

Constanz looked at her, thinking that Francesca seemed less tense today. Did she feel safer away from the city?

"Yes, go ahead," Gianni said. "That's why it's here, to be played."

"Well, just for a moment." Constanz sat and played a few phrases of a Beethoven sonata. "I never thought to find such a fine piano here—and it's in tune."

"Now, Celeste," Gianni said. "We may be in the countryside, but we're not in the jungle. Do you like it?"

"Yes, more than I can say. I love playing. It somehow makes me feel whole again."

Monica chimed in, proudly telling everyone that her mamma had had a chance to be a concert pianist, but she wanted to marry Papà instead. After a few minutes, Francesca interrupted the playing, wanting Constanz and Monica to get settled upstairs.

As Constanz left the room, Francesca added, "And then we'll talk about preparing the rooms for Herr Hauptmann."

Constanz's heart sank. How could she do this? Where would she find the strength to stay in the same house with a German?

*   *   *

The morning after his meeting with von Mühlenberg, Ben stepped out of his chalet to enjoy the invigorating mountain air, so crisp he could see his breath. He intended to take a long hike, hoping to ease his worries about his family. Perhaps he could even assuage his lingering bitterness about the Bacchus sketch. He shifted his rucksack to rest more comfortably on his shoulders and walked away from the shadow of the chalet.

"*Buon giorno,*" a young woman's voice called from behind him. "Are you out for a walk?"

Ben turned to see who had spoken. It was the dark-haired young woman who had caught his attention in the Caffè Montagna. She was sitting on a bench alone, wearing walking shorts and a heavy sweater. She stood, giving him a radiant smile, and walked toward him, her hand outstretched. "I'm Silvia Bellini."

He decided that she must be about nineteen or twenty. "I'm Ben," he said, not wanting to give the last name on his Aryan papers.

"I know you're Ben," she said, lifting her rucksack from the bench and putting one arm through the strap. "Your friend Bruno told me you were joining his group."

Ben laughed. She had called him by the familiar *tu*, something in Padua you did only with childhood friends. "So Bruno was talking about me before I even arrived. Here, let me help you." He hoisted the rucksack onto her shoulders.

"Thanks. He told me you live in Padua. I've never been there, except passing through on the train to Venice."

"Do you go to Venice often?"

"I live there now, with my aunt, Zia Brigida. Rome is so difficult. You know, the Germans, rationing." She had the lilting accent of southern Italians. "I'm glad I left Rome, but I worry about my parents."

"You live in Venice?"

She gave him a puzzled look. "That's what I said. Is that so surprising?"

"Well, I work in Venice."

"Oh, really?" She paused a moment, contemplating him, and then laughed. "Well, I suppose Venice has room enough for both of us."

"Where are you going now?" he asked.

"I'm just taking a walk. It's a little too quiet at the Hotel Tirol."

He fell into step with her. "How is it you came to Bolzano?"

"Zia Brigida thought it would be nice to spend the weekend here. We came with my cousin."

"Is that the fellow you were with at the Caffè Montagna?" As soon as the words were out of his mouth, he wanted to kick himself for sounding like an adolescent.

"I noticed you there too," she said, not embarrassed. "Is this the first time you've been to Bolzano?"

"No, I used to come through here all the time." He heard Giorgio and Bruno calling to him from the steps of the chalet and shook his head, waving them off. "I don't have any plans for this morning. Would you like some company?"

"That would be nice."

They set out through the meadow, making a path through the

tall grass. The sun, climbing higher, warmed the air. Occasionally a cool breeze drifted across Ben's back, carrying with it the scent of pine from the hill above.

"What brings you here this weekend?" Silvia asked.

"I'm here on business, but I finished it very quickly." He was still feeling the flush of success at selling the painting in such a short time. "Are you a student?"

"Yes, the University in Rome transferred all my credits. I'm studying English literature." She looked at him, her expression serious. "I suppose you don't want to hear about that."

"Why wouldn't I want to hear about what you're studying?" He walked ahead to pull back a branch blocking their way.

"Well, we *are* at war with the Allies. A lot of people don't want to hear me talk about English literature."

"Don't worry," he said. "My mother has a lot of English novels at home." He quickly changed the subject. "How is it that you say '*tu*' to me? Most people use '*tu*' only with old friends."

"In Rome we say '*tu*' with anybody our own age."

"Well, how old are you?"

"Twenty. And how old are you?"

"Twenty-one."

She nodded, as if she approved. "In Rome we only say '*Lei*' to strangers."

"All right, then, '*tu*' it is."

He pointed to a sign saying Bar Rustico. "We could go there and have a cappuccino. It can't be too far."

"I'd like that."

As they walked Silvia learned that Ben had an eight-year-old sister and he learned that Silvia had no brothers or sisters. When she asked Ben about his mother and father, a hollow feeling hit him. It was the first time he had allowed himself to say that his father had died and that he missed him terribly.

Silvia touched his shoulder, asking if he took care of his mother and sister now. Ben's guilt at not being with Mamma and Monica rose again, and he quickly changed the subject, asking about Silvia's family. Her father was an officer in the Italian Navy, working in Rome at the moment.

The words, "an officer in the Navy," fell heavily on Ben's ears. Could her father be working closely with the Germans? It was just as well he was leaving soon.

"How did you get interested in English literature?" he asked.

"I got that from my mother. She loves the English poets, and the Italian ones, too, especially Leopardi. That's why she named me Silvia, you know. She was the girl he loved."

"It's a beautiful name." He saw another wooden sign nailed to a tree. "We're almost there."

"The only other Ben I've known was the son of Jewish friends," Silvia said.

He studied her expression and drew up his courage. "What if I told you I was Jewish?"

She looked at him, considering the thought. "I'd say— everybody is something, and that's what you happen to be."

"Would you say that just not to offend?"

She frowned. "I always mean what I say."

"Well then, I am a Jew." Why had he said that? he asked himself. How did he know he could trust this girl?

She shrugged. "And I'm telling you that I'm Catholic." She pointed to a chalet at the end of the meadow. "I think we're here."

The Bar Rustico was a welcoming place with wrought-iron

tables on a flagstone veranda. Ben and Silvia climbed the steps and found a table in the sunshine. Pulling back a chair for her, Ben beckoned for the waiter and ordered two cappuccinos.

After a moment, he asked, "Shall we do something this afternoon?"

"I'd like that, but I promised Zia Brigida we'd go shopping under the arcades down in Bolzano. Not that there's much to buy, now that the German soldiers have scooped up almost everything. We won't be back until evening." She smiled. "But we can walk until lunchtime. There's a beautiful waterfall everybody talks about that's not far from here." She broke a cookie in two and offered him half, smiling again.

Their coffee finished, they walked through the woods toward the waterfall. Ben put his arm around her, telling himself it was just a friendly gesture. He was surprised at the slenderness of her waist. She slipped her arm around him. They walked, not talking, for a few minutes. The silence was companionable, as if they had known each other for a long time.

"How long will you be here?" he asked.

"We're leaving tomorrow morning, right after breakfast."

He couldn't hide his disappointment. "Can't you wait until the evening?"

"No, my aunt wants to get back in time to prepare dinner for my uncle. Look, there's the path we want."

They followed the trail through the pine forest until they heard a roaring sound. Farther on, in a clearing, a cascade of water thundered over the rocks and plunged down to a stream. Silvia ran ahead, calling to Ben to hurry.

A few minutes later, they sat together on a rock and dabbled their bare feet in the icy water. She laughed, telling him how she used to do this in the summertime in Ostia and that her family had a villa overlooking the place where the Tiber flowed into the Mediterranean.

Ben smiled and sketched his own summers for her, how he used to catch frogs and go rowing in his grandfather's rowboat. His *nonno* would read to him the leaves in the trees.

She grinned. "Is that like reading clouds? What did he say about them?"

"He said he saw a war coming."

"Oh, wasn't he right! Where did your family go in the summer?"

"On the canal near Padua. A hundred years ago the canal was used to take the wealthy Venetians into Venice."

She looked at the pine trees overhead. "I used to think the summer would never end." She lay back on the wide, flat rock and tucked up her knees. "What else did you do?"

"I hiked with my friends and we used to explore in the woods." Was she inviting him to lean over and kiss her? He picked up a broken branch and leaned forward to move it slowly in the water. "And I went to art galleries with my father. That's how we spent a lot of Sunday afternoons."

"Do you mind telling me what he was like?"

Ben swallowed hard. "He was old-fashioned ... and much more religious than I am. And very smart."

"He sounds wonderful. My father must have taken me to every art gallery in Rome. I used to hate going every Sunday afternoon, but finally I got to like it. My favorite paintings are the ones in the Borghese gardens."

"Which painters do you like?"

She frowned in thought. "I like the French painters. Am I too modern for you?"

"No, of course not."

"How about you?"

"I'm partial to the Italian painters. I like Canaletto, but my favorite artist is Caravaggio." The stab of loss hit him again, once for Papà, and then for the drawing. It meant more now that his father was gone—the drawing had somehow tied them together. "After the war, I want to open my own gallery and offer only paintings of unknown artists." He wished he could tell her that he always imagined opening his gallery with his Caravaggio framed for all to see and admire.

She looked at him, curious. "Why?"

"Because I think I'm good at spotting talent. Wouldn't it be great to introduce a new artist to the world?"

"Pretty daring, I'd say. I admire that." She sat up, reaching for a pebble to toss into the stream. She took the ribbon holding back her hair and wrapped it around her wrist. When she bent over to throw another pebble in the water, her dark hair fell forward. Suddenly she announced that it was time to go back and find her aunt.

He tried to mask his disappointment with a smile. They put on their shoes and scrambled to their feet. He took her hand—it was small and soft in his. They walked through the woods for a while, with Ben thinking maybe it was just as well they wouldn't see any more of each other. The last thing he needed was a friendship with a Catholic girl whose father was a naval officer.

"I have an idea," she said. "I'm going to have dinner in Bolzano with Zia Brigida and we're coming back to our hotel around nine. Maybe afterwards you could meet my aunt and we could all go to the Caffè Montagna."

He hesitated. "I'm not sure. Look, I don't know how your aunt would feel about me being Jewish."

She stopped walking and looked up at him. "As a matter of

fact, since you're asking, my whole family is disgusted with the government's attitude toward our Italian Jews." She took his arm. "You know, you ought to trust me a little more."

He smiled. "I don't even know you."

"I'm easy to get to know. I don't keep secrets about myself."

"Is it because you're from the south that you're easy to know," he asked, "or is it because you're you?"

"It's just the way I am," she said, smiling at him. "And my aunt's the same way."

Ben walked her to the hotel, listening to her talk about the shops she wanted to go to with her aunt. What was it like to find life so simple and to be so carefree?

She put her hand on his wrist, asking him why he suddenly looked so sad. When he shrugged and wouldn't answer, she touched his cheek and ran off, calling back that she'd meet him at the hotel at nine that evening.

During the rest of the afternoon, he told himself that she seemed so attractive only because his own life had been turned upside down. He mustn't allow himself to lose his head. She was just a carefree, pretty girl who could never begin to understand his complicated life. Maybe he shouldn't have agreed to see her again. It could even be unwise. But he had said he would meet her at nine o'clock, so he'd go ahead and be there.

CHAPTER 18

On Tuesday Aldo Lupino elbowed his way through the tightly packed crowds in the Padua station, muttering to himself. Unruly, for heaven's sake. People had lost all their manners since this war began. He claimed his seat in first class and set his black bowler hat on the overhead shelf.

As he glanced at the two SS officers sitting across from him, a deep sigh escaped him. He thought he had himself under better control. The increasing guilt he felt about Cantarini's death made him edgy and irritable. Awful that it had gotten out of hand like this. If Eric Feltzer hadn't become greedy and asked for money from the family, Claudio would have made it back to Padua sooner and might not have had that heart attack. It must have been the fright of the whole thing.

Lupino set his briefcase on the seat next to him. If no one sat there, he'd at least have some space on the long train ride. The idea of being so close to strangers for God knew how many hours was oppressive. Even in first class, you never knew who had bathed before starting a trip and who hadn't.

He thought about Feltzer, who always had to have everything

his way, as far back as university days. If Feltzer had just kept the Caravaggio and waited for the check—but no, he had to get more out of it. Really, Lupino decided, Claudio's death was Feltzer's doing. It had been such a simple arrangement. The SS men were to stop Claudio on his way back to the station, take the Caravaggio from him, and let him go on his way. Feltzer would have had the drawing with no problems. Probably Feltzer had caught wind of Kappler getting all that gold from the Jewish Community and decided he'd go for a little extra himself.

Lupino lowered his eyes. It wouldn't do to let those two SS officers see how agitated he was. Those fellows were said to have a nose for situations. In a way, their jet-black uniforms and black riding boots impressed him, but the white death's head on their caps sent a chill down his spine. He looked out of the window, pretending to watch the crowds walking up and down the platform. The engine whistle screamed, hisses of steam arose, and the conductor leaned out of the carriage, yelling *"A-bor-r-r-do."* Lupino remembered people saying that since the Germans had arrived, everyone was heading north, but it looked to him as if the world wanted to go south to Rome today.

The SS officer closer to the door stood up and slid it shut. Good, they were under way, so they'd have the compartment to themselves. Patting his breast pocket where he had put the check and Feltzer's letter, Lupino sat back, feeling more relaxed.

Eight hours until he had the drawing in his hands. He remembered the day he had first heard about Ben's amazing discovery, recalling his mixture of burning curiosity and envy. It irked Lupino the way Claudio kept saying, "My son and his discovery!" Lupino remembered the evening Claudio had invited his friends and colleagues to see Ben's drawing—first the Champagne, and then the grand showing. Now, sitting in the train, he felt again the same rush of awe, the stunned awareness of the master's outrageous love of life. Good God, it exploded from the simple sketch! Oh, rarity of rarities! Bacchus was not so much a god as a sensual young man from the streets, with his pale but muscular body and sunburnt hands. He was a real person, probably chosen from some group of workers near Caravaggio's studio in Rome. The pen and brown wash drawing was as small as Lupino had always heard, a little larger than a man's hand. But its impact was huge. By the end of the evening, Lupino knew he would give anything to possess it.

He shifted uncomfortably in his seat, feeling almost trapped by the way his thoughts always went back to the drawing. During the day, his mind returned to the sketch over and over, and when he closed his eyes at night he ached to see it again, to have it in his hands, to be able to call it his own. It still burned him that Claudio would never have sold it to him. Lupino knew it was because Ben disliked him. Unfortunate that the story of the Griffino situation started making the rounds of the art world. But he wasn't the only art dealer who had sold a painting with a questionable provenance.

He hoped that Ben wouldn't cause any trouble about wanting the gallery back again after the war. The boy could work for him, if he wanted, and that would help the family. At least one thing comforted Lupino—signora Cantarini was a real beauty. She'd find another husband before two years were out. Maybe sooner. Where did a Jewess get that chestnut hair and those startling gray green eyes?

Lupino noticed the SS officers eyeing each other and realized it must be his own movements attracting their attention. Perhaps he looked agitated. He took a newspaper from his briefcase and sat back against the cushions, trying to look more at ease.

From time to time he sneaked glances at the officers. He always wondered what they were thinking. They looked arrogant, as if they were just about to make trouble for a person. One was reading a German newspaper, the other perusing some official-looking documents. He had to admire those officers, the way they were always spit and polish no matter what the circumstances. Yes, he really liked that.

The younger of the two officers lowered his newspaper. Lupino quickly reached into his breast pocket for his silver cigarette case and opened it, revealing a neat row of Nazionali. He leaned forward to offer one to the officer. After all, he told himself, they might also be going as far as Rome and the three of them should stay on pleasant terms.

"Ah," the officer said, plucking a cigarette from the case. "*Danke schön.*" The other soldier looked up, shook his head, and went back to his documents. "I appreciate your decency," the younger officer said, smiling with a movie star's set of teeth. "We were told that the Italians would welcome us." He gave an ironic laugh. "I've seen more cold shoulders here in one week than in my whole life in Germany."

Lupino drew out a cigarette for himself and snapped his case shut. He lit the officer's cigarette and then his own, saying, "Myself, I admire the Germans tremendously." He inhaled deeply, feeling the little surge of excitement that came as his lungs filled with the first smoke of the day. "You see," he added, "my father was Italian, but my mother was Swiss, Swiss-German, that is."

"*Schwyzerdütsch,*" the young officer said in Swiss dialect.

"No," Lupino said emphatically. "We spoke no dialect at home. High German only, and Italian, of course, because of my father."

"*Ja, ja, sehr gut.* For a real man, it's German, *nicht wahr?*"

Lupino leaned forward. "I'll tell you something. I think that the Germans being in Italy is going to be a good thing." He could tell that this pleased the young officer. "Yes, I grew up in Bern, and in the summer my cousin and I would come across to Italy to Minusio to visit family on Lago di Como. Do you know it?"

"Nein, but I hear it's beautiful."

"Well, when the train stopped at the border, my cousin used to say, Thank God we're in Italy. I can drop my empty cigarette pack and no one will say anything." Without waiting for a response, Lupino added, "The Swiss—like the Germans—know how to run a country, make things work, you know. The Italians are casual as hell."

The fellow lifted his chin and blew out a circle of smoke. "So your mother was Swiss?"

"And very beautiful. She was the toast of Bern. Everyone envied me." He laughed. "My friends from school wanted to come and play at my house just to talk to my mother." He thought of Mutti, her red hair twisted in a French braid, always well dressed in smart suits. He loved the way she patted his friends' heads and called them *Schatzi* or *Bonbon*.

The young officer was speaking again. "And so where in Bern did you grow up?"

"Outside the city, quite high up in the hills. Yes, we were always more German than Swiss-German, which my father considered ... " Lupino searched for the correct word. "Well, rather provincial. Father admired the English system of bringing up children, you know, supper for me in the nursery at six and dinner for them in the dining room at seven." Lupino was surprised at the details he was giving a perfect stranger. Well, a train was almost like a ship, where you told your life story and then the ship docked and you went your own way, your confessions safely gone with the departing passengers.

"*Ja*, my family was a great deal like that, too, my father being a count."

Lupino was impressed, but kept his response to a slight nod.

The train was slowing down. The conductor stuck his head into the compartment to say that the problem was a broken trestle. All three men looked outside. On the road, a quarter of a mile beyond, a line of cars and trucks struggled its way north. Here and there cars were abandoned by the side of the road, people were piling out, their arms full of clothing and suitcases.

"It looks as if you are one of the few Italians going south." The young officer smiled, questioning Lupino with his eyes.

"I have business in Rome," Lupino responded, suddenly wanting to draw back from the intimacies of his conversation.

"Indeed?" The older officer set his documents in his lap and looked at him steadily. "What line of business are you in?"

It was a demand and not a casual question. Lupino's scalp began to sweat. Perhaps he had gone too far. "Oh, I'm just an art dealer, but not a well-known one."

"What a modest fellow you are," the younger officer said. "Art dealer."

Lupino shrugged and smiled. Was the tone of voice the officer used in saying "art dealer" the same deprecating one his father used? It took Lupino back to his father's book-lined study fifteen years earlier. He was twenty years old, standing in front of the paterfamilias who was seated at his desk, discussing what he would do now that he had finished university. His father was exploding with anger. "An art dealer, indeed! A sissy, that means you're a goddamn sissy!" In his fury, his father had slipped into the Swiss-German dialect. "You might as well be a dancer!"

"Father, I'm talented. I understand art."

"I'm beginning to understand you! There's something the matter with you."

"Well, that isn't the way Eric Feltzer's father talked to me, the time I went to Berlin over the holidays. He was impressed by how much I know about art history—and the art world today!"

"Feltzer? That fellow from Berlin? Why is he going to a Swiss university anyway? Can't get into a German school?"

"He wants to go into the Foreign Service. His family wants him to have experience outside Germany." His father tapped his fingers on his desk, the sign that he wanted the conversation to end. "So what would you have me do, Father, be a lawyer like you?"

"Don't you dare put down my profession. I'm doing real work with real men. The only reason Feltzer's father encourages you is because you're not his son."

In a steady voice, Aldo Lupino said to his father, "Your idea of beauty is hunting in the mountains, killing animals."

His father sucked in his breath, his face red from his hairline down to his stiff collar. "Be any goddamn thing you want, but don't look to me for support. In fact"—he waved him away—"get out of here. I mean out of this house!" He turned his face from his son.

Lupino remembered his mother hanging onto the window of his car, weeping, clutching his arm, crying out, "Don't go like this! You know his temper, just apologize." In answer, Lupino revved the motor. "Please, darling," his mother begged. "Where will you go?"

"Venice is where the art world is," he said, and gently pushed her away before swinging out of the driveway and into the night.

Now Lupino was aware of the young SS officer leaning toward him, asking, "Where are you staying in Rome? Unless you're German, it's difficult to find accommodations."

"A hotel reservation has been made for me." He didn't like the turn of the conversation.

"Is the person German then?"

"Yes, he is," Lupino said, putting his hand on his briefcase.

The officer raised an eyebrow. "I see that you are well connected."

"Yes and no." Lupino stood, thinking that the fellow was getting too damn curious. "Excuse me, a friend just walked by in the corridor. I'm going to join him." He pulled down his suitcase and bowler hat. "It's been a pleasure talking to you."

The officer nodded. *"Auf Wiedersehen, mein* Herr."

Lupino found an empty compartment and settled in, relieved to be by himself. Really, Eric Feltzer should have ordered a courier to bring the drawing to Padua. Instead, here he was, forced to make this unpleasant, dangerous trip to Rome. But then maybe Feltzer was right—you don't entrust the only Caravaggio drawing in the world to just anyone.

Lupino reached inside his jacket for the letter he had received the day before. He opened it and read it again.

Dear Aldo—Yes, it has been a long time, too long. All the conversations on the telephone aren't quite the same, are they? I hope your parents are well. I've often spoken to my friends of your beautiful mother. Too bad you didn't get her looks, old friend! Yes, I miss the old days in Switzerland, and now the world is such a serious place. Here's the address where you'll find me. I know of an excellent restaurant not far from my office and with a good bottle of red wine, we can talk over everything…

He thought of the Eric Feltzer of his university days, a rake and a daredevil, always getting what he wanted without counting the cost. Wasn't it a good thing they'd kept up their friendship throughout the years? All those buying trips to Berlin had been more than worth it. Interesting that Eric had become a Nazi right at the beginning. He sure had guessed it right. By joining the party early, he got to be the big shot at Gestapo Headquarters in Rome.

Lupino smiled, folded the letter and put it back in his breast pocket, giving it a little pat of satisfaction.

*   *   *

Ben crossed his arms, wishing he could hide his sweater, wondering why Silvia hadn't asked him to meet her at the Caffè Montagna. What was he doing here in this fancy hotel with all its well-heeled clientele, waiting for a girl he barely knew? Why was he even bothering to make a new friend when he'd soon have to give up all his friendships? No, it was time he faced honestly the idea of going into hiding, of living in a strange place and postponing any hopes of a career.

It was quarter past nine and still no Silvia. Maybe he should just leave. Besides, she was bringing her aunt along. It wouldn't be much of an evening, having to make conversation with her aunt. He turned to leave.

"*Buona sera.*" Silvia, her dark shoulder-length hair shining, and wearing a long blue skirt and high heels, called to him from the landing of the wide staircase. Smiling and waving, she came down the long flight of steps with a tall woman in her fifties who walked with a self-assured gait.

"Zia Brigida, this is Ben. Ben, this is my aunt, signora

Aucello." Silvia's cheeks turned red. "Ben, I'm sorry—I don't know your last name."

"Campano," he said, the name making him feel uncomfortable.

"Campano?" the aunt asked, raising her eyebrows. "So this is the young man my niece met this afternoon." Her tone was cool—she was taking sharp notice of him.

"*Piacere,* Signora," he said in response to her tight smile.

"How long will you be here?" she asked.

"Well, Signora Aucello, I don't know. Maybe another day, maybe not. I'm on business and—"

"I see. Well, we're leaving in the morning. Now, I'm going up to my room to stretch out with a book. Silvia, I hope you won't stay too long at the Caffè." She looked Ben hard in the eye. "May I say, young man, that times are not what they were a few years ago."

Ben thought of Giorgio and his broken engagement. Flustered, he said, "I wasn't thinking of anything like that."

"One never does in the beginning," she shot back. "The two of you mustn't start something you can't finish. *Buona notte.*"

Ben watched the woman glide up the stairs without a backward glance. He stood still for a moment, and then came to life. "Whoa! What am I doing here?"

"I'm sorry." Silvia took his hand. "My aunt can be pretty outspoken."

"I can see that. Well, the best way not to start something I can't finish is not to start it at all. I hope you have a good book to stretch out with yourself." He turned and started for the door to the street.

"No, Ben, don't!" She reached for his hand again and held him back. "I know she was rude. It's just that she worries too

182

much. But I do what I want—and I want to go dancing with you at the Caffè Montagna."

"No, I don't take a girl dancing when I get that kind of a reception. Please let go of my hand." He shook himself loose and pushed through the door, intending to return to his *pensione*.

"Stop!" She ran after him, reaching for his shoulder. When he stopped and turned to her, she went on. "You're not being reasonable. You're judging me by my aunt's behavior. You're not being fair."

"Would you go dancing with me if my parents had roughed you up like that?"

"Yes, I would, because I had such a wonderful time with you this afternoon. I was just beginning to know you and I want to know you better."

They stood quietly in the middle of the dark lane. Nothing moved but the pine branches over their heads. Ben's heart still pounded with unforgiving anger. "Did you tell her that I'm Jewish?"

"Yes," Silvia said softly. "Was that my mistake?"

"No, because it's true. There's no point in our talking now. Go back to your hotel."

"Please do something for me. I'm not a little girl doing the bidding of my aunt. Pretend with me for just this one evening that we live in another country and we're good friends. Just give us this one evening. After all, I'm leaving in the morning."

She was so sincere, and she was right that she was going away. He'd soon be leaving for Turin himself.

"Is it really possible to pretend like that?" he asked.

"Yes, Ben. Aren't you tired of being pushed around? Can't we just talk and dance and you can tell me about yourself and I'll tell you about me? Would you like that?"

"Yes, I would." Now his heart was beating hard for a different reason. "All right, let's walk to the Caffè."

Inside the Caffè Ben led Silvia onto the dance floor. He didn't speak as he took her in his arms, since he didn't know quite what to say. Then he pressed his cheek against hers, and they moved easily together with the music. After a foxtrot and a waltz, he asked her if he passed her test.

"My test for what?"

"For being a dancer. You said you wanted to dance."

"Yes, but my other tests are more important," she said, shifting closer to him.

"I'll want to know what they are." The delicious scent of her hair and the softness of her skin made Ben forget the warning he had been given.

Each time the music stopped they walked back to their table arm in arm, and sat telling stories about their families and friends. Once in a while Ben looked up at the door, half-expecting the aunt to come marching in and take Silvia away. But as the evening wore on, he worried less and less about signora Aucello. He was increasingly comfortable telling Silvia about his family, his friends, and how he had just made a successful sale of a major art work. He thought for a moment about the Caravaggio drawing, but knew that telling her about its loss would bring too much unhappiness to their evening.

"Ben, how wonderful to make a sale like that! I can see why you want to make this your life's work."

"I am excited about selling a Monet, but my career is on hold because of this horrible war." He paused. "Silvia, what do you want to do after you finish your studies?"

"I'd like to teach English in the university. I really love the nineteenth century women writers."

"Then you'd have to get a graduate degree, wouldn't you?"

"Yes, and I would enjoy the work."

"I can see that you have a serious side."

"We have a lot in common, don't we?"

He nodded. "It's getting late and they're going to close soon. Let's have another dance."

Finally, when the last stragglers were leaving, Ben led Silvia outside. They strolled in the direction of the hotel until Ben paused, looking up at the sky. "Bolzano is known for beautiful stars," he said, putting his arm around her.

She leaned into him, turning her face up to his. It happened easily, naturally. He kissed her, breathing in her sweetness, stroking the soft skin of her face.

"I can't believe I met you only this morning," she whispered.

"I've never met a girl like you," he said, and kissed her again.

She pressed herself against him. He couldn't say it to her, but he wished he could know everything about her, every detail of her life. "You really are a surprise for me, Silvia."

"You didn't surprise me. I liked you when I first saw you. My aunt and I almost didn't come. We thought of going to Lago di Garda." She traced the outline of his jaw, her fingertips coming to rest on his lips. "But I asked if we couldn't come here. I don't know why."

"I wish I didn't have to take you back to your hotel."

He gave her another long kiss, and then pulled himself from their embrace, fearing that if he didn't, he would never be able to let her go. He kept one arm around her shoulders as they walked to the hotel.

"Perhaps we can see each other in Venice," she said tentatively.

Happiness welled in him. For the moment he didn't care about her aunt, or signor di Stefano, or the war, or even going into hiding. "Maybe we could meet one day after I finish work."

"We're going to the seaside for a couple of days, but I'll be back on Wednesday."

All the promises he had made to himself about leaving for Turin the next day or the day after dissolved. "I finish work at twelve thirty on Wednesdays. My gallery is near the Calle dei Nomboli. I could meet you in the courtyard of the Doges' Palace at one o'clock. We can have lunch."

"I just won't go home for lunch that day." He caught the excitement in her voice. "Just think, Ben, the next time we see each other, we'll have all of Venice to walk in."

It seemed that the world was opening up again, the same world that for five years had been closing in on him, had pushed him down into darkness. "Meet me by the *Scala dei Giganti,*" he said.

"Yes, I know the Giants' Staircase."

They had reached the hotel, where the night doorman waited impatiently outside for the last guests. Silvia gave Ben a quick kiss on the lips. "Until Wednesday at the Doges' Palace." She ran to the door, turned, and waved.

He watched her disappear into the hotel. Now what had he done? This wasn't what he had intended to happen. Instead of leaving for Turin immediately, he had made a promise to see a woman he had known for one day. He touched his lips where she had kissed him and then walked slowly to his *pensione.*

CHAPTER 19

The two men embraced, slapping each other on the back. "*Mein Gott*, you look good," Lupino said. "A little tired but good, anyway." He set down his briefcase in the middle of Feltzer's office and took a step back. "*Ja*, really good, even though you're losing that golden hair that used to set the girls wild."

Feltzer's grin broke his usual somber expression. He stroked his high forehead. "All my brain power keeps it from growing! But it doesn't keep the women away, I can tell you that."

Lupino gave him a playful shove. "That's what counts, isn't it?"

"So," Feltzer said, putting a hand on his friend's shoulder, "it's been two years since we got together in Berlin. You're not looking so bad yourself, maybe a little serious, as if you're working too hard."

Lupino touched the hair just above his ears, smiling when he admitted to getting a little gray. But for an art dealer, he confided, it lent distinction.

Feltzer parried with a comment about seeing from Lupino's papers that he had a Swiss passport. Now how was it that he called himself Swiss when his father was Italian? Lupino started to answer, but Feltzer interrupted, saying money could buy anything. His smile unsettled Lupino.

Feltzer looked around the room, asking if Lupino had ever imagined seeing him at Gestapo Headquarters.

Lupino shrugged, thinking, You *Scheisse*-filled cock of the walk. "What the hell did you do with all the furniture?" he asked. "This place used to be filled with antiques—well known for that."

"We're safeguarding them in Germany. In storage you might say. Frankly, I wish they were still here. You know how much I like beautiful furniture."

And art? Lupino wanted to say, but no, that was a touchy subject for Germans nowadays.

Feltzer continued, "Did you like the hotel I found for you?"

Lupino grinned. "Very much. The staff couldn't move fast enough to make me comfortable. I'm in a room on the top floor overlooking the Spanish Steps."

"Good." Feltzer reached for his hat and coat. "Now I'm eager to go to dinner. You must be starved after that long train trip. You won't believe the Foro Romano III—a wonderful wine cellar and cognac from the last century."

Ten minutes later they entered the restaurant. The street outside had been dark, like all of Rome, with only a faint blue light coming from the almost blacked-out street lamps. But the restaurant was well lit, smoke filled and alive with conversation. In spite of the unsettling sight of so many German uniforms, Lupino was pleased by the oil paintings on the walls and the soft piano music rolling out American love songs.

Feltzer nodded toward the piano, laughing as he said that

even though the Germans hadn't won the war yet, they already had the Americans' best ballads.

The maître d'hôtel was at their side, stiff but smiling so broadly that the gold teeth in the back of his mouth gleamed. My God, Lupino thought, when you stepped into a place with this old school chum, the goddamn world fell at your feet.

"Corner table," Feltzer said to the maître d'hôtel. When they were seated and had taken the menus, Feltzer glanced down the list, beckoned to the waiter, and ordered a bottle of Möet and Chandon and the house's prosciutto-wrapped bread sticks. Lupino's mouth watered as Feltzer ordered the rest of the meal. He hadn't eaten like this in years.

When the waiter left, Lupino cleared his throat and began. "Too bad about Cantarini. His wife is shattered."

"Yes, unfortunate," Feltzer agreed. "But he looked like hell when they first brought him to us."

The waiter poured the Champagne, set down the plate of hors d'oeuvres, and melted away again. The two men raised their glasses. "Let me ask you something," Lupino said after they drank. "I was surprised that you didn't just keep the briefcase and let Cantarini go. We had talked it out to the last detail, you know."

Feltzer waved dismissively. "These SS boys can't always think for themselves. They were confused when they saw that Cantarini was with his son."

"What? Didn't you tell them that they might find father and son together?"

Feltzer's voice took on an edge. "Dammit, Lupino, the SS aren't used to taking something and leaving people behind."

"But why the ransom?"

"Lower your voice, Lupino. You have no idea the expenses I

have." He poured more Champagne for both of them. "Come on, old friend, what's done is done. Let's talk about the next step."

It took a moment for Lupino to control his irritation. "You brought the drawing with you, didn't you?" he asked. Not good, he thought. This conversation was off on the wrong foot.

Without answering the question, Feltzer said, "You ought to know that nothing goes as smoothly as it used to. Nothing's all that easy."

Lupino shifted in his chair, as his anger mounted. "Eric, you're talking in circles. Look, I came all the way down to Rome—traveling is dangerous as hell nowadays with the Allies bombing the tracks and the Partisans dynamiting the bridges—and you sit there and tell me that it isn't all that easy." He felt his neck swelling under his starched collar.

Feltzer reached for Lupino's elbow and squeezed it tight. "Don't make a scene in here. People know who I am."

"But what the hell is this?" Lupino hissed. "I agreed to pay you. You get the money and I get the drawing."

"Of course you'll get the drawing." Feltzer raised his glass. "Here's to Caravaggio." The two men were quiet while the waiter set their filet mignon dinners in front of them. When they were alone again, Feltzer said, "I'll explain, but look, let's eat first before our dinner gets cold. Come on, enjoy your meal." He waved Lupino on with his knife.

Feltzer opened his jacket and pressed his napkin across his chest, snugging it tight under his arms. "Don't get this fine cuisine in Germany anymore. Pleasure before business." He ate steadfastly, looking up after a few minutes to ask about Lupino's mother. "Still as beautiful as ever?"

"She's fine."

"And your father? I always had the feeling that he didn't care for me." Feltzer smiled. "Am I right?"

Lupino shrugged. "By the way, did you keep the ransom money? That was a terrible hardship for the Cantarinis."

Feltzer raised his eyebrows. "What's done is done. Don't question my authority!"

After an eternity of small talk, Feltzer finished his dinner and suggested they look at the dessert trolley. Lupino shook his head. "Well then, cognac and a cigar?"

"No, thanks."

Feltzer took a cigar from his breast pocket and waved it in front of Lupino. "Cuban. The Reich has connections all over. Unfortunate for those Jews who took a boat to Cuba and were turned away in the harbor." He clipped the end of the cigar and lit up. "But some good came of the whole thing. The captain sent me a box of these." He blew a circle of smoke toward the ceiling. "Now we can talk." He contemplated his cigar. "I need something else—in addition to your check."

Lupino eyed him suspiciously. "What do you mean?"

Feltzer leaned forward. "I need a list of the members of the synagogues in Padua."

"What?"

"You heard me."

"What does that have to do with the drawing?"

Feltzer looked around before proceeding. Speaking through clenched teeth, he told Lupino that orders had come from Berlin. "I have to get that list and you have the connections to do it. When you give me the check and that list, you'll get your drawing."

Lupino stared at him for a long moment, trying to take it in. "Oh, come on, Eric, what makes you think I can do that?"

Lupino's stomach muscles had contracted with fear. Feltzer was silent. "Look, the Italian government has turned on the Jews, but I'm not going to make it worse for them."

"You didn't mind ending up with an art gallery."

The remark stung. "I was only doing Cantarini a favor."

"Consider this a favor."

"What will be done with the list?"

"Oh, for God's sake, we're efficient. You know that's the word for us Germans. *Ordnung*. We want things in order, that's all." He paused. "Look, Lupino, I know you have dual citizenship."

The comment stunned Lupino. "Are you threatening me?"

"I'm not threatening you," Feltzer fired back. "You may have dual citizenship, but you could be treated like any other Italian."

"You son of a bitch!"

Feltzer lowered his voice. "Goddammit, Lupino. The rules have changed. We're here now. If we don't get the list, you don't get the drawing."

Lupino beat out his words in a whisper. "I cannot get that kind of list." He looked into Feltzer's narrowed eyes. "Impossible, do you understand? You might as well ask me to close off the Brenner Pass single-handedly."

"I have orders to get that list, so you'd better start thinking."

Lupino looked at his eyes, dark now. "Why didn't you tell me this before I came all the way down to Rome?"

"I didn't know about it until this morning." Feltzer shrugged. "I know, you'll have to go all the way back to Padua, but I'll make it easy for you. My driver will pick you up at your hotel in the morning. I've reserved a seat in first class for you."

Lupino stood, wondering how he'd let himself be sucked into this ugly mess. Feltzer rose and shook his hand, telling him he'd better be back in forty-eight hours. And that there was a car outside, waiting for him.

Lupino spun around and strode toward the coat room, muttering, "*Scheisse!*" He picked up his coat, tipped the hatcheck girl, and headed for the door. Bastard, he thought, threatening him like that. Could they really do anything to him? He didn't want to find out. Stepping onto the sidewalk, he mentally named his clients who were Jewish. It was a beginning, but it wouldn't satisfy Feltzer. Who else? Let's see ... He climbed into the waiting car, scouring his mind for other Jewish acquaintances. Dammit, he wasn't going to give up that drawing. No, not after all he'd been through. Besides, if he didn't give the list to Feltzer, the bastard would only find some other way to get it.

"Driver, take me to the Hotel Hassler."

*   *   *

After lunch the next afternoon Constanz decided to distract herself by playing the piano. Entering the library, music in hand, she was soothed by the old brown velvet furniture and the well-worn books filling the shelves around the fireplace. She placed the sheets of the *Appassionata* in front of her, and let her fingers find their way through the chords and runs. The familiar sounds enveloped her with pleasure. So much trouble, so many horrible changes in her life, but Beethoven was always the same, a faithful friend. Slowly, subtly, the dread of the past months began to subside. The music spilled out around her, filling the room like flowing water, and at last she was in a safe place, soft with shadows and dappled moonlight.

"*Bitte entschuldigen Sie.* Excuse me for interrupting such beautiful playing."

Her body tensed, her hands freezing above the keys. The man's voice could have been her father's. Those were exactly the words he used when he had to interrupt her playing. She dropped her hands to the bench and turned around.

A tall man, his blond hair turning gray, stood in the doorway. His military bearing and straight Germanic features were those of the schoolboys of her youth. He strode confidently across the room and rested his hands on the top of the piano. "What a lovely sight and sound!"

So, he had been watching her. For a few minutes she had let down her guard and this had happened. He must be the guest from Germany. She rose quickly and closed the piano lid. He was studying her face. She was certain he was deciding she was Jewish. Wasn't that the first thing Germans thought about nowadays? He would run to the authorities and they would all go to jail. She leaned against the piano, grateful for its support.

"I am Hans Hauptmann," he said, putting out his hand.

She gave him her hand, cold against the warmth of his. Her name? What was her new name? Her mind had gone blank.

"And you must be signora Campano."

"Yes, oh yes," she said. "That is exactly who I am."

He clicked his heels and bowed over her hand. "Gianni told me there was a new housekeeper here, but he didn't say she played the piano."

"Yes, I learned as a young girl," she managed to say.

"My wife ... I know this music well."

"Your wife plays the piano?"

He shook his head. "My wife died two years ago, but she loved to play."

"Oh, I'm so sorry."

"Once she gave a concert, just for me. Imagine, she wrote an invitation in her finest handwriting, saying the dress was to be formal, and placed a candelabra on the piano. She wore a long rose gown."

Constanz was surprised by the man's openness. He must have a great need to talk to someone about his wife. But why to her, a total stranger?

"Of course," he continued, "I had to dig my tuxedo out of mothballs for the occasion. You know, we're not having formal parties with the war going on. Well, my wife introduced herself as the artist for the evening and she played, starting with a Schubert impromptu."

Constanz looked at him, unable to speak, not wanting to react. He was confessing the tenderest of memories, and yet she felt no sympathy for him. Instead, it chilled her to hear his German accent. "What else did your wife play?" she asked.

"Beethoven, of course. The *Pathétique* and the *Appassionata*. She left me with wonderful memories." He took a few steps toward the sofa. "Would you play more while I sit and listen?"

"No. I mean … I haven't touched the piano in so long that I'm not playing well."

He motioned for her to sit again. "I don't mind."

She shook her head. "I really don't have time. I have work to do now. Excuse me, please."

"Do I detect a German accent in your Italian?" he asked, smiling.

"People say that."

"How long have you been here?"

"Why … here? In Montebello? Just a few days." She tidied the music on the piano. "Please excuse me, I have to set the table for dinner."

He followed her into the dining room. "Here, I'll help."

"Thank you, but it's easier if I do it myself."

"*Ach*," he said in mock despair, "one of those ladies who can't bear to see a man work in the house." He walked to the other end of the dining room where the French doors led to the garden. "Have you been outside today? We seldom have such warm days in November."

She shook her head. Why hadn't Gianni protected her from him? Couldn't this man see that she wanted to be left alone?

He was holding the door for her, saying, "Please, come outside for a moment." It was more like a command than a request. "Gianni told me that your husband is in southern Italy. What division is he with?"

Division? They had never thought about that! Shaking inside, she told him that she worried about her husband too much to talk about him. Did the lie show on her face? She tried to think of a question to ask him to stop his probing, but her mind had gone blank again. She passed in front of him, stepping onto the grass. The scent of sandalwood followed her. Oh Lord, how many years since she had smelled Vati's sandalwood cologne? She remembered standing with her father in front of his shaving mirror, while Mutti prepared breakfast downstairs. She had loved watching him open the bottle of gentlemen's scent and pat it on his cheeks. It was part of him whenever he kissed her good morning or good night.

Hauptmann motioned for her to come over to the fading geranium plants, the blossoms long gone. "How is it that the flowers are so bright and charming in summer?" He picked a leaf and pressed it between his fingers. "And yet they smell so dreadful."

"Nasturtiums are worse," she offered, afraid to be completely silent.

"Yes, 'nose twisters' in Latin, correct? So, tell me, is it a German accent in your Italian, or English?"

"I was born in Germany," she admitted.

He grinned with delight. *"Nein! Wo in Deutschland? Sprechen wir Deutsch!* Let me hear a little of my native tongue."

"I prefer speaking in Italian." She couldn't take this any longer. Brusquely, she turned. "As I said, I have work to do."

He smiled at her clipped manner and gave a slight bow.

Constanz walked quickly to the kitchen and leaned against the sink, her hand on her chest, waiting for her heart to stop pounding.

CHAPTER 20

On Wednesday, two days after leaving Bolzano, Ben was alone in signor di Stefano's art gallery, surrounded by beautiful paintings and the smell of turpentine. He'd managed to talk to his mother on the telephone. She told him that she was doing well in Montebello being a housekeeper, something she'd never imagined for herself. She said she was always afraid of being caught and it numbed every sinew in her body every moment of every day. But it wouldn't help for him to be in Montebello. She insisted he stay for the month in Venice.

Filled with guilt and worry, he was filing and typing letters, waiting for the time when Silvia had promised to meet him. Her aunt's last words kept returning to him: "Don't start something you can't finish." Here he was, a Jew, a member of an ancient and moral people, and yet all he could think about was a beautiful Catholic girl and how he would see her in less than an hour.

Quarter before noon. He was turning the key in the lock when the telephone rang. *Càspita!* He ran back and picked up the receiver, disappointed to hear signor di Stefano's voice.

"Take a few minutes to tell me everything that's been going on this morning," his employer said.

Now he was going to be late. Through the window he saw that the lunchtime rush had begun. Serious-faced businessmen, women shoppers, and schoolchildren scurried in all directions, bent on making it home for the middle of the day meal so sacred to Italians.

When Ben arrived at the Doges' Palace a half hour late, the courtyard was empty except for an elderly gentleman next to the Giants' Staircase. He turned to leave, when a young woman stepped out from under an arcade. She wore a close-fitting, stylish dress that showed off her slender figure and a fashionably tilted hat. She was a cool, collected presence. Only the tapping of her foot gave away her impatience. She waved her hand, folded her arms across her chest, and waited for him to come to her.

It was Silvia! He had forgotten how beautiful she was! Ben walked quickly across the wide courtyard.

"I'm so glad you waited," he said, wanting to embrace her. "Signor di Stefano called and I couldn't get him off the telephone."

Her look of impatience melted into a smile. "I was afraid you had forgotten, or changed your mind." She threw her arms around him.

"I've had a hard time getting you out of my mind since Bolzano," he said, holding her tight.

"Me too, Ben. I thought Wednesday would never come." She surprised him with a long kiss. "You look so handsome, all dressed up like this."

Taking her hand, he walked with her toward the street. "There's a café near here. Let's go there and talk. I have to tell you something."

She looked up at him. "You seem so serious. What is it?"

"Wait until we're in the café."

She stopped walking and broke away from him, insisting that he tell her right away. He saw that no one was nearby and blurted out what he had dreaded telling her. His mother and sister had already left Padua, and before too long he would have to join them in another city.

Silvia looked confused and angry. She took a step back, her eyes darkening with hurt. "So it was just a weekend in the mountains for you?" She grasped her pocketbook, ready to walk away.

He reached for her hand. "Please don't be angry. I didn't know how to tell you. I'm not even used to the idea myself." He added, "I have to take care of my mother and my sister."

The hurt was still in her eyes. "How long will you be gone?"

He lowered his voice. "With the Nazis here, who knows how long anyone will have to hide. Don't you understand? I'm a Jew."

She squeezed his hand. "I understand, but why didn't you tell me in Bolzano that you would be leaving Venice?"

"I can't talk here in the street. Let's go to the café."

When they were seated, he reminded her in a low voice that in Bolzano she had wanted to concentrate on just that one evening. He hadn't wanted to spoil their time together.

Tears filled her eyes as she told him that it was such a big thing for him to have to go away, and she couldn't believe he hadn't even given her a hint.

He took her other hand, reminding her that they had pretended they were in a place without a war, without problems. He hadn't known then that he would care for her so much. His face flushed as he admitted that her aunt was right, he had nothing to offer her. There it was. He was in Giorgio's shoes, loving a girl he would soon be forbidden to see.

She swore she wasn't afraid, even when he told her that she could be persecuted too. "How much do you care for me?" she asked.

"I care for you much too much to make trouble for you." He took his Aryan document from his breast pocket and handed it to her. "You see what I have to do? I have to use a new name on Aryan papers that say I'm Christian. You don't even know my real name."

She read, "Campano, Bernardo—factory worker." She gave back the document. "Do you think I don't know about people having to do this? How long will you be in Venice—really how long? We have to be truthful with each other."

"I should go right away, but signor di Stefano told me this morning that he wouldn't be ready to get around by himself for a week or more and my mother wants me to work here a few weeks longer."

"I'm sorry for him, but glad for us. If you won't tell me where you're going, at least tell me how far away you'll be."

He shook his head. "I can't say anything. It would be dangerous for my mother and sister—and maybe for you, if you knew something you ought not to."

"But you have to tell me. I won't tell anyone, not even my aunt and uncle."

"I wish it weren't like this." He was quiet for a long moment. "At least I'll tell you that I'll be about five hours away."

Her face lit up with hope. "Then you'll come back to see me."

He shook his head. "You know what *clandestino* means. Once I go, I'll be in hiding."

She fixed her eyes on his. "If something happens to you, I won't even know about it."

He hesitated, and then leaned in close to her. "Well ... we'll be in a village in the west of Italy."

"So far away? You won't go across the border, will you?"

"No, I'm sure we won't."

"You can write to me."

"Silvia, the mail is being read all the time. The last thing I want is for you to be hurt by knowing me."

"Then don't hurt me." She put her hand on his cheek and leaned closer.

"How can I not?" he asked.

She turned her face up to his. "Like this." She pressed her lips to his.

He kissed her, slipping his arm around her waist.

Ben pulled away. The waiter was standing in front of them, smiling.

"*Signori?*"

"Um, two pasta Bolognese and two *aranciate*. All right, Silvia?"

She nodded. When the waiter left, she said, "Please come for dinner this evening. Zia Brigida found porcini mushrooms for the risotto."

"Silvia, you know I can't go to your aunt's tonight, or any other night. I have no right to."

"Caring for someone isn't a matter of right or wrong. Whose business is it, anyway?"

"Nowadays I'm everybody's business."

She looked at him with determination. "Until you have to leave Venice, we'll simply be together as much as we can."

Ben smiled in spite of himself. "You don't give up easily, do you?"

The waiter brought them their food and left. "I can't say good-bye right now," Silvia said. "Can you?"

He gave her a long look. "No."

"We'll go out walking tomorrow. What time can you meet me?"

"Five o'clock."

"Good. Come on, start eating." As soon as he lifted his fork, she said, "Now I feel better. Tomorrow I want to show you a wind garden."

"What's a wind garden?"

"You'll see. It's a specialty of Venice and I discovered a new one just last week."

They ate in silence for a few minutes, until Silvia looked at her watch. She had another class in a half hour. She finished her lunch and agreed to meet him in the same café the next day.

She smiled and stood, picking up her fashionable little hat. When Ben stood, she stepped close to him, putting a hand on his shoulder and asking him to promise they wouldn't talk about his leaving.

The words caught in his throat. "I can't say I won't think about it."

"Thinking doesn't make it so. Now, promise?" Suddenly, she looked panic-stricken. "What *is* your real name? Can't I at least have that, in case we lose each other?"

He considered whether to tell her. "No. The less you know, the better for you. I know your name and I would always look for you." He lifted her hand and kissed it.

"It's all so ... " She shook her head, and then turned and left.

Ben watched her hurry through the café and disappear beyond the awning.

*   *   *

Ben kept his promise. In the following weeks, he never spoke to Silvia of having to leave her. He never mentioned again that they would not be able to telephone or write to each other. Sometimes her expression became a little lost and faraway—he had hurt her—but she seemed determined to enjoy each day.

One evening they took the *traghetto* ferry through the lagoon to the port of Chioggia. Venice had never looked so beautiful to Ben, with Silvia admiring everything and holding his hand. They crossed the Ponte Vigo, the curved bridge overlooking the harbor, and walked by the artists' paintings lining the Piazza Vescovile. So much to see, but Ben saw only Silvia.

They strolled through the narrow streets, stopping to embrace and kiss in the privacy of archways, or sometimes under leafless wisteria vines cascading from high iron fences. Ben drank in Silvia's graceful walk. Her delicate features, her smile, everything about her was enchanting. She returned his glances as she led him to the wind garden she'd promised to show him, where wind chimes tinkled and yellow starbursts and crescent moons danced on strings, twirling in the evening breeze. When they walked past a group of barges tucked away under colorful striped tarpaulins, he said, "I wish it were summer and we could climb under that tarpaulin and hold each other all night."

She squeezed his hand tighter. "I wish we could too."

When he gave her a good-night kiss outside her apartment, he was content, knowing they still had more time to enjoy Venice and each other.

But later, as he stood alone at the window of his *pensione,* staring at the broken reflection of the moon in the wavelets of the canal, his thoughts turned dark, almost desperate. Could he put off going to Turin? No, that would be disloyal to his mother and his sister. But to think that he might never see Silvia again was unbearable. When, if ever, could they walk arm in arm and watch the gondoliers push their long oars, murmuring "*Gondola, gondola*" and reciting love poetry in their lispy Venetian dialect? He thought about how happy they were together. What he had told her was true—the more he saw her, the more he cared for her, and the more difficult it would be to leave her.

The next days went by too quickly. They spent their late afternoons walking through the narrow streets, watching the barges ferry their goods along the waterways, peering through the windows of the flower stores and antique shops, and looking through the stalls in the outdoor markets. Even in wartime there were gloves and scarves and umbrellas to tempt the Venetians, and spices and cinnamon filled the air with their heady scent. Anytime they spotted Nazi soldiers patrolling the streets, they paused, pretended to look in a shop window, and turned back to walk the other way.

Sometimes they found a quiet street and stopped at a gelato bar. After having their ice cream they sat alone on a bench, holding hands, talking, and kissing.

Soon only two days were left before Ben was to leave for Turin, and they took a boat to the island of Murano. In the glass factory, Silvia paused to admire a small mermaid, just born from the hands of the glassblower. Ben bought it when she wasn't looking and later, over dinner in their favorite trattoria, presented it to her.

The heaviness in his heart returned, because it was really a farewell present. "I would never leave you willingly," he told her.

His sadness seemed to bring with it all the sorrow and pain he had felt at Papà's death.

Concerned, Silvia touched his hand. "Please Ben, what are you thinking?"

"There are things I have to tell you about myself. Do you know the *Bacchus* painting in the Uffizi?"

"Of course. I love it."

"You probably never heard that someone found the preliminary sketch for that painting."

"What do you mean 'found' it?"

Ben felt again the excitement of his discovery. "It was always said that Caravaggio never made preliminary drawings before he painted … "

She frowned. "But I thought all artists drew a sketch first."

He leaned forward, speaking quickly. "Yes, but supposedly Caravaggio always went straight to the canvas when he had an inspiration. But over the centuries art historians have talked about the possibility of the existence of one Caravaggio preliminary drawing—made prior to painting the *Bacchus*—and that it was somewhere in Europe, maybe in a private collection."

"Oh, how intriguing."

"Well, one day, five years ago, I was walking in Venice about two blocks from here and I was looking in the window of a mask shop—and a small, framed drawing of Bacchus caught my eye."

"Ben, you don't mean to tell me … "

"I thought that maybe … I didn't really think it could be, but I ran and got my father and took him to the shop. He was skeptical but we bought it anyway, for a very modest price. Then my father asked the opinion of his friends—they're all art historians and well-known curators and experts—and to a man they agreed that this had to be the authentic lost Caravaggio drawing."

Silvia grabbed his hands. "Ben, that's amazing! Why didn't you tell me about this before?"

"It was the most unbelievable thing that's ever happened to me. It was right there in a simple wooden frame lying between a mask of Arlecchino and one of Pulcinella."

"It's so wonderful! But you're not looking … well, like I'd expect you to look. Aren't you still thrilled about—"

"Silvia, it's really not a good story. So far it has brought us nothing but trouble." He looked up to see that the waiter was bringing their dinner. They ate in silence for a minute, and then Ben told her everything—about going to Rome, the Gestapo keeping Papà and the drawing, and his father dying on the trip home. When he finished telling the story, he sat in silence, looking down at the table.

"It's too much, Ben. I'm so sorry." She reached her arms around his neck and put her head against his chest. Her tenderness deepened his affection for her and gave him the courage to tell her the whole story, about the gold in Rome, how much he had liked being with Foà and Ascarelli, and how proud he was of his tradition.

"My father was a faithful believer, and now that he's gone, I feel an obligation to understand things the way he did. I could never have the faith that he had, but at least I was able to do what was necessary."

She sat back to look in his face. "*Caro mio,* I understand you so much better now."

"I've been wanting to tell you, Silvia. No one knows about this except my family."

"It means so much to me that you told me all this."

"I don't know where the Caravaggio sketch is now, but by rights it belongs to me and I *will* find it again."

"You've been through so much, and I know you'll get your drawing back someday."

She hugged him again, and Ben realized that if he had to choose between the Bacchus sketch and Silvia, he wouldn't hesitate to choose Silvia.

CHAPTER 21

"Twenty miserable hours to get from Rome to Padua," Lupino muttered, hailing a cab at the Padua train station. "Three in the morning, for God's sake."

Inside the cab, he leaned forward to say, "Can't you go faster?"

"Not when my headlights are shuttered for the blackout," the driver growled. The taxi crawled through the dark, the two small beams from the headlights barely showing the way.

At the end of the short ride, Lupino smacked the fare and a tip into the driver's hand and slammed the door. He hurried through the cloud of soot from the retreating cab to the doorway of his apartment building. And then, of course, the damn elevator still wasn't working. "*Merda!*" he cursed. He dashed past the cage elevator and hurried up the stairs to his third floor apartment.

Inside his living room, he threw down his luggage near his worn brown leather easy chair. He made a mental note to buy all new furniture and draperies as soon as the damned war was over. He'd already made enough money from the Cantarini gallery to replace the faded blue plush sofa and the striped draperies, streaked by the sunlight. He walked to his desk, reached for a pad of paper, and penned the Jewish names he had been thinking of on the long train ride from Rome to Padua. He opened the file drawer of his desk to search for their addresses. Fatigued from the journey—thank God no bombings, no Partisan activity—he couldn't get his hands to move as quickly as he needed them to go. He copied down the Padua addresses. Not enough. So many were from Venice and Vicenza, and this one was from Bassano del Grappa. Another family probably lived too far away to go to a synagogue in Padua. Damn, he thought. That gave him a total of thirty and that wouldn't begin to satisfy Feltzer. He tapped his foot and looked out the window at the apartment across the street. Lights were just coming on in their breakfast room. Maybe he should make some coffee to clear his head.

Sitting at his kitchen table, Lupino thought how years ago he never would have done anything so devious. He let his mind wander to more pleasant days, to vacations in Germany, where everything was done in such a correct way. It was hard to believe the Nazis were the same race of people. In the old days children wore little white sailor outfits, were not allowed to get dirty, and everyone stayed on the path, behaving the way civilized people should, yes, everything as it should be. But now the rules had changed. *Si salvi qui può* ... Everybody had an expression for that, even the English, who thought they were so honorable, said "Every man for himself" and jumped into any lifeboat. Sure, this year it was different, and who knew how long this bloody war would drag on. He had to help himself or things were bound to get worse for him. He stood up with new resolve and returned to his list of Jews.

Now why hadn't he thought of that before? From the bottom shelf of the telephone table, Lupino pulled out the last telephone book to allow entry of Jewish names. He would pick out fifty. Even their addresses would be there. It was perfect. He smiled and nodded at his own cleverness.

When he sat down at his desk, a worrisome thought intruded. Suppose those Jews didn't belong to a synagogue? Never mind, they could explain that for themselves. Besides, hadn't Feltzer said the list would just as likely sit in an empty drawer somewhere and never be used? Anyway, if he didn't give Feltzer the list, someone else would. For a moment he flirted with the idea of forgetting the Caravaggio and not going back to Rome. No, he was too close to the prize now. And he assured himself that he certainly deserved it more than that tub of lard Hermann Göring, prancing around Rome in a fur coat, looking like a prostitute. For God's sake, he was calling himself Arminio, the Latin name for Hermann—the pompous ass.

Lupino opened the telephone book to the letter A. He turned the pages easily, his fingers moving with their usual deftness. It would be best to take a few from A, then some from B, a couple of Cs, yes, the list would look quite authentic. This was getting easier and easier to accomplish.

At six o'clock in the morning, after he had made his way to the Ks—Kahn, Kupferman—Lupino sat back to release the tension from his neck and shoulders. With his fingertips, he massaged the nape of his neck. He could relax a few minutes since he was making good progress.

At nine o'clock he went to the gallery to attend to some important business and at three o'clock treated himself to lunch at a nearby trattoria. Afterwards, he went back to his apartment to resume work on the list. Finally, at ten in the evening he had sixty-five names and addresses. By midnight, he had assembled the list and put it in a folder.

He no longer questioned what he was doing, but his qualms had been replaced by nagging worries. Was Feltzer just using him? Might he make other demands of him? What did Feltzer really want of him?

Late the next afternoon at the entrance of Via Tasso, Lupino thrust his Swiss passport into the hands of the stern-faced SS man, who pointed to the hallway behind him. Waiting for Feltzer on the polished bench, Lupino rubbed his eyes, gritty from lack of sleep. He opened the briefcase and looked again at his list of Jewish names to reassure himself.

"Ah, there you are." Feltzer was standing over him.

Lupino quickly shut the briefcase and stood up to shake his hand. The smile on Feltzer's face said that all would go smoothly now. He motioned for Lupino to come into his office.

Standing alone by his desk, Feltzer held out his hand. "I'll take the list, old friend—and the check. I'm in a hurry. Things are happening fast nowadays."

Lupino's flush of success turned to annoyance as he gave Feltzer the folder and the check. "Well then, where's my Caravaggio drawing?"

Feltzer wagged a finger at him. "Hey, old buddy, you didn't tell me how valuable it was." He slid open the bottom drawer of his desk. "You really are a clever fellow. I'll be damned, you never let on."

"It's not German art," Lupino snapped back. "You like your paintings dark and Wagnerian."

"Well, as you say, a deal's a deal." Feltzer took a cardboard tube from the drawer and held it in the air. Somewhere along the line, the frame had been chucked and the sketch was in a tube.

Lupino reached for the tube, opened it, and carefully

unrolled the Caravaggio drawing. He was overwhelmed to be holding it for the first time. He felt his face burning, thinking of others who may have held it before him—and the first was the master artist himself! Oh God, that this extraordinary moment should take place in Gestapo Headquarters. How unfortunate. He stroked the edge of the yellowed paper, taking in Bacchus's wanton expression, the negligent folds of his robes, his slender, somehow uncaring fingers holding the glass of wine. Amazing that the master could convey such sensuality with only brown wash and paper.

Feltzer smiled indulgently. "The drawing has an effect on you, doesn't it?"

Lupino managed to shrug. He rolled up the drawing as fast as his fingers would allow him and carefully replaced it in the tube.

"Well, it's yours now, my friend," Feltzer said. "But tell me, what do you intend to do with it?"

"At first I just want to enjoy having it. Later, I don't know." Lupino knew that as soon as he was safely out of that place and alone on the street with his Caravaggio, he would be the happiest man in the world. Even his irritation with Feltzer had vanished in the glow of possession. "How about a ride to the station? One of your men must surely have a moment to take me."

"Sorry," Feltzer said. "Can't help you. The quickest way to get there would be to go around the Colosseum. Take a left just beyond it and keep going."

Once on the street, Lupino walked quickly past the Arch of Titus, thinking that if all went well he would be in Switzerland by late the next day. Sleeping on the train overnight wouldn't be pleasant, but leaving the Caravaggio in Switzerland for the duration of the war would be the safest plan.

Good that the drawing was in a tube. When he reached the border, he could just slip it up the sleeve of his jacket. Customs could root through his luggage all they liked and he would pass on through.

Lupino hurried past the Colosseum, just as the workers and shoppers were heading home for the evening. When he arrived in Bern, he would call his mother and she would be there in a half hour. If he arrived at the Rome station in time, he could even get a bite to eat. No, more than a bite. He'd see if he could find a piece of steak, or even that horsemeat they were passing off as steak nowadays — but mostly a glass of wine so he could celebrate! Yes, he had his glorious prize and he was almost home!

CHAPTER 22

"Of course we'll see each other again." Signor di Stefano rolled his wheelchair to the front door of his gallery where Ben was waiting to say good-bye. He reached up to clap Ben on the shoulder. "You're such a fine young man and a very dedicated worker. I only wish you could have stayed longer. The month went by so quickly." He pulled an envelope from his pocket and handed it to Ben. "Here, you deserve this bonus. Remember, be careful, whatever you do. And wherever you go, may God be with you."

Ben remembered Papà's words in Rome, "May the God of our Fathers bless you."

"Thank you, Signor di Stefano." The envelope was thick. Good, that meant cash. The man understood that Ben wouldn't be able to cash any more checks. "And thank you for letting me have the afternoon off."

"Well, I knew you'd have a lot to do on your last day."

"Yes, I do. Good-bye."

"When this war is over, please come back to me. I hope ... " Signor di Stefano stopped, his voice choking. "Go on now, Ben.

Good-byes are difficult for me." He turned his wheelchair and rolled himself back to his desk.

Ben gave a final wave and shut the door behind him.

In the Caffè Serenissima, Silvia was seated at a table, leaning on her elbows, eyebrows drawn together in thought. She looked more beautiful to Ben every day. When she saw him, she jumped up and kissed him full on the lips. He held her close, telling himself to remember the fresh scent of her skin and the way she slipped her hand to the back of his neck when they kissed.

She broke away from their embrace. "I have a surprise."

"What?"

"You'll see. Let's walk." She took his hand and led him out to the street. "Just come with me."

It was the hour of the siesta and the streets were empty, except for an occasional cat scurrying by. The metal lattices were pulled down in front of the shops, hiding luxurious bouquets of flowers and lush paintings of gondolas.

She leaned in so close, he could smell her sweet breath. With a mischievous smile, she asked if he remembered her friend Isabella. They had seen her in the glass factory in Murano with her family. Ben laughed, remembering the loud-voiced young woman examining glass fish bowls with her mother and father. They'd been in a heated discussion—should the artist put three or five glass fish in the bowl?

Silvia stopped in front of a Moorish apartment building near the Piazza San Marco. The only movement around them was the breeze from the canal. "Isabella and her family went to the seaside for four days and I have the key to their apartment. They asked me to water the plants." She bent her dark head over her purse, digging in its depths and then lifting up an antique key. Brushing

Ben's cheek with her fingertips, she said, "I'm going to skip my class. We can spend the whole afternoon there alone."

Excitement rushed through him. "You're wonderful! That's everything I could wish for!"

Walking past the concierge's door, Silvia whispered, "If the concierge asks what we're doing here, we'll just say that we've been asked to water plants."

They entered her friend's apartment. Silvia led Ben into the living room, darkened by the almost-closed louvers, and then down a hallway until she stopped in front of an open door. "The guest room," she said, stepping ahead of him into the room. The walls were painted a soft Pompeian red that matched the overstuffed pillows piled on a large half-tester bed. Cologne bottles and powder boxes sat in front of the mirror of a cream-colored dressing table. Several enormous bergere chairs were decorated with brown silk and velvet pillows. A terracotta Cupid was perched on the high frame of the headboard, chin in hand. As Silvia pulled back the thin ivory curtains and opened the window a few inches, her body was outlined under her silk blouse and her long skirt stirred in the light breeze.

"Silvia ... are you sure this is all right? I mean ... will we really be alone?"

"It's fine, Ben. Don't worry." She reached up to take the pins from her hair, letting it fall onto her shoulders.

He embraced her. "Silvia, I love you."

"I love you so much that I can't imagine ever being with anyone else."

"Your beautiful face ..." He kissed her cheek and neck, but then felt her arms tense. "What is it?"

"I'm just not sure I'll know what to do."

"You mean you never ..."

She shook her head. "No, never."

"Are you afraid?" he asked gently.

"Yes, but I want to be with you." She slipped her hands up to the first button of his shirt. Slowly, her gaze locked on his, her breath warm and moist against his chin, she undid the buttons and nuzzled her face against his chest. Ben tightened his embrace and kissed the top of her head.

She took a step back and unbuttoned her blouse, letting it slide off her shoulders. Her skirt slipped to the floor and, with her eyes down, she removed the rest of her clothes. His arms encircled her waist and he kissed her mouth, and then moved his lips down to her breasts. Stepping back, he fumbled for his belt buckle and removed his own clothing.

She stroked his chest with both hands, and then pulled back the velvet coverings on the bed. Lying on the linen sheets, she opened her arms to him. Ben lay down next to her, leaning on his elbow, while she grazed her fingertips along his neck and onto his shoulder. He could feel her heart beating rapidly under his hand as he touched her breast.

"Please," she said. "Touch me everywhere. I'm not afraid anymore."

He stroked her back, her waist, and her hips. When he put his hand on the dark triangle between her legs, he felt her stiffen.

"Maybe I am a little afraid," she whispered.

He pulled away from her. "Shall I—"

"No, don't stop."

He kissed her and waited for her to ask him to caress her again. When she did, he was lost in the perfume of her skin, the heat of her body. Finally he made himself one with her and felt her hips moving against his. They were both lost in desire and tenderness and the rhythm of their lovemaking, until the moment of final pleasure.

Exhausted, they lay back on the cool pillows. The linen was a balm against Ben's hot cheek. Reaching for Silvia's hand and entwining her warm fingers in his, he gazed at her beautiful body stretched next to him, her dark hair spread like a mantle on the pillow.

"I can't believe we found each other," he whispered.

"Ben, I'm so happy. I can't give you up, I won't ever give you up." Her voice broke as she embraced him.

"Shh," he said. "Sweetheart, we don't have to give each other up. We'll only be apart for a while."

She leaned on one elbow, her eyes wet. "How do we know that? How do we know anything?" It was the first time he had heard her sound desperate.

Sudden footsteps in the courtyard below silenced his response. He tensed as he lifted his head to listen. Men's voices echoed against the walls outside.

"Are you sure no one else has the key?" he asked, reaching for his clothes.

"As far as I know. But we'd better leave now." She began dressing, while Ben hurried to put on his clothes.

She quickly straightened the bed. They hurried to the living room and Silvia opened the door to the hall. "Here, let's go out the back way."

*   *   *

The next morning, Ben and Silvia stood locked in an embrace on the railroad platform. The steam from the engine mixed with the early morning mists.

"My heart is breaking," she murmured.

"I know," he whispered, "but we mustn't be sad, because we've found each other." He pushed a strand of hair back from her forehead. "Wait for me, that's all."

Her voice caught in her throat. "I'm afraid you'll get there and forget me. I'll never want to be with anyone else now."

"Never, my sweet love."

"Ben, you're the only person I've ever loved. Should I have, I mean, should we have … Did it mean everything to you like it did to me?"

"Of course. I love you, Silvia. I can't imagine ever loving anyone else."

"Then tell me where you're going. Please don't abandon me like this. How will I even know if you're all right?"

"Somehow I'll let you know, I promise. The train is leaving now." He kissed her once more and walked toward the train.

She followed, not letting go of his hand. He kissed her quickly on the lips and jumped onto the train steps. Over the final blast of the engine, he mouthed the words, "I love you." He rushed inside the train and leaned out the window to wave until he could no longer see her.

As the train rolled alongside factories and smokestacks, he sank onto a seat, overwhelmed by a deep sense of loss. Yesterday when he was with Silvia, the world had been bright with meaning; now he felt only a sickening loneliness.

The train sped west, the dark Adriatic backwaters giving way to farmland, but Ben saw nothing.

* * *

Constanz was preparing luncheon for the family, but her mind wasn't on what she was doing. The day and night strain of expecting German boots on the gravel outside was taking its toll.

And furthermore, she was still bothered by Herr Hauptmann. He came to the house quite often and always left with Gianni for several days. What was their unnamed business? Who went out so late in the evening, and to do what? This time Gianni had been gone for four days. Francesca seemed preoccupied, but didn't give a clue as to her thoughts. Living in hiding was making Constanz jump at every noise. Oh God, how long would this go on?

"Hullo!" a man's voice called, sending a shiver down her back. She looked up to see Gianni standing in the doorway next to Herr Hauptmann. "I'm back and we have a guest for dinner, Celeste."

Her heart sank. Now she'd be in the middle of pretending again.

Gianni remarked on the mild weather and said he wanted to take Maria to the park. He insisted that Hans and Constanz join them. Constanz begged off, saying that her son had managed to get a telephone call through from Venice and would be arriving shortly. But Gianni's expression told her she should join them. He insisted that a little fresh air would be good for her. Francesca would stay at home and tell Bernardo where they were.

It had been one month since she'd seen Ben, and now she wouldn't even be at the house to greet him when he arrived. It irked her to hear Ben called Bernardo. Something else for her to accept. She went to the hall closet for a light sweater, and followed Gianni and the others outdoors.

Gianni walked briskly ahead on the path with Monica, calling back, "Hans, you keep Celeste company."

"Wir sprechen Deutsch, nicht wahr?" Hans asked her. "Where in Germany were you born? You never did tell me."

"In Berlin." Her heart was pounding in her throat. Suppose

he asked her what street they lived on? They had had so many Jewish neighbors.

"I wish I knew Berlin better," he said. "Believe it or not, I've been there only a few times. *Ich bin aus Essen.* Since the war started, the weather in Essen has been unusually bad. That's one reason I like Italy so much."

In spite of herself, she enjoyed speaking German again. He spoke a lovely German, like the cultured friends of her youth. His speech was occasionally touched with old-fashioned expressions from his part of Germany.

He turned his face up to the surprisingly warm autumn sun. "May I call you Celeste? I'd like it very much if you'd call me Hans."

"Yes, of course." She couldn't imagine calling him by his first name.

"Celeste is such a beautiful name. Means 'heavenly' doesn't it?"

"Yes, it does."

"You're fortunate. Every other little German boy is named Hans. Have you been happy in Italy?"

"Sehr glücklich, very happy."

He picked a small branch of oak leaves. "Too bad these are not flowers, but even a spray of leaves could bring cheer. Do you have a little vase for them in the kitchen?"

She took the branch, finding it awkward that he seemed always to be talking to her about flowers. "Perhaps signora Baldissera does."

She heard footsteps on the path behind her. She knew those footsteps well and turned around to see her son walking quickly toward her.

Opening her arms to him, she remembered not to call him

by name. "*Amore mio!* You're early, how wonderful!" She was overwhelmed with relief. "You're here, safe and sound!" She turned to Hans. "Herr Hauptmann, this is my son."

Hans shook the young man's hand. "So this is Bernardo. Delighted to meet you."

"Hello." Ben dropped the man's hand quickly and excused himself to greet Monica and introduce himself to Gianni. When he returned, he took his mother's arm. "Let's go back to the house so we can talk."

As soon as they were out of earshot of the group, Ben turned to her, demanding, "Who is that man?"

"You weren't very polite to him. He's a guest here. Signor Baldissera invited him."

"Signora Baldissera met me at the front door and told me I'd find my mother walking toward the park. I go out there and what do I see—you, taking a bouquet from a German. Are you crazy?"

Constanz felt her face turn red. She chided him, telling him he had no right to talk to her that way. Holding up the branch, she pointed out that it was hardly a bouquet! And furthermore, she reminded him, she had been in charge of their family while Ben was in Venice and she knew how things worked in the Baldissera household. He should have more faith in her.

But she wondered about the truth of her next words. She asserted that Gianni knew exactly what he was doing.

Ben leaned back against a tree trunk. His arms folded, he listened to her explain that Herr Hauptmann sometimes came to Turin on business. He wanted to know what the hell kind of business he was doing. Did his mother know that the Nazi would figure out that that they were Jewish?

With a sigh of exasperation, Constanz reminded him that

they had to make the best of the situation and that they had no other choice.

Ben asked through gritted teeth, "Did the rabbi know about all this when he sent us here?"

"All I know is that we're here now and we have to be grateful and accept whatever it is. Let's walk back to the house. I'll show you which room is yours. Please be civil during dinner. Herr Hauptmann will be leaving very soon."

Ben found it painful to make small talk with Hauptmann over dinner. It was obvious the rabbi had picked the wrong family to hide them in. At the end of dinner, he was relieved when Hauptmann said good-bye and drove off.

Within minutes Gianni came to Ben and invited him into the library for a talk. Following his host down the hallway, Ben felt the man's strength and authority. In the library the small lamp on the desk cast shadows on the mahogany leather chairs and the spines of the well-read books on the shelves. This was a serious room.

Gianni closed the door and gestured for his young guest to sit, and then stood next to his desk and studied Ben for a long moment. Ben's heart quickened. Was there more trouble? Gianni began speaking in a measured way. "Ben, the reason I chose your family from among the many who needed to hide is that your rabbi assured me that you were a person of exceptional character. He said you were passionate in caring for your family and for our beloved Patria. You detest everything the Nazis represent."

Ben nodded, and Gianni went on to explain that he was part of a clandestine effort to undermine the Nazi occupation of Italy and to help save as many Italian Jews as possible. The work was dangerous. Gianni could very much use Ben's help, but if he chose not to be part of that special operation, he could work with the gardener instead.

Ben answered with enthusiasm, "Signor Baldissera, I want very much to be a part of what you are doing. I've been waiting for a chance like this."

"Don't say yes yet. You must understand that if you agree, you'll have to give me your solemn promise not to let a single word of this pass your lips. You might be tempted to speak to your mother, a sweetheart, a close friend ... This could put them and the rest of us in grave danger."

"Signor Baldissera, you can trust me. I won't disappoint you."

"Good. And just what I was hoping you would say."

He went on to explain to Ben that the Italian government had ordered him to work for the Germans. He had to retool the factory in Turin to make tanks, and Ben would start his work for Gianni by working in the factory. He would also help Giacomo in the garden, enough for appearances.

Ben didn't see how working in the factory would help the country, until Gianni explained that Ben would slip a faulty gear into every fifth tank he worked on. After riding a few kilometers into battle, the faulty tanks would shut down and be unable to move. In a few weeks Ben would start the real work.

Now that Ben was in the man's confidence, he dared to ask, "Why do you have a German guest coming to this house—with our family being Jewish?"

"Don't ask about that. You must trust me. But, another thing, your mother and sister were baptized. That's because your sister goes to school with the nuns and your mother has to take Communion when she goes to church with her. You know that Italian men don't go to church as often as the women do, so your

Aryan papers will be sufficient to show that you're Catholic." Gianni looked around the room, as if he had talked enough. "Are we clear on all this?"

"Yes, I understand. I want very much to help."

"Good. And call me Gianni. No more signor Baldissera." He put out his hand. "This is all for now. I like you, Bernardo. Together we have a chance to do good things."

Ben stood and shook Gianni's hand. Gianni wheeled around and strode from the room, calling, "Francesca, is there enough coffee for another cup?"

Ben walked to the window and snugged the blackout curtains, wondering what he would be asked to do. He hardly knew Gianni and yet he had just committed himself to follow his orders.

A feeling of excitement touched him, until he remembered how far away he was from home—and Silvia. For the past few weeks he'd been obsessed with plans for keeping track of the Bacchus sketch. Now his head was filled with thoughts of Silvia. What was she doing? When would he see her again? He tried to picture her face and couldn't. Soft dark hair, he remembered, and always an aura of sweet freshness about her. But her face? Bright, inquiring eyes, tender lips. What else? He didn't even have a picture of her.

His thoughts returned to Gianni saying, "What you need to know, you will learn ... " Maybe someday this would lead him to the Partisans. Giorgio must already be working with them near Bolzano, throwing the four-pointers and blasting German trucks with grenades. Maybe it was only a matter of time for Ben.

CHAPTER 23

Thankful to be distancing himself from Via Tasso, Lupino held onto his briefcase with the precious Caravaggio. He walked as fast as he could past the Colosseum and turned into the side street Feltzer had recommended as a shortcut to the station. Shopkeepers were pulling down their iron lattices for the night and clerks were scurrying to get home before the curfew.

Lupino heard the screech of tires. Through the dusk, he could make out two road blockades—a canvas-covered military truck with German markings had pulled up at each end of the street. German soldiers armed with rifles sprang out of the truck nearer to him and rounded up the men on the sidewalk.

"*Hinein*, get in!" they shouted, prodding the men with their rifle butts. Lupino backed into an empty doorway, trying to hide and make sense of the scene.

"Wait! Wait!" the men were shouting as they fumbled for their papers.

"*Nein*, get in!" The soldiers shoved them into the van.

My God, Lupino thought, it was true. They were starting to round up Italians.

He tried to open the door to an apartment behind him, but heard the lock being latched as he turned the handle. "Help! Let me in!" he screamed, pounding on the door.

"*Andate via!* Go away!" came the muffled cry from the other side of the door.

In an instant, two soldiers were upon him. "*Papiere!*" they demanded. "*Wo sind Ihre Papiere?*"

"Here," Lupino said, reaching into his briefcase for his passport. "I'm not Italian! I'm a Swiss citizen!" One soldier grabbed the passport and looked through it, while the other one kept the butt of his rifle in Lupino's stomach. "You can't do this," Lupino shouted.

Snatching Lupino's briefcase, the soldier ordered, "Get in!"

Lupino reached for his briefcase. "I said, I'm Swiss!"

"Without a passport, you're *Scheisse,*" the soldier said, and pushed him into the back of the truck.

"Where are you taking me?"

"Shut up!"

Rough hands shoved him farther into the dark interior of the truck, already crowded with other men. The canvas covering was yanked shut; Lupino and the other prisoners were in blackness. The driver ground the truck into first gear and, horn blasting, took off, spilling Lupino and the other men on top of one another. When they had righted themselves on their benches, Lupino heard a boy wailing, "Mamma! Mamma!" Good God, they had even taken a child.

"*Cáspita!*" a man's voice called out. "Stop peeing in your pants, my shoe is soaking wet!"

"I can't help it, I want Mamma."

The smell of urine mixed with wool assailed Lupino's nostrils. He leaned back against the metal rod behind him. What in hell was this all about? Were they being taken to a German labor camp? Those clumsy oafs had his passport and his Caravaggio drawing. He had to make them understand that they had made a horrible mistake.

Hours later, the truck carrying Lupino and the others pulled over to the side of the road. The driver and his assistant yanked open the canvas and beamed their flashlights into the men's faces. "All right, two by two, you can take a leak and get water from that faucet." The driver moved the beam of light to a spigot next to a cattle trough. Lupino climbed stiffly out of the truck, urinated next to the trough, and then bent down to drink from the spigot.

His stomach was growling. "When are we going to eat?" he called out.

"You think this is the spa at Baden-Baden?" came the answer. The driver and the other soldier laughed.

Lupino tuned his ears to what the two of them were saying to each other. "Bologna, then the road north … they speak German there." Good God, they were taking him way up north toward the Tirol. Why there? That was up near the Brenner Pass, on the way to Austria.

The driver waved his flashlight, ordering Lupino and the man with him to get back in the truck. Inside, Lupino positioned himself close to the end of the bench, hoping to get a whiff of fresh air now and then.

Much later, when the truck had once again slowed down, Lupino put his eye to a rip in the canvas and saw a sign: 2 km. Bolzano. The air had grown cold and the smell of pine reached his nostrils. When the driver pulled to a stop, Lupino heard him ask, "*Wo ist das Lager?*"

The answer came back, "*Heil* Hitler! The barracks are north of the town, first graveled road on the left."

The truck followed the main road, made a turn, bumped along a winding road, and finally stopped. The bewildered men were let out in front of a long, narrow one-story building. Two weary-looking German soldiers shoved their captives into a dimly lit, bare hall where piles of straw were pushed against the walls. Looking at his watch, Lupino saw that it was three in the morning. He had lost his hunger pangs, but his anger remained.

Striding over to one of the soldiers, he demanded, "Why are we here?"

"Go lie down and be quiet."

Furious, Lupino went over to one of the piles of straw and sat with his back against the wall. He pulled out a Nazionale and lit up.

"What the hell are you doing, trying to burn us all up?" one of the guards yelled.

"All right," Lupino grumbled, tamping the cigarette against the bottom of his shoe, careful not to crush it. The guard left, leaving the light on. Lupino lit up again and leaned back. First thing in the morning, he'd tell whoever the hell was in charge that he was a Swiss citizen and that they'd better call Feltzer in Rome. He cursed the prickly straw and ran his tongue over his coated teeth. Animals, those Nazis. He hugged himself for warmth, his teeth chattering. How could they have made a mistake like this? Those low-class bums couldn't distinguish between the common little people and somebody like Lupino. Why hadn't Feltzer made a driver available to take him to the railroad station? Instead, he'd told him to take a shortcut.

Lupino's blood ran cold. Suddenly he realized what had been done to him. *Jesus, Maria, und Josef!* Feltzer had set him up! Why hadn't he realized this sooner? Feltzer must have thought he was going to get something out of it—the filthy bastard! If it was to get the drawing, why hadn't he just taken it? Why send him up to this godforsaken spot?

The next morning the sound of coughing and throat clearing awakened Lupino. He looked down the long, half-darkened room at the men rising from their piles of straw, brushing the dust from their clothes.

"*Scheisse*, it's freezing in here," he muttered. "I can even see my breath." He stood and stamped his feet for warmth. As soon as he could find a place to take a piss, he would call that filthy Feltzer. He saw a guard in the doorway. "So where do we wash up?" he called.

The guard pointed toward the other end of the room. Lupino hurried past the other men, now standing in little groups, grumbling and blowing their noses. He found one small toilet in the corner of the freezing bathroom. "For God's sake, a child's toilet," he muttered. "They must have put us in some kind of abandoned school." He relieved himself, threw water on his face at one of the low sinks, and strode back to the guard.

"Listen," he said to the guard, "I have to get to a telephone. There's been a terrible mistake."

The fellow shrugged. "*Ja, ja,* there's been a mistake for all of you."

Goddamn son of a bitch, he had to get through to this blockhead. He felt a tap on his shoulder. It was the fellow who had been peed on by the young boy in the truck. He was beckoning to him.

Edging close, he whispered in Lupino's ear. His breath was rank. "The fellow next to me last night, he's been here for a week and he told me what this is all about. They're waiting for a train from Novara, that town near Turin."

"Of course I know where Novara is," Lupino snapped.

"It's the same train that took German troops to Turin three days ago and it's coming back this way tomorrow. Everyone they rounded up in Rome and Bologna is going on it to Germany."

"Not me!" Lupino said. He turned away and walked back to the guard. In his most polite German, he said, "Officer, may I speak to you?"

The guard gave him a wily look. *"Ja, was ist los?"*

Lupino pulled the corner of a large bill from his pocket. "I have to get to a telephone. Help me out and you'll have plenty left over from this."

Under his breath, the soldier asked, "Are you trying to bribe me, you idiot?"

"This is no bribe. It's gratitude from a Swiss citizen to a soldier of the Third Reich." Lupino pushed the lira note toward the fellow's hand, which was cupped and turned palm down. "When do you get off duty? I need to get to a telephone."

The guard put the note in his pocket. "I can't get you to a telephone. Tell me the number and the message."

You bastard, Lupino thought. "Come on now, I have to make the call."

"Do you expect me to take you out of this holding pen? Give me the number and message and make it short."

"All right. Ask for Herr Feltzer at Via Tasso in Rome."

The soldier's face froze. "Are you crazy? He's a big man in the Gestapo down there."

Lupino continued sotto voce, telling the soldier that he was a personal friend of Feltzer. He gave his name, Lupino, Aldo, adding that Feltzer was waiting for his call. The soldier must tell him that there had been a mistake, that he had been taken to Bolzano. Feltzer must send for him right away.

The soldier nodded and shoved the lira bill deeper in his pocket, warning Lupino to go away. They had talked too long already.

Lupino walked away from the soldier, doubts beginning to haunt him. What if the telephone lines were down, or suppose Feltzer refused to take the call? Looking out the dirty window, he saw nothing but woods and snow on the mountains. But they beckoned to him, because they meant Switzerland and home. Escape would be dangerous, but he had to keep thinking. He had to do something, but what?

*   *   *

A week later, as she walked down the hallway toward her room, Constanz heard a muffled sound. Was that Monica sobbing? She went quickly to the bedroom she shared with Monica. Pushing open the door she saw her little girl curled into a ball on the bed, cuddling her doll.

Constanz sat next to her, caressing her cheek, and whispered, "What is it, my little sweetheart?"

"A girl at school said everybody knows we're Jewish."

Oh no! If one girl was saying it, soon everyone would be. "But you're not Jewish! Don't you remember, we went to the priest and now we're Catholic."

"Will someone hurt us now?"

"No, of course not." Constanz stood. "We have to ..." What *did* they have to do? What *could* they do?

She embraced her daughter, promising that Mamma would

take care of it. Hastily, she left the room and paused on the landing, gathering strength.

Somewhere downstairs a door slammed. Could it be the authorities already? She ran to the window and looked out. No police van. The gravel driveway was empty. But she heard a man's voice downstairs. What was he saying?

She stood swaying at the top of the stairs, trying to decide what to do. She went down a few steps and made out the voices of a man and a woman—Ben and Francesca! How could she not recognize her own son's voice?

She went downstairs and walked into the library where the other two were. "Where's Gianni?"

"He's gone," Francesca said. "He'll be back in a day or two."

Constanz heard the news with deep disappointment. "Excuse us, Francesca, but I have to talk to … " She motioned for Ben to follow her.

In the dining room, Constanz lowered her voice, telling Ben that someone at school had been saying that the Campanos were Jewish. What would they do about it until Gianni returned?

They would just have to wait.

Still whispering, she asked what Gianni did when he took Ben away with him.

Ben shook his head and said nothing. Constanz begged him to tell her at least that he was safe in what Gianni wanted him to do. In reassuring her, he reminded her that if he were Catholic like Giacomo's son, he would have been sent to the Russian front and would probably be dead by now.

Constanz embraced her son, grateful that he wasn't in the army. She prayed that Gianni would return soon.

CHAPTER 24

Gianni returned two days later. Constanz and Ben waited until Monica was in bed before speaking to him. They found him with Francesca in the library, listening to the war news on Radio London.

Ben spoke first, telling Gianni that a girl in Monica's school was saying that a Jewish family was staying with him.

Gianni shut off the radio and looked from Constanz to Francesca. "Oh, my God!" he groaned. "I was afraid of this."

Francesca's face had paled. "Some of those parents at the school are fascists!"

Gianni pushed himself out of his chair. He strode over to his desk, pulled out a folded map, and spread it on top of his ledgers and papers. Muttering that he had started planning for this before they arrived, he gestured for Constanz and Ben to look at the map. He jabbed his finger at Switzerland, saying that was where Maria would have to go.

Constanz stared at him, trying to understand, protesting

that her little girl hadn't done anything. Ben looked at Gianni, bewildered, asking why his mother and sister had to go to Switzerland.

"Not your mother—just your sister."

"Oh no, my little girl can't go without me."

Gianni raised his hand for silence. "I know a family in Switzerland who will take Maria in and treat her like their own. They'll take a child, but not an adult."

"But I don't want strangers taking my daughter in! I'm her mother!"

Gianni was firm. "Don't you understand, we may have to act quickly. If the authorities come after us, it will be easier—and safer—without Maria."

"No," Constanz said. "I can't do this." She turned to Ben. "You and I can find a place to stay with her in Switzerland, Ben. We'll stay in a hotel." Her voice was shaking.

"Mamma," Ben said, "we don't have the money to stay in a hotel."

"We'll find work. After all, suppose she gets sick or hurt. I have to be near her." She looked at Gianni. "Ben and I will find a way to get to Switzerland."

"No," Gianni said firmly. "Switzerland is overloaded with foreigners trying to get work. The Swiss might send you to Germany, to a labor camp."

Constanz clutched Ben's arm. "How do I know they won't do that to my daughter?"

Gianni shook his head. "She wasn't born in Germany."

"Well, Ben wasn't born in Germany either and I'll take my chances in Switzerland."

"Mamma," Ben said, "Gianni's right. It would be worse if you were sent back to Germany."

"Celeste dear," Francesca said, "we only want what's best for you and your family." For the first time since Constanz's arrival, the woman's expression held genuine compassion.

Constanz grimaced. "And what if the authorities come for us here? Suppose they send me back to Germany? Then my daughter won't have a mother!" She was near tears.

"*Coraggio*, be brave," Gianni said. "We'll get Maria safely into Switzerland. You must trust me."

He pushed back the map, saying that it was decided. The next day, which was Saturday, Celeste, Maria, and he would go on the train to Como to the home of an Italian woman, signora Chiara, who had a large property outside Como. Part of one of the fields behind her house was actually in Switzerland. She had been allowing Gianni to help refugees cross over the border at night.

Thinking of all the tricks the Nazis were playing on Jews, Constanz, her voice shaking, asked if the woman could really be trusted. She did not voice her fear that perhaps she shouldn't trust Gianni.

He looked directly into her eyes, explaining that he had been doing this for almost a year. Signora Chiara had risked her life over and over to help a lot of people to safety.

Constanz studied Gianni's face, demanding to know why this woman would put herself in such danger for people she hardly knew.

Gianni spoke in a quiet voice. "Because you people are innocent victims of the fascists, and the fascists are ruining our beloved Patria. We Italians have to do something. Celeste, you *have* to let go and trust."

Ben put his arm around her. "Gianni, how far away from here will my sister be?"

"Six, maybe seven hours."

"It's too far," Constanz said, her eyes burning.

Gianni continued, "She'll be in a farmer's family, so she'll be well fed. They're Catholic, so she won't have to learn a whole new set of prayers."

Constanz stared at Gianni, realizing that he meant it. Oh dear Lord, he really meant that she would have to give up her precious daughter.

"Let's all go to bed now and get some rest." Gianni turned to Ben. "You'll take the first bus into Turin in the morning. Giacomo can get along without you in the garden until spring. Except for helping him bury the fig trees—he'll do that in a week or so. For now you're needed at the factory."

Numb with shock, Constanz walked upstairs. She stood at the foot of Monica's bed for a long time. Her daughter's face was so peaceful. Still hugging her doll, she turned, but didn't awaken. Had the world gone insane? Shakily, she lay down next to Monica. Her last night to be near her—until when? She stayed awake, fearing the sound of a car pulling up in the driveway or boots marching toward the door. Stroking Monica's hair, she asked herself how she could possibly tell her precious daughter that she had to send her away.

In the morning, Constanz helped Monica dress and then sat with her on the bed. Putting an arm around her daughter, she steeled herself to begin. "My little sweetheart, I want to tell you something. Gianni has decided that it's safer if you ... " She forced herself to say it. "If you go for a little while to a family in Switzerland, a nice family, with cows and chickens."

"No, Mamma, tell him we don't want to go."

"It isn't a matter of wanting to go. We have to do what's safe."

"I want to stay here. I like signora Baldissera. She's starting to be nice to me."

Constanz held her closer. "*Amore mio*, you must do this. Now, listen to me. Gianni says Mamma can't go right away. I'll come later."

Monica looked stricken. "No, you have to go with me or I won't go!"

Constanz shook her head. "I want to, but I can't."

"Then Ben can go with me."

Constanz held her close. "No, there's no place for Ben or for me right now. The family in Switzerland can only take children." She added, "You want to be safe, don't you? We hope it won't be for long. Your brother sent you a hug and a kiss before he left for Turin this morning. He said to tell you to be brave."

Monica started sobbing. "I don't want to go!"

Suddenly, Gianni called from the landing. "Hurry up! There's just time for breakfast. I'll see you downstairs, hurry now."

In Como, four hours later, Gianni, Constanz, and Monica took a taxi from the train station to the outskirts of the busy town. As they drove through the quiet countryside, wretched thoughts reverberated in Constanz's head. One by one, she was losing her family. First Claudio, now Monica. When would she lose Ben?

At the end of a long driveway, she saw a stone villa in the midst of vast, rolling fields. Beyond the fields rose hills and, in the distance, snow-covered mountains. Switzerland. Her insides were tearing apart, but she told herself that she must appear brave for Monica's sake. The taxi pulled up in front of the villa and a young woman, blond hair piled on top of her head, long skirts floating behind her, rushed down the flight of steps. Smiling, she called out loud enough for the cab driver to hear, "Cousins! Welcome!"

"Signora Chiara," Gianni murmured to Constanz, as they stepped out of the taxi.

Constanz was surprised. She had imagined a serious, older woman, not one her own age, cheerful and full of energy. Signora Chiara embraced Constanz, saying how long it had been since they had seen each other. And how big Maria had grown. Wasn't she as beautiful as her dear mother! She gave Gianni a kiss on each cheek.

After Gianni had paid the driver, signora Chiara took Monica's suitcase and led the way up the steps. Setting Monica's bag against the wall in the hallway, she said to Constanz, "Maria should rest this afternoon. She has a long, hard night ahead of her."

"Yes, but for the moment it would be good for her to move around a bit. We've been a long time on the train."

Putting a hand on Monica's shoulder, signora Chiara said to Constanz, "There's a moon tonight, but the clouds are coming in so it should be dark. It's a half hour walk to the end of the property."

Monica pressed herself close to her mother.

Signora Chiara smiled at the girl. "I'm going to give you a good dinner, Maria, because you mustn't get hungry. And of course," she continued, "if anyone comes to the door this afternoon or during dinner, just say you're my cousins." She turned to Constanz. "Does she understand?"

"Yes," Constanz said. "I've told her to pretend she's shy and let me answer any questions."

"Good. Well, we don't have to stand here in the hallway."

In the long low-ceilinged living room signora Chiara sat on the striped blue sofa next to Constanz and Monica, with Gianni across from them in a high-backed chair. She smiled at Monica. "You look like a brave girl who will do exactly what signor Baldissera asks you to do."

Constanz put her arm around Monica. "Yes, she is. Signora Chiara, I want to thank you for helping us."

The other woman put her hand over Constanz's, explaining that she didn't do this for thanks. It was simply something that had to be done. She removed her hand. "Now, the walk is over rocky soil, and when Gianni and Maria get to the end of the property ... "

"I'm going too," Constanz said.

Signora Chiara shook her head. "I don't advise that. The locals know that my property is partly in Switzerland. If you're caught, the border guards have orders to send you back to the country you came from. Gianni and Maria would end up in the police station in Como, but you were born in Germany, weren't you?"

"I'm an Italian citizen," Constanz answered.

Signora Chiara pressed her lips together and gave Constanz a long look. She insisted that she didn't mean to offend, but she had noticed a strong German accent in her Italian. Would she please stay in the house that night? No, Constanz was definite. She was going with her daughter to the border.

Signora Chiara's look was dubious, but then it softened. "Well, for everyone's sake, be careful." She stood and beckoned for Constanz to follow her. "Would you help me with the tea trolley and biscotti? I was fortunate enough to find ingredients for biscotti." She smiled. "Maria likes cookies, doesn't she?"

"Yes, of course." Constanz rose to follow her. Good Lord, she thought, tea trolleys and border guards. How could she keep her mind from breaking in two?

*　　*　　*

Lupino sat up on the straw, angry and agitated, unable to sleep any longer. The hall where the captives were being held was still in shadows, hidden from the rising sun by the sharp outline of the gray Dolomites to the east. "A week, for God's sake," he muttered to himself. It had been a week of watery minestrone, no bath, no shave, no exercise, and worst of all no information. A week of waiting for a telephone line through to Feltzer. If that damn soldier told him one more time that the lines were still down …

He looked over at the pile of wallets and papers in the corner of the room, grown larger since a second load of prisoners had been put on trains departing for Germany. Thank God they hadn't sent Lupino with his group or the one that arrived after him. He remembered the guards saying that their belongings would follow. Filthy liars. He was sure the prisoners' money would end up in the commandant's pocket.

Lupino felt a heavy hand on his back. "Come with me," a guard ordered. "Herr Feltzer is in the commandant's office right now. He arrived on the train last night."

Lupino stood, thinking that dammit, it was about time. He did his best to brush the dust and straw off his jacket and walked with the guard.

After knocking on the door, the guard left him in front of the commandant's office. As Lupino waited for the door to open, he was suddenly aware of what he would look like to Feltzer—a scarecrow, with his suit rumpled and dirty. He pushed his straggly hair behind his ears.

Someone called out to come in. It was Feltzer's voice, all right. Lupino pushed open the door.

Feltzer was alone, sitting behind an old schoolmaster's desk. The flag of the Third Reich hung on the wall behind him and a photograph of the frowning Führer dominated the room. Feltzer didn't rise to greet him. He looked different to Lupino, hardened, with deep circles under his eyes.

"It's me, it's Lupino, for God's sake."

"Well, if it isn't you!" Feltzer said, leaning back in his chair.

Lupino could tell that the man was repelled by the sight of him. "You bet it's me. Why the hell did you send me into that trap? Do you know what I've been through? And your thugs stole my briefcase."

"I … send you into a trap?" Feltzer looked surprised. "Really? I only heard about you being here two days ago. Anyway, I've got your briefcase. It was turned in last week in Rome."

"Look at me! Thanks to your SS, I've got lice and I've been sleeping on a pile of straw! *Scheisse*, Feltzer, you got your goddamn list, so—"

"Easy, Lupino," Feltzer cut in. "Everything will work out. Don't think you're the only one having a hard time. If I told you about the work I have to do, flushing Jews out of that ghetto in Rome, always pushed to go faster, never enough help—"

"Shut up!" Lupino yelled. "What is that to me?" He took a step toward the desk.

Feltzer put out his hand to stop him. "Don't get too near me—old friend. You don't smell so good, you know."

"Get me the hell out of here!" Lupino's voice was gravelly

with anger. "Give me my briefcase!" He gave Feltzer a sharp look. "The Caravaggio is still in there, isn't it?"

Feltzer waved away the question. "Listen to me. I'm giving you an escort to take you to the Park Laurin hotel here in Bolzano. You know it, big, fancy hotel near the railroad station. We'll send you there with some clean clothes. First thing, you'll take a nice long shower—"

Lupino cut in, "What are you talking about?"

"We can't have the SS getting a reputation for bringing lice into a place—and then the bar is yours and so is the dining room. Look, I'm trying to make it up to you."

Lupino's head was swimming. He protested that he just wanted his briefcase and his drawing and a train ticket to go to Switzerland.

Feltzer gave him a mocking smile. Did he really want to greet his family in that filthy suit? No, not when there was a room waiting for him at the Park Laurin. He'd be there about a week, maybe less. Feltzer opened a drawer, pulled out a cigar, and offered it to him.

Lupino grumbled, asking if Feltzer really thought a cigar would make up for what he'd been put through.

Feltzer shrugged. "I have to go back to Rome on official business. While I'm gone, I want you to go over to the tailor shop on the piazza. They'll measure you for a suit—I suggest banker's gray—and a couple of nice shirts."

Perplexed, Lupino asked, "Why are you suddenly trying to be nice to me?"

Feltzer stood. "Compliments of the SS. Buy some socks and a couple of handkerchiefs while you're at it." He gave a short laugh. "Go all the way." He looked down at Lupino's feet. "Even polish isn't going to help those shoes. Buy yourself a new pair. Go to the Gardena shoe store, under the arcades, just past the open air market."

Lupino stared at him. "Wait a minute. What the hell is this all about?"

Feltzer continued, as if ticking off a list. "The food is still good at the Park Laurin. Go to the dining room for all your meals. Oh hell, have breakfast in your room, order it up. I hear that some very pretty fräuleins and signorinas hang out in the bar after dinner."

Feltzer walked to the door, opened it, and called out into the corridor. "*Kommt her!*" The sound of marching footsteps, and then two soldiers appeared in the doorway. "Here's your escort," he said to Lupino.

"What about my briefcase?"

"I'll give it to you when I return from Rome. It's safer that way. Besides, you don't need it now." Feltzer barked an order to the soldiers, telling them to take Lupino away.

Lupino was marched out of the room and ordered to sit in the backseat of a limousine, between the two soldiers. After the limousine had been underway for a few minutes, Lupino saw that they were approaching the train station. If they were putting him on a train, then Feltzer was sending him to a German labor camp. Was Feltzer crazy enough to promise him clothes and a way out of Italy, just so he wouldn't have to tell him to his face that he was being sent to a camp in Germany? But maybe Feltzer had given the soldiers orders to take him out in the woods and shoot him. He could say "shot while trying to escape." Either way he could get rid of him and keep the Caravaggio. A shudder threatened to split his spine.

Gott, hilf mir. Please God, I beg you, help me! I know I've done some bad things, but I won't anymore. Help me, please!

CHAPTER 25

Constanz and Monica stumbled behind Gianni, making their way through a meadow in the inky darkness. The pleasant days of November were gone, bringing the cold, dank air of early winter. Constanz pulled her tweed coat tightly around herself, wishing it were heavier. She kept her arm around Monica for warmth and made sure the little girl's collar was snug around her neck. Who would do this for her little girl when her mother no longer could?

Cold moisture from the damp grasses crept into the bottom of Constanz's shoes. Occasionally she could see the silhouette of a tree against the horizon, and then all was obscured again. She heard the tall grasses rustling under Gianni's boots as he pushed forward, carrying a huge rucksack on his back. Monica moaned softly, the way she did when she was unhappy. It would soon turn into crying.

She bent down long enough to give Monica a quick hug and told her to be brave, the way a big girl could.

"But, Mamma, I'm so tired. And I'm afraid."

"Be brave, my precious sweetheart." Constanz called out

softly to Gianni, "How far are we from the border? Can't we use the flashlight? Wouldn't that help?"

"No. Stay close to me. I know the way by heart." He walked on.

A tearful sob erupted from Monica, who clung to her mother's coat. Constanz shushed her, trying to keep her voice steady, promising everything would be all right. Gianni turned around and put his face close to Monica's, saying firmly that if she made any noise, bad people could get her. Not a sound, did she understand? He reminded Constanz that they were coming to a very rocky area. She should walk extra carefully.

Constanz's throat hurt from breathing the raw air. They pushed on for half an hour longer, and then Monica complained that her legs hurt and she couldn't go any farther.

Finally, Gianni reached back to help them over a rock-filled embankment. "See that?" he whispered. "We're almost at the border." In the background of the dark night, the faint outline of mountains shot into the sky. "Maria, look—that's Switzerland. You'll be safe there. You two wait here for a minute. If anyone comes around to talk to you, don't answer."

As he walked away, Constanz rocked her daughter against herself, wondering who on earth might be near them in the dark. Other people trying to get to Switzerland, or Italian police looking for fugitives? Oh Lord, that's what her daughter was now, a fugitive—an escapee.

In the darkness she heard heavy breathing coming close. When a hand grabbed her sleeve, she held in a cry. The gravelly voice of an old man demanded, "*E` qui il confine? Dov'è?* This is the border?"

Monica gave a little scream and hid her face in her mother's coat. Constanz, her heart in her throat, turned away. The man's hand slid down her arm until he was grasping her wrist. He pulled her close, his breath rank with cigarettes. A woman near him whimpered. "*Il confine?*" the man insisted. "We want the border."

"No, over there," Constanz whispered, trying to free her wrist.

He refused to let go. "My wife wants to cross the border. I heard that man you were with. He knows, doesn't he?" The old man's body rocked with a paroxysm of coughing. Finally, he drew a breath and said, "I'm too sick to cross." He pushed the woman, still whimpering, against Constanz. "Take my wife with you." It was a command. "On the other side, friends will meet her. Her name is Lena."

"No, I'm not going," Constanz said, prying the woman away from her, desperate for the couple to leave her alone.

"If you're here, that means you're going." The man grabbed Constanz's hand, forcing her fingers open. "You can change this into Swiss money after you cross. Ask for signor Weibel."

"Go away," Constanz whispered, stumbling back, clinging to Monica.

"*Puttana!*" the man spat in her face. The couple disappeared into the blackness, the man cursing, the woman crying.

This had to be a nightmare. Constanz strained her ears and eyes for Gianni. She became aware of a sound in the distance—water rushing and tumbling. If that was what Monica had to go through, she'd never make it. She'd be too afraid. In a small break between the clouds, the moon allowed a glimpse of Gianni's hefty shape looming twenty feet ahead. Constanz saw that he was kneeling down and digging in his rucksack.

"Come here," he called in a loud whisper. She led Monica closer. "Wire cutters," he muttered. "They've set fences—chicken wire—all along the border. I can cut a hole to get through, but since I was here two days ago they've lined the top of the wire with cowbells. You'll have to steady the wire while I cut."

He led them several yards farther into the darkness. Constanz set down Monica's suitcase. She felt Gianni grip her wrists and raise her arms above her head, until she was touching the top of the wire mesh. He ordered her to hold as many bells as she could while he cut an opening close to the ground.

She held the wire taut, stopping the noise of two small bells under each palm. In the cold night air, the bells felt like ice cubes. With each snip, bells down the line tinkled. Gianni cursed softly each time.

In between snips, she heard the rushing water, much closer now. A cold mist was rising around their feet and her aching arms began to burn.

At last Gianni said, "The opening is big enough. Let go very slowly."

Constanz opened her hands and lowered her arms. Gianni told Monica to say good-bye to her mother and come with him. A wave of panic swept through Constanz, and she grabbed her daughter's hand. "Maria," Gianni continued, "after we go through the fence, I'll take you across the stream. A nice family will be waiting on the other side."

Monica flung herself against her mother, locking her arms around her waist. Constanz held her tight, forcing back her tears. She couldn't bear to let go. Her chest hurt with the sobs she couldn't release. Thinking of Claudio, she choked out the words, "May the God of our Fathers bless you."

The little girl began to wail. Gianni leaped toward her, clapping his hand over her mouth. "Listen," he whispered, "if she can't control her crying, I have something to make her sleepy, but then I'll have to carry her."

Monica shook her head vigorously and Gianni took his hand away. "All right, but not one more sound."

Constanz kissed the girl's wet cheeks. "Sweetheart, you must go with signor Baldissera now. Mamma will be thinking about you and loving you every minute of every day."

Gianni dropped his rucksack next to Constanz, pushed the suitcase through the opening, and crawled through himself. Constanz helped Monica slip through the opening after him. Suddenly every bell lacing the top of the wire tinkled and sounded. "Damn!" Gianni snapped. "Her foot's caught in the net. Get it loose."

"*O Dio,*" Constanz whispered, stooping down, feeling for Monica's foot. The toe of her shoe was jammed into the chicken wire. With her cold fingers, she struggled to free the little girl's foot, cringing at the sound of the bells jingling up and down the line.

The crack of rifle shots broke the night air.

"It's a warning shot," Gianni said. "They want us out of here."

Constanz bit her lip and, holding back her tears, forced herself to keep untangling the shoelace. Finally, the shoe was free. Constanz tied the lace and guided Monica's leg through the hole. Unable to leave her, she followed her through the opening.

"Celeste, you go back!" Gianni said harshly. "I'm taking her across the stream now."

Constanz gave Monica one final embrace and crept back through the hole. She could just make out Monica's small shape next to Gianni's bulk, and saw that he had taken her hand. They pushed through a rushing stream, hands above their heads holding suitcases—like the ghostly souls in Dante's Inferno crossing the river Styx. Then the clouds hid the moon and it was dark again.

She waited anxiously for Gianni to return. Finally, a shadow appeared in front of her. "Let's move away quickly," Gianni whispered.

"Is my little girl all right?"

"Yes, she's safe with her new family." He pulled at her elbow, moving her along.

The words "her new family" stung Constanz. "What did they do when they saw her?"

"They said they would take good care of her. They helped her into the cart and slapped the horse to set off."

"Was she crying?"

"Don't worry, Celeste, she'll be fine."

When they reached the meadow, Constanz asked, "Were they welcoming?"

"Yes, yes, they're farm people, Celeste. They have seven or eight other children and she'll be part of the family."

Looking up at the sky, Constanz asked God why He'd let this happen to her people. She would never understand. Did He think they were crazy? Did He think they'd love Him more because they were suffering?

Gianni strode ahead. The night was without sound. There was her answer, she told herself bitterly. The Master of the Universe offers you silence.

*   *   *

Lupino lay back in a tub of steaming water, glad to be alive, but still shaking after his ride from Feltzer's office. What a beautiful sight the veranda of the Park Laurin had been. *Gott im Himmel!* He sat up, soaped, and rinsed his head under the faucet, thinking how much he'd like to put Feltzer in that bug-filled school for a week.

He heard the heavy creak of a floorboard outside the bathroom door. Was there someone in his room? Couldn't be. He had chain-locked the door from the bedroom to the hallway. The balcony. Someone could have come in from the balcony. Another creak. He stood up in the soapy water, threw a towel around himself, and stepped into the bedroom. Nobody in sight. It must have been the heat going on.

He had to get hold of himself. Why would Feltzer put him in the hotel, just to have someone come after him? The heat in the tall-standing iron radiators was coming on, hissing and banging, filling the whole room with noise. He toweled off his body, chagrined to see how prominent his hip bones were, how pale his skin was. Naked, he felt vulnerable. He hurried to put on the underclothes that Feltzer had sent over with him. He shaved with the hotel razor and patted his face, wishing he had some cologne. The whole business still didn't make sense.

He wanted his papers. At least Feltzer could have given him his passport. Lupino knew he couldn't go one block without it, not with those Nazis everywhere. He put on the clean suit the SS men had given him. How would he shop for new clothes without his papers? Was Feltzer hoping he'd get caught and end up in that schoolhouse again? What the hell was going on here? Feltzer always knew how to put people off balance and take advantage of them, but he wasn't sadistic. Or was he? All Lupino wanted was to get out of there with his drawing. But, after this madness, it was better to be alive and without the Caravaggio than to die fighting for it. Maybe that was what Feltzer wanted. Maybe he was wearing him down to make him give it up.

Going down the stairs to the dining room, Lupino discovered

how weak his legs were. He should have been doing exercises while they had kept him in that pig pen. He held the railing and eased himself down to the main floor. Walking past the bar, he cast a glance into the smoky, velvet-lined room. *Scheisse,* nothing but strutting SS officers, lightning bolts and death heads all over the place. Girls? Mmm, yes, over there by the bar, one with a nice pair of legs. But that would be for another time. For now he just needed to get out of there. Tomorrow he would get to work on the clothes and shoes. How fast could a suit be ready?

He walked into the dining room and sat down to order his dinner and formulate a plan. The shopping would be a good test. If no one stopped him for the next two days, he'd leave before Feltzer returned. There probably wouldn't be a direct train to Switzerland, but he knew the Bolzano people had to go there sometimes. If he was asked for his papers at the border, he'd say they'd been destroyed when his house was bombed.

Three days later, Lupino took off the fine clothes that Feltzer had instructed him to buy and hung them in the closet of his hotel room. Then he put on the heavy windbreaker, hiking boots, and rucksack he had purchased with his own money. He glued on the moustache he had fashioned from his own hair clippings and pulled the windbreaker hood tight around his face. He was sweating as much from nervousness as from the heavy clothing. But during his strolls around Bolzano, he had never been asked for his papers and was quite certain no one had followed him. He glanced again at the train schedule that he had picked up from the front desk. His alpine walking stick in hand, he closed the door behind him, walked past the elevator, and took the service steps to the rear garden of the hotel. A few minutes later he'd reached the train station.

He bought a second-class ticket for the first leg of his trip and walked through the station hall, following the signs for platform #2. He waited until the last minute to push his ticket into the cancellation machine, to minimize any chance of being detected getting on the train. That done, he followed the passengers to the platform. So far, so good, no one looking at him, no one following him. He welcomed the sound of train wheels squealing into the station.

When the train stopped, he walked with a small group of travelers toward the second-class car. In a few more minutes, he would be safely out of there. As he put his foot on the bottom step, a man in a business suit approached him, smiling like an old friend.

"*Guten Morgen,* Herr Lupino."

A shiver ran across his shoulders. He ignored the man and pushed his way up the steps.

The stranger grabbed the hood of Lupino's windbreaker. "Won't you step down, please?"

Lupino almost lost his balance backing onto the platform. He realized that he'd seen the man before—in Bolzano, under the arcades and outside the shops. He had seemed to be just another tourist, but he'd been following him.

"*Bitte, kommen Sie mit.* Herr Feltzer will be disappointed if you're not in the hotel when he returns."

Now Lupino knew he had been Feltzer's prisoner all along. He dreaded what might lie ahead.

CHAPTER 26

"I know it's been a horrible, never-ending five days, Celeste dear."
Francesca took her raincoat from the hall closet and gave Constanz
a sympathetic smile. "I'm certain everything's all right with your
little Maria." She pulled out an umbrella. "If I haven't been very
kind to you, it's because I've been so terrified. But watching you
and seeing how brave you are, I've been very comforted, even
inspired."

"You were kind to take us in, Francesca." Constanz continued
dusting the hall table. Staying busy kept her from going mad
with worry over Monica.

Francesca sighed with exasperation. "Celeste, it does you no
good to be constantly cleaning the house." Gently she took the
rag away from her. "Come to Turin with me. We'll have some
coffee together and when I go to Gianni's office, you can enjoy
walking around on your own, even though it's raining again. Just
make sure you catch the bus for Montebello well before dark and
the bombings."

"But Giacomo and Bernardo are burying the fig trees this morning and they'll need lunch."

"No, Bernardo is going to Giacomo's family for lunch before going to Turin." She handed Constanz a heavy coat. "Here, it's getting cold out there. This coat of mine will keep you warm. I'll tell Bernardo where we're going."

In Turin, as soon as she and Francesca had finished their coffee—or rather, their wartime chicory—Constanz thanked her and left to walk under the arcades. She was not interested in the few fabrics and furniture still remaining in the shops. Instead, she headed directly for Via Regina Vittoria.

Standing outside a dark Gothic building, she pressed the buzzer. A gray, timeless face, hair pulled back in a bun, opened the door, eyeing Constanz as if she were an intruder.

"Please, I have to see Monsignor Pietro. I'm Celeste Campano."

The old housekeeper opened the door just enough for her to enter. "Wait here. I'm not sure he has time to see you."

While Constanz waited for Monsignor Pietro, gusts of wind and rain beat against the high windows. The minutes dragged by, and her annoyance rose that the Monsignore was making her wait so long.

"This shouldn't be," she said aloud.

"What shouldn't be?"

She hadn't heard the priest enter the room. He put out his hand as she stood. "Good morning, Celeste." Leading her into his office, he asked again, "And so, what shouldn't be?" He motioned for her to sit.

She raised her hands in a helpless gesture. "Gianni sent my

little girl off to Switzerland and I don't even know if she's being well cared for."

"Gianni did the right thing, Celeste." The priest's tone was kindly. "Your daughter is with a decent family."

"Did Gianni get the name of the Swiss family from you? He won't tell me anything, but you can tell me, can't you? I have to know if my child is all right." She sat forward. "Please, Monsignore, I have to know."

"Celeste, I understand your anguish. Maria will be fine. And when this horrible war is over, she'll come back to you." He nodded. "She won't forget you. Gianni has told me what a wonderful mother you are."

"Then please help me. I'm losing my mind with worry."

"Tell me, have the instructions given to you by the priest in Montebello in the past weeks helped you?"

"What on earth do you mean?"

"Do you feel any closeness to the Blessed Mother?"

"No, I do not. Of course, I know that she was a mother who must have suffered every day, worrying about her child. I've often thought that she, too, was Jewish, but it doesn't help me. After all, look what happened to her son."

He put up his hand. "Celeste, can you not see the close relationship of Catholicism and Judaism? After all, one grew from the other."

Constanz tried to control her irritation. "I understand, but it seems to me that your church has added on to my belief—as if it had embellished the truth."

"In what way?"

"I could never be Catholic in my heart. After all, you say that the only way to get to heaven is through Jesus. That means that my Claudio is lost forever. How could I ever believe that?"

Monsignor Pietro became more insistent. "Celeste, did the priest in Montebello not speak of baptism of desire, baptism of blood, baptism—"

"Yes, but those beliefs are too thin a thread for me to hang onto."

The priest stood up. "All right. I see that what you need is consolation and hope, not theology. Go to the church. Can you pray in a Catholic church?"

"I can't pray anywhere anymore. I was never good at it, and certainly not now."

"Then go into the church and just be still. Sit and look around you and open yourself."

"What do you mean? That isn't an answer."

"I'm not giving you an answer. I'm sending you in a direction."

"But I want answers," she said. "You must know something. Tell me!"

"I've told you what I can. You'll hear the choir practicing. Gianni tells me you're a musician. They're preparing for Brahms's *Ein Deutsches Requiem*. It's for the living, not the dead." He held out his hand to her. "Come with me."

The Monsignore guided her out of his office and down a corridor toward a side door of the church. When he left her, she opened the oak door and stepped inside. Her gaze was drawn upward to the ornately carved golden dome where Christ in glory was depicted in fresco. She glanced around the musty, empty church as the numbing dampness of the paving stones seeped into her feet. Sitting in a back pew, she knew she couldn't pray—she could only talk to Claudio. Where was he? He had her alone with their children, and now their daughter had been torn from her.

She shivered from the cold, or was it from the feeling of utter desolation? Standing, she wrapped her coat more tightly around herself. Flickering lights from a side altar caught her eye, their waxy scent mixing with the dank smell of the air. She wished she could feel the mystery of Catholicism, but her thoughts always went back to the synagogue in Padua. It was so welcoming with its wooden floor and large windows letting in the light. It had been like Claudio's second home. She walked to a side altar and sat on the bench, thinking that she had been open to everything and look what had happened. Only her son was left to her, and her memories. She wished she had learned how to pray. Here she was, as mute to prayer as if her tongue had been cut out.

The heavy main door of the church creaked open. Footsteps shuffled on the paving stones and climbed the circular stairs just beyond the altar not far from where she sat. She heard phrases being played on an organ, and then the haunting, urgent chords of Brahms's *Requiem* filled the somber church. She fixed her gaze on the wavering flames of the votive candles, remembering an evening when she was young and Vati had taken her to hear *Ein Deutsches Requiem* in Berlin. He had ordered a carriage for the ride to the Schauspielhaus. The lights of the city were just coming on as the horse clip-clopped down Friedrichstrasse. Her father belonged to her that evening, elegant in tails and top hat. Sitting next to her in the carriage he explained that some of the words of the *Requiem* were from the New Testament, but that there was no mention of Jesus Christ. The great Brahms had written not a Christian requiem, but a human requiem.

She heard a rustle of pages, people clearing their throats. The organ music started again, this time sweet and lilting. She knew what would follow. Voices rose, singing in German, gentle as a lullaby—"*Wie lieblich sind deine Wohnungen* (How lovely are Your dwelling places)." And then Claudio's beloved prayer—"*Meine Seele verlanget und sehnet sich nach den Vorhöfen des Herrn* (My soul longeth, yea, even fainteth for the courts of the Lord)." Those were the words he prayed when he entered the synagogue, or when he wanted to calm his thoughts and fears.

Her heart beating fast, Constanz walked to the bank of flickering candles. The back rows reminded her of a menorah. She chose to light one of those, whispering, "Since I am unable to pray, since I am mute, this will be my prayer."

A soprano voice soared above the rest of the choir. "*Ihr habt nun Traurigheit, aber ich will euch wieder sehen* (You now have sorrow, but I will see you again)." She thought of Claudio lying on their bed in the apartment in Padua, his eyes just opening, murmuring the words of his first morning prayer: "Lord, thank you for opening my eyes." Was he thanking God for giving him understanding, or for waking him to another day?

She sat again. Had something brushed against her back? She turned to see if someone had walked by, but no, there was no one. The choir sang, "*Ich will euch trösten, wie einen seine Mutter tröstet* (I will comfort you as one whom his mother comforteth)."

Claudio, you were like a mother to me, a father and a mother.

She became aware of a warmth starting at her feet and a sense of tranquility rising all around her, touching her face—and then it was gone.

The sensation of someone or something having entered the church lingered. Was it just her imagination, her mind playing tricks? And yet a sense of peace enveloped her. She walked slowly from the side altar to the great wooden portal. Outside the church, she saw that the rain had stopped. She touched her eyes with the backs of her hands.

"Thank you," she murmured. "I don't understand, but I thank you."

Riding out to Montebello on the bus, past the bombed out industrial sites and onto the mountain roads, she was glad for the silence—nothing to break the calm in which she was enveloped. She knew somehow that Monica was safe. And that Claudio was near. She whispered words remembered from Dante. "We're in a dark forest, but we're not alone. Yes, Claudio."

In Montebello she stepped from the bus and walked quickly down the wet, windy street. Fifteen minutes later, she pushed open the iron gate to the Baldisseras' villa, and then stopped abruptly. Something was not right. A black Mercedes-Benz with a German license plate was parked on the gravel driveway. Hans Hauptmann's car at this time of day, unannounced? He had found out she was Jewish! Who would help her? Gianni was at the office. Francesca wouldn't be home for another hour. Ben had already left for Turin. At least he would have a chance to run. She was pinned to the spot, unable to move in any direction.

The front door of the villa opened and Hans stepped out. He beckoned to her. "Celeste, I didn't expect you to be here. I just spoke to Francesca on the telephone and she said you were in Turin for the afternoon. Come in."

Slowly, Constanz walked toward him.

He took her arm and ushered her into the front hallway. "I'm so glad to see you," he said, shutting the door behind her. When he snapped the lock, her heart squeezed. In front of them, in the shadows behind the hallway credenza, stood two men.

Constanz's knees started to give way. In a faint voice, she said, "Please, I'd like to sit down."

*   *   *

Lupino and the stranger who had stopped him from boarding the train walked together in silence to the hotel. What was there to say? It didn't matter who the fellow was, he was from the Gestapo, sent to keep Lupino from leaving Bolzano. He eyed the man without turning his head. Leather coat, brown fedora, melt-into-the-crowd face. He should have looked for someone like him, should have known he was being watched.

In the lobby of the hotel, the stranger left Lupino and walked over to the newspapers rolled on wooden sticks for the hotel guests. Picking up *Die Zeitung,* he sank into an overstuffed chair near the door, opened the paper, and began reading.

Lupino, too deflated to walk up the stairs, took the creaky cage elevator to his room. Dropping onto the bed, he wondered what his next move might be. Should he try to get past his guard and take the cable car to the village on the mountain? It wasn't Switzerland, but perhaps he could hide out there in some *pensione* until the end of the war. No, if they caught him again, the Gestapo might just shoot him. The anger he felt toward Feltzer was so strong, he was nauseated.

He sat up and stared at the telephone. "I'll call him," he said aloud. Lifting the receiver, he asked the operator to get him Via Tasso in Rome.

"We have no authority to call long distance," the operator

informed him, "unless the SS presents itself to the reception desk." Lupino slammed down the telephone.

A thought—at least, since they'd gone to all this trouble, they didn't mean to kill him. But what did they want from him? He stood up and began pacing the floor. He looked at the clock. It was past dinnertime. Maybe his appetite would come back when he saw food.

He ripped off his moustache, threw his hiking clothes onto the bed, and dressed for dinner. Walking down the stairs toward the dining room, he wished he could vent his anger. If he couldn't get out of there soon, if he couldn't have his drawing, at least he wanted revenge. He glanced into the bar. Since the tab was completely on Feltzer, why not treat that redheaded fräulein, the one with the nice legs, to drinks and dinner? Not much revenge, but at least it would be something, having a romp at Feltzer's expense. He stepped into the noisy bar, threading his way through the SS officers, who seemed to pay no attention to him. Ah, there she was, sitting alone, twisting her beer glass, staring into space.

"Fräulein?"

She turned and smiled.

He got right to the point. "Would you care to have dinner with me?"

She stood abruptly, giving him her arm. "Yes, I've waited here long enough."

"Waited long enough?" he asked, walking her to the dining room.

"Yes. Some SS officers think a girl will sit around waiting for them at any time, any place."

"Well, that kind of person I'm not." He pulled out the chair for her.

She sat, pushing back her hair with one hand. He leaned forward. "I have a soft spot for red hair," he said.

"Your mother?"

"How did you know?"

"It's always the first thing a man says to me when his mother has red hair." She laughed, giving him a look as if he were a naughty child.

Dinner went well, with talk of how she was from Berlin and how she came to be in Bolzano—an SS friend had invited her to see the sights. She confided that her friend came around less and less often to chat with her, as she put it, and tonight had stood her up. She was glad to get away from the SS, so arrogant, think they're the rulers of the world. She gave him an engaging smile.

By the time dessert was offered, he had found out all about her. He told her that he was impressed that she had studied at the university for a year. He wanted to know what she had studied, but wouldn't she come up to his sitting room where they would be more comfortable and enjoy a *Schnäpschen* together.

"Don't get the wrong idea," she said, sitting back, away from him, "just because I said I'd have dinner with you."

"Of course not, I know a lady when I see one." He signed the check and asked the waiter to bring two schnapps to his room.

When they arrived at his room, Lupino was surprised to see that the door was ajar. The waiter, so soon? He pushed the door open, ushering his redheaded friend in ahead of him.

A man stood at the window, a briefcase resting against his leg, peering out at the dark night through the edge of the curtain. The broad shoulders, the chunky body, the bald spot in the back of his graying blond hair gave away who he was. Arms folded, Feltzer lifted his head at the sound of their footsteps. He turned to face Lupino.

"I—I didn't know you'd come back," Lupino said.

Feltzer looked the girl up and down. "I'm back and you look like a different man. Excuse us, fräulein, but we gentlemen have business to discuss."

The woman stared angrily at Feltzer. "You're all the same!" She tossed the words over her shoulder and walked out, slamming the door.

"So," Feltzer said, "enough small talk. It's time we got down to business."

Lupino looked at Feltzer, reminding himself to stay calm. Feltzer had everything, and for the moment Lupino had nothing.

CHAPTER 27

Ben knew it was risky but he had decided to call Silvia. He approached the clerk behind the counter and asked to make a telephone call to Venice.

"*Il numero?*" The man handed Ben paper and pencil.

As Ben wrote down the number of Silvia's aunt, the clerk studied his face and asked if he wasn't living with the Baldisseras.

Ben's heart leaped with fear, but there was no use in lying. "Yes, I'm the gardener's helper. Are the telephone lines up at the moment?"

"Earlier today they were. Go into booth number two and wait."

Ben sat inside the small booth, facing the telephone on the little shelf. Through the glass, he watched the clerk, hunched over his switchboard, working at making the connection. He heard the sound of his own breathing, magnified inside the narrow space. Let it be that the clerk didn't denounce him. Maybe it was just a casual question. And let Silvia be home—she was always there at that time of day.

When the telephone in his booth finally jangled, he jumped. He reached for the receiver and heard, "*Pronto,* Silvia Bellini here."

"Silvia, it's me."

He could hear her take in a little breath, the way she did when something delighted her.

"*Amore mio,* how are you?" she asked.

Ben looked up at the clerk and saw that he had the receiver pressed to his ear. If only Silvia understood the Veneto dialect that he and his father used when they didn't want to be understood. "I'm fine," he answered. "That's really all I can say at the moment."

"I've been waiting and waiting to hear from you."

A click. Ben saw that the clerk had put down his receiver. "I was told not to write or call anyone, but I couldn't stand it any longer. I had to hear your sweet voice."

"I can't think of anything but you, my love. Tell me what it's like where you are."

"Our house was once the manor house. We're on the outskirts of town. We have a nice garden and I help the gardener sometimes. Oh, I miss you so much. Today I learned how to bury fig trees. Maybe in the summer I'll be bringing you the new figs."

"I'd love that, but I can see you sooner than that."

"What do you mean?"

"It was my birthday yesterday," she said. "I'm twenty-one now and I can decide what I want to do—legally it's my own choice. Tell me where you are and I'll come to you."

"You mean it?" He felt his spirits soaring.

She laughed. "Of course I mean it."

Just as quickly, his spirits plummeted. "No, you really can't come here. It would be dangerous for you. You know my situation." He thought again of Giorgio having to give up his Catholic fiancée. He was putting himself in the same terrible situation.

"Then you don't want me to come?"

"Of course I do!" He paused. "But the people we're with wouldn't allow it."

"Didn't you say you're near a big city? I'll stay there. All the cities want workers in the hospitals, with all the casualties from the bombings."

"And how about your university classes?"

"Don't worry, I'll go back later. I'd rather be with you."

"I want to be with you more than anything in the world, Silvia —but how about your parents? What will they say?"

"My aunt was very upset, and so was my uncle. I've never heard him so angry before. But they can't get through to my parents on the telephone, so I'm ready to come to you. I've made up my mind—unless you don't want me. Are you happy that I want to see you?"

"Yes, yes. It's the most wonderful thing I can imagine." Would it be so dangerous for his family if Silvia knew where he was? If he could see her, if she could stay nearby, it would be a dream come true. He looked over at the clerk. He was reading a newspaper. "Silvia, I'm near Turin. But it isn't safe. The Allied bombers come every night. How can I put you in danger?"

"Is it really so bad?"

"They fly right over our village on the way to Turin. Everything in the house rattles. We have to get the glasses and vases off the shelves. And then we see the explosions."

"Well, find me a place to stay near you. I'm not afraid."

He really didn't want her to change her mind, so he said, "I'll meet you in Turin. What day will you be here?"

"Saturday."

"I'll meet you at Porta Nuova station, my love. I'll call you tomorrow at just this time to find out when your train comes in."

"I love you, Ben."

"Ciao, amore mio. I love you too."

He hung up the telephone, staring at it for a moment, wondering at the unbelievable news that he might soon see Silvia. He wanted to hold her in his arms and never let her go. He'd kiss every inch of her beautiful body. She shouldn't stay in Turin, with the waves of Lancaster bombers coming every night. But maybe Gianni could find her a place away from the industrial sites.

Crossing the street, he played their conversation in his mind, over and over. Silvia's sweet voice, her loving words ... he wanted his mother and Silvia to meet. He knew they would love each other. But perhaps Gianni would be angry and say that Silvia's coming jeopardized everyone. In that case, even if Gianni insisted that she leave, at least they would have been together one more time.

*   *   *

"Celeste," Hans said, "please do sit down."

The two men, their clothes wrinkled and worn, stepped from the shadows into the dim light of the hallway. Frozen with fear, Constanz looked at their faces. She put her hand to her mouth because they reminded her of her German cousins—they were Jewish! What was Hans doing with two Jewish men? Had he captured them and now wanted to take her along with them?

Hans cleared his throat. "Signora Campano, this is Herr Gruen and Herr Wallach. We have traveled a long distance. We stopped here to rest for a few minutes. I'll be taking them to a hotel." The men shifted from foot to foot while he continued. "I saw Gianni at the factory on my way here. He said that Francesca won't return until very late."

Why was he telling her this?

"Gianni will be late too. I should be back in about two hours. Would you be willing to give me some dinner when I return?"

She nodded, remembering to play her role.

Hans gestured for the men to follow him. As they moved toward the door, he paused and reached into his coat pocket. He handed her an envelope and left with the two men.

As they drove off, Constanz put her hand on her chest and sank back into the hall chair. She tore open the envelope. The message was terse: "Maria is well, already going to school. Be hospitable to Hans. I'll be home as soon as I can. G."

Thank God Maria was well! Be hospitable. Well then, she would try.

At six o'clock, the doorbell rang. Constanz looked out of the library window and saw that Hans had returned. Opening the door, she studied his face, trying to see him not as an enemy, but as someone to whom she must be welcoming. After greeting her, he took her by the elbow and led her toward the library.

Sitting next to her on the leather sofa, he said, "First, my dear Celeste ... may I say that?"

"I'm not sure you may." She was surprised at the sharpness in her voice.

"Excuse me. I just want to tell you what I know."

She was trapped. Why hadn't she run away while he had taken the strangers to their hotel?

"After I first met you, I thought about you, quite a lot. I was sorry to hear that your husband was separated from his family, stationed in southern Italy. I knew how much you must miss him and how difficult it had to be for you, so I made inquiries about him."

She stiffened. "Why did you do that? You had no right."

"I wanted to do something for you."

She stood and walked quickly to the window, looking out at the darkened garden. She folded her arms across her chest, steeling herself for his next words.

In a low voice, he said, "There is no Colonel Arturo Campano in the Italian army—anywhere in the Italian army. I learned that your husband had died, probably in his efforts to retrieve the Caravaggio sketch his son had found years before in Venice."

Constanz's heart stopped. She was bared, unmasked. How easy it was to be caught.

He continued, "I told no one—because then I supposed you were Jewish."

She didn't dare to look at him.

"It wouldn't mean anything to me," he said quietly, "except that I hope and pray that you stay safe."

She froze. This was how informers started out. She had heard those stories.

"I ... Believe me, Celeste, I mean you no harm." He hesitated. "All right, let me tell you why I really come to Italy."

She turned to face him. "Gianni already told me. You're seeing that tank parts are made for the German war effort."

He shook his head. "I do that in order to come to Italy. Let me tell you what I'm really doing. Then I'll have your secret and you'll have mine."

"Secret?"

"Yes. You saw those two men. I bring Jews across the border

with me, saying they're my assistants. Then I send them to safe houses in Genoa, until they can escape to Portugal and safety."

She studied his face. He could be lying.

He rose from the sofa and she stepped back. "Don't expect any secrets out of me."

"I don't," he said softly.

"Nobody wants to go the way of Count Hofer's refugees."

He frowned. "You've heard of Count Hofer?"

Her voice rose. "A catcher! Meeting wealthy Jews at cocktail parties, promising them safe passage to Switzerland. Then he takes their money and hands them over to the SS."

"Do I seem like someone who would do that?"

"A lot of Jews thought Hofer was trustworthy," she snapped.

"If that were my game, I wouldn't bother bringing Jews across to Italy."

"You could be putting them in the hands of the SS."

He shook his head. "My dear Celeste, don't you know that Hofer hands them over the next day? He doesn't go to all the trouble of taking people across the border and then turning them in."

She began to breathe more easily. Hans continued, "Gianni took Maria across the Swiss border. Who do you think introduced him to signora Chiara?"

"How would I know?"

"I introduced them to each other."

He went on to tell her why Gianni was absent so many nights. Like Ben, he was taking refugees to signora Chiara, leaving them off, and returning home at the end of the day.

Constanz cringed at the idea of Ben doing something so dangerous. She remembered that when she washed Ben's clothing, it often smelled of soot. She had wondered what was sooty in the factory. Now she realized that the smell came from his hours on the train.

Hans smiled at the light of realization in her eyes. "You never ask me much about myself. Did you know that my special love is art? I taught sixteenth-century art at the university in Switzerland. If not for the war, I would still be teaching art history." He was silent for a moment. "I have connections with the Gestapo." The breath went out of her. "None that would cause you harm," he said quickly. "The Gestapo think I work for them. I'm playing a dangerous game, but it's worth it for the information I get. In fact, I have my feelers out to locate the whereabouts of the Caravaggio drawing. I know that means everything to your son." He smiled again. "Bernardo and I have shared some interesting moments talking about Caravaggio. You can be proud of your son. He's an exceptionally fine young man."

Constanz shivered at the mention of Caravaggio. Should she really let herself trust this man?

He spoke softly again. "I've admired you since the first moment I saw you." His hand touched hers.

He seemed sincere, but was she being courted by the devil? She wanted to say that she believed him and that she wanted him to keep her family safe, but she looked down and didn't move. He put his fingers under her chin and turned her face up to his. "In another time, in another world, we would … "

She looked into his eyes and saw for the first time how deep a blue they were. He slowly drew near, but then broke away, saying, "We have important work to do, to see that this terrible war ends and that as few people as possible are hurt."

The horror of her husband's death washed over her again. She had just learned to make her grief more bearable by talking to Claudio and remembering his little sayings. And now this man was reminding her of feelings she wanted to put aside. She turned away from him and walked to the kitchen, grateful for the silence. The fire in the wood stove had gone out and the icy air cooled her cheeks.

By the time she had put the chicken and salad on the dining room table, she felt stronger. But when she stepped into the library and saw Hans standing at the bookshelves, his back to the doorway, she felt her face grow warm. She thought of the risks he was taking to bring Jewish refugees out of Germany. And because of him, her daughter was safe.

But she mustn't think about his goodness or his kindness. It was better to turn her mind to other matters. "I've put dinner on the table," she said in the lightest tone she could find.

He turned, and from the expression on his face, he seemed to have pulled back too. "Good. I've had a few hunger pangs. It's been a long day."

She felt confused again when he held the chair for her. "Did you not have lunch?" she asked.

"The one café we found open didn't have much to offer." He looked at her earnestly. "I have to return to Germany tomorrow, but I'll be back as soon as I can."

"I see." She looked down at her plate. "Tell me, are there any art galleries still open in Germany?"

He frowned. "No. Well ... only the approved art is being shown. I miss being able to see whatever paintings I like."

She smiled, because it was good to hear about the art world. It took her back to her long conversations with Claudio, all the museums they had explored together. "Where did you study?"

"In Florence and Rome, but of course I've never stopped studying. And then I'm always in contact with art historians like Berensen."

When Hans had finished his last bite of dinner, he pushed back his chair. "Celeste, you can't imagine how deceived we feel in Germany, my friends and I."

"What do you mean?"

"You haven't lived in Germany since when?"

"I went back and forth visiting until twelve or thirteen years ago."

"Of course you don't remember the days when you needed a suitcase to carry enough money for dinner in a restaurant."

"The early twenties? I knew about that. It was dreadful."

He talked on, trying to make her see how hard it had been for the German people. Millions were out of work; people on the street dropped dead of hunger before his eyes. Of course the Germans thought Herr Hitler would keep his promises and do something about the hunger and the gangs in the streets. Seeing her expression of disbelief, he insisted that, had she been there, she would have understood. There had been no order, no *Ordnung*. She was German, she would have had the same desire for order. So many people honestly believed this man could solve the problems.

She sat forward, saying that the Germans never should have believed that order could come out of strongarm tactics.

Hans shook his head. "I'm only saying that in the beginning, many people thought we needed a strong man—but then Hitler let the lowest elements of society take over. Some people didn't care because they were grateful to get heat for their homes. And so many homeless, where were they to turn?"

Constanz banged her fist on the table. "How could you have been so naïve? The German people should have seen from the beginning that everything Hitler did was terrible." She pointed a finger at Hans. "For heaven's sake, look how it's ending! In violence and degradation!"

He was firm. "You don't understand, because you didn't live there."

"Don't you tell me that! I have cousins who lived there and they understood." She stiffened her shoulders. "They've disappeared."

"Of course, you're right, Celeste, and I feel terrible guilt." His eyes grew dark. "That's why I'm doing everything I can to get people like your cousins to safety."

She stood. "It's not enough. Somebody has to get rid of that madman."

Hans's voice became quieter. "Celeste, there's a limit to what anyone can do. He has an iron grip on German throats."

"German throats? How about the rest of us? All of Europe!" Hastily, she lifted their dinner plates. "Somebody should have stopped him long ago." She glared at him. "And somebody should stop him now. You're even helping his war effort, coming down here getting tank parts from Gianni's factory."

He took the plates from her, explaining that what she was saying was not entirely true. He and Gianni were deliberately slowing production at the factory and helping the Partisans.

"Please give me those!" Plates in hand again, she walked to the kitchen, Hans in her wake. Close to tears, she scraped the dishes with a vengeance. She pushed past him to remove the rest of the things from the dining room.

When she returned to the kitchen, he was there, waiting. "I think you're determined to find some fault in me," he said.

"I'm just the housekeeper here, or whatever you like, and you're the guest and let's leave it at that."

She turned quickly to the sink.

"The last thing I want to do is upset you." He turned the faucet off. "I respect you and I sincerely care for you. Please know that I'm your friend and not your enemy." He stood close enough that she could feel the warmth of his body, but when she said nothing, he shook his head and retreated to the library.

Relieved that he had gone, Constanz stayed in the kitchen. She could hear the first wave of Allied planes coming in for their nightly bombing of Turin. The *poum-poum* of the first explosions sounded within minutes.

Finally she heard the doorbell ring and went to unlock the door. Gianni rushed in, saying, "Home just in time!" As he shut the door, Constanz heard the drone of the second wave of bombers.

From behind her came Hans's voice. "I've been waiting for you, Gianni. Can we talk for a few minutes?"

"Of course." Gianni joined him in the library.

After a few minutes, Hans reappeared in the kitchen. "Goodbye, Celeste," he said. "Thank you for dinner."

As she put Gianni's supper on the table, she heard Hans drive away. A feeling of emptiness swept over her. It was because she missed Monica so much, she told herself. It had nothing to do with Hans.

CHAPTER 28

Lupino's heart drummed hard in his chest, as Feltzer set his briefcase against the wall. To break the silence, Lupino asked, "When did you get back?"

Feltzer shrugged. "Do you remember our professors in Switzerland in the university?"

"Some. Why do you ask?"

"You took a course in Renaissance Art."

"Right, not my favorite."

Feltzer's voice rose. "I'm not talking about what you liked."

"Well, then, what the hell are you talking about?" Lupino retorted.

"Do you remember the professor?"

"Of course, a real stickler for research papers. He never went to the bar with the students. Spent all his free time going back to Germany to see his girlfriend." Lupino could still see the tall, aristocratic, straight-shouldered fellow. "Wasn't he from Essen? I remember that his father died during the term and he left to take over the family factory."

"Right, ball bearing factory," Feltzer said. "So you'd know him if you saw him?"

"Of course, if he hasn't changed a lot. Why?"

Feltzer took the chair next to the desk, while Lupino sat on the edge of the settee, wondering what the hell he was going to be told next. Feltzer rubbed his palms together and cleared his throat. He explained that the Gestapo had found out something very unfortunate about Professor Hans Hauptmann. It seemed that the Third Reich thought Hauptmann was doing his job for Germany, getting the Italians to move along on making tank parts, but it turned out he was behind the strikes at the Mirafiori factory in Turin and helping with slowdowns in other factories. He'd been collaborating with the Italians for over a year now.

Lupino was bewildered that he was being let in on state secrets.

Feltzer grimaced, telling him that even worse things were reported about Professor Hauptmann. He was taking Jews across the border, and furthermore was even giving the Italian Partisans information about German troop movements. He had enlisted a young Italian man to set up shop making four-pointed nails. Göring was incensed that the Germans had lost two hundred soldiers when truck convoys bringing troops into Turin had been sabotaged two weeks ago. Feltzer's voice rose as he stamped his foot and announced that any one of those acts was treasonous.

"I don't understand," Lupino said, bewildered. "Why are you telling me all this?"

"He has to be stopped and it has to be done quietly. We must avoid murders like we had last week—six SS men were gunned down in reprisal in a Turin café." Feltzer stood and strode across the room.

"But why—"

Feltzer put up his hand. "Wait. There's more. Two weeks ago I took the best German historians and art experts down to Rome to go through the Jewish libraries and select the books and papers to be taken to Germany. While they were there, I asked several of the art experts to have a look at your Caravaggio drawing."

"You didn't have to do that," Lupino said in a tight voice. "It was better to keep it quiet. I know art, for God's sake."

"No, no, no. It was done in strictest confidence. But you're correct—they agreed that the drawing is undoubtedly the real thing. My God, it's a fantastic, priceless treasure. They had all heard of the one Caravaggio preliminary drawing."

What was Feltzer trying to do to him? He stood. "Listen, Feltzer—"

"No, you listen to me! I asked my people to search out the Cantarini family, to see what else they might have."

Lupino stared at him, stunned.

"I found out that they had sold everything, except for some unimportant paintings in their summer villa." He lifted his briefcase onto the desk and looked away, lost in some other thought. "Listen, a lot of valuable paintings have passed through my hands this year, on their way to *Reichsmarschall* Göring, and it's my job to get more."

Thieving bastards, Lupino thought.

"This will interest you. Signora Cantarini and her son are hiding with a Catholic family in Turin."

"What? How long have they been there?"

"A few weeks. We understand that her daughter was living there, too, but she hasn't been at her school lately. She appears to have vanished. We don't know where she is, but in a matter of time, we'll find her."

"What the hell difference does it make? She's just a child."

Lupino remembered meeting the little girl on several occasions, a sweet, polite child.

"Jewish girls have babies when they grow up. We don't want Jewish grandchildren someday retaliating against the Third Reich." Feltzer drew a quick breath and continued. "I suspected that Hauptmann was working hand in glove with Gianni Baldissera, an industrialist in Turin, but imagine when I discovered that the Cantarinis had moved into the Baldisseras' household! For a year Hauptmann has been saying that Baldissera's factory was completely retooled and producing parts for German tanks—says he can't find the source of the slowdowns and strikes." In a barely controlled voice, he said, "He's the source! He's a traitor to the Third Reich. He has to be done away with."

"Done away with?"

"Killed."

Oh God, Lupino thought, the Cantarinis hiding in a house marked by the Gestapo.

Feltzer continued, "Hauptmann visits the Baldissera family frequently. We know exactly when he will be there again. This is where you come in."

"Where I come in?"

"Yes, you're going to help me."

"Oh, no—no!"

"For God's sake," Feltzer said, "we hunted together in Switzerland and you're a good shot. You rarely missed the mark." He paused. "It'll be over quickly and you'll have your Caravaggio and your passport and be on your way to Switzerland."

Lupino shook his head vehemently. "Are you crazy? I'm not a murderer!"

"This isn't murder. He's a traitor. We have to get rid of all traitors, so we can build our peaceful society." Feltzer's expression was hard and cold. "You want to be with us, don't you? Besides, you don't have a choice."

"No!" Lupino protested. "Look what you've done to me already. I give you a list of Jews, and instead of giving me the drawing, you put me in the middle of a roundup and leave me in that stinking school for a week. Now this! What next?"

"This is it. Look, it's fortunate that, at our level of society, we all eventually get to know each other, at least hear of each other. You have a splendid entrée, a perfect reason to visit your friends the Cantarinis and your old professor Herr Hauptmann."

"You can't mean that you want me to walk into that house and kill Professor Hauptmann!"

"Yes. We'll take care of everything else. We'll make it look like a robbery. That way the Partisans won't take reprisals."

"Good God, do you want the family too?"

"Not your worry, dear fellow."

"Look, take Hauptmann into police headquarters if you're so determined, but for God's sake leave me out of this. No, I won't do this."

Feltzer picked up the briefcase and walked to the door. He promised Lupino that the only way he'd get his drawing, passport, and safe passage home would be to take care of Hauptmann. Opening the door, he said he would be back tomorrow. If Lupino wanted him sooner, the reception desk would put him through to the commandant's office.

Lupino leaned against the wall, listening to Feltzer's footsteps fading down the corridor. He grasped his chest with both hands. "*Ach!* The bastard could give me a heart attack. How can he think I want the drawing enough to kill for it! He's crazy!" If Hauptmann were aiming a gun at his head, he could shoot to protect himself. But Hauptmann wasn't, so how could he do this?

He sank into the chair next to the telephone. Not to have the drawing? What was that compared to being forced to kill someone? He looked at his watch. Twenty minutes had gone by. He reached for the telephone, asked the reception desk for Feltzer's number, and hung up. The operator would call back when she had the connection.

He paced the creaking floorboards of the old hotel, pressing his clammy hand against his jaw to stop the involuntary twitching, as he waited for the telephone to ring.

*   *   *

Outside Turin's Porta Nuova train station, Ben stared at the black and red graffiti that greeted the crowds entering the building. *Not to the concentration camps, but up against the wall— give the Jews the flamethrower!* He shuddered with anger. What would Silvia think?

An hour later, the train from Venice pulled into the station. Ben looked into the face of each passenger stepping down to the platform. Where was Silvia? Suppose she had decided not to come after all. In the last group of passengers descending from the train, there she was! Flooded with relief and joy at her safe arrival, he ran toward her.

She set down her suitcases and fell into his embrace, saying that she had worried all the way from Venice that he wouldn't be able to meet her and that she'd never find him.

Holding her tightly, he asked how he could *not* be there. Then he whispered in her ear that she must remember to call him Bernardo.

"Yes, I remember," she said softly.

"I'm so glad you came," he said, pressing his cheek against hers.

"You really are?"

"Of course I am. I can't believe you decided to do this. It's wonderful and you're wonderful!"

"And you haven't met anyone else since I last saw you?" She looked at him with a worried expression.

"Never. I care only about you." He kissed her warmly. "What did your aunt and uncle say when you left?"

She lowered her voice. "I never heard my uncle yell like that—and at me! My aunt begged me to think of all the Catholic boys I could go out with. They feel so responsible for me." She looked down. "They're afraid for me."

He thought of the graffiti. "If I ever made trouble for you, I'd never forgive myself."

"I told them that it was my decision." She smiled. "I wouldn't be happy with anyone else."

"And your parents—did you ever reach them?"

She shook her head. "Telephone calls between Padua and Rome are forbidden by the Germans. Besides, I'm twenty-one now. It's my decision, you know."

He picked up her suitcase. "I'm so glad you're here, but I wish there was no war, no hatred, no fear. I wish your family wasn't so against us."

She gave him a long look. "I am here, my darling. And I'm here to stay."

"I love you, *amore mio*." He kissed her again. "Let's walk a bit. Do you know Turin at all? There are so many beautiful places. I want to show you the Piazza San Carlo, you'll love it." When they went out to the street, he remembered the graffiti and walked over to it. "I hate to have you see this, but you have to know what's going on. You could be in danger because of me."

She looked at the graffiti. "That's horrible! It makes me sick." She put her head against his shoulder.

"Silvia, I don't know what kind of future we can have. The war news is worse all the time."

"That doesn't matter. I just want to be with you." She looked at the graffiti again. "You told me what your father used to say. 'When there are no human beings present, let me remember to be one.'"

"If you're sure, *amore mio*."

"Oh yes, I'm absolutely sure." She smiled, taking his arm.

"Good," Ben said. "Silvia, I want you to meet my mother—soon, maybe tomorrow."

She frowned, saying she was worried Ben's mother would try to stop them from seeing each other.

He promised her his mother would love her, the way anybody would love her. He thought for a moment, and then said he'd tell his mother that evening that they'd both be at the Baldisseras' house tomorrow, around three in the afternoon. Signor and signora Baldissera would be home—and their house guest, Herr Hauptmann. Everybody would meet Silvia.

A cloud fell over her eyes at the mention of a German.

Ben assured her that Herr Hauptmann was all right. She had nothing to worry about. "I do believe you," she said. "And I know where I can stay. At the hospital in Venice they told me that I'd have no trouble getting a job as a nurse's aide at the University Hospital in Turin. They provide meals and a cot. They're desperate for workers."

"Good. It's only a five minute walk from here to the University Hospital complex." He picked up her suitcases again. "But we have to talk about tomorrow. The family I'm staying with is extremely nice, but signor Baldissera can be tough. He may worry that your being here will call attention to our family."

"I'll stay here in Turin and you can come visit me."

"Yes, but I want you to meet my mother tomorrow. We'll just see what happens then."

CHAPTER 29

Feltzer entered Lupino's room, a smug look on his face. "I'm glad you made up your mind to call me so quickly. Now let's talk about how you'll do this."

Lupino shook his head. He told Feltzer that he was mistaken. He had only called to say he wasn't going to do it. He just wanted his Caravaggio drawing and his passport. Feltzer shouldn't think he could buy him off like a whore, with nice clothes and a vacation in a fancy hotel. Lupino could afford all those things himself.

Feltzer's voice was hard-edged when he snapped back that Lupino wasn't getting anything unless he did as he had been told. After all, Feltzer was only trying to protect him.

"Protect me?" Lupino cried. "I was in that hell hole because you let me get trapped by your thugs and now I'm your prisoner in this hotel. I want no part of this terrible business. You have a hundred men who can do the job."

"Now listen, Lupino, be reasonable. The SS refuse to do the killing, because Hauptmann is working closely with the Partisans. If word got out that the Germans had executed one of the Partisans' key informants, there would be no end to the reprisals. That's unacceptable to Berlin."

"But why me?"

"Because you know Hauptmann. There would be no mistake. We will get the word out that this was a failed robbery and your name will never be mentioned. You'll be safely away in Switzerland."

"But it's insane. What if there are other people in the house?"

Feltzer waved away the question. "Hauptmann will be in Montebello in two days. I'll give you a driver to take you there." His voice took on a tone of strained patience. "I don't have time to go on about this, but you will do it. Everything's set in motion."

Beads of sweat trickled down Lupino's temples. He shook his head. No, he wasn't going to do it.

Feltzer raised his voice as he told Lupino he was doing him a gigantic favor. Why did Lupino think he'd been in that school for a week? Feltzer had been working on a way to keep him out of Dachau. He pointed to Lupino's hands. "You, with your soft art-dealer hands, do you think you'd last two weeks hauling rocks in that *Lager*—on two bowls of watery soup a day and a piece of stale bread?"

Lupino went numb. "You wouldn't let that happen!"

"Don't you realize that the Third Reich can do anything it wants, that all the power is in our hands now? If you don't do this, you'll go to Dachau, and if by some miracle you survive, we'll see that you'll be a pariah among your art dealer colleagues."

"You could never make my colleagues turn on me!"

"Oh, couldn't we? After we win the war, I'll be here and I'll let it be known that you arranged to have Claudio Cantarini taken by the SS. His blood is on your hands."

"But that's a lie and you know it! I only told you that Cantarini was on his way to Rome to get the drawing. I never asked to have your thugs beat him up. And I even told you that he had a heart condition! You were just going to question him for a few minutes and then let him go. But you got greedy and asked for a ransom." Blazing with anger, he shouted, "What about our friendship? I thought you were—"

"Dammit, you know that I'm your friend, but friendship has nothing to do with this. This is what Berlin has decided to do."

Lupino stared past Feltzer, picturing himself after the war—his reputation ruined, his business destroyed, heads turning away as he passed by, people whispering that he had betrayed his partner and caused his death. He glared at Feltzer. "You son of a bitch!"

"Wartime leaves us with few choices."

"How do I know that you won't hold Hauptmann's murder over my head?"

"Why would I do that? This episode will be forever behind us. Many things are happening these days that are simply swallowed up, gone, forgotten."

Lupino turned his back on Feltzer and walked to the other end of the room, arms folded and head down. He didn't deserve to die of starvation in a *Lager*. He hadn't gone through so much to be rejected and despised by his family and friends. He thought of the years of study he'd gone through, the never-ending effort to build his reputation, to make the right connections.

Feltzer's words cut into his thoughts. If he refused ... Well, why should he and Hauptmann both lose their lives?

Lupino reasoned to himself that either he did this or he'd have no life worth living. He was trapped. He turned back to Feltzer.

"All right, dammit, I'll do it."

"That's a wise decision, old friend." Feltzer reached into his briefcase and pulled out a Beretta. "You'll use this."

Lupino stared at the Beretta and shook his head. "I've never used one of those."

"Nicest pistol I've ever fired—easy to use. You'll have no trouble." He gave Lupino a reassuring clap on the shoulder. "We know that Hauptmann is right now taking some Jews into Turin and that he'll almost certainly stay with the Baldisseras for a day or so. That's his pattern." Feltzer set the pistol on the desk. "As I said, the driver will take you to Montebello. He'll wait while you make a surprise social call. When the job is done, you'll run out to the car and he'll drive you to Switzerland."

"You haven't answered my question. What will I do if other people are there?"

Feltzer shook his head. "Signor Baldissera and his wife and the Cantarini son have been going into Turin every day. They don't return from the factory until seven in the evening. I told you that they've sent the child away somewhere, so it's just signora Cantarini and Hauptmann. Signora Cantarini will be so surprised, she'll cause you no trouble."

"Then signora Cantarini will know I did this."

"We'll see that she will never tell anyone."

"Good God, what does that mean?"

"That's our business. Don't lose track of what you have to do."

"How will I know Hauptmann is in the house?" Lupino asked.

"Good," Feltzer said. "You're beginning to focus on the details. Hauptmann drives a black Mercedes-Benz. If it's parked in the driveway, he'll be inside."

"And if the car isn't there?"

"The driver will know what to do." Feltzer lifted the Beretta from the desk. "He'll hand you the pistol as you leave the car to go into the house. Oh, by the way, your driver will be downstairs in the lobby of this hotel until tomorrow, so don't get any foolish thoughts about not doing this job." He added, "All the hotel doors are locked, except the front door."

Lupino nodded numbly, feeling as if he was suffocating.

Feltzer returned the Beretta to his briefcase, reminding Lupino to be ready early in the morning to leave for Montebello. If he did a good job, he'd be rewarded with his passport and his Caravaggio drawing and he'd be on his way to Switzerland.

He opened the door, and then turned around again. "I forgot to tell you that this pistol throws a fraction to the left."

After the door clicked shut, Lupino was still for a moment, unable to think. Pull yourself together, he told himself. *Ach, mein Gott!* He remembered a story. Was it true? Who had told him? As punishment for not working hard enough in Dachau, they made you stand up for a day and a night, no food, no water. No, he wasn't going to Dachau, whatever he had to do. He tried to picture Professor Hauptmann. He'd had such respect for him. How many years since he'd seen him? Twelve, fourteen?

Lupino's insides were churning, twisting in his gut. He staggered to the bathroom, a bitter taste rising in his throat. He leaned over the toilet, his hands braced on the wall. He retched and vomited, and then sank to the floor.

*   *   *

The day after Ben met Silvia at the train station, Constanz, in her best suit, was sitting on the sofa in the library, trying not to seem nervous. Looking from Francesca, to Gianni, and to Hans, she said, "Silvia may be a bit intimidated with all of us here when she comes in. I mean …"

"Celeste dear," Francesca said, "didn't Bernardo tell you that he hoped we would all be here?" She waved a hand to include Gianni and Hans. "You know that we'll all be welcoming to Silvia."

"Yes, of course."

Ben had come into her bedroom the night before, telling her the news. He'd met a girl in Bolzano and her name was Silvia. He'd seen more of her in Venice, and now she'd come all the way to Turin to be with him.

"I suppose," Constanz went on, "the war makes everything seem more important, more urgent, but this certainly is not the time to become so attached."

"He's twenty-one," Hans said. "Old enough to know his mind, I should think. Look," he added reassuringly, "he even seemed glad that I would be here this afternoon."

Gianni grinned. "He admires you, Hans. After all the trips you and he have taken together over the past several weeks to signora Chiara's, he should. And when I think of all the trouble you've made together for the Nazis … "

Constanz looked at Hans, saying she was proud of the work Ben was doing with him, even though she dreaded the danger. But couldn't he see that the presence of this young lady would call attention to the household?

Gianni agreed that girl or no girl, Bernardo shouldn't be seen too much around the village. But if he and Silvia stayed out of the public eye, he thought it was manageable.

Constanz turned to Francesca, hoping that, as a woman, she would understand that Ben asking his mother to meet Silvia made it so …

Smiling, Hans reminded her of the German expression about love coming unbidden and when least expected.

The sound of the doorbell cut in. Constanz jumped up from the sofa and looked at her watch, saying as cheerfully as possible, "Right on time, two thirty." Smoothing down her skirt, she added, "Here we go."

Francesca patted her. "Go on, answer it."

She opened the door, wondering what Silvia would look like, hoping she would be a sensible girl. The two of then stood on the front steps, Ben's arm around a pretty young woman.

"Mamma, this is Silvia."

"Hello, Silvia." She took the young woman's hand, impressions racing through her mind. What a beautiful, compassionate face— and such a radiant smile. No wonder Ben was so attracted to her. But he hardly knew her. No, the whole thing was impossible. "Come in, children," she almost said, but realized that her son and Silvia were hardly children.

"Hello." Silvia's voice was undeniably sincere. She pushed back her long dark hair in a way that showed she, too, was tentative about this meeting.

"Please come in and meet signor and signora Baldissera, and Herr Hauptmann."

As they walked toward the library, Ben took his mother by the elbow. Lowering his voice, he said, "Mamma, stop a minute. I want to introduce Silvia as my fiancée. We've decided on that."

Constanz's smile faded from her face. "Oh dear … But can't we talk about this first? I mean, in these times, you know. Silvia, you're a lovely young lady. I have nothing against you, but this is so unwise."

"Silvia and I are engaged." Constanz knew that tone of voice.

Ben sounded exactly like Claudio when he had made up his mind.

She wanted to ask how they could be engaged when they couldn't even be married, but then she looked from her son to Silvia. The love in their eyes said that they had given up any consideration of the real world around them.

Constanz tried to imagine the years ahead. Suppose the bombings were in vain? Suppose they never were liberated? No home of their own, always running and hiding, pretending to be what they were not?

What would Claudio say of all this? Did anyone else take Claudio into account anymore?

Ben put his arm around her shoulders and reminded her that she had left her parents to go with Papà. He loved Silvia as much as Papà had loved her. His love was as strong as theirs, and he would be careful.

"Careful?" She shook her head, and then straightened up. "So be it." She walked into the library with Ben and Silvia, saying, "Francesca, Gianni, Hans—Bernardo is here with Silvia."

"Silvia is my fiancée," Ben added, his voice resolute.

"Oh my, this is a surprise," said Francesca.

Gianni grinned. "One look at the two of you and there's nothing to be said, except that this calls for Champagne. I've been saving a nice bottle in the cellar for the end of the war, but this is an important occasion too."

Constanz gave Gianni a warning look, hoping to avoid a celebration. He either didn't understand her message or chose not to.

Francesca took Silvia's hands. "My mother once told me that something about love is always wrong, and it's what's in the heart that counts. Do you truly love this young man?"

"With all my being," Silvia answered.

"Congratulations!" Hans held out his hand to Ben and nodded encouragingly.

"Thank you," Ben said, shaking his hand.

In a moment, Gianni returned with glasses and the Champagne. The cork flew across the room, hitting a book. *"Evviva!"* Gianni cried. "The cork got Nietzsche square in the spine. Too bad it wasn't the man instead of the book." Even Constanz had to laugh.

She held the silver tray while Gianni poured. He lifted his glass. "A toast to this lovely couple. May they live long and always know happiness together! May they have many loving children!" He took a breath to say more.

"Lovely, Gianni," Francesca said. "Now let us have a chance to raise our glasses to what you've said so far."

"Oh yes, of course." They all sipped their Champagne, and then Gianni continued, "Just a surplus of enthusiasm. A beautiful woman makes me talkative. An old habit, can't help it." He opened his arms to Silvia, who shyly embraced him. He gave her a resounding kiss on each cheek. "Welcome to our family." He looked at Constanz. "Do you mind if I call you family?"

"I'm honored, Gianni." She could see that Silvia was probably the right girl for her son, but she thought of what Ben had told her about his friend Giorgio. What kind of trouble would this bring?

"Sit down, everyone," Gianni said, "and let's get to know Silvia."

Constanz sat next to Silvia. Listening to her, she was struck by the young woman's sincerity and the way she spoke of her parents with great pride. It was a wonderful moment, but she couldn't help wishing Monica were there. Did Ben miss his sister as much as she did? She stared at the fire in the fireplace. How kind of Gianni to think of lighting it. And how good of him to call her family part of his family. She was grateful for what he had given her—warmth and kindness and safety.

CHAPTER 30

Lupino stood on the front steps of the hotel, staring into the cold November morning. He had finally accepted that he must kill Hauptmann in order to obtain his own freedom. Yet he was bothered by a lingering concern that Feltzer would demand something more before letting him cross the border. He looked up at the sky. The sun was struggling through gray clouds. Rain or snow would have suited his mood better.

Beside him was a suitcase holding his new clothes, all paid for by the Gestapo. He'd get rid of the valise as soon as he reached Switzerland, no reminders of bad times once he was home. There would be plenty of work then, with wealthy Jews spiriting their paintings across the border from all the European countries. Yes, dependable Swiss neutrality, and he would be there to take advantage of it.

"Guten Morgen." A dark-complected man in a leather coat approached Lupino. "Your car is across the street."

Lupino's heart sank when he saw his driver. It was the same man who had forced him to go back to the hotel from the train station. Gestapo, but he would still demand that the man show him the contents of his briefcase.

"Good morning," Lupino responded. "I need to see my briefcase."

The man nodded in agreement and led the way to the car park. He opened the trunk of his limousine, retrieved Lupino's briefcase, and handed it to him.

Lupino was going to take his time. He unlatched the briefcase and looked inside for the Caravaggio.

"We have a schedule to keep," the driver said.

"That may be," Lupino snapped, "but I have to see something here." He pulled out the drawing and unrolled it, thinking that Feltzer had better not have replaced the original with a copy. He examined the Caravaggio closely and satisfied himself that it was the authentic one. "All right."

He replaced the drawing in the briefcase and the driver returned it to the trunk. Lupino slid into the backseat of the limousine. When the driver took off his leather coat and sat behind the wheel, Lupino spotted the holster and gun he was wearing.

"Your gun is in the glove compartment," he announced to Lupino.

As the car descended toward Verona, an autumn mist of the area rolled in, turning the empty stalks of the vineyards into skeletal figures. The thickening fog muffled the sound of the engine, making Lupino more aware of the constant thrumming in his stomach. To reassure himself, he repeated an old refrain, taught him by his father: "When comes the moment to decide, the brave man chooses, the coward stands aside." Yes, those English knew how to face a difficult situation. Once he got through this, it would be as Feltzer had said, swallowed up and forgotten. Then his life would be his again. Let's see. Lupino ran through the plan he and Feltzer had worked out.

Feltzer had said only Professor Hauptmann and signora Cantarini would be at the house. The driver would park out of sight, and Lupino would hide the Beretta in his pocket. Professor Hauptmann was certain to open the door. No one sent a woman to the door in these times. He would ask Hauptmann to step outside for a talk, about business. That way signora Cantarini wouldn't see him.

As the car followed the road curving along Lago di Garda, speeding in and out of tunnels, Lupino went over the plan again and again, adding more details each time. Feltzer had said that in case signora Cantarini saw the shooting, he would "take care of things." Lupino allowed his mind to stay vague on what Feltzer meant by that.

At the southernmost end of the lake, the fog lifted and he saw the majestic snow-capped Dolomites falling away to the north. After another half hour, the wide plain of the Po Valley stretched out in front of them.

Seemingly endless hours later, Lupino looked at his watch. Only one o'clock. They'd be in Montebello by three—if the Allies hadn't bombed the roads last night. He looked at the back of the driver's head and wondered how much the man knew. The fellow must have details of their mission, because he had mentioned Lupino's pistol in the glove compartment. In two hours Lupino would confront Hauptmann. He had his plan and it would be all right. But he would have to make certain no one in Switzerland found out—especially Mutti and Father.

Now the driver called over his shoulder, "See the sign?" The wooden road sign indicated that Turin was one hour's drive away.

Lupino looked at his watch. Soon they would be in Montebello. His breath began coming quickly. Putting his head back, he told himself that he mustn't panic. In fact, he must be eager to arrive there and get it over with.

At a few minutes before three, Lupino and the driver were bumping over the dirt roads of Montebello. Although it was only mid-afternoon, the sun was already beginning to disappear behind the mountains to the west. The driver slowed and stopped in front of a small stone building. Lupino saw over the entrance *Posto di polizia*, and realized that the SS must have taken over the police station here too. Without speaking, the driver left the car and disappeared into the building.

Five minutes later, he returned. "I called Herr Feltzer. He wanted to know when you arrived." He started the motor, backed up, and drove down the narrow street, toward the outskirts of the village. Several minutes more, and Lupino saw that the road had become a narrow lane edged by fields and very few houses. The driver pulled up outside the entrance to a half-timbered villa, stopping ten feet short of the front gate. Turning to Lupino, he said, "I'll wait for you here on the road—I'll park behind the wall." He took his gun from his holster and with his other hand reached into the glove compartment and drew out a pistol. "Here's your Beretta. I'll expect you back within fifteen minutes."

Lupino's hand was shaking when he took the pistol. He slipped the gun into his coat pocket and got out of the car. He walked to the iron gate and pushed it open, hoping he wouldn't find Hauptmann's car in the driveway. It was there, a black Mercedes-Benz parked under the porte cochere. *Scheisse*, he thought, swinging the gate against the inside wall to allow himself a quick exit. He crossed the driveway, treading carefully on the gravel.

He stopped short. Through the front window of an office or perhaps a library, he saw a group of people laughing and talking. He was shocked. He saw signora Cantarini. But who were those others? This was terrible! Now what should he do? Go back to the car? Somehow he'd have to get Hauptmann alone. He would get him to come outside. He approached the front door, feeling for the Beretta in his coat pocket, and then told himself to take his hand out of his pocket. He mustn't give anything away.

He rang the doorbell. Footsteps approached. The door inched open, far enough for Lupino to see an older man, a ring of gray hair and a reddened face. It must be Baldissera.

"Yes?" the man inquired, opening the door farther. Next to him was a tall, aristocratic man. Despite the years since university days, Hauptmann had changed little.

"*Buona sera,* Signori," Lupino said. "Sorry to intrude, but I am looking for Professor Hauptmann. I was a student of his at the university."

Hauptmann stepped forward to hold the door, looking confused and guarded. "I am Professor Hauptmann. What is it you want? You're coming at an awkward time."

"I took your Renaissance art course."

"And so? What are you doing here?"

"I have to speak with you privately, a matter of urgent business. Let me explain. Just step outside, please."

"No. You can tell your business right here." Hauptmann turned to Baldissera. "Why don't you go back with the others? I'll take care of this."

He wasn't going to come out. Lupino reached into his coat pocket, feeling for the Beretta, but before he could grasp it, Hauptmann gripped him hard by the elbow. "Come in. We'll talk inside." As he urged Lupino inside the house, Hauptmann scanned the front yard. "Who are you?" he asked. "How did you know I was here?"

Lupino was prepared. "You might remember Eric Feltzer, another student at the university."

"Yes, what about him?"

"He told me that you were working with signor Baldissera and I took a chance that you'd be here when I came to Turin."

"Really?" Hauptmann's fingers were beginning to hurt his elbow. "How did you get here?"

"My driver is over there, outside the gate." With his other arm, Lupino pointed to the entrance.

He knew he had to act quickly. Freeing his arm from Hauptmann's grip, he pulled the pistol from his pocket. He lifted the Beretta to the level of Hauptmann's chest. Lupino told himself to pull the trigger, but his hand was shaking too much.

Hauptmann took a step forward. "Feltzer sent you here? Why?"

"Don't move."

"I have a right to know why you've come here with a gun!"

Spittle gathered at the corners of Lupino's mouth. "You're a traitor to your country."

"Ah!" The other man's eyes lit with understanding. "You know that if you kill me, they'll kill you, that's how they work. Do you want to die?"

Lupino's tongue wanted to cleave to the roof of his mouth. "They're going to take me to Switzerland."

"Don't be a fool! They'll want you dead so you can't tell what they've done. Don't you see?" Hauptmann said quietly. "Once you do this, you're worthless to them. They'll kill you."

Lupino's hand wavered. Christ, he was right! The driver was out there waiting to kill him.

Hauptmann walked slowly toward him, his eyes fixed on him, his voice authoritative. "Aldo Lupino, I remember you. You're no killer. You're a gentleman from a fine family."

Lupino tried to pull the trigger, but his fingers had frozen. Hauptmann's hand covered Lupino's hand and lowered the pistol. "Aldo, listen to me, I'm the only one who can get you to Switzerland safely."

Lupino's legs were shaking under him. "But they're coming any minute now," he whispered.

Hauptmann quickly took the pistol from him and pushed him into the living room.

"Listen, everyone," he said, as Lupino stumbled into the room. "This son of a bitch was sent here to kill me, but I've made him change his mind. The SS know all about us. There's an armed Gestapo agent at the gate."

Lupino looked in horror at the assembled group, his mind and body frozen.

Constanz jumped up from the sofa. "Oh dear God, it's Aldo Lupino."

Ben sprang at Lupino.

"No!" Hauptmann yelled. "We have to get out of here right away. Francesca, you three women close up the house. Bring warm clothes and blankets and be at the front door in three minutes. Gianni, Bernardo, come with me to the back of the house."

Ben turned to Silvia and told her to follow his mother.

Baldissera took two pistols from a gun case on the wall, quickly loaded them, and handed one to Ben. As he left the room, forcing Lupino ahead of him, Hauptmann called back, "We'll be firing off shots. Don't worry."

Lupino thought, *I'm going to be a shield!* He felt the nose of the pistol grinding between his shoulder blades, pushing him through the hallway toward the back of the house. When the four men reached the back door, Hauptmann said, "Gianni, once we're outside, I'll take Lupino to the left. He and I will cross the garden and stay close to the wall until we reach the gate. Lupino, is the gate open or closed?"

"I left it open."

"Gianni, you and Bernardo go around the other side of the house. Stop just inside the gate where you can't be seen from the road. We'll cover the driver from two angles. Then I'll send Lupino out."

"The driver has a gun!" Lupino warned.

"We'll take care of him. We'll give him a chance. If he cooperates, we'll leave him tied up. If he resists … "

Baldissera nodded, and the four men moved outside.

"Go ahead, Gianni, fire two shots now," Hauptmann ordered.

Lupino flinched as the shots went off, the reports echoing against the house.

"All right, get in place," Hauptmann said. "Walk on the grass. The gravel is too noisy."

Without another word Hauptmann pushed Lupino through the grass until they stood behind the wall to the left of the open gate. More than twenty minutes had passed since Lupino had left the driver. Was the driver alone, or were there SS men with him now? Ben and Baldissera crouched at the other side of the gate.

"Go out to the road," Hauptmann whispered harshly in Lupino's ear. "Wave for the driver to come to you. Tell him the job is done, but you need help. If you do anything else, I'll kill you. Now go!"

Lupino walked out to the road and waved frantically, yelling, "Help me! I need help!"

The driver jumped out of the car, slamming the door. "What is it?" he shouted. "Did you do it?"

The driver walked toward him, and even in the fading light of the afternoon, Lupino could see the pistol in his hand. "What's wrong?" the driver called.

Hauptmann rushed out to the road, shouting, "Drop your gun! If you move, we'll shoot."

The driver lifted his gun and fired. Lupino felt the sting of the bullet graze his arm and collapsed against Hauptmann, whose return shot went wild. When the driver lifted his gun again, Baldissera stepped forward and aimed. Another loud report rang out in the cold November air. The driver staggered, waving his gun wildly, blood spouting from his neck. He spun around and dropped, his neck awash in blood. A rivulet of red pulsed from his mouth, puddling in the shell of his ear. Baldissera lowered his pistol, muttering, "Damn! This gun kicks like hell."

Lupino struggled to his feet and leaned against the wall, holding his wounded arm.

Hauptmann searched the driver's pockets, found his official papers, and quickly studied them. Next he told Ben to help carry the driver's body across the road to the ravine. "Gianni," he called, "you take Lupino inside and wrap his arm."

Ben watched Gianni and Lupino walk toward the house, tempted to put another bullet in Lupino. But Hans was right, they had to hurry. He lifted the dead driver's legs, surprised at how heavy the man was. At the steep part of the hill, he and Hans released the body, and it quickly rolled on its own, bouncing over the rocks on its way to the bottom of the ravine.

When they returned to the car, Hans put on the driver's coat and hat and climbed behind the wheel. Ben got in beside him. They pulled up to the front of the house. The three women ran out, followed by Gianni pushing the wounded Lupino. Ben saw his mother's eyes widen with fear as she caught sight of Hans in the driver's leather coat.

Hans saw it too. "This way I'll look more like Gestapo," he explained. "Everybody in the car. Hurry!"

"Lupino's elbow is grazed, that's all," Gianni said. "I bound his arm enough to stop the bleeding."

Hans told Gianni to get in back with Constanz and Francesca. "Silvia, you sit in the jump seat. Lupino, lie on the floor in the back." As the car spun off, spitting gravel, he added, "Gianni, if we're stopped, throw that blanket over him."

Hans slowed the car and turned onto Montebello's narrow main street. Ben was grateful that the sun had already gone behind the mountains. The limousine was moving along in semi-darkness, and a cold wind whirled dust against the car. The smell of the air meant snow. As they drove in silence through the village, Ben saw the shutters of the stone houses lining the road were closed tight. Smoke from the chimneys meant that the families were drawn in by their fireplaces for the evening, enjoying their family supper.

Hans glanced at the empty sidewalks. "Good, no patrols outside, too busy staying out of this freezing air." He drove to the bottom of the hill, peering through the growing darkness for the turn onto the highway. "Celeste," he called back, "are you all right?"

"Yes," she answered in a subdued voice. "I'm all right."

Ben looked back, trying to see his mother's face. He reached behind him to hold Silvia's hand. "I didn't think you'd be in danger like this, and so soon. I'm sorry, *mia cara.*"

She leaned forward to whisper in his ear, her voice shaking, "I'm scared. Just promise you won't leave me."

"You'll be all right, Silvia," Hans said. "But I'm afraid you'll have to go with us and work your way back to your family later."

"Herr Hauptmann," she asked, "where are we going?"

"Switzerland, I hope." He checked the rearview mirror, and then looked at the gas gauge, shaking his head. "I don't know where that driver thought he was going to find gasoline at this time of the evening. It's already below half a tank."

A few minutes later, he swung onto the highway, saying, "This is the best time to travel, when soldiers stop for supper."

Lupino groaned. "Be quiet," Hans snapped.

A half hour later, Ben broke the silence to ask Hans if he knew where they were.

"Soon we'll be on the roads we use to get to signora Chiara's."

Within a few minutes they were passing a stretch of open land, and Hans announced they were near Lugano.

Suddenly, Ben saw beams of light swinging in arcs in the distance, illuminating the road and surrounding fields. "Should we turn around?" he asked in a low voice.

"No, we don't have enough gas to retrace our way. I think we're coming to a roadblock." He slowed down. "Gianni, throw the blanket over Lupino. I'll talk for everyone. Bernardo and Gianni, be ready to shoot."

"To wound or to kill?" Ben asked, his breath short.

"Kill if you must. But do nothing until I tell you to. You women, be ready to drop to the floor."

"What do you see?" Gianni asked.

"I see two soldiers and a guardhouse. There could be more men inside."

"I'm terrified," Francesca whispered.

"Stop it," Gianni commanded. "Act calm, these soldiers can smell fear."

Hans stopped next to the guardhouse. Ben gripped his pistol and waited.

CHAPTER 31

One of the soldiers walked toward them, tossing away his cigarette. The sweep of a searchlight caught the other soldier standing against a wooden barricade. "Now quiet everyone," Hans whispered, rolling down his window.

The soldier leaned toward the car, shining his flashlight on Hans's face. "*Wohin farhen Sie?*"

Ben saw the fellow was just a teenager. In spite of his effort to sound manly, his diction revealed that he was no more than a well-brought up schoolboy.

Hans drew himself up behind the wheel. "I am on official business—orders from Berlin."

The young soldier thrust his hand into the car. "Let me see your documents."

"My orders come from the Führer himself." Hans handed him the driver's papers.

The soldier frowned as he played his flashlight over the papers. "This says you are to go to Turin."

Hans raised his voice. "Well, we are coming from Turin and now I'm doing what I must do next."

The soldier flashed his light into the backseat. The beam fell on the blanket below Francesca's knees, hesitated for a moment, and then moved on. "Who are these people with you? I want to see their papers."

"They're my responsibility. For God's sake, young man, you're interfering with Gestapo business! How many ways do I have to say it?" Hans put the limousine in neutral and revved the motor.

The other soldier, a man in his thirties, even more stern and authoritative, stepped away from the barricade and approached the car. "What's going on here?"

"What's going on," Hans roared, "is that I have important Gestapo business and this fellow is delaying me."

The younger soldier said, "His papers say he's on Gestapo business in Turin, but he's heading toward Lugano."

"Give me the papers," the second soldier said. "I'll call in and see what this is all about." He took the papers into the guardhouse. Hans could see his flashlight swinging around inside the room, settling on a desk. The younger soldier walked to the back of the limousine, beaming his light on the tires as he went.

"Everybody get down!" Hans yelled. He threw the car into first gear and took off. Francesca and Constanz pressed themselves down as far as they could. Gianni pushed Silvia down. Ben gripped the dashboard as Hans crashed through the wooden barricade, sending it flying into the air.

From behind the speeding limousine, shots rang out, raining on the trunk. Hans pushed hard into second gear.

Ben took a hurried look behind him. "One of them is on a motorcycle. He's gaining on us."

"He's hit our tire!" Gianni shouted.

The car veered from left to right and back again, slowing

down even though Hans kept his foot on the accelerator. "Go ahead, Bernardo, shoot!" he yelled.

The soldier was even with the back of the car. He fired off two more shots at the tires. Ben leaned out the window, the night air slamming against his face. He fired at the soldier's chest. The man's hands flew off the handlebars, his body catapulting into the air and out of sight.

"I got him, he's down," Ben yelled.

The car bumped helplessly, swinging over to the left side of the road. Hans went fifty feet farther, gripping the steering wheel, grinding on metal rims. The car finally shuddered to a halt.

"Everybody out!" he shouted.

Ben and Gianni jumped out of the car. The women and Lupino scrambled after them.

"My briefcase!" Lupino shouted. "I must have my Swiss passport! Get it out of the trunk!"

"We don't have time for this," Gianni grumbled, but he took the key from Hans, opened the trunk, and thrust the briefcase at Lupino.

"Come with me—hurry!" Hans ordered. Constanz and Francesca followed him into the high grass at the side of the road.

"Bernardo, go ahead with Silvia," Gianni said. "I'll be right behind you. I'll take care of Lupino."

Ben took Silvia's hand. "Are you cold, sweetheart? Do you want my jacket?"

"No, I'm all right."

"This field is a farmer's acreage," Hans called back. "Quite flat, no streams or rocks. Just stick close to me."

Feeling like a blind man, Ben walked ahead in the dark, his face wet with the first snowflakes. From time to time Hans assured the group that they were going in the right direction, that they mustn't lose courage and that they were nearing signora Chiara's house. In between the assurances, Ben listened for the *shush-shush* of Hans's footsteps through the grasses ahead of him. When Francesca called out that she had a stitch in her side, Hans said that he was sorry, but she must keep up the pace. From time to time Ben glanced behind him, fearing any sight of flashlights.

The field had become a bog. "My shoes are being sucked into the mud," Silvia murmured.

"It can't be much farther," Ben said, holding her hand more tightly.

As the wind picked up, bringing the snow in earnest, Hans called out, "The house is just ahead, signora Chiara's house."

"Who is signora Chiara?" Silvia asked Ben.

"She's a friend of Gianni and Hans. Her property is partly in Switzerland. We'll keep walking past her house to the back of her property."

"There it is, not much farther," Hans said. "Keep going."

Between the gusts of snowflakes, the outline of the villa appeared.

Silvia caught enough breath to say, "Thank goodness."

Ben put his arm around her shoulders. "We have to go half a mile beyond the house, then we have to get past the border guards."

CHAPTER 32

TWO WEEKS LATER—OUTSIDE BERN

"Mutti, I'm going to work in the library." Lupino picked up a sheaf of papers from the console table in the hall and put them under his good arm.

"Turn on the lights, *Schatzi*. It's already getting dark. You don't mind if I leave you alone for a few hours?" His mother reached for her gloves and hat in the hall closet. "I'm so glad you're home."

"No, I'm fine. It's good to be here." Once more Lupino felt a wave of relief to be safe at home in Switzerland. The Caravaggio was in the vault behind the portrait of Grandfather Lupino in the library. Mutti and Father had asked no probing questions about it, and Father had even surprised him by being delighted to have him home again.

Now his mother pulled on her kidskin gloves and, looking in the hallway mirror, gave a final tug to the half-veil of her velvet hat. She smiled with satisfaction and pursed her lips to send him a kiss. "I won't be late, let's say midnight. If Father telephones from his meeting, tell him I'll be home soon."

"Good night, Mutti." Lupino felt a pang of regret at being left alone. The manservant had built a roaring fire for him to enjoy while he worked in the library, and it would have been good to sit sipping a schnapps with Mutti, chatting about this and that. Or perhaps he should have looked up some old friends and invited them over for drinks. He shuddered, thinking of how close he had come to being killed. Suddenly, in this house where he had grown up, far from the center of Bern, he felt very alone.

He turned on the desk lamp and put down his papers. Stepping over to the bar, he poured himself a schnapps—"an angry schnapps," one of his girlfriends used to call it, when you have to drink by yourself. He sat at the desk and twirled the glass in his hand. The little movement hurt his wrist, reminding him of the pain he had felt stumbling through the blinding snow and wading through the icy stream. And then, thank God, Hans had said, "You're in Switzerland, go on your way."

He took a sip of schnapps and lifted his pen, tapping his chin. As he looked around the room, he began to feel more settled. The familiar dark furniture was a balm to his soul. Home, thank God, home. He turned off the desk light and walked to the French doors on the other side of the room. Peering through the slightly parted draperies, he looked out at the night and the falling snow. Yes, it felt safe to be in the weather he knew so well from his childhood, lovely new-fallen flakes nestling into the snow banks. He drew the dark velvet draperies together, turned on the light again, and bent to his work.

Some time later, he looked up, startled by—what was that noise? It was almost as if the wind had slammed a door shut. Where had it come from? Some other room. Perhaps the hallway. Footsteps? So soft, but he heard footsteps.

"Hullo!" he called out. No answer. It must be Mutti coming

back for something, tiptoeing down the hallway so as not to disturb him. "Mutti, is that you?"

Silence. Nervousness tingled at the nape of his neck. He'd heard of refugees breaking into houses, desperate for food. So many foreigners now fleeing Germany. No one had come to any harm. Still, you never knew. He opened the drawer of the desk. Father's gun, where was it? *Scheisse,* Father must have moved it. He walked across the room to the hallway. It was quiet now, but cold, as if the frigid Alpine air had crept into the house.

He narrowed his eyes, straining to see into the dark hallway. A figure was silhouetted against the dining room door and was moving toward him. The manservant must have come back from his evening off. "Johann, is that you?" Lupino called out, but there was no response.

It must be an intruder! *My house, damn you!* At least they never had guns, those refugees, that's what everyone said.

Lupino called out again. "What do you want?" He was surprised that his voice had no depth, none of the fierceness he intended.

"Aldo Lupino?" a man answered.

"Who is it?" But he knew before the answer came.

The figure continued down the hallway and stood in the half-light not far from him.

"Eric Feltzer! What are you doing here?"

"No, no, no. What are *you* doing here? I sent you on an errand and you failed me. You killed a member of the Gestapo and one of our soldiers."

"No," Lupino cried. "I had nothing to do with it. They forced me into the car. Everybody was there. You said only Hauptmann and maybe signora Cantarini would be there!"

"Shut up, Lupino. Never mind. I've come for the Caravaggio."

He shook his head vigorously. "I don't have it." He could see Feltzer well now, the balding head, the plump face.

"Did you give it to Hauptmann?"

"No."

"Give me the drawing, Lupino. I didn't come all this way to be disappointed."

"I told you, I don't have it. It's in the bank. My mother took it down last week and put it in the vault in Bern. It really belongs to the Cantarini family."

"Do they know where it is?"

"No. If you come back next week, I'll have it for you." By then he could have the Swiss police waiting for Feltzer.

"I don't believe anything you say." Feltzer's hand moved to his coat pocket. "I know you. You kept it in this house." He stepped closer. "Where is it?"

Lupino stood frozen. "No!" he pleaded. "It's in the bank in town. If I had it, I would gladly give it to you, but I don't have it. Please go!"

"You are a useless, lying bastard." Feltzer withdrew a pistol from his pocket, a Luger. "I'm sick of you, I'm sick of everything about you!"

Instinctively, Lupino turned toward the telephone on his desk.

"Don't think you're going to call the police."

"Oh no, I won't, I never would!"

"I remember that vault." Feltzer pointed to the portrait of Grandfather Lupino. "Your mother went to it one day when we were on vacation here. Go open it."

If he gave Feltzer the drawing, he'd go away. His life was worth more than the damn sketch. "My mother said she was taking it into town, but maybe she hasn't yet." Lupino walked shakily to the portrait. Feltzer followed, pistol trained on him.

"I can't remember the combination. Lower that pistol." Lupino turned the dial several times. Finally the metal door opened. "What luck," he said, trying to sound surprised. "Here it is." He held out the sketch, still rolled up in its tube.

All in one motion, Feltzer snatched the sketch, lifted the pistol, and pulled the trigger. A muffled sound followed—*pfft*—a little explosion.

Lupino saw Feltzer glaring at him, but his face was wavering, like something under water. *Tears in my eyes,* he thought. Something made him put his hand on his stomach. He looked down. His hand was red. He felt a bit weak. It was nothing, he told himself. He was just tired. He moved carefully to an overstuffed chair. He saw Feltzer walk away, yes, he seemed to be going back down the hallway. The sound of his footsteps grew softer and finally disappeared.

Good, he's going away. Oh God, I'm so cold. Lupino sank against the back of his chair. *Mutti, hurry back and bring me a blanket.* He closed his eyes. *Mutti, if you'd just bring me something to warm my body. Oh please, please, Mutti!*

CHAPTER 33

Gianni sat with Ben and the three women at the wrought iron table in the breakfast room of the seedy hotel he had managed to find in Bern. "Sorry that you ladies all have to sleep in the same room, but we're lucky to have any place at all to put our heads. Refugees are pouring in from everywhere. Before he left this morning, Hans said I snored like an engine. Hope I didn't keep you awake, Ben."

Ben raised his eyebrows and grinned. "I couldn't comment on that!"

"I just wish we weren't so far from your sister Monica," Constanz said.

"Constanz," Gianni reminded her, "this is where Hans has his best connections. We were fortunate that he found someone to drive us here from the border—and that this hotel owner will let us stay longer."

Constanz was filling coffee cups from the metal urn on the buffet. "I know you're right. Where is Hans?" she asked.

The door to the breakfast room burst open and Hans entered, his face flushed with excitement.

"I've just been at the German Embassy. Thank God I'm not yet on their list of wanted persons. They're used to seeing me come through on factory business and they told me everything I wanted to know."

"Here, sit down." Francesca set a cup of coffee and a roll in front of him.

Sitting, Hans waved his hand to get everyone's attention. "First of all, Lupino was killed last night in his home outside Bern by an intruder."

Constanz put her hand to her mouth. "Oh dear God! What a shock! Who would do such a thing?"

"I thought of Feltzer right away and I asked if he had been at the embassy recently. Sure enough, he was there last night asking for papers to go back into Italy and on to the Brenner Pass."

"Why would he go to the Trentino area?" Ben asked. "Isn't he supposed to be in Rome?"

"The Allies are fighting well north of Rome. A lot of Germans see the end of the war in sight and they want to get out. I'm surprised he isn't running for Genoa, it would be easier to get there." Hans stirred sugar into his coffee.

Ben abruptly realized why he had had a sick feeling in his stomach ever since they'd pushed Lupino out of the Gestapo limousine. He kept seeing Lupino running off, clutching his briefcase. What a fool he had been! Lupino must have had the Caravaggio with him. Ben cursed himself for not taking the briefcase.

Hans furrowed his eyebrows. "If Feltzer was the intruder, you can bet he has the drawing now. He probably wants money to last out the war. Maybe he knows somebody to sell it to in the Trento area."

Ben jumped to his feet. "The man I sold a Monet painting

to—Heinrich von Mühlenberg. He kept asking me about the Caravaggio drawing. Feltzer knows him."

Hans nodded. "Yes, von Mühlenberg is a well-known collector and a Nazi too."

"How do you know?" Ben asked.

"The Partisans make it their business to know everything they can."

Ben was puzzled. "My friend Giorgio works with the Partisans in Trento. He knew I had sold a painting to von Mühlenberg. I saw Giorgio two weeks after I started working in Venice, but he never said anything about von Mühlenberg."

"People like your friend Giorgio aren't supposed to know everything. On his level they're cogs in the wheel." Hans drew in a deep breath. "We're going to have to get rid of Feltzer. He's a vicious criminal, responsible for the torture and killing of God knows how many people. When the Partisans find out they can get hold of one of the perpetrators of the Ardeatine cave massacres, they'll know what to do with him."

Ben grimaced. "I'd like to go after him myself—after what he did to my father and mother."

Hans shook his head. "There isn't time to get you down there, and you don't know the area as well as the local Partisans. They can swarm the area and locate Feltzer." He gave a tight smile. "My friend at the embassy gave me the make of Feltzer's car—a BMW—and the license plate. As long as he doesn't exchange it for another car, we'll find him."

"How will you get the message to the Partisans?" Ben asked.

The door to the kitchen opened and a maid entered with a tray of clean coffee cups.

Hans motioned for silence. "Ladies," he added, "excuse us while we leave the room for a minute."

In the bedroom where the men had spent the night, Hans, Ben, and Gianni sat on the beds while Ben described to Hans the road leading to von Mühlenberg's castle, the places where a car would have to slow down, the dogs at the gate, and the distances to the neighbors on either side.

Hans nodded when he had finished. "I'll take the information to my contact here who has a wireless transmitter and I'll put it into code. The Trento-Bolzano partisans will have the information by this afternoon."

"Wait," Ben said. "If I can't do this, I want my friend Giorgio to go after Feltzer. He knows what the man did to my father." And his mother, he added silently.

"Your friend isn't just a raw recruit, is he?"

"No, he's been in the thick of it for some time."

"Do you know your friend Giorgio's code name?"

"I'm not supposed to know, but I do."

"For God's sake, man, let's have it."

"His code name is Emilio."

"I'll ask for Emilio to do the job, if it's possible."

The men walked toward the breakfast room. "Can you remember everything I told you?" Ben asked Hans. "You didn't write it down."

Hans shook his head. "Most important part of the job—never write anything down. You wouldn't want me to get caught with your friend's name on a list, would you? Now, I'll go and see if I can reach the Partisans."

CHAPTER 34

Giorgio leaned his bicycle against the wall of the fountain in the central square of Bolzano. After filling his thermos with water, he tightened the straps holding the bike's saddlebags. He glanced around the piazza to make certain he wasn't observed before he lifted the flap of each saddlebag. One bag held four-point nails and in the other was nestled a nine millimeter semi-automatic Beretta. A leather pouch behind the seat held salami, cheese, bread, and the thermos of water.

The journey up the mountain was going to be long, but Giorgio was used to taking the steep ascents of the Dolomite area, and was unafraid to kill a Nazi target. Four months of pedaling between Trento and Bolzano had given him thighs like ham hocks. His aim with his pistol was near perfect. He could throw down the four-pointers, lie in ambush, waiting for the car tires to burst, and shoot a car's occupants while bicycling away. He and his friends had perfected the stratagem.

This time the action would take place in daylight, and Giorgio would carry it out alone. He knew that in the past two days Eric Feltzer's car had been spotted twice driving up the steep road to Heinrich von Mühlenberg's castle. What a tremendous satisfaction it would give him to hunt down the man responsible for the death of Ben's father. Ben had spoken also of a humiliation Feltzer had forced on signora Cantarini. It had hurt Ben too much to explain it to Giorgio, but anyone could imagine what the bastard had done to her.

For a handsome sum of money, signor von Mühlenberg's groundsman had let the Partisans know that Herr Feltzer would make his last visit to the castle today, for lunch and business matters. After that he would be on his way north to the Brenner Pass. The groundsman had learned from von Mühlenberg's valet that Feltzer had cousins in the former Sudetenland of Czechoslovakia, reliable people, German sympathizers, who would take him in until the war was over. There was always the slim chance that the Caravaggio had not yet changed hands, so Giorgio knew he mustn't use a grenade when stopping the car.

It would be easier if Feltzer's visit were taking place for dinner instead of lunch. The cover of darkness would have helped, but Giorgio would simply have to be extra cautious. He was dressed like a woodsman's helper with loose flannel trousers gaitered at the ankles, a countryman's rough wool shirt, and a thick cap with a stiff beak.

Two hours later, a half mile from the allee of trees leading to the entrance of von Mühlenberg's castle, Giorgio found the sharp hairpin turn mentioned in the message his leader had read to him. A deep gorge lay on the other side of the road. He threw his bicycle behind the roadside bushes and lay down, waiting and munching on his salami and cheese. It was eerily quiet. The only sound in the freezing air was the whispering of the pine boughs overhead.

After waiting nearly an hour, he began to worry that Feltzer wasn't coming after all. But then a new sound broke the silence. Giorgio cocked his ear and heard the whine of a car motor straining to climb the hill. Now he heard the purring of a BMW motor close by. Peering through the underbrush he saw a black BMW slowing for the hairpin turn. It crawled past him, only the wheels visible to him. The car went into first gear, pushing its way toward the castle. After a moment, he heard signor von Mühlenberg's wolfhounds barking. The groundsman must have yelled at them, because the racket soon ceased. Giorgio checked his watch. Lunch with von Mühlenberg would probably take an hour. He lay down and waited.

When the hounds began yapping again, Giorgio clicked off the safety catch of his Beretta. He retrieved the four-pointers from his saddlebag and tossed them onto the road. Kneeling behind the bushes, he listened for the sound of the car beginning its descent.

At the hairpin turn, the car slowed again, and Giorgio lifted his head above the underbrush. He saw only the driver in the car, no passengers. The BMW bumped its way through the nails and began veering to the right ten yards ahead of Giorgio. One tire was flat and the others were losing air fast. The car swerved more and more out of control, finally slamming against the trunk of a pine tree.

Giorgio had to make certain the driver really was Feltzer. He also had to catch the man by surprise before he stepped out of the car and thought to pull a gun. Crouching, Giorgio quickly made his way around the rear of the car, stopping behind the driver's door.

"Get out of the car," he shouted, "and keep your hands up!"

The man leaned toward his glove compartment. Giorgio fired a warning shot into the plush seat of the back of the car. The man pulled his hand back and slowly stepped from the car, his hands raised. Fat, thinning blond hair, piercing blue eyes. The description fit.

"Give me your papers!" Giorgio demanded. "And not a false move."

The driver pulled his documents from his breast pocket. "My dear young fellow, what do you think you're up to? If it's money you want, I'll give it to you, but put down that gun."

Giorgio pointed the pistol at Feltzer and glanced at the papers. ERIC FELTZER, VIA TASSO, OFFICIAL OF THE THIRD REICH … "You're a criminal and an enemy of Italy."

"Come now, you have no idea what you've gotten yourself into. You won't make it down this hill if anything happens to me. I have people watching me at every moment. I'll give you money, but only if you put that damn thing down."

"The Partisans have ordered you to be executed."

"Oh God in heaven, stop it! Let me go and I can promise you anything you want. Don't you see, a man in my position … you can tell by my papers that I have a great deal of power."

"You helped plan the Ardeatine cave massacres!"

For the first time fear flickered in his eyes. "I admire the Italians!"

"I'll give you a choice, like the one you gave others, you barbarian."

"What the hell do you mean?" Feltzer pretended he was somehow in control, but Giorgio saw a wet spot on his pants.

"Either I shoot you or you can jump off this precipice." Giorgio pointed to the deep ravine, where far below the Adige River tumbled over rocks and boulders.

The look on Feltzer's face changed. "No, no!" he cried, shaking his head. He dropped to his knees.

"You want me to show you mercy? Did you show Ben Cantarini's father and mother any kindness? You animal calling yourself a human being!"

"You don't understand!"

"Where is their Caravaggio drawing?"

"Von Mühlenberg has it. I'll go back there and get it for you. Right now!"

"Shut up and get off your knees!"

Feltzer began crawling away from the edge of the road.

"Stand up, I said!"

He stood on shaking legs, two feet from the edge of the cliff. He faced Giorgio, sobbing, his hands outstretched.

A single shot rang out from Giorgio's Beretta, echoing across the valley. The impact sent Feltzer flying over the edge of the road, sailing into the ravine below. In the distance the wolfhounds began barking again.

Giorgio made a quick, thorough search of the car. Satisfied that the Caravaggio drawing was not there, he jumped onto his bicycle and rode away. His feet flying on the pedals, he made for the hut deep in the woods where his fellow Partisans awaited him.

CHAPTER 35

NEW YORK —Five years later

Constanz's heart leaped as she heard the stewardess's voice on the loudspeaker: "Ladies and gentlemen, we are about to land at New York's Idlewild Airport." She leaned into Hans and tucked her arm under his.

Across the aisle from her mother, Monica pointed out the window. "All I see is water!"

"I'm sure it's all right," Constanz reassured her, even though she too saw only gray ocean all around them. They were descending with no sign of land.

"Don't worry," Hans said. "Hundreds of planes land here every day." At the very last moment the plane was over a runway and touched down.

On the taxi ride into Manhattan, Constanz realized how weary she was from the long trip across the Atlantic. The strangeness of the foreign city made her almost dizzy. She thought she knew about cities, but Padua and even Turin were nothing like this. Taxis and cars weaving in and out and people cramming into busses. Everyone in a hurry.

When their taxi turned onto West End Avenue, her spirits lifted. The neighborhood was quieter. They were stopping in front of a handsome apartment building on the tree-lined boulevard. While Hans helped the driver with the suitcases, Constanz took Monica's arm. "This reminds me a little bit of our old neighborhood in Padua, only there are trees here."

Monica looked up and down the street. "I wonder what it's like to live here."

Hans answered her. "Ben and Silvia said in their letters that they're very happy here." When he had finished counting out the unfamiliar American dollars, the three travelers picked up their suitcases and walked into the high-ceilinged vestibule of the apartment building. Constanz looked at the list of names next to the elevator—Bodzin, Campbell … She took in a breath when she saw the next name—Cantarini, third floor.

She turned to Hans. "It's been three years. I'm so anxious to see them."

"It's going to be wonderful, sweetheart." He smiled at Monica. "Your first trip to America and your first look at your little niece. Just think, you're an aunt now."

Monica nodded. "Mamma is going to show me how to hold her."

As the elevator rose, Constanz said, "I hope they're doing as well as Ben says. He always wants to tell me just the good news." The elevator stopped and she stepped out first. "Look, there it is, 3-B." While Hans pressed the buzzer, Constanz adjusted Monica's collar, patted her own hair, and then stood straight, waiting.

Inside the apartment, Ben called to Silvia, "Finally, they're here." Would Mamma like New York, or would she say that he should have opened his art gallery in Italy instead?

He started to walk toward the door, but Silvia put her hand on his arm. "Promise you'll wait before you say anything about what happened."

"I won't say a word before lunch, *amore mio,* but as soon as we've finished, I'll have to tell them."

"Of course." Silvia picked up little Francesca from her high chair and went with Ben to the door.

He swung the door open, grinning broadly. "Mamma! Monica! Hans! Welcome!" He hugged and kissed his mother. As he stepped back to look at her, he felt a pang to see how she had changed. She was still lovely, but he could see the strain of the past years in her eyes. "You're here now, safe and sound," Ben said. Turning to Monica, he threw his arms around her. "Look at my baby sister, in a grown-up tweed suit!"

"Ben," she protested, "I'm not a baby anymore! I'm thirteen years old."

He laughed. "Monica, you'll always be my little *briccona!*" He shook hands with Hans, surprised to see that his hair had turned completely gray. The kindness in Hans's eyes made Ben think of all that they had done together.

Ben stood aside so that Silvia could give everyone her hugs and kisses. Constanz took the baby, saying, "Oh, look at this beautiful angel!"

Ben beamed at the sight of his mother holding his little girl. "She's our greatest joy, Mamma." He saw a shadow fall across his mother's eyes and knew what she must be thinking—how much Papà would have loved this baby.

Silvia promised a nice luncheon for their reunion and a bottle of Champagne on ice to toast the bride and groom. Hans smiled at Constanz, reminding everyone that they'd been married for three years and were hardly newlyweds. "*Liebe* Constanz," he added, kissing her on the cheek.

Constanz rocked the baby in her arms, telling how Francesca sent all her love from Turin and how thrilled she was to have her little namesake. She was doing very well, even though she missed Gianni terribly—they had been so close.

Hans frowned. "I should never have gone back to Turin with Gianni. But he was so determined to start another slowdown at the factory. Terrible that he was killed by a bomb a week before we were liberated."

Silvia leaned in from the kitchen to say, "Francesca was so good to me in the two years we lived in Switzerland. When our papers finally came through after the war, I was very sad to leave her."

Ben explained to Hans that he and Silvia had grown to love New York, although they still missed Italy. Hans promised them that Italy was not yet a good place to live, that it was still recovering from the war. There were signs of destruction everywhere and bulletin boards with pictures of missing relatives.

Constanz nodded, adding that there were shortages of everything and people wandering the streets looking for work. Hans was fortunate to have a professorship in Renaissance Art at the university in Florence. They loved their little apartment in nearby Fiesole, and Constanz even had a very nice piano.

In the moment of silence after the last plate was taken away, Ben crossed the room and picked up a page from the Arts section of the *New York Times* from the week before. He handed a circled article to Hans, who read it intently.

"Good Lord!" Hans cried out. "Sotheby's is auctioning the Caravaggio drawing!"

"What?" Constanz exclaimed. "What does this mean?"

"Just what it says." Ben took the paper and handed it to her. "I went down to Sotheby's yesterday afternoon and I saw the drawing! It's *my* drawing! Here, in New York, just minutes away from our apartment!"

"Well, who's auctioning it?" Hans asked. "They don't say anything about the provenance here. It just says 'attributed to Caravaggio.'"

"I know several of the appraisers at Sotheby's," Ben said, "but they wouldn't tell me much, just that it's being offered through a Swiss bank. They have an idea what it will fetch. The reserve is huge. Not decided on yet, but enormous."

"A Swiss bank ... it must be von Mühlenberg," Hans mused. "Lupino lost his life over the Caravaggio and so did Feltzer. Probably von Mühlenberg must be desperate for cash." Hans rubbed his chin. "Ben, do you think that if you pursued it further with Sotheby's, you could find out who is behind this sale?"

"No. I pressed them hard, but they wouldn't tell me anything more." Ben looked at his mother. "Remember the day Papà and I found the drawing? We paid for it, legitimately. It is mine, and I have every right to it! Von Mühlenberg bought stolen property and he knew it. It should be returned to its rightful owner and that's me."

"Hans," Silvia asked, "how can Ben prove that it belongs to him?"

"It may be impossible. Looted art works are moving around all over Europe and South America. People are trying to prove ownership—without much success." He put a hand on Ben's shoulder. "Do you have money for a lawyer?"

"No, of course we don't. But since I saw the drawing again, I've thought of nothing else."

"You could spend years fighting for it."

"I realize that."

Hans pressed further. "Do you want to go to hearing after hearing, reliving the war, explaining everything to the courts, dragging yourself and Silvia through all those horrible years again?"

Ben walked around the table, agitated. "I don't know."

"And then, at the end, chances are likely that the Caravaggio might never be returned to you."

Constanz walked over to Ben and took his hands. "You remember what Papà used to say—'We own nothing, neither possessions, nor people.' And now I think he would say, if he knew you had to give up the Caravaggio drawing again, that you have so many other wonderful things in your life." She looked from Silvia to little Francesca. "You see how much you have now, a lovely wife, a beautiful baby, and a promising art gallery."

Silvia nodded. "Ben, now we don't have to hide or run or wait for papers to go to America."

Ben sighed. "I do think often of how Papà would say I should be grateful for all that I have. Still, the thought of not going after the Caravaggio hurts badly. It feels like losing Papà all over again, because ... I don't know exactly why, but that's the way it feels."

No one spoke. Finally, Ben broke the silence. "I certainly don't want to risk our happiness by reliving the past. So ... I'll leave things the way they are."

"Are you sure, Ben?" Silvia asked.

"Yes, I am sure."

"I think you've made the right decision," Hans said.

He nodded. "Yes, it is the right decision."

"Now," Hans said, "you know what you'll want to do next. Tomorrow you'll write down all you know about the history of the drawing and give it to Sotheby's. And then the name Cantarini will be forever associated with the drawing—Beniamino and Claudio Cantarini."

"Yes, of course. You're right, Hans. I must at least do that." Ben embraced his mother and gave Hans an *abbraccio*, and then put his arms around his little sister. He thought of how his father used to say, "In the evening, when I come home to my family, I thank the Master of the Universe for all he has given me."

CHAPTER 36

NEW YORK—2009
The Winthrop Art Gallery, just before lunchtime

Tullia Cantarini smiled at Henry Prentiss and Adelaide Bunning. She could tell that they had been thoroughly caught up in her story. "My grandfather, Beniamino Cantarini, always tells me that it was a bittersweet day—*una giornata agrodolce*—when he decided that his family's happiness meant more to him than the Bacchus drawing. I'm so proud of him. In many ways he's always been my best friend. He's taught me how to be true to myself and stalwart—and determined too. I was hoping you would give me the time I needed to explain that the Bacchus drawing belongs to the Cantarini family. And so I persuaded my grandfather to come here at noon just about the time I figured I would be finishing talking to you. Would you like him to join us?"

Henry Prentiss's eyebrows shot up in surprise. "Well, of course."

Tullia opened the door to the waiting room and Ben entered. Tall, silver-haired, and straight-backed, he walked with Tullia toward the two people who had listened so intently to her story.

She introduced him, saying that she wanted her grandfather to explain how he knew the name of the most recent thief of his Caravaggio drawing.

Ben began to talk, his accent British with overtones of Italian. "As my granddaughter has probably told you, in 1948 I gave up hope of recovering the Bacchus sketch. Yet a small persistent part of me always hoped to find it again. I scoured the newspapers for word of the Bacchus. I listened to every jot of supposition in my friends' conversations, every shred of information that came my way. I felt quite certain that Heinrich von Mühlenberg had offered the drawing to Sotheby's in 1948, and then had withdrawn it." Ben looked at Henry Prentiss. "Perhaps Sotheby's was afraid of a lawsuit and the bad publicity."

Prentiss shifted uncomfortably in his chair while Ben continued. "Of course, von Mühlenberg eventually died and his final estate became public knowledge. How curious, I thought, that the Bacchus drawing was not mentioned in the list of possessions. Why not, when he had been so anxious to have it? Tullia may have mentioned to you that on the day I sold von Mühlenberg the Monet painting, he offered me a handsome sum if I could get him information of the drawing's whereabouts. Oh, he wanted it badly, all right."

Henry Prentiss rubbed his forehead. "Are you certain that von Mühlenberg ever had it?"

Ben leaned forward and smiled at Tullia. "I've told my granddaughter that von Mühlenberg was the logical person to buy it from Feltzer. He was the only one who could quickly get Feltzer the money he needed to escape to Austria. Also the only person who would help him. Feltzer was a desperate fugitive."

He bent down for his briefcase. "Before I tell you the name of the person who must have brought the drawing to your auction house, I want to show you my documents which establish that I bought the drawing in 1939 and that it surely is Caravaggio's sketch."

He pulled a notebook from the briefcase and laid it on the table. The first pages told the history of the families said to have owned the drawing over the first years of its existence. The next pages told how Ben and his father found the drawing in Venice in a mask shop. The mask shop was named and a bill of sale, yellowing but still legible, said: "200 lire—brown and white wash drawing of a young boy." The succeeding pages were written by Claudio Cantarini's associates, all of whom were renowned art experts. They had set down descriptions of the drawing and their reasons for believing in its authenticity.

"You can find the names, backgrounds, and degrees of all these men," Ben said.

Henry Prentiss leaned over the pages, nodding. "Yes, I know these names, almost all of them. But what makes you think you know the name of the person presently claiming ownership of the Bacchus sketch?"

Ben smiled. "I have followed the fortunes of von Mühlenberg since 1948 and saw his obituary in the *New York Times* in 1970. I read in an Italian newspaper that he had left all his art works to a museum in Berlin, so naturally I made it my business to see the list of those works. The Bacchus was not in that list and was never mentioned in any newspaper, museum bulletin, or scholarly tract that I saw. Of course it was possible that he had sold it on the black market, but that wasn't von Mühlenberg's style. He would always want his name attached to the sketch as part of his legacy as an accomplished collector. After all, he paid for it, so he felt that it was rightfully his, despite his certain knowledge that Feltzer had stolen it. My strong suspicion is that someone in his household spirited the Bacchus away between the time von Mühlenberg died and the Tirol authorities came in to make an inventory of the belongings in his estate. As you know, the wealthy often don't list all their valuables in their household appraisals, not wishing to pay the enormous taxes that would follow.

"Did Tullia mention to you that von Mühlenberg had a driver, a factotum who doubled as butler and sometimes, I suppose, bodyguard? Von Mühlenberg mentored him in a small way, teaching him something about art, no doubt enough to whet his appetite. This man, Konrad Grünewald, was the only servant living full-time in the castle when von Mühlenberg died. Grünewald had a wife and son in Austria and went back there after von Mühlenberg passed on. Later Grünewald's son married and had a son of his own—Josef. That grandson, Josef Grünewald, would be forty-six or forty-seven years old today."

Prentiss's face had lost all its color. He turned to Adelaide Bunning. "Has anyone revealed the name of the person who brought us the Bacchus drawing?"

She shook her head, trying to keep her composure. "Only you and I know the name."

Ben leaned forward. "Then I may assume that I am correct? I would like to add to my supposition. It is possible that Josef Grünewald, the grandson, does not know that he is in possession of stolen goods. He will have to learn that."

Henry Prentiss had gained control of himself. In a steady voice, he said, "Mr. Cantarini and Ms. Cantarini, we want to thank you for coming to us with all these details. As you can imagine, we must discuss this situation with the owner of the Winthrop Auction House." He stood, offering his hand to Ben. "We will be in contact with you in a very few days."

Tullia, shocked at the abruptness of the man's dismissal, took the hand he offered her. "Thank you for listening to us," she said. "We certainly look forward to hearing from you." She took her grandfather's arm and walked with him through the waiting room. She pressed the button for the elevator, unable to speak, the breath gone out of her.

"Now," Ben said, "we did the best we could. I'm so proud of you."

"And I was so happy you were there, Nonno."

CHAPTER 37

NEW YORK 2009
Two days later – Ben Cantarini's apartment

Tullia was due to arrive for lunch at Ben's apartment. At last the buzzer sounded and he opened the door to welcome her.

"Nonno!" she said, throwing her coat on the chair near the door. She looked again like the cheerful, high-spirited girl he had always known, instead of the tense young woman measuring every word at the Winthrop Auction House. "Where's the letter, Nonno? You're wicked that you wouldn't even give me a clue as to what it said. You knew I'd come for lunch even without all the suspense!"

He kissed her on the forehead. "*Vieni,* come sit in the study."

When they were both seated, he handed her a letter typed on ivory stationery, with the heading Winthrop Auction House, Ltd. "Now, my dear, read it to me aloud and tell me what you think."

Tullia began:

Dear Mr. Cantarini:

We are most grateful that your granddaughter was kind enough to relate so vividly the details of the provenance of the Caravaggio Bacchus as you see it. It is indeed a remarkable story, as are so many stories coming to us—and to others—nowadays. The lives turned upside down because of the theft of works of art, as well as the destruction of works of art, make up a sad and sordid part of the events of the Second World War.

Although it is not in the power of the Winthrop Auction House to make any legal determination as to who is the rightful owner of the Caravaggio Bacchus, we are removing the drawing from auction on the basis of the valuable information and documentation provided by you and your granddaughter. If you decide to seek justice in the courts, Winthrop Auction House, Ltd. is willing to lend support to your claim.

Thank you for bringing this matter to our attention. We wish you and your granddaughter success in the future.

Sincerely,
Henry Prentiss, Esq.

Tears filled her eyes. "Oh Nonno! This is wonderful! Wait until Dad comes home from Padua to hear this. Let's telephone him right now!"

Ben smiled. "Yes, I thought of that too. It's eight in the evening in Padua. He'll still be at his evening course for an hour. We'll call him later."

"And tomorrow morning we'll call Aunt Monica in Switzerland.

She and her family will be delighted to hear about this. If only Nonna Silvia were still here. She would be so happy!"

"I know," Ben said with regret. "You know how much I loved your grandmother, my dearest Silvia. If this had only happened two years ago, she would still be here and able to share our excitement. She always wanted this. She told me several times that she hoped I would leave the Bacchus to you, should it ever come back to me."

Tullia jumped up and hugged her grandfather. "Nonno! Thank you, but don't you think it should go to the Metropolitan or some other museum, to honor you and to honor your Papà?"

"You can do that someday, if you still think it's best—when you're a very old lady." He smiled. "But now, you're a very young lady and capable of accompanying me to a great Italian restaurant I've just discovered. It has wonderful northern Italian cuisine and we can celebrate your fine work at the Winthrop Auction House. We'll have a bottle of Brunello di Montalcino, 1990. It won't be from the year you were born, but it will do nicely." For a moment his thoughts were far away. "I wish my father could be here too." But then he smiled again, saying, "But he always said that we should be thankful for what we have and not grieve over what we don't have. We'll raise our glasses to him and to Nonna Silvia and to my lovely granddaughter who pled our claim and did it so well."

"And I'll raise my glass to my dear grandfather, Beniamino Cantarini, and to all the Cantarinis—and of course to the return home of the Caravaggio Bacchus."

Breinigsville, PA USA
20 May 2010
238362BV00001B/2/P

9 781440 164217